# AMERICAN HORSE

## A NOVEL

—— BY ——

WILLIAM
PANZARELLA

ISBN: 978-0-578-09425-0

Book design by Maureen Cutajar
www.gopublished.com

This book is dedicated to all the
brave men and women who have served
in the United States Armed Forces,
especially those who have paid the ultimate price.

Our country is forever
in your debt.

# PREFACE

They were called the Greatest Generation. They grew up during the Dust Bowl and Great Depression. They came of age during the most prodigious and bloodiest war the world has ever known. Many of their young lives and stories ended on desolate beaches in the Pacific, or Normandy, or countless other battlefields.

Those who did make it back returned to a new America, which had risen from the ashes of Pearl Harbor like a Phoenix to become the most powerful nation in the world. Their generation would bare witness to the United States' most expansive and illustrious time. But it would not last. After years of relative peace, advancement, and prosperity, the nation would be cast into its darkest and most divisive days since the Civil War.

Within a decade's time, America would experience the assassinations of John F. Kennedy, Martin Luther King, Jr., Robert Kennedy, unparalleled protests, deadly riots, Vietnam, and the first and only resignation of a president, Richard M. Nixon. The nation would be brought to the brink of self-destruction and its resolve tested like never before.

Frank Keller was only seventeen when the Japanese attacked Pearl Harbor. After graduation, he had planned on working fulltime at his father's hardware store, perhaps one day even taking over the business. Once eighteen, he dreamt about asking his girlfriend's hand in marriage so they could start a family of their own. But those plans would have to wait, as like millions of other young men across the country, Frank first had to help save the world.

Frank was one of the fortunate ones who made it back home from the frontline. He was part of the Great Generation, living through, and benefiting from, America's vast expansion and prosperity. But in time, he and his family will be plunged into the chaos and division of the Sixties and early Seventies.

While Vietnam was fought with guns and bombs in the battlefields of Southeast Asia, its ideology was fought in the streets, campuses, and homes across the United States. It pitted sons against fathers, brothers against sisters, the government against its citizens.

The Keller household will be no exception. As the world around him starts to unravel, Frank will travel on his own dark journey of confliction, grief and regret. And like America itself, he will try to make sense of it all and find redemption.

# CONTENTS

# 1

# PRECIPICE

The year was 1941. America had managed to survive both the Great Depression and the Dust Bowl. Though the unemployment rate was still over fourteen percent, it was a far cry from its peak in 1933, when it reached the unprecedented rate of nearly twenty-five percent. Roosevelt's New Deal appeared to be working. Across the vast Great Plains, the skies had finally reopened, quenching the dying land's thirst, as some of the Dust Bowl refugees, as they had come to be called, started returning to their farms and homes. Across the nation, though there was still much work to be done, the feeling was that things were finally getting better. But new storm clouds were already on the horizon.

America was at peace, but she was an exception. For an ocean away, the world was already at war. Germany had already invaded and conquered Czechoslovakia, Poland, Denmark, Norway, and France. Great Britain was under relentless and devastating aerial attacks from the Luftwaffe and teetering on the brink of collapse. Beyond Europe, in China, the invading Japanese were committing atrocities. Several years had already passed since the Nanking massacre, when more than 300,000 people were slaughtered and countless women raped. The Italian Army had pushed into East Africa, taking Ethiopia and invading Egypt and was now at war there with British troops.

In America, notwithstanding a few muffled voices, isolationism was the mantra of the day. Though the government was already shipping supplies to Britain to aid in its struggle, the vast majority of adults, with the carnage of the Great War (and the Great Depression) still fresh in their memories, both deplored and feared the thought that distant winds of war could once again sweep them into action. Let Europe's problems stay in Europe, the citizens clearly and loudly petitioned Roosevelt. What was happening in China and the small, obscure islands of Japan was hardy even an afterthought for most civilians.

But open-mindedness rests with the young and for the youth of America the idea of isolationism was not so cut and dry. Enter Frank Keller and Robert Davenport, best friends from Bayside, New York. Seven months away from graduating high school, they were on the precipice of a watershed moment, not only in their own lives, but of all history.


It was an unusually warm day for mid-October in New York. It was late Saturday morning and a bright sun was bursting through the azure sky, which was dappled only by a few, thin, transparent clouds. On the sidewalks people walked to and fro, carrying groceries, newspapers, holding their children's hand, almost always greeting each other with a short pleasantry.

"Good morning, Mrs. Tyler."

"How are you today, Mr. Thompson?"

"Beautiful day isn't it, Mr. Rossatto?"

Chevrolet Clippers, Chrysler Highlanders, and Buick Coupes glided sporadically along the coarsely paved roads. Stores bustled with business.

For kids, other than a few chores, Saturday meant free time. As they often did when they had idle time, Frank and Robert—or Bob, as everyone called him—arranged to rendezvous at their favorite meeting place: American Horse, a horse ranch not far from their respective homes.

Frank, a tall, slender seventeen-year-old with thick, straight brown hair had already been there for nearly half an hour, waiting for his best friend since third grade. Not that he minded the wait. With crossed arms, leaning against the weathered, wooden fence that stretched along the entire perimeter of the property, Frank gleefully gazed at Old Man Baxter placidly leading a lone horse from the stable. The rancher spotted the familiar young man and waved. "Hello Frankie," he hollered in a coarse voice.

"Hi Mr. Baxter," Frank responded enthusiastically, as he waved vigorously. "It's a beautiful day, huh?"

"Yes. Yes it is."

The high school senior watched with a smile as Baxter and his horse sauntered farther into the background. Ever since he was a small child, Frank had had an obsession with horses—and so did his best friend. He and Bob would often come to the ranch and fantasize about how one day they would own a ranch of their own. Maybe they would even buy American Horse from Mr. Baxter. Oh, the dreams of the young.

"Hey Frank!" rang out a close, chipper voice, snapping the teen out of his trance. Frank turned around to see the person he considered a brother. "Sorry. I was held up. My mother asked me to pick up some groceries."

"No bother."

The two friends stood together, leaning against the fence, staring out towards the sprawling ranch. On some days Old Man Baxter would come over and chat with them, maybe even let them help out in the stables. But this day he seemed too involved with his own work. After admiring a gray, spotted mare trot about, Frank and Bob discussed the local rumor mill. But then, as it often did in such unsteady times, the conversation turned more serious.

"Hey Frank, you know Mr. Rosenbaum, he runs the five and dime on Hanson Street?"

"Sure. He's a nice fella."

"Well I overheard him talking to this man about how the Germans were taking anyone Jewish to these prison camps and then killing them. Just because they were Jewish."

Frank turned to his friend, so that just his left arm was against the wood fence. "Yeah I heard that too. But those Nazis seem to be killing everybody. I heard on the radio the other day that the Krauts are advancing further into Russia. They're almost at Moscow."

"Russia? Forget Russia. What about England? All you hear is how the whole city is bombed out and that it's only a matter of time before the Germans invade." Bob paused. "It's crazy what's goin on," he continued in a low, somber voice. "It's just crazy."

"You know it's only a matter of time before we get dragged into it. We're already sending supplies over there. Next thing you know it'll be troops."

It now seemed as though the two seventeen-year-olds were a world away from the serenity and refuge of the horse ranch that almost disappeared into the landscape. Their thoughts were now of a foreign land of which they had only read about and seen photographs.

"I mean, what if we don't get involved? The Germans will conquer all of Europe—and everywhere else—and then they'll be comin' for us anyway. If someone doesn't defeat them the whole world will be eating sauerkraut and sausage. And salutin' Hitler."

"Frank, you sayin' that we should send our boys over there?"

Frank looked at his friend and pondered the question. "I don't know," he replied in a tone of almost defeat. "All I know is that if we do send boys over there, those boys will include us. We'll both be eighteen soon."

Bob just looked down and nodded in agreement.

The duo continued their discussion of the war in Europe, and its ever-expanding dark cloud—a cloud that seemed to be drawing closer and closer to their own country, as if the arms of Ares were reaching across the Atlantic. They spoke of radio reports, newspaper headlines, and newsreel footage played before movies. They also talked about conversations they had overheard, in the candy store, in the barber shops, in school, even between their own parents at home, wondering aloud what was fact and what was fiction. But regardless of the details, they knew that thousands of people were dying each day and nations seemed to be falling like dominos under Nazi control.

Though Frank and Bob were rightfully concerned about a devastatingly spreading war, they were afforded the luxury of switching topics from the Blitzkrieg to what to do on Saturday night, or girls, or what they were going to get for Christmas. There were no bombs dropping on their heads. Tanks were not rolling down their streets. Their neighbors were not dying like flies. In October 1941, the war in Europe was no longer abstract, but it was still not affecting the daily life of the American citizen.

After leaving the ranch, Frank and Bob met up with some other, younger kids from the neighborhood and played a game of stickball. At seventeen, they were the oldest of the group. But it was hard to turn down a game of stickball. Besides, Frank and Bob thought it was neat how the younger kids looked up to them. After about an hour of play, the two best friends went their separate ways, though with plans to meet up again later that evening for a double date.

Frank stopped by his father's hardware store, which was about a mile away. Frank had worked at the store since he was fifteen. During the school year, he worked only two days during the week, after class for a few hours, and sometimes on Saturdays. But that past summer, he had worked five days a week, at least six hours a day. Despite his childhood fantasies of owning a horse ranch, Frank accepted that his future was to work full-time at the hardware store until the day that he would eventually step into his father's shoes. But he had no complaints; to the contrary, he was more than grateful. Many people around the country were still out of work and those that did find new jobs were slaving away in factories and on construction projects, six, seven days a week, just to be able to afford the barest of essentials. During the depths of the

Depression, countless businesses had closed, especially small mom-and-pop stores. It seemed a miracle that his father's hardware store had not only survived, but was starting to do well again. Frank was five years old on Black Thursday and had grown-up in the throes of the Great Depression, and though his family fared better than many, he had seen up close the true meaning of hard times. So even with the grandeur of youth, he knew inheriting a successful hardware store was a blessing.

Frank helped his father and chatted with some of the regular customers. It was all small talk and pleasantries.

"How are you today, Mr. Holland?"

"Very well Frank, and you?"

"Hey Mr. Farnsworth, how is Billy doing?"

"Frank, your father tells me that you are doing very well in school. That's my boy."

Around a 4:45 p.m., Frank and his father started preparing to close the store.

"Hey Pop?"

Mr. Keller, who was putting something away, turned his slender frame around and looked at Frank through his round glasses. "Yes?"

"Remember how I asked you and Mom yesterday if I could take Mary out to the movies tonight, after dinner?"

His father smiled, glad that it was not something more serious. "Yes son, I do. And that'll be fine. Just as long as it's okay with Mary's parents."

"Oh yes sir, of course."

Frank had been dating Mary Capelli, a girl from the neighborhood, for almost a year. Though Mary's mother was born in New York and was of Irish descent, her father was from Rome and came to America as a boy. Although there was not the same prejudice against Italians as there were the Germans at the time, Italy was part of the Axis and Mary did find herself in the crosshairs at times, because of her last name. One time at school two boys started calling her "WOP" and "Nazi Lover" as she walked by. Frank, who happened to be a few yards away talking to Bob, overheard the deriding and immediately ran over. Though he could handle himself, Frank was not known as a fighter or tough kid, but when one of the boys made another derogatory comment towards Mary, Frank punched him in the mouth, knocking him to the ground. When the other boy tried to stand up for his friend, Frank gave him a pounding as well. No one at school ever messed with Frank, or more importantly Mary, again.

Naturally, he did get in trouble over the incident and his dad gave him a tongue-lashing, but inside he was also extremely proud of him. And after reading Frank the riot act about fighting in school, he added: "With that said, I want you to know son that even though you might have gone about it the wrong way, I didn't raise you to be a coward. And I respect that you stood up for not only yourself, but for Mary."

As for Mary's parents, who already liked Frank, they would never forget what he had done for their daughter. In fact, from that point on, her father thought of Frank as a son and bragged about him whenever the chance arose.

After closing the hardware store, Frank and his father headed home, where his mom had dinner waiting for them. It was just the three of them. Frank had had an older sister, Ellen, but she died before he was born. She was only eleven months old when she succumbed to complications brought on by scarlet fever.

As they did before every dinner, the family of three sat around the table and clasped their hands as Mr. Keller said grace. "Dear Lord, we thank you for the food we are about to eat. We thank you for the roof over our head and that we are together. We know so many others have it much worse than us—and we pray for them, too, Lord."

As the potatoes, bread and cabbage were passed around the table, the conversation was started by Mrs. Keller asking her husband Harold, then Frank, how their days were. However, inevitably, the dialogue turned to the war in Europe. "So I heard today that the Germans are almost at Moscow," Frank proclaimed with inquisitive enthusiasm. "It doesn't seem like anything is going to stop them."

"Do we have to talk about war at the dinner table Frank?" His mother responded.

Frank had always been obedient to his parents' wishes, but how could they not talk about the War? It was all over the newspapers, the radio, the schools. It seemed to find its way into every conversation. In fact, he was certain that Bob and his family were sitting around the dinner table discussing it, as was Mary's family. Frank knew that his mother was just sick of hearing about it and on some, small level he could understand. But the unprecedented conflict in Europe wasn't going away. To the contrary, it seemed as though it was getting even worse.

"Pop, do you still think there's no way we're sending troops over there? I heard we're sending more and more supplies each day."

Mr. Keller swallowed his bite of food and placed down his fork. "Let me tell you something son, where was Europe and the rest of the world during the Crash, during the Dust Bowl? I didn't see anyone sending over any food or help to us. You know how many young American boys died over there during the Great War, fighting for the French and the Brits? But when America needs help who came to our aide? No one. And they never will. You think if we were attacked the Brits or the French would send their boys over here?" He went on, his voice gradually rising after every word. "Well son, I think we both know the answer to that."

"Your father's right," his mother submissively chimed in.

Frank understood what his father had said, but still felt the urge to talk about what was going on, seemingly a world away. "I heard that the Nazis are going around killing people just because they're Jewish. They're actually rounding them all up so they can kill 'em."

"Oh Frank," Mrs. Keller quickly interjected. "You should know better than to believe everything you hear or read."

"Your mother's right son. They want everything to seem even worse than what it really is so the American people will buy into it and demand that President Roosevelt send our troops over there." His father began to cut a piece of potato. "Besides, the Jews can fend for themselves. Don't get me wrong, I got nothin' against them, but again, do you think they would help us out?"

Frank had always heeded and been influenced by his father's words. Early on it may have been out of sheer instinct, nature. But the older he became, the more he came to understand and respect his father, the only real role model in Frank's life. But, at seventeen, though he still respected his father immensely, he was old enough to form his own intellectual opinions of the world, of how things worked. Nonetheless, Frank sympathized with his father's words about the war not only because he was his son but also because his own mind and experience said his father was probably right. If the shoe *was* on the other foot, perhaps no one would come to America's aid. But another part of him said there was too much death and suffering in Europe and elsewhere just to stand by. One part of him knew with certainty that if the United States sent troops to Europe thousands, maybe tens or hundreds of thousands of young American men would never make it back. But he was also convinced that if America didn't intervene and stop Hitler, no one could. Frank was torn. The issue of the war made him realize more than ever that things are not always black and white. Sometimes there is no clear, definitive choice.

After dinner, Frank walked over to Mary's house to pick her up. It was less than a ten minute walk. Her father greeted him warmly as usual and invited him in. While Mary finished getting ready, Frank exchanged pleasantries with her parents. They did not discuss the war.

The two high school seniors then started their walk to the movie house, where they were going to meet up with Bob and Annette, Bob's girlfriend. Like Frank and Bob, Annette and Mary were close friends and the four often went on double dates and hung out together. When they did, there never seemed to be any disagreements or friction. It was always a good time. When the four were together they were always encompassed in their own little bubble of laughter and glee, no matter what else was going on in the world.

When Frank and Mary arrived at the movie house, Bob and Annette were already waiting out front. The movie, *Dr. Jekyll and Mr.*

*Hyde*, was not going to start for another forty minutes, so the four hung out by the entrance. As Frank and Bob talked about school, the girls discussed Mary's older sister Mildred's upcoming wedding. Mildred, who was twenty-two, was getting married in the beginning of November. Mary was terribly excited. Not only was it her only sister's wedding, but also she was the maid of honor.

The next morning, as he did every Sunday, Frank put on his only suit and accompanied his parents to church. As with the majority of Americans at the time, Sunday Mass was as routine as sitting down for dinner or saying hello to your neighbor. Religion, especially Christianity, had been engrained in the American culture since before the Revolution. And it was faith, that beckoning light of hope, that most Americans clung onto during the darkest depths of the Great Depression.

# 2

# A DAY OF INFAMY

The next few weeks flew past in the routine blur of school, work, and occasional leisure time. Then, on the second weekend of November came Mary's sister Mildred's wedding. It was of course, a special and long awaited day for the Capelli family. Frank arrived at the house several hours before the ceremony to accompany his bridesmaid girlfriend to the church. The house was abuzz with people and activity. As Frank, himself caught up in the excitement, waited in the foyer, Mary appeared from the kitchen. Frank stared at her, his eyes blocking out everything else, soaking up her stunning image like a sponge. She looked angelic in that long, flowing, turquoise dress. Its tranquil color seemed to accentuate her pale, blue eyes, which peered from her soft, white face. Her long, black hair was in a loose perm, each strand perfectly placed.

"You look beautiful, Mary," Frank spoke in a slow, floating voice.

Mary usually never wore lipstick, but for the occasion her lips were flawlessly painted bright red. She smiled. "Thank you."

"I…I mean you always look beautiful, but…"

"It's okay. I know what you mean. And thank you."

Mary grabbed hold of Frank's hands and shone an ever bigger smile as she practically jumped out of her high heels. "Isn't this exciting! I'm so happy for Millie."

Frank smiled back and nodded. "Yes. Yes, I'm happy for her, too. How is she?"

"She's fine. Just busy getting ready. She looks so beautiful."

After the reception, Mary and Frank went for a walk. It was a pleasantly mild night for mid November. A clear, black, silk sky flickered with countless stars. Hand-in-hand the two young lovers strolled down the still and silent streets. The clamor and excitement of the wedding had already faded into what would be an everlasting memory. Outside, in the star-speckled darkness, the world seemed so small. To Mary and Frank it was as if no one else existed but them. Frank took a deep breath of the crisp air as if he was inhaling the very moment, trying to keep it forever in his soul.

As free and content as Frank was, Mary felt the same. It was a perfect end to a perfect day. Her family had been all together. Her sister had finally married, in a wonderful wedding. And now she was alone with the young man of her dreams, the only lover she had ever known. But sometimes, even in dreams we dream. "Frank," she said in a gentle voice that seemed to float through the night.

"Yeah, Mary?"

"Do you think we'll get married?"

Frank stopped and faced the only girl with whom he could ever see himself with. The question caught him off guard and in his own unique way, he responded the way he always did when taken by surprise—with sheepish humor. "Well Mary Capelli, are you asking me to marry you?"

Mary smiled and jokingly hit Frank's arm with her purse. "Frank. You listen mister, I am a lady and a lady does not ask for a man's hand in marriage. It's the other way around. And if you—"

"Listen Mary," Frank cut in, putting his hands on her shoulders. "You know I love you and that I want to spend the rest of my life with you. God," he went on, shaking his head, "I can't ever imagine being with anyone else. But as you are a lady, and you are, I am a gentleman. And as such, when that day comes, I'm going to do it the right way. First, I'm going to ask your father for his approval. Then, I'm going to come to you on my knees, with a ring in my hand. And I'm going to make sure that I'm able to provide for us and our family."

Halfway through Frank's words Mary began to cry.

"Mary, what's wrong? Did I say something wrong?"

Mary just threw her arms around him. "I love you, Frank," she cried into his shoulder. "I love you so much."

"I love you too, Mary. You know that. I'm sorry if I said something wrong. What's the matter?"

Mary lifted her head from his shoulder and looked straight into his eyes with a smile. "Nothing's wrong Frank. Nothing at all. In fact, I couldn't be happier."


December 7, 1941. It started off like any other Sunday. Frank and his parents dressed up and went to Mass. Afterwards, outside the church they conversed with some of the congregation, making pleasant small talk. As usual for a Sunday, the hardware store was closed, so after changing into casual attire, Frank walked over to Mary's house. The two hung out there for a while before deciding to go to the local soda shop for lunch. On the way, they talked about Christmas. What an exciting time of year they both agreed. Though it had not snowed yet in New York, the electricity of the holidays could not be escaped. They were also one more year removed from the depths of the Depression, which made it that much more special. Though still by no means prosperous times, there would be presents under the tree. Of course, winter recess was also cause for celebration.

The soda shop was alive with kids and teens, but Mary and Frank managed to find two seats at the counter. As they awaited their hamburgers and fries, a couple of friends from school came over on their way out and chatted for a while. Then, over lunch,

Mary and Frank talked about what to do with the rest of the day. Mary said her parents were going to visit some friends in Brooklyn and suggested the two go back to her place. Naturally, Frank quickly agreed.

Just as Frank was about to pay the bill, a young man burst into the soda shop. "Do you have the radio on?" He yelled frantically. "Did you hear what happened?"

The man behind the counter, dressed in all white, flung a hand towel over his shoulder. "Hey, what's this all about?"

"The Japs just bombed our naval base in Hawaii!"

In an instant, all the bustle of the luncheonette fell completely silent. Just as the last words left the stranger's mouth, Frank noticed people stopping on the sidewalk and talking to each other, all with the same pale face of disbelief.

"What did you say?" The man behind the counter asked, piercing Frank's mesmerized focus.

"The damn Japs! They bombed our base! Hundreds of planes! Turn on the radio."

Suddenly another stranger burst upon the scene. "Did you hear?"

As the cook appeared from the kitchen, the man in white scrambled to turn on a radio that was on a shelf, behind the counter. It took him only a second or two, but it felt like minutes. As a crackling voice came over the airwaves, the soda shop was still deathly silent, in disbelief, perhaps hoping this was all some sort of sick prank. But it quickly became apparent that there would be no such fortune.

*Again, for those of you just tuning in, at seven fifty-five this morning, Hawaiian time, scores of bombers and torpedo planes from the Empire of Japan attacked the United States naval base in Pearl Harbor. Approximately an hour later came a second wave of planes. At least one battleship, the Arizona, has been sunk and numerous other ships are said to be on fire. Though there has been no official death count thus far, it may very well be in the thousands...*

The silence of the soda shop was replaced by collective gasps, moans and crying. Though many of the patrons had never heard of

Pearl Harbor, it might as well have been in their own backyard. Those were American men and women that had been killed, and whether they came from Hawaii, Illinois, Texas or New York, it was irrelevant.

Mary clutched onto Frank's bicep and buried her head in his shoulder. "Frank," she cried unabashedly, "is this really happening? Is this for real?"

Frank could feel Mary on him, but her words did not register. He was too fixated on the radio. But his thought was the same: *Is this really happening*? A cold, numbing sensation washed over his body, from his head down to his toes. Each crackled word from the reporter hung in the thickness of the air. The seventeen-year-old knew already that things would never be the same. No matter what happened from that point on, history would be judged before Pearl Harbor and after Pearl Harbor. He also realized, instantly, that this day was just the opening salvo to America's entry into a now complete, global war.

After a few minutes of listening to the news report, people started flooding out of the soda shop. Many of them were crying. All of them were awestruck.

"We should go home, see our parents," Frank suggested in a shaky voice.

Mary reminded him that her parents had gone to visit friends.

"It's okay. Come with me to my house. If your parents start looking for you, they'll figure out that's where you are."

Mary, still crying, agreed.

As soon as Frank and Mary walked through the front door, Mrs. Keller ran over to her son and gave him a hug. "Oh, Frank, have you heard? It's just terrible!" As she then said something to Mary, Frank could tell that his mother had been crying.

Mrs. Keller then led the pair into the living room, where Frank's dad was sitting, listening to the radio. "Can you believe it? Can you believe those damn sneaky Japs?" He yelled, without ever turning around. "That's not war, that's murder! Those damn cowards!"

For the next hour Mary, Frank and his parents huddled in the living room, glued to the radio. It was all so surreal. The carefree mundaneness of that morning already felt like a lifetime ago. How to spend a lazy, Sunday afternoon and talking about Christmas had been replaced with unspeakable thoughts and images. What would the total number of dead be: A thousand, two thousand, five thousand? And what about their poor families? The suffering seemed unimaginable. Then there were the ships; how many would wind up sinking or badly damaged? Would the Navy even be able to defend itself going forward? And speaking of going forward, there was of course the gut-wrenching fear of the unknown. Was another attack on Hawaii imminent? Were the Japanese going to attack the Mainland next? At that point, anything seemed possible.

As the day pressed on, in houses throughout the country, disbelief turned to anger. There was still shock, still sorrow, and even fear. But rage and vengeance started to percolate from the depths of nearly every man, woman, and child until it began to explode like a collective volcano. As Admiral Yamamoto was infamously credited with saying, Japan had awoken a sleeping giant. And that giant wanted revenge.

That night, Frank met Bob by the local park. When he arrived, Bob was already there, underneath a streetlamp, pacing about, shaking his head. "Can you believe those Japs?" Bob dived right into a diatribe. "Those cowards are gonna pay for this! They're gonna pay, I tell ya! This is war!"

Frank was less animated, but felt the same emotions. "I know. All those poor fellas over there, just gettin' ready for a relaxing Sunday. But I still don't understand how this coulda' happened. I mean how didn't we have any warnings at all?"

"Because those Japs are sneaky bastards, that's how. They're probably planning another attack right now, as we speak. Maybe next it's gonna be California."

It was a sobering thought, but Frank realized his friend was probably right. Why would the Japanese just attack Pearl Harbor? What was their end game? Were they actually thinking of invading and conquering the United States? In one aspect that scenario sounded extremely far-fetched. But then again, if someone had suggested the day before that Japan was going to attack Hawaii, Frank probably would have laughed at the thought.

"Here we are all this time so worried about the Nazis and what's happening in Europe," Frank said in an almost defeated voice. "Has the whole world gone mad?"

For the first time since Frank's arrival, Bob stopped pacing and stood toe-to-toe with his best friend. "You know what this means Frank? We're going to war with Japan. And they're gonna need all the young men they can get to join the service." Bob paused. "We have to enlist right away," he added in a matter-of-fact tone. "It's our duty. Besides, I wouldn't miss kicking those dirty, slant-eyed Japs ass for anything."

"Bob, I wanna kick their ass as much as you do, but we're not even eighteen yet. I don't turn eighteen till April and your birthday isn't till June. Plus, we're still in high school. They're not gonna let us join the Army."

"I don't care. I'll drop out of school. I'll tell them I'm eighteen. I don't care what I have to do! My country is counting on me!"

The two high school seniors continued their emotional dialogue well into the night. It was a similar conversation being played out in countless parks, houses, and taverns.


The next day hardly anyone went to school or to work. Instead, families throughout the country gathered in front of their radios and television sets—those that had TVs—and listened as President Roosevelt addressed the nation in front of Congress and gave his now historic "Day of Infamy" speech. Though the fervor and angst of the attack on Pearl Harbor was obviously the focal point, new news made matters even worse. The Japanese had also attacked Hong Kong, Guam, the Philippines, and somewhere called Midway Island. An hour after the speech, at Roosevelt's request, Congress passed a formal declaration of war against the Empire of Japan.

That night, as the Keller family sat down for dinner, after saying a special grace, Frank announced to his parents his decision to enlist in the military. At first, his parents just looked at each other, though neither one was surprised. They knew that that night, across the land, boys were informing their parents of their intention to join the war effort.

"Son, I understand you're intentions," his father calmly said, "and I admire them. I really do. But you're only seventeen. You have to be eighteen to join the military. Plus, you're still in high school."

"But I'll be eighteen in a few months; maybe you and Mom can sign some papers giving your permission. And I know school's important, but this is bigger than me. This is about the defense of our country. It's my duty. I know you can understand Pop. You served in the Great War. And no one even attacked us then."

Mrs. Keller latched on to her husband's arm. "Harold."

Harold cleared a dry lump in his throat. He realized that barring some miraculous, quick end to the war, the inevitable could only be staved off for only six months, when Frank graduated from high school. He knew his son well enough to know that he would not have a change of heart. Harold had raised his son well, to stand up and fight for what he believed in, to be counted for when responsibility and duty called—to be a patriot. But what would all those values mean if he never lived to see twenty-one, if he never lived to get married and raise a family of his own? As were countless parents at that time, Mr. Keller was conflicted to the core.

"Harry?" His wife tugged at his arm, waiting for him to say something.

Feeling like everything was going in slow motion, Harold let out a deep breath. "Frank, I'd like to have a moment alone with your mother."

Frank stood up from the table, which had on it his still untouched dinner. Before leaving, he looked straight into his father's eyes and a connection was made. He knew his father, though understandably conflicted, understood where he was coming from. No words were necessary.

Once Frank left the room, Harold turned and faced his wife, his hands on her arms. She too, could read her husband's eyes. "Oh no, Harold," she said in a low, but frantic voice. "He's our baby. He's our only son."

"Marge, he's not a boy anymore. Our son has grown into a man…and in a few months, when he turns eighteen, he's going to enlist whether we approve of it or not."

Margaret Keller's eyes began to swell with tears. "I don't care. He'll listen to you. You tell him you need him to stay here to help you with the store."

Harold gently rubbed her arms. "It doesn't matter Marge. If this war lasts any amount of time, they'll probably expand the draft anyway. Besides, how can we let our neighbors, our friends…how can we let everyone else send their sons to war to protect us, but say it's not okay to send our own?"

Margaret burrowed her head into her husband's chest. "I don't care about anyone else's son. I only care about Frank," she cried.

"Come on Marge, you don't mean that. You think I want anything to happen to our son? You know how much I love Frank. Who knows, maybe this will all be over sooner than we think."

After gaining her composure, she retrieved Frank from his room. Then, as dinner still waited on the table, Harold told his son that after graduation, if he still wanted to enlist and the war effort was still in need, he would have his parents' blessing and support. It pained Mr. Keller to even say it. But if Frank was hell-bent on enlisting and he and Margaret could not stop him, then how could they not support him? He wanted to make sure his only son understood that they would always stand by him.

After dinner, Frank excused himself and met Bob at the same place he had the night before.

"Well, did you tell your parents?" Bob asked.

"Yeah, they said that after I finish school, if I still wanted to enlist that they would give me their blessing. What about you? Did you tell your folks?"

Bob shook his head in a defeated manner. "Yeah. They said pretty much the same thing," he replied in a frustrated voice. "What if the war's over by then?"

"I don't think it'll be Bob. I mean, we still have to repair our fleet. And these Japs are pretty crazy. I think this thing's gonna last longer than most people think. And don't forget Europe. Who knows what's gonna happen over there."

To Frank's bewilderment, his friend pulled out a small pocket-knife. "What the hell's that for?"

"We're gonna take a blood oath. The day after we graduate— we'll both be eighteen by then—you and I are going to the recruiting office together and we're both going to enlist."

Frank let out a fleeting laugh. "Bob, we've been best friends forever. If I give you my word I'm gonna do something, I'm gonna do it. And I give you my word." Frank looked straight at Bob. They had been best friends forever, through thick and thin. "Ah, hell, let's do it," he said while sticking out his left hand.

Then, as if some ancient ritual, the boys made a small cut on each other's palm and clasped their hands together.

"We go in together and we leave together," Bob proclaimed.


The next day, after school, Frank went for a walk with Mary. He had debated even telling her his intentions to enlist. What if the war was over before June? There was no need worrying her for nothing. Maybe he should only tell her if and when the time came. But in the end, Frank would feel too guilty keeping it from her. Frank had not kept any secrets from Mary.

The cold, December afternoon was already darkening as the two young lovers walked hand-in-hand down the boulevard. For the first time, Frank started to realize how much he would miss Mary. Since they had started going out, the longest they had not seen each other was four days. And as their time together pressed on, so did their love. For Frank, telling Mary that he was going to enlist was going to be harder than telling his own parents. But he knew it had to be done. His heart racing, Frank led Mary down a side street.

"Where are we going?"

"Mary," Frank said in a solemn voice as he stopped and faced her. "There's something I have to tell you."

Instantly, Mary's heart sunk. Though she had no idea what Frank was about to say, she could tell it was bad news. "What...what is it?"

Frank peered into those pale, blue eyes and tried to muster the strength to tell her. "I...um...I..."

"What is it?" Mary asked with quivering lips, afraid to hear the answer.

"I'm going to enlist in the service. Me and Bob. We're going to enlist together the day after graduation."

In one instant, shock, fear, anguish, and loneliness exploded together like a bomb inside Mary's heart and overcame her entire body. For a few seconds she just stood there paralyzed by those emotions, as tears began to form.

"Oh, Mary, please don't cry." It killed Frank to see her in such distress. "Who knows, maybe the war will be over by then anyway," he said to appease her.

Mary grabbed hold of Frank and squeezed as hard as she could. "What if something happens to you over there? What if..."

"Shhh, shhh," Frank combed his hand down her long, silky, black hair. "Nothing is going to happen to me. I promise."

# 3

# THE OMNIPRESENCE OF WAR

On December 11th Germany and Italy declared war on the United States. There now seemed little doubt that America would be fighting a war on two fronts; two fronts that could not have been farther away from each other. But before the U.S. could go on the offensive, against Japan or Germany, she had to bolster her military, which before World War II, paled in comparison to the two main nations of the Axis. And that did not just mean adding men to its armed forces. After the attack on Pearl Harbor, the United States began what would be undoubtedly the largest and most ferocious buildup of warplanes, ships, submarines, and tanks the world had ever seen, outdoing even the Third Reich. Overnight, countless citizens, still left unemployed by the Depression, went to work in newly formed factories and shipyards. For the war effort, the wheels of industry were cranking like never before. Bombers, fighters, battleships, destroyers, submarines, landing vessels, tanks, Jeeps, trucks, bombs, guns, ammunition, and uniforms could not be manufactured fast enough. Soon, with many young men going off to war, the nation called on its women to work on the factory floors. For the war could not have been won without them.

If the country was preoccupied by the conflict in Europe before December 7th, it was now worked into a feverish pitch by the war. It was omnipresent, in the fields of the Great Plains to the Mississippi Delta, from Los Angeles to Chicago, from the Great Northwest to the East Coast—and in Bayside, New York, where the Keller family resided. As Pacific Islands fell to the Japanese like dominos, and with the United States' inevitable involvement in Europe, Harold's and Margaret's thinly held pipe-dream that the war would be over before their son had a chance to enlist no longer even entered their mind. They were all but certain now that not only would Frank join the military, but he would be shipped to the front line.

As much as the Kellers tried to avoid the thought of their son fighting for his life in some foreign land, the daily events of war were inescapable at the dinner table, or at church, or at the hardware store. Everyday seemed to bring with it new bad news. In early January, Japan attacked Bataan in the Philippines, which would soon lead to the infamous Bataan Death March, where nearly 80,000 Americans and Filipinos were forced to march night and day to awaiting prison camps, under the harshest conditions and the relentless brutality of their Japanese captors. Less than 55,000 would make it there alive and many more would perish in the prisons. After the invasion of Bataan, in succession, in January alone, the Japanese attacked the Dutch East Indies, Burma, North Borneo, and the Solomon Islands. And by late January, seemingly a world away from the Pacific, the first U.S. troops arrived in Britain.

Though, like everyone else, Mary could not escape the news and rumors of war, but she and Frank hardly ever talked about it. It was a hard topic to avoid, however, especially since the two started spending even more time together. But Frank's commitment to enlist remained the two-hundred-pound gorilla in the room. They just wanted to spend as much time together as possible before Frank went off to basic training. And they wanted that time to be filled with joyful memories. After all, though neither one wanted to entertain the thought, the reality was that if Frank was shipped off to the Pacific or Europe, there was a chance he would never make it home.

Frank was torn. The more time he spent with Mary, the more he realized how much he would miss her. Yet on the other hand, he was not only resolute, but eager to join the service and help in the war effort. It was not just to honor some pact he had made with Bob. Like most young men at the time, patriotism was part of Frank's DNA. And that was his country the Japanese attacked on December 7th. Though he had never met anyone of them, those were his brethren that were slaughtered that day. But it was not just what happened that infamous December day. It was also about the future—the future of not only the United States, but the entire free world. To him, every American citizen, including his family and Mary, were in jeopardy of one day saluting Hitler or bowing to the Emperor. And no matter what small part he played, or even if he had to sacrifice his own life, Frank was determined to make sure that did not happen.

Inevitably winter gave way to spring. On April 17th Frank turned eighteen. His parents had a party for him at the house. Mary, Bob and Annette were there, as well as other friends and relatives. At one point, Harold and Margaret found themselves in the kitchen, away from everyone else. "I can't believe our little boy is eighteen," Margaret said as she dried a dinner plate.

"Yeah, it seems like just yesterday he was running around in the backyard playing cowboys and Indians and hide-and-seek." Harold paused, as if he was reliving those days in his mind. "We raised him well though, Marge."

"Yes, he's a good boy." Margaret caught herself and let out a fleeting laugh. "I mean a good young man. He's done so well in school. He should be going to college when he graduates. The sky is the limit for him. But this stupid war!"

Harold put his hands on his wife's shoulders. "Marge, I thought we weren't going to talk about that today. This is a celebration."

Margaret looked at her husband and took a deep breath. "You're right," she said with a smile. "You're right."

The days, weeks and months continued to pass. As Frank's enlistment day approached, his father asked his son to work less and less at the hardware store. Harold wanted to spend as much time with his son as possible, but he also understood Frank's desire to share more time with Mary before joining the war effort. Harold was once himself young and in love. And in 1917, at the age of nineteen and madly in love with a beautiful Irish girl named Margaret O'Malley, he was drafted into the Army and shipped off to Europe to fight in World War I. Luckily, she was still waiting for him when he came back. Mr. Keller knew how much Mary meant to Frank, and he also admired her.

Between school, studying, and spending time with Mary, Frank found time to start working out. He was always slender and good with his hands, but that was from being young and having natural ability, not from any training. In fact, though Frank followed professional baseball, he had never enrolled in any team sports. His fitness had come strictly from gym class, moving boxes around the hardware store, and walking everywhere. But not long after agreeing to enlist, Frank and Bob agreed that it would be a good idea to start working out, to get in shape for basic training. They hoped that this would make it a little less difficult. So on their own, Bob and Frank would do pushups, sit-ups, jumping jacks, and even run.

By June 7th, news of the United States' victory at Midway spread across the land. Though Japan had already suffered its first defeat a month earlier during the Battle of The Coral Sea, Midway was heralded as a turning point in the Pacific War. To celebrate the news, Frank bought some beer, now that he was of legal drinking age (which was eighteen at the time) and took it over to Bob's, whose parents were gone for the day. Neither Frank nor Bob were big drinkers. In fact, Frank had been drunk only once before. But it seemed like a special occasion.

Frank arrived to find another friend of theirs, Murray, already at the house. They all greeted each other and wasted no time cracking open a beer. "To our boys at Midway," Murray raised his bottle and cheered.

"Here, here," Frank and Bob replied in unison.

"I knew it was only a matter of time before we started kicking those Japs' behinds!" Frank proclaimed.

Bob took a swig of his beer. "Yeah, we better hurry up and get over there before the war's over."

"Well, only one more week before graduation," Frank added.

"So you guys decide to join the navy?" Murray asked. He knew about his friends' commitment to enlist, but did not know what branch of the service they would be joining.

Frank and Bob looked at each other. "Well we thought about it," Bob began to answer, "and we don't wanna be stuck on a ship. We wanna be on the ground, fighting. So that rules out the Navy. We figure that the best chance of us being deployed to some island or even Japan, when we invade them, is with the Army. I mean, even with all these naval battles going on, you know it's only a matter of time before we have to fight those bastards on land."

"Yeah," Murray agreed, shaking his head, "there sure are plenty of islands over there to fight on." He finished off his beer. "But what if you guys get shipped to Europe?"

Again, Frank and Bob looked at each other, only this time with a more serious look. "Don't even talk like that," Bob snapped back. "I ain't got no problem shootin' Nazis, but I'm joining the service so I can kill as many Japs as possible!"

"Yeah, they're the ones that bombed Pearl Harbor," Frank heatedly added.

The three friends continued to guzzle down beers in the living room. However, after a while, the conversation changed from war and killing to girls and baseball. Soon they found themselves laughing, joking around and acting like…well, a trio of teenagers.


In the second week in June, Frank, Bob, Mary, Annette, and the rest of the Class of 1942 graduated. Though it marked an achievement of four years of hard work, what should have been purely a joyous occasion was marred by the reality of the times. In his speech, the principal said,

"I know that some of you will soon be joining the service and that you will be sent to fight in the Pacific or in Europe. And I know that you will make all of us here at home proud. I ask that God be with you on your journey and that he brings all of you home safely."

Harold and Margaret looked around and knew that they were far from the only parents that would have their son torn away by the hands of war. But that brought them no comfort; it only made the moment that much harder to bear.

After the graduation ceremony, Frank, Bob, Mary, and Annette went to a party at a friend's house. Both Frank and Bob tried to abstain from war talk in the presence of the girls. Mary and Annette put on a front, pretending that all was well. But it wasn't.

The day after graduation, just as they had planned, Frank and Bob went to the local recruiting office. They were not the only ones; the small storefront had a line going out the door. As agreed, the two best friends signed up for the Army, with the caveat that they serve together, in the same unit. Needing as many men as possible, the recruiter promised them it would not be a problem. So after completing some paperwork and a physical, Robert Davenport and Frank Keller were enlisted in the United States Army. Their lives would never be the same again.

Less than two weeks later, the day had finally arrived. Mary accompanied Frank's parents to drive him to the bus depot. There, he would board a Greyhound to Fort Devens in Massachusetts. When they arrived, the terminal was already bustling with young men carrying backpacks and duffle bags, saying goodbye to their families. Mr. Keller looked around and knew that only some of those brave men would make it home. His only wish was that his son would be one of them.

Almost immediately, Bob came walking over and greeted everyone.

"Where are your parents, Bob?" Mr. Keller asked.

"They already left."

"Well, I'm sure they're very proud of you."

Bob shook his head. "Yes sir, Mr. Keller. Thank you." Bob paused and looked at the group. "Well listen, I'll give you guys your space to say goodbye. Frank, when you're ready, I'll be over there," he pointed, "by the check-in."

Before Bob could turn around, Mrs. Keller gave him a hug. After all, both she and her husband considered Bob part of the family. They had known him since he was in third grade. "You take care of yourself Robert, you hear?"

"Yes ma'am."

As Margaret let go, Harold extended his hand, which Bob proudly shook. "We're all real proud of you too, son. You were always a good kid and you're going to make a fine soldier."

Bob's face lit up. "Well, thank you, Mr. Keller. I appreciate that."

After saying goodbye to Mary, Bob turned around and started to walk away. But before he made it more than two yards, Mr. Keller called out to him. "Robert!"

Bob immediately turned around.

"You take good care of my son. You guys take care of each other."

"Of course, Mr. Keller. Of course." With that, Bob turned back around and faded into the crowd.

Harold faced Frank and had to fight to keep his composure. "Well son, you're in good company."

"I know, Pop."

Then, one man to another, Harold shook his son's hand. "You just do what your commanding officer tells you to do and stay alert. You'll do just fine, I know you will." Harold could no longer help himself and gave his son a hug. "I'm proud of you son. Damn proud."

Next it was Margaret's turn. She had already started to cry when she embraced her son. "Don't cry, Mom."

"I can't help it. You know how much me and your father love you, don't you?"

Frank pried his mother apart, so he could look her in the face. "Of course I do. And I love you guys, too."

It was hard saying goodbye to his parents, but as he turned to look at Mary, he knew that his most difficult farewell had yet to come. "Mom, Dad, do you think I could have a minute alone with Mary?"

"Of course," Margaret replied as she and her husband walked away.

As Frank turned and faced Mary, he could feel a tugging at his heart. When he thought about how much he loved her and how he would miss her it was almost too much to bear. But with every fiber of his being, he fought to put on a stalwart front, for her sake. "Don't think of this as goodbye."

As soon as the words left his mouth, Mary collapsed in his arms. "Oh, Frank, I don't want you to go," she cried. "What am I going to do without you? And what if something happens to you? I love you so much."

Frank wiped a tear from her eye and smiled. "I told you, nothing is going to happen to me. You hear me? Just get those negative thoughts out of your head. And I'll write every chance I get, I promise."

Mary tried to stop herself from crying. "I know. I know. It's just going to be so hard being without you."

"Believe me, it's going to be hard for me, too. I just hope you're still waiting for me when I get back," he said half-jokingly.

Mary's distressed face instantly morphed into anger. "Don't you ever talk like that, Frank Keller! I will wait for you till hell freezes over. You hear me? I will never leave you."

It was time. Frank found Bob, checked in and then piled on one of the awaiting Greyhounds. As the bus slowly pulled away he looked through the window and saw his parents and Mary still standing in the parking lot. They had waited and watched which bus he had boarded. As with many of the other young men, Frank waved through the open window. Mary and his parents feverishly waved back. Then, as the driver turned onto the main street, they faded from sight.

With a simple sigh, Frank leaned back in his seat and collected his thoughts. After a few moments he turned to look at Bob, sitting beside him. "So I guess it's too late to change our minds now, huh?"

Bob smiled then let out a laugh.

# 4

# FATHER TO SON, MAN TO MAN

Frank had expected the worst about basic training, from a grueling, physical standpoint. Those expectations, coupled with the workout regime he had started that winter, made the experience less difficult than he had imagined. Still, his days were filled with training from sunrise to sunset. There was little downtime. But what time he did have, Frank spent writing letters to his parents and Mary. He had yet to see combat, so the letters were all lighthearted, joking about the terrible food, who ran or did the obstacle courses faster, he or Bob. He also asked how they were doing, what was going on back home. As light as he kept the subject, Frank always had to tell Mary how much he missed and loved her.

Frank had always been sociable and basic training was no exception. Despite the rigorous schedule, living in barracks and seeing the same faces all day, everyday, bonds—as well as rifts—were formed. Frank and Bob befriended two men in particular. One was Charlie Hudson, a twenty-year-old from Hazleton, Pennsylvania. Charlie saw and admired how hard Frank pushed himself during training and started conversing with him. The two instantly hit it off and, of course, it was not long before Bob was in the mix.

Throughout time, whenever boys and men spend a lot of time together, nicknames are sure to be found. From the first day he arrived at basic training, Charlie started telling anyone who would listen how much he loved to fish, what kind of fish he would catch and the details about his favorite fishing spots. Soon, some of the guys started calling him "Fish", and the name stuck. Once Frank told Charlie where he was from, Charlie started calling him "Bayside".

"What about me?" Bob asked. "I'm from Bayside, too."

Charlie looked him over. "No, you're just Bob." And from that point on, Robert Davenport was known as "Just Bob."

The other person whom Frank and Bob formed a particular bond with was an eighteen-year-old from Brooklyn, New York, Vincent Pertucci. Of Italian decent, some of the guys would call him a WOP. Others would try to start fights with him. Vincent would stick up for himself and explain that he was born in America and that most Italians hated Mussolini. Most of the guys relented and would just shoot him dirty looks and talk behind his back. But there were a few who still tried to make life more difficult for him. From going out with Mary and remembering the incident at school where she was being picked on because of her Italian heritage, Frank immediately felt compassion and a kinship towards the fellow New Yorker. At first though, he stood on the sidelines, afraid that if he said anything, the guys would ostracize him as well. However, after about two weeks Frank felt ashamed for feeling that way and started befriending Vincent.

Then one day, while Frank was talking to Fish, he saw three young men giving Vincent a hard time. Vincent, never one to back down, pushed one of them. Immediately, the three piled up on him and one quickly got him in a headlock. Frank rushed over, shoved one of the guys aside and then grabbed the one who had Vincent in the headlock. One of his cohorts jumped on top of Frank, but Charlie had instinctively followed his friend and pulled the thug off him. Now three-on-three, a melee ensued. Punches were thrown and landed, bodies grappled on the ground, and ob-scenities flew through the air. But it lasted only a few minutes be-fore the drill sergeant caught wind of it and roared over. "What the hell is going on over here?"

They all recognized that voice. And even in the heat of a fight, all six stopped, quickly brushed themselves off, and stood at atten-tion. "Nothing Drill Sergeant!" They said in unison.

One of them added: "We were just horsing around Drill Ser-geant!"

"Well I'm glad you all came here to horse around!" He yelled at the top of his lungs, as spit flew from his mouth. "But if you horse around out on the battlefield it will get you killed! Or get the man next to you killed! Is that what you want?"

"No Drill Sergeant!" They all yelled back.

"Now you sorry ass excuses for recruits, drop down and give me forty!"

From that point on, Vincent, or Vinny as they came to call him, became close friends with Charlie and Frank, and thus also with Bob. As for the three instigators, they would flash Vinny and his new friends evil looks, but it never again became physical.


As the weeks passed by, news of the war kept flooding in. Though every new story and rumor was listened to, it was news regarding the battle of the Pacific most the men were interested in. As news of the Marines' landing and ongoing campaign on Guadalcanal came in, Bob and Frank, starved for combat, joked that perhaps they should have joined the Marines. But they sensed that their time to join the fight was fast approaching.

By late August, it came time for Frank's and Bob's graduation. Unfortunately, because of the war, after graduation, their unit would have to stay on base to wait for deployment. There would only be a weekend pass and there would be no going back home for a few days. But unbeknownst to Frank, his parents decided to surprise him by driving up to Massachusetts for his graduation.

Moreover, they were bringing Mary.

During the outdoor ceremony, Frank aimlessly scanned the nearby bleachers and was shocked to catch sight of his parents and Mary. For a second, he literally thought he was dreaming. When he realized it was real, they were real, his entire body surged with warm euphoria. Frank wanted to run over to the bleachers. But then he remembered where he was and fought to remain at attention.

After the ceremony was over, Frank went to find his parents and Mary in the crowd. As he did, he kept telling himself: *Okay, when you greet them don't start crying like a baby. You're a soldier now. Hold it together!* Suddenly, he felt a tugging at his sleeve. As he turned around, Mary jumped into his arms.

"Oh Mary, I can't believe you guys came. It's so good to see you," he said, hugging her back.

"I had to see you before you got deployed."

Just then Frank opened his eyes and saw his parents standing there. He let go of Mary and hugged his mother.

"Oh Frank, we're so proud of you," she said before prying herself from him. "Look at you," she added, staring at her son. "Look at you in that uniform, you look so handsome."

"Son," Mr. Keller said, while extending his hand.

Frank firmly shook his father's hand. "Dad."

"Congratulations."

"Thank you," Frank replied with a smile.

"You're part of the First Army now."

Frank just nodded in response.

As they caught up, Frank saw Charlie walk by. He grabbed his friend and introduced him to Mary and his parents. Charlie had already heard much about them. Before the crowd dispersed, Frank also introduced them to Vinny. Of course, Bob also came over and said hello.

With a fresh weekend pass, Frank went with his parents into town. Mr. Keller insisted that Bob also come and they would all have dinner together. At first Bob balked, wanting to give them their privacy. But the Kellers would not take "no" for an answer, explaining that Bob was part of the family. In the car, Mary said Annette also wanted to come, but her parents would not let her. Annette's parents never approved of Bob, because they did not think he had a good enough pedigree. Her father, a wealthy land developer, thought only a young man from high society was good enough for his daughter. Naturally, Bob was upset about Annette. He was also disappointed that his own parents did not come for the graduation, though he understood, because his mother had recently fallen ill with meningitis. However, Bob was grateful he was not alone and was proud that the Kellers considered him part of the family.

Mr. Keller treated everyone to dinner at a seafood restaurant. For one night, he didn't care what he spent. The atmosphere was jovial. Frank and Bob joked about basic training. Harold ordered the boys beer. At first, Frank felt uncomfortable drinking in front of his parents, but Harold told them that they were now men and if they were old enough to fight for their country, they were old enough to drink beer.

At one point, Mary excused herself to use the powder room. A few minutes later, Frank said he needed to use the men's room. But he really went to meet Mary. By the hallway to the restrooms, he devised a plan with Mary so they could spend the night together.

By the time dinner was over, it was already 8:00 p.m. On the way out of the restaurant Frank was able to pull Bob aside just long enough to whisper in his ear, "Play along with me."

By the entranceway, Frank announced that he and Bob had promised Charlie and Vinny that they would meet them at a bar in town. Mr. Keller offered to drive them, but Frank said it was okay, that the bar was within walking distance. Not thinking anything of it, his parents said their goodbyes for the night, as did Mary.

Once they were gone, Frank turned to his best friend. "Listen Bob, you gotta do me this favor please."

"Sure, what is it?"

"I'm not going back to the base tonight. I'm going to catch a cab to the motel they're staying at and sneak into Mary's room to spend the night." Though both Frank and Mary were eighteen, in 1942, an unmarried couple sleeping together was still frowned upon, especially by one's parents.

Bob smiled and patted his friend on the cheek. "You devil, you."

"Is it okay if you find your way back to the base by yourself?"

"Of course. Don't worry about it. What are friends for?"

"You're the best," Frank proudly proclaimed. "You sure you'll be all right?"

Bob laughed. "Yeah, I think I can handle myself. Maybe I will walk around town and try to find some of the fellas. Maybe have a few more drinks and see if I can't get myself in some trouble."

Frank thanked his friend again. He then found a local and asked the address to the motel. When they told him that it was about a mile away, he asked for directions.

On the way to the motel, Frank stopped at a local store and bought a cheap bottle of Champagne. After quietly sneaking around the outside of the motel, Frank made his way to Mary's room, which was on the first floor and luckily not next to his parents' room. Mary gingerly opened the door to find Frank standing there with a devilish grin and a bottle of Champagne raised in his hand.

"Oh, Frank Keller, you're so bad."

"Well, you gonna let me in?"

Mary smiled and ushered him into the small room. There, the two drank the entire bottle and made love all night.

Frank was used to waking up at five, sometimes four in the morning. But after a night of drinking and Mary snuggled beside him, Frank was way too comfortable for his internal alarm clock to wake him up. It was not until 10:00 a.m. when Frank slowly lifted his eyelids to the bright light splintering in from the motel blinds. He looked over to a still sleeping, still naked Mary and closed his eyes. But then somehow, through his hazy mind, Frank realized he was supposed to meet his parents for lunch. And what if they called or knocked on Mary's door? He quickly panicked. Frank shook Mary awake. After a few moments of her gaining full consciousness, he explained the situation.

Mary was more nonchalant. "Don't worry about it, they're not just goin' to barge in here. You can hide in the bathroom. We can take a shower together," she smiled seductively, "and then we can meet them. You can make up some story about how you just took a cab to the motel."

"But I have no clothes. I can't show up wearing my same formal dress that I wore the night before. They're not stupid."

Reluctantly, Mary saw Frank's point. The revised plan was for him to take a taxi back to the base, change and then come back to the motel. Not planning ahead, Frank realized that with buying the bottle of Champagne, he did not have enough money to pay for a cab back to the base and then back to the motel. Mary went in her purse and gave him five dollars.

"No way. I'm not taking money from you."

"Don't be silly. Frank, please, it's no big deal."

Frank thought about the situation and though he felt embarrassed to take money from Mary, he saw no other choice. But before he went to find a cab, the two did take that shower together.

By the time Frank arrived back at base it was 12:30 p.m. Frank showed his pass and scurried to his barracks. There, he ran into Bob, who was a sight for sore eyes. "What are you doing here?"

"I had to come back to put on my civilian clothes. I'm supposed to meet my parents and I couldn't be wearing the same uniform as last night."

"You have a good night?" Bob asked with a dry smile, as he slapped his friend on the shoulder.

"That's none of your business." Frank looked his friend over. His eyes were completely bloodshot, his uniform un-tucked, and he was swaying. "What the hell happened to you?"

Bob snickered. "I found a bar in town and actually ran into Fish, Frenchy and a few of the other fellas. I feel like a truck ran me over. I've never been so shit-ass drunk in my life. Fish was making me drink whiskey."

Frank smiled and laughed. "You guys are fucking crazy. Just as long as none of you got picked up by the MPs."

Frank met his parents and Mary back at the motel and the four went to lunch. They then jaunted about town for a few hours, taking their time, mostly lost in lighthearted conversation. Frank's parents expected him to stay the night at the motel with them. Understandably, they wanted to spend as much time with their son as possible. After all, there was no doubt he would soon be heading to the frontline. Wanting to spend his last free night with Mary, Frank explained that he found out that he actually had to be back at the base that night. His pass was only good through that evening. He felt guilty lying to his parents, especially not knowing the next time he would see them. But he could not resist spending another night with Mary.

After dinner, Frank said his goodbyes. But before Frank left, Harold asked Margaret and Mary if he could go to the bar and have one drink with his son. "I know you have to get back, but…"

"Of course. I have time."

The small town's only three taverns were abuzz with service men on leave. But, Harold and his son found a place at the bar. With foam overflowing from his mug, Mr. Keller raised it for a cheer. Without saying a word, Frank raised his glass. "God be with you, son," Harold proudly said.

The two mugs clanked together. "Thank you, Dad," Frank replied over the roar of the tavern. The father and son then took a swig of their respective beers.

"I really am proud of you, son. And though God knows I wish there wasn't a war—and me and your mother will worry about you every day—what you're doing is noble."

"Thank you, Pop. I know it's not easy for you and mom, but I'm in good hands. Just like you said when you dropped me off at the bus depot. Those are great mean I'll be fightin' with."

Mr. Keller nodded. "I know they are son. I know they are." He then took another drink of beer, but after he was finished he stared down at the bar.

Frank could sense that something was wrong. "What is it, Dad?"

Mr. Keller took a moment before answering. "It's just…well…I know I was always working and, well… I just wish I coulda been there for you more."

Frank put his hand on his father's shoulder. "Dad, look at me."

Mr. Keller lifted his head from the bar and stared at his son.

"Don't you ever say that. You've always been there for me. I would never be the person I am today without you, without your support, your advice and wisdom. And I can never in a million years ever repay you for that."

Harold smiled as he fought not to cry. Besides his marriage and the birth of his daughter and son, this was the next most proudest moment in his life. And they were words that in the inevitable passage of time, he would take with him to the grave.

The father and son, one a veteran of the first World War and the other soon to be of the second, had another few beers and talked some more. However, they now laughed and joked about their respective experiences of basic training. That was before the conversation turned to the Brooklyn Dodgers. Frank had always thought that he and his father had a good relationship, but this was the first time they had ever talked together, man-to-man. And that was a memory he would treasure forever.

As Harold and Frank left the bar, squeezing their way through a sea of drunken servicemen, the elder put his hand on his son's shoulder. "You have fun tonight and don't worry, I won't tell your mother."

"What are you talking about?"

Harry pushed open the door and the two stepped outside. "I was once a young man in love myself. I understand."

After saying hello to someone he recognized going into the bar, Frank looked at his father. He knew what he meant. "Thanks for understanding, Pop."

"I just hope that after you get back from the war, you and Mary get married. She's a good girl."

Frank smiled. "Yes she is."

Mr. Keller took a cab back to the motel, but Frank decided to walk again. He was glad his father understood about him and

Mary, but it was still too weird to take a car back together so he could have sex with his girlfriend—even if it was the woman he was planning to marry.

For what would be the last night, Frank showed up at Mary's motel room. Mary was pleased to find him ecstatic about his time with his father. "It was great," he kept repeating. But eventually, it became all about she and him. After the thrill of that morning, they decided to take another shower together. Then, they had long, passionate sex.

In the morning, both realized that this would be goodbye for a long time and though they dared not say it, possibly forever. Mary promised herself before she even came on the trip that she would not cry. She knew that Frank had enough on his mind.

"You know, Frank," she said as she lay under the covers next to him, "I meant what I said at the bus depot—I will wait for you no matter what, no matter how long it takes. I know you're not always going to be able to write. But know that I will always be with you. And when you come home, whenever that may be, I'll be standing there waiting for you."

Frank was overcome by a calm sensation of gratefulness. He felt truly blessed for having someone so caring, so devoted, so amazing as Mary. He believed every word that she said, without a splinter of doubt. And he knew that no matter what the war brought him, she would indeed always be right there beside him, maybe not in person, but in spirit.

# 5

# THE LONG WAIT

A week after graduation, Frank's unit was on a converted cruise ship, headed for Britain. Frank, Bob and quite a few of the other men were bitter that they were being sent to Europe instead of the Pacific. Many young men joined the service after Pearl Harbor with hope of playing a small, but personal part in exacting revenge on the Japanese. But stopping Hitler and the Third Reich's merciless conquest was the next best thing.

It took over a week to reach Britain, but for Frank, it felt much longer. It was a large ship, but every crevasse seemed jammed with servicemen. Men were piled up several to a cabin. Some slept in the auditorium and even on deck. Moreover, most showers were a luxury that not everyone was afforded and only officers were able to bathe once a day. But more than the cramped quarters and the stench of body odor, it was the sheer boredom that played on Frank's mind. Used to rigorous daily exercise, men on the boat had to make themselves workout and there was little space. Like most others, Frank did pushups and jumping jacks. He also walked around a lot, but after the first few times around the ship, the scenery quickly became old. Mostly, Frank bided his time by writing letters and playing cards with Bob and the other guys. He even made some new acquaintances. But if Frank thought that the boat ride to Europe was uneventful and long, he had no idea what lay ahead for him in the next year and a half. It would be a time that some of the men would refer to as "The Long Wait."

Immediately after arriving in Britain all the servicemen on the ship were ushered to a large base in the countryside of England, where they were housed with other elements of the First Army, as well as British soldiers. It would be their home for longer than any of them could have imagined.

Fortunately, Frank and Bob were housed in the same barracks, as was Fish. Vinny was a few barracks over, but during the day everyone mingled. As Frank and the rest of the new arrivals settled into their post, rumors swirled about just when and where would be the first major joint mission. Most agreed that it had to be soon. They were wrong.

Two weeks after their arrival, Frank, Bob, Charlie, Vinny, and a few other men went on a day tour of London. It was the first time they had seen the devastation of war up close and personal. Frank walked around the narrow, dust-filled streets and gazed in awe at the ruins left behind by the Luftwaffe. Some buildings had been reduced to mere rubble. Others looked like ghostly, skeletal remains, silent facades protruding with twisted, steel. *Were people in them when they were bombed* Frank wondered? As he strolled down the street, the whole scene was so surreal. Despite the backdrop of war-torn stores and buildings, some still smoldering, locals walked about, seemingly unfazed. Next to a demolished two-story building, half of it lying in bricks, was a bakery opened for business. Frank asked their guide, Fredrick, about the store.

"Obviously, everything is heavily rationed," replied the tall, slender Londoner, who looked to be about nineteen. "But people still have to eat. Life still has to go on. When the air raid sirens go off, people put on their gas masks and run to the nearest shelter. But other than that, we can't just hide in a closet."

"What's it like?" Asked one of the Americans. "What's it like during a raid? I mean how close have you been?"

Fredrick, who was in the lead, came to an abrupt stop and turned around. "The Germans first started bombing London in August of nineteen-forty. Like every other Londoner, I've lived through my share of air raids. And though after a while you come to accept it and even get over it quicker, while it's happening, it's as terrifying as that first time." Fredrick paused and looked up. "Usually, you hear the siren first and it's loud. You put on your gas mask—everyone in London has one, they even have masks fitted for babies—and depending where you are, you head for a shelter. But you think maybe it's just a false alarm, or maybe they're gonna hit another part of town. But when you hear those roaring engines overhead"—Fredrick's voice grew deeper and slower—"you know it's for real. And then your heart starts pounding out of your chest and you wonder is this going to be it? I mean how many raids can you escape unscathed? Sooner or later your luck has to run out. And make no mistake about it, shelter or no shelter, with hundreds of bombs falling out of the sky, whether or not one falls right on top of you is sheer luck."

"How long do they usually last?" Bob asked, with a somber voice.

"It all depends. Usually not more than twenty minutes. But believe me, it feels like a hell of a lot longer. And if you're nearby when those bombs start falling, you can feel the concussion throughout your whole body, like somebody's actually punching you in the gut. And the sound… well I don't even think I know the words to describe that sound. Not only of the bombs themselves, but entire buildings crashing down. The whole word seems like it's shaking."

Everyone was hanging on Fredrick's every word.

"And then when it's finally over, sometimes that's actually the hardest part. You look yourself over to make sure you're still in one piece. You wonder if you're trapped, if your neighbors survived, if there's gonna be a second wave. Then finally you make your way outside to assess the damage. There's fire everywhere. And all you can hear is the roaring of the flames—that and children crying. People are walking around like zombies, some holding the injured and dead." Fredrick let out a deep sigh. "I've lost an uncle, two cousins, and several friends. That's why I can't wait to get some payback and start killin' some Nazis."

The group walked around some more through the war-ravished town. Frank remained mesmerized by the bombed-out buildings and how, as Fredrick had said, life went on all around them. But also as his guide pointed out, what choice did the people have? After a few more blocks, Fredrick stopped and pointed out across the street to a hollowed-out, two-story building that had only partial west and east walls still standing. "That used to be a school. Luckily, it was a night raid that leveled it, so none of the children were in it. But there are other schools that weren't so lucky and got hit during the day. And sometimes the air raid sirens go off too late. Sometimes, especially early on, they didn't go off at all."

On the bus ride home, Frank silently stared out the window at the smoldering city. He had known about the air raids on London for a long time. He had even seen footage of the aftermath. But being there, seeing the brute devastation was completely different. He had walked atop the same ground where people had been killed. He had come face-to-face with decimated houses where entire families had been wiped out. Frank's heart went out to the people of London. He tried to imagine the horror they had been living with for the past several years. Then, he could not help but think of France and the other European countries overrun by the blitzkrieg. *How many people had been devoured by the Nazi war machine*, he wondered? Frank had been so fixated on Japan, but he was now re-focused on the human plague killing all of Europe. No longer bitter about not being sent to the Pacific, he was proud to play his part in hopefully helping to defeat the Third Reich.

It was not just compassion for the European allies and determination to fight against Germany that Frank was feeling as he stared out that bus window. For the first time since enlisting, the eighteen-year-old felt fear. In touring London, he realized now more than ever, that death was neither abstract nor glorious. It was very much real, very much indiscriminate, and very much brutal. But more than anything, it was final. For the first time Frank thought long and hard about the possibility of not making it home, of never seeing his parents or Mary again, of never living past his teenage years.

Throughout the rest of the day Frank wrestled with the fear of dying. But by nighttime, what bothered him the most was the fear of being afraid. What if he froze up on the battlefield? What if he cowered the first time someone started shooting at him? The other men were depending on him. He was part of a team, a unit. How he acted could literally mean life or death for the man standing next to him. That's when Frank realized that no matter how scared he might be stepping onto the battlefield for the first time, he had to suck it up, if not for himself, than for his comrades.

Each passing week came with the arrival of new servicemen. As more men, artillery, and supplies accumulated at the base, so grew the sense that something big was going to happen soon. But then another week would pass, then another month. Life at the base became monotonous. There was a lot of training, but there was also plenty of downtime. There was a lot of card playing and joking around. Some of the British soldiers played cricket, while the Americans mostly played baseball. Some men kept to themselves, reading books and writing letters. But even the most recluse could only read so many books, write so many letters. Inevitably cliques were formed, as well as divisions. There were the occasional arguments and even fights. Spending so much time together, sometimes even friends came to blows.

Frank hung out with Bob naturally, and also Charlie and Vincent. But in time, he also made new friends. One in particular was a fellow eighteen-year-old who occupied the bunk next to him. John Harrison was a tall, redheaded high school graduate from Montgomery, Alabama, with a strong southern drawl. Frank quickly learned that John's family lived on a ranch and had five horses. Frank told him about American Horse and his infatuation with equines. John was more than happy to tell his new friend all about life on the ranch. But in the end, what they wound up talking about most were their girls back home. However, unlike Frank, John married his sweetheart right before he went off to basic training. Her name was Beverly. John eagerly showed Frank a photograph and in return, Frank let him see a picture of Mary. Of course, almost all the men had girls waiting back in the States—or at least said they did. But whereas many of the other guys seemed to mention their women in passing, neither Frank nor John could talk enough about them. John would go on about the "world's best" blueberry pie Beverly could make, or how beautiful her blonde hair looked blowing in the breeze. Frank would gush over Mary's hypnotic eyes, her perfect figure, and how caring and smart she was.

"So you gonna ask her ta' marry you?" John asked with his southern accent in one of their first conversations.

"As soon as I get home," Frank instantly replied with a smile. "We're gonna get married and we're gonna start a family."

John let out a cloud of smoke from his cigarette. "Yeah, I can't wait to have kids. I want at least three of them, at least two boys. Man, it'd be great teachin' them baseball and how to ride a horse." John paused and smiled, as if he was picturing himself running around with his two, yet-to-be-born sons.


Fall inevitably gave way to winter, and winter to spring. Then, one day, Frank looked at the calendar and realized that eight months had passed since he had arrived in Britain. Eight, long months without seeing any action. But outside the confines of the base, the tides of war appeared to be changing. In Europe, Germany had been defeated at Stalingrad. Montgomery's Eighth Army had taken Tripoli. America had joined Britain in launching massive air raids on German cities. The Third Reich had begun withdrawing from Tunisia. When was it going to be their turn to join the fight, Frank, Bob, and the others wondered? It seemed the war was passing them by. They were tired of training and sitting around on their hands. By now, they were frothing at the chance of some action.

A tension had started brewing between some of the American and British soldiers. Things were said like, "I guess you Yanks are here just to go into town and take our women." Though most of the Americans wanted more than anything to jump into battle, there was a growing sentiment amongst the locals that they were just there for show. Of course, this did not sit well with the Americans. But it was not just the tension between the two allies. Everyone seemed to be getting on everyone else's nerves. And everyone was asking the same question: *What the hell are we doing here?* Without the enemy firing a single shot, morale began to unwind.

In early July, Frank, Bob, and Fish were playing cards in the barracks when Vinny walked over. "Well, I'm shippin' out," he said matter-of-fact.

All three men put down their cards and looked up at him. "Whaddaya mean your shippin' out?" Asked Bob with the same puzzled look Frank and Fish had.

"I'm bein' transferred to First Division."

Fish stood up. "What are you talkin' about?"

"I got called into command. They asked me if I spoke Italian. I said yes and the lieutenant said that I was to report to First Division headquarters and that I would be shipping out tomorrow morning."

Frank, Bob, and Charlie looked at each other.

"I guess that means only one thing: We're off to Italy."

"What about the Twenty-Ninth?" Frank asked about their division. "Only the First is going?"

Vincent laughed. "You think they debriefed me? They didn't even tell me where I was goin'. But I mean, why else would they want me and specifically ask if I spoke Italian? Hell, I probably shouldn't even be telling you guys, so please keep it on the down low."

They all agreed they would.

Vinny looked at his watch. "Well I should really be goin' and gettin' my shit together. We're supposed to be headin' out at oh-four-hundred hours… I just wanted to come and say goodbye."

Frank put his hand on his friend's shoulder. "Take care of yourself, Vinny."

"Yeah, stay safe," Bob added before Charlie chimed in.

"You too, fella's. Maybe we'll run into each other somewhere on the front."

"Yeah, in Berlin," Fish said emphatically. "When we raise the American flag!"

All four cheered and laughed. Then, unceremoniously, the eighteen-year-old from Brooklyn, New York, who they had all considered a good friend, walked off to join the battle. None of them knew if they would ever see him again.


A week later, Frank ran into Bob outside the mess hall and could instantly tell that something was wrong. "I can't believe it!" Bob ranted.

"What? What's the matter?"

Bob shook his head. "I just got a letter from Annette. She said she found someone else. You believe that shit?"

Frank was shocked. He had certainly not seen that coming. "Are you serious?" He could tell that Bob was not playing around, but he did not know what else to say.

Bob let out a heavy sigh and shook his head again. "Yeah. She said she's sorry, she didn't mean for it to happen. What does that even mean? If she didn't mean for it to happen she wouldn't have done it."

"Ah man, I'm sorry." Bob was venting and showing his anger, but Frank knew how despondent he must have also been. He knew how much Bob loved Annette and that he was planning to propose to her after the war. Frank would do anything for his best friend. However, he found himself not knowing exactly what to say, what to do. "You're a good guy, Bob. You'll find someone even better."

Bob knew his friend was trying to help. "I know. Thanks buddy. I'll be all right." He was lying. Inside, Bob was crushed.

That evening, Frank was still dwelling on what Bob had told him. He felt horrible for his friend. But for the first time, Frank started to wonder if he would some day receive a similar letter from Mary. He had already been gone a long time and who knew how much longer it would be before he would return home. He hadn't even yet seen any combat. Frank did not doubt that Mary loved him, but she was a beautiful, young woman. Certainly, she had many suitors. How long could she really wait and put her life on hold?

For the next day and a half Frank wrestled with the fear of Mary finding another man, or simply not being able to wait for him. But by the second night, he chose to believe the promise that Mary had made, that no matter how long it would take, she would be there waiting for him. That night, as he lay in bed, before lights out, he wrote another letter to her.

*Dear Mary,*

*I guess you heard about Annette running off with another man. Bob received a letter from her the other day. I feel so bad for him. I also feel so helpless. I mean what could I say or do to make him feel better? I wish there was something. If you have any suggestions, please let me know. I realize that if you did know about it, you didn't mention it in any of your letters, because you knew I would have to tell him and how crushed he would be. I'm so glad that I have someone like you. I can't tell you how lucky I know I am.*

*As for what else is going on, I guess by now you've all heard about the Allies landing in Sicily. About a week and a half ago Vinny was shipped out and I'm certain he was part of the invasion. I really hope he's ok. He's a real good guy and I'm sure he's doing a fine job. I hope I will see him again one day.*

*When Vinny was shipped out we all started thinking that it was only a matter of days before we received our orders. But so far it's just been more waiting. However, now with us landing in Sicily and the ground offensive underway, I'm sure the time will come soon for the rest of us get our marching orders. So if you don't hear from me again for a little while, don't be alarmed. It'll just be because there will be a blackout from writing home, or there will be no way to send mail. But I'll write again as soon as I can.*

*Give my love to your mother and father. And as always, all my love to you.*

Three weeks passed and it was still the status quo for Frank and his friends at the base. They started wondering if the war was going to be over before they even had a chance to see any combat. The boredom and frustration kept mounting. However, at least for a day, Frank's spirits were lifted from receiving a letter from Mary.

*Dear Frank,*

*I was so sorry to hear about Bob. No, I did not know about it until your letter. Though Annette had been acting very strange, not returning my calls and suddenly not wanting to get together with me. I should have known. But after your letter, I went to her house and gave her a piece of my mind. She's always been a good friend, but I don't know how she could have done that to Bob. He had always been so good to her. And here he is putting his life on the line, fighting for our freedom and she's off with some other man.*

*Frank, I feel bad even saying this, because I know you trust me. But I have to tell you anyway. I never want you to have to worry for even one second about me. Like I've told you before, no matter how long I have to wait, you are the only man I want to be with.*

*As for not seeing any combat yet, I know you don't want to hear this, but I would be more than happy if you never left that base. But if you do, be careful and know that everyone back home is praying for your safe return. By the way, mom and dad are always touched how you ask about them and that you send them your love. They always ask about you as well. They're very proud of you. But then again, they were always very proud of you.*

*I am doing well, still working four days a week at the factory. It's the least I can do to contribute to the war effort. Besides, it's not that bad. In fact, I actually enjoy keeping busy. And don't worry, all the guys know I'm taken. In fact, I talk about you so much that sometimes I think my coworkers get sick of it. Too bad!*

*Frank, I dream about the day you come home and I can fall into your arms. I dream about the day I can once again touch your face and kiss you. Until then, you will be in my every thought and I will keep writing.*

*Love always,*
*Mary*

After reading the letter, Frank closed his eyes and imagined holding Mary's soft, delicate frame. He imagined sifting his fingers through her long, black hair. He imagined breathing her subtle perfume. "When are we going to launch the big offensive and put an end to this goddamn war," he muttered to himself. It already felt like he had been away from home and Mary for eons.

# 6

# HELL ON EARTH

It was 1944. Over two years had already passed since Pear Harbor. In the Pacific, sea and land battles had been raging for some time. In Europe, British and American bombers had launched a long and seemingly effective air campaign on Germany, as Soviet troops fought bloody battle after bloody battle, pushing back the Third Reich on the Eastern Front. But until the recent landings in Sicily, Taranto, and Anzio, major U.S. and British ground forces had been abeyant. And even with Allied troops now fighting throughout Italy, the bulk of the British and American armies sat in bases in Britain, waiting for "The Big One", the big ground offensive against the Wehrmacht that surely had to be coming. The wait was over.

As May came to a close, nearly everyone at Frank's base received notice that they would be shipping out within days. No one but high-ranking officers were privy to the destination, but everyone knew that this was the big one. By now, with fresh servicemen and equipment arriving on a continuous basis, even with the recent deployment of troops to Italy, the buildup had become massive. Frank's base was abuzz with activity. Endless rows of crates were being stacked on pallets twenty feet high and a block deep. Countless tanks, cannons, Jeeps, and trucks were lined up and inspected. Runners were sprinting through the grounds carrying messages from post to post. Mail call had been halted. Electricity was pulsating not only through the air, but within the veins of every enlisted man. They were finally going to get the chance to prove themselves in battle, finally going to do what they had signed up for.

It was the early morning of June 6th, off the coast of France. Under a dark, rainy sky, Frank Keller stood on the rail of a transport ship along with hundreds of other men, staring in disbelief at the colossal armada in which they were a part. They were heading towards the beaches of Normandy.

As the sea pitched, most men were quiet, each reflecting on his own thoughts. By now, most of them had been frothing over the chance to finally see combat. But now that it was upon them, they wondered what really waited for them.

As a faint, foggy image of land appeared, Frank turned to Bob, who was standing by his side. "Well, I guess this is what we came here for," he said with a half smile.

Bob patted his friend on the back. "Just be careful out there. Remember, I promised your old man that I would get you home in one piece."

The two looked at each other and laughed, breaking up the seriousness of the moment, if only for a second.

As the morning began to hazily illuminate through the thick clouds, the orders were given to start boarding the awaiting landing crafts. In an instant, organized chaos broke out. With the seas still churning, men, bogged down with rifles and other equipment, began to make the descent down the rope nets to the jerking crafts. As they did, nearby battleships and destroyers started shelling the shore. Frank could not believe how loud their guns were. He could feel their concussion throughout his entire body. The orders being yelled by commanding officers had been replaced by a constant, high-pitch ringing. Until his hearing came back, Frank just followed the group of men in front of him.

With an overpowering surge of adrenaline, Frank looked across the horizon. Even in the dim light of morning, he could see that there were even more ships than he realized. In fact, his eyes could not even reach the end of the flotilla. There were battleships, destroyers, cruisers, transports, frigates, hospital ships, and tankers. There were so many ships, jammed so close together that one could almost jump from one to the other. The commanding officer had told them before boarding the ship in England that they were going to be making history—and now Frank knew it was true.

Still fixated on the enormity of the invasion, Frank felt a push from behind.

"Let's go," someone yelled.

It was his turn to climb down to the landing craft. With a full backpack and a large, heavy M1 Garand slung over his shoulder, Frank climbed over the rail and onto the rope net, which was already crowded with other men making the same descent. Immediately, his left foot slipped off the net, as the entire ship pitched in the white-capped waves. Then his right foot came loose. Gripping onto the rope rungs with all of his might, Frank fought to swing his feet back into place.

"Come on!" The person above him yelled. Though the boat and net continued to sway, he managed to regain his footing and continue the descent. But Frank noticed that he was far from the only one having trouble making his way down. It was like trying to climb down a net in an earthquake—with people above and below you and on each side. Finally, when Frank was almost to the now half-full landing craft, he felt someone grab his ankles. "Come on, I've got you." He let go as two infantrymen grabbed his legs and eased him the rest of the way down.

"Thanks!" he said as the same two men were already helping another soldier.

"Watch out!"

Frank instinctively looked up to see someone completely lose his footing and grip, and fall off the net. It was about a fifteen-foot drop and though he did not take anyone else with him, his head hit the metal side of the landing craft. Blood spurted in the air as if someone had slapped a sink full of red water and the poor soul violently tumbled into the ocean in between the craft and the ship.

"Let's go, keep 'em coming! He's gone!" Yelled an officer.

Bob ended up on a different landing craft. After Frank's was full, it jettisoned from the transport ship, joining the countless other landing crafts racing towards the shoreline. The waves were turbulently rocking the small vessel and the only thing keeping the standing men from falling was that they were too jammed next to each other. Frank knew it would be a short ride to the beach, but time seemed to slow. As the deafening roar of the battleships' enormous sixteen-inch guns continuously thundered through the air, planes roared overhead, and plumes of smoke covered the seemingly endless beach. Frank once again found himself filling with fear. But this was a much more intense, a much more physical fear than what he had felt after surveying the aftermath of the air raids on London. His heart pounding, he fought not to vomit. *Pull yourself together*, he told himself. *Don't be a coward! You're a soldier! This is what you signed up for! Your country is counting on you! The men next to you are counting on you! Look at them, they're not afraid!* But as Frank looked around at the other men, he noticed that nearly everyone one of them had the look of fear in their eyes. A few of them were throwing up.

Before Frank had another second to ponder his thoughts and feelings, the landing craft came to a stop and the large, metal ramp at the bow flew open. "Come on, get your asses out!" A sergeant yelled.

In the middle of the craft, Frank blindly followed the stampede of men out the front opening. But he soon realized that instead of landing right on the beach, they were about twenty yards away. As soon as they ran off the ramp they fell into the churning water, almost up to their chins. Like the men in front of him, Frank held his rifle over his head and slogged through the frigid water.

As Frank approached the beach, he thought one thing: *This must be hell on Earth*. Cannons, mortars, machine guns, rifles, and exploding mines all roaring at once made it so he could not even hear the person next to him. Nearly every foot of shoreline was filled with man and machine. Acrid smoke and the stench of diesel and death filled the air. A squadron of warplanes roared low overhead before dropping earth-shattering bombs on the ridgeline, from where German artillery were peppering the beach. Men all around him were being hit by unseen fire. Instinctively, he went to the ground, lying on his stomach. As the sounds of rounds whizzed passed him, Frank looked for a place to take cover—but there was none.

From the corner of his eye, Frank saw the figure of someone falling down next to him. He turned to look; it was John Harrison, who had been in the same landing craft. "We gotta get the hell off this beach!" John yelled at the top of his lungs, just to be heard over the explosions and gunfire.

"How the hell are we supposed to do that? Where's the lieutenant?"

A shell landed a few yards away, erupting earth and shrapnel into the air in a smoky, fiery plume. Frank and John held onto their helmets and burrowed their heads into the hard, rocky sand, as the sound of the blast thundered through in their ears.

After a second, John lifted his head. "I don't know where he is! I don't know who's givin' the orders! But we can't just lay here like sittin' ducks!" John pointed to a small sand dune about thirty yards away, where about a dozen men were already taking cover. "I say we make a run for that dune! It's not much, but it's better than right here! Maybe there's a CO over there!"

Frank nodded in agreement.

"Okay, on the count of three we run like hell!"

"Let's do it!"

John counted to three as loud as he could and the two friends sprang to their feet and started running. John was about three steps ahead when Frank saw a wide spray of blood and chunks of meat burst from his midsection. Instantaneously, John flew backwards and landed on his back. Frank dropped to his knees over him. Suddenly, somehow everything fell silent. "John!" He yelled, as he looked down at his convulsing friend, blood spitting from his mouth.

John grabbed his arm. "Frank," he gargled through thick, red blood. "I don't want to die." Then, almost immediately, John stopped moving.

Frank was in horrified disbelief. He had seen other men go down, be shot, step on a land mine, or have their limbs ripped apart by shrapnel from nearby exploding shells. But this was John! This was his friend! In a split second all the times they shared, all their conversations, raced through his mind. What about his new wife Beverly, he cried inside? He was supposed to make it home and start a family.

But Frank did not have the time to kneel there and grieve for his friend. A battle was ranging on all around him. Frank turned and looked at the dune that they had been running towards. But as the sounds and smell of war snapped back to his consciousness, he felt paralyzed. It was as if he was just kneeling there, waiting for that inevitable bullet that would render him another victim lying lifeless on the beach. But then, something came to him: They were the faces of Mary and his parents. *You can't just lie down and die! Whatever is going to happen is going to happen, but you owe it to them, you owe it to your comrades and your country, you owe it to yourself dammit, to go down fighting!* Then, with his hand, Frank touched his head, shoulders and heart making the holy cross and said aloud, "God, give me the strength to do what I'm about to do." With that, Frank stood halfway up and in a crouched position, zigzagged to the dune.

As Frank hid behind the crowded dune, a sergeant was already shouting orders. "We gotta leave this position and get to those cliffs! You"—he pointed to a private—"come with me and Charlie! We'll lead the way!" Rapid fire sprayed the top of the dune, but luckily, none of the men were up high enough to get hit. "Gunner," the sergeant yelled to a soldier holding a heavy machine gun, "you cover us and fire everything you've got at that ridge!"

With his heart pounding like a jackhammer, Frank left the relative cover of the dune and sprinted towards the base of the cliff. Hell was still raging all around him. Men—alive, dead, and wounded—littered the exploding beach. Every second felt like minutes. Suddenly, he tripped and fell. Frank looked to see what it was he had tripped on; it was the upper half of a man, blood and intestines spewing out of his torso. Where his legs were, Frank could only imagine. With no time to dwell on the horrific sight, he sprang back up and started running again.

Frank was almost to the foot of the cliff when a shell landed about five yards to his left, knocking him down once more. The explosion felt and sounded so close that this time, instead of continuing his run, Frank crawled to the smoldering remnants of a Jeep to take cover, just to make sure he was still in one piece. To his exaltation, he was unscathed. Before getting fully back up, Frank peered around the back of the Jeep and fired several shots from his M1 towards the German positions at the top of the cliff. The area was heavily fortified and Frank was not aiming at anyone or anything in particular. He told himself it was necessary to join the suppressive fire in which the Allies were continuously spraying. But part of him just wanted to shoot at the enemy who was trying to kill him.

Just as Frank was about to leave the Jeep he saw an American soldier sprint right past him and get hit by a round. Without any hesitation, Frank ran over to the fallen man. He had been shot in the left thigh. As Frank crouched over him, he could hear other rounds whizzing all around him. Without wasting any time, and without exchanging any words, Frank threw the six-foot man over his shoulders and using all his strength and adrenaline, stood up and started running. But after about only five yards, Frank felt what seemed like a hammer hit him in the head and the two men tumbled to the ground. Frank was sure he had been shot in the head and was breathing his final breath.

The wounded man grabbed his arm. "It's okay. It only skimmed your helmet."

Frank could feel himself smile. With a new lease on life, at least for the moment, he once again strapped the stranger over his shoulders and took off running. Before he knew it, they were at the base of the cliff, along with dozens of other men. After placing the man on the ground, Frank took off his jacket and then his shirt. "We gotta get this around your leg," he said, working feverishly to tie a tourniquet around the top of the man's thigh.

"Thank you for saving my life," he said through grimacing pain. "I would've been a goner had I stayed laying another minute."

"No problem." As soon as the words left Frank's mouth, for the first time, he realized the stripes on the man's sleeve. "No problem Sergeant!"

"I got separated from what was left of my squad when our position came under heavy artillery fire. I don't know if there's any of them left." He paused. "My radioman took one in the head. I tried to..."

The sergeant said he needed to go look for any surviving members of his unit, but he could not even stand, let alone walk. Frank assured him that he would ask around, and for the first time the two exchanged names. Eventually, Frank transferred him to a medic and wished him well. Though Sergeant Thomas J. Elmer would lose his leg, he would never forget that Frank had saved his life—while risking his own—and officially put in a recommendation for a Silver Star, which Frank later received.


By the next morning, though fighting still remained, the continuous carnage and mayhem of the previous day had subsided. From a position atop a cliff, with sporadic heavy and small gunfire echoing through the nearby distance, Frank looked down on the still smoldering beach. It had been turned into a macabre cemetery of men and half-burned vehicles. Bodies and body parts were strewn everywhere. Some were covered with white, but most were not.

Medics were busy evacuating the wounded, trying to help even those who were destined to die. On the shoreline, landing crafts brought fresh meat and supplies, and trucks tried to maneuver between the dead bodies, rolls of barbwire, shelled-out vehicles, and craters. Sitting on a large rock, rifle on his lap, Frank could hear the faint voices from the beach and engines of the tanks and trucks. However, notwithstanding the occasional bang of artillery fire, the landscape seemed silent compared to the deafening chaos of the initial landing.

As Frank stared down at the countless bodies littering the pockmarked earth, he was not filled with elation that he had survived. Instead, he was overcome with one resounding question: Why did he survive when so many others had not? It was not some special skill or training, not some superhuman power that let him escape even injury. Was it fate, he wondered? Or was it simply luck of the draw?

Frank reunited with what was left of his unit, but he could not find Bob. Fearing the worst, he frantically asked one person after another if they knew what happened to his best friend. Several people said they had seen him on the beach during the landing, but did not know his whereabouts after that. Suddenly, Frank felt a hard slap on his shoulder. He turned around to see a dirty, but familiar face. "Fish!" It was his friend, Charlie Hudson.

Charlie greeted Frank with a bear hug. "Bayside, damn is it good to see you!"

Frank smiled. "It's good to see you too!" But the smile quickly ran away from his face. "Hey, have you seen Bob? I can't find him anywhere and no one knows what happened to him." Frank was afraid of what the answer might be.

"Me, Terry, and Rupert were with him. One of the other guys we were with stepped on a mine and some of the shrapnel got Bob and Terry." Charlie could see the immediate look of anxiety on Frank's face. "But it just wounded him. Some of it hit Bob in the arm and shoulder. It looked pretty deep, but we managed to get him to a medic." Charlie paused. "But a piece of shrapnel hit Terry in the face, right in the left eye. He probably still would have survived, but as he was running with us—on his own, even with blood gushing from his head—he was hit with a round right through the midsection." Charlie looked down and shook his head. "There was nothing we could do for him after that."

"I'm sorry to hear that. He was a good guy." Frank then told Charlie about what happened to John Harrison. Sadly, it was a similar conversation that countless friends were having that day—and would continue to have for some time.

"So what happened to Rupert?" Frank finally asked.

"He should be around here somewhere. He twisted his ankle, maybe sprained it, but that's it."

Frank would later find out that though he did not lose his arm, Bob's wounds were serious enough to get him sent home. He would never return to the frontline. Fortunately, besides large scars on his left shoulder and arm, the only permanent damage Bob would suffer was a slight loss of hearing in one ear.


Over the next couple of weeks, Frank's unit, along with most of the initial invasion force, fought to completely secure the beachfront and surrounding areas. However, day by day the fighting faded and was never near the hell of June 6th. As more troops, tanks, artillery, and supplies arrived from ships, the men awaited their next assignment. But for most of them, their pent-up bravado and enthusiasm about war had been left on Normandy's shoreline.

# 7

# SO THIS IS WAR?

In the beginning of July, Frank was part of a large infantry, and mechanized force heading towards the city of Saint-Lo. However, on the grassy, hilled outskirts of the city they were met by heavy German resistance, in what would come to be known as The Battle of the Hedgerows.

Under mortar and cannon shelling, Frank's unit took a position by a splotch of dense hedges and shrubs, between two open hillsides. The artillery battery they were attached to returned fire. Howitzers roared as thick clouds of fire and smoke erupted from their muzzles. The whole ground shook.

"All right listen up!" Frank's lieutenant shouted to a group of about thirty men, trying to be heard over the thundering of artillery fire. "Our platoon is going to follow those two tanks over there through those lines of hedgerows," he yelled while pointing, "and come up on those Germans' right flank! We're gonna be noisy with those Shermans rolling with us, but hopefully with all this shelling going on they won't hear us till we're right up on them!" The lieutenant then shouted the go ahead to the two men sprouting out of their respective tanks.

With Fish and the lieutenant, Frank found himself at the head of the pack, about ten yards in front of the slowly rolling lead tank. In the middle of thick hedgerows, the men could see only straight ahead. As Frank crept in a crouched position, he wondered what awaited them; a platoon, a company, maybe an entire battalion? No matter how many troops there were, they definitely had some heavy firepower. Were the Germans going to see or hear them coming and unleash their artillery, killing the whole platoon before they even knew what was coming? Was this going to be the day he died? Was it going to be a slow, painful death? These thoughts raced through Frank's mind, like his heart racing in his chest. All the while the nearby pounding of tank, cannon, and mortar fire was nonstop.

As the unit turned a corner, Frank heard the distinct sound of small arms. Simultaneously, he saw the platoon's second in command jerk backwards.

"Down!" The lieutenant yelled. But Frank was already on the ground, his rifle at the ready.

"I'm hit!" Someone else screamed as the fire continued.

"It's comin' from ten o'clock, in the brush!" Yet another voice rang out.

Lying in the middle of a grassy path, with no cover to protect him, Frank aimed his rifle towards ten o'clock and fired several rounds. Just then at least one of the Browning heavy machine guns atop the tanks opened up, drowning out all other noise. As Frank scanned the tall, deep hedges, looking for the enemy, he saw two German soldiers, partly camouflaged by the brush, kneeling and shooting at his platoon. Frank fought to slow his breathing and keep his hands from shaking as he aimed his M1 Garand. He felt the kick of the gun and saw one of the German soldiers go flying back. It was a direct hit to the chest. As the other soldier looked back at his comrade, Frank took aim and fired at his second target. Another kill shot. It was the first time that Frank had shot anyone, at least that he could actually see. But there was no time to dwell on it; he was still in the middle of a firefight.

Eventually, Frank's unit was able to destroy the small German contingent. But three of their men had been killed and four others wounded, including Fish, who had been shot in the right shoulder. Also, unbeknownst to them at the time, one German soldier had escaped and would soon tell his command about the Americans.

After some thought, the lieutenant ordered several of his men to help the badly injured back to their main position, report the skirmish, and request another platoon to follow their rear. But unsure if the request would be granted, or if it was delivered, how long it would take, he decided to forge ahead to their objective. So with two tanks and now only eighteen infantrymen, the group moved to attack an unknown number of German troops and artillery.

The lieutenant did not know that an enemy soldier had escaped and alerted his comrades, but realized it was a possibility. And his fears came to fruition when a Panzer came barreling out of the brush, about thirty yards in front of them. Luckily, before the Panzer could fix its turret on either of the American tanks, one of the Shermans fired first. The Panzer had crossed directly in front of the Sherman's main gun and suffered a close hit. The firing of the round and subsequent explosion was deafening. But though the Panzer had been rendered inoperable, enemy soldiers were everywhere. A hail of rifle and machine gun fire rang through the air.

Just as Frank was about to shoot, his eyes caught a German kneeling on the ground, aiming a bazooka. "Watch out!" He yelled, as he fell to his stomach.

At the same time, a white puff of smoke came from its barrel. It was followed by a whoosh and then a violent explosion. Frank twisted his neck to look behind. The lead Sherman's turret was in flames. Fearing that all the tanks' ammunition would soon detonate, Frank sprang to his feet and ran into the brush.

By now, both German and American soldiers were spread out in an area of at least two acres. Squads were fighting squads. All hell was breaking loose. Men were being hit, some cut down by machine gun fire. The remaining Sherman would sporadically unleash its main gun at a pocket of infantrymen. Finally, the Americans were able to repel the Germans, but at a heavy cost. Seven more men had been killed, five others wounded. What started off as a platoon was now down to less than a dozen men. They had also lost one of their tanks. With perhaps more Germans on the way, the lieutenant had little choice but to retreat back to their main position.

For the next week and a half, fierce battles continued, the Allies fighting to gain control of the next field or hill, trying to inch closer to Saint-Lo. Almost daily, U.S. warplanes would drop bombs on the city. Giant plumes of black smoke rose high into the air, as the ground quaked. On both sides, the casualties and wounded were piling up. But day by day the Allies were pushing through the German defenses.

As for Frank, by now, the ravages of war had become woven into his daily existence. He heard so much gunfire and bombs exploding that it became background noise. He had seen so many dead bodies and people getting killed that it no longer shocked him. Every morning he asked himself the same question: *Is this going to be the day that I die?* But the question seemed less profound with each passing day. Frank no longer knew what "normal" felt like. Fighting on two hours sleep, eating maybe one ration a day, wearing the same uniform for weeks, having continuous cramps, all put him in this constant foggy, almost inhuman state of being. But still, he not only continued to perform his duties, but did so with valor and without question. Then again, what choice did he have? He couldn't go home, couldn't stand up and tell the Germans to stop fighting. But Frank did find strength in praying every night, even though he was starting to question God's existence. Another thing Frank did every night was take out and look at a photograph of Mary. And when he did, he could feel her presence.

On July 18th, the Allies finally entered Saint-Lo. The city was in ruins. Frank remembered seeing the devastation in London left by the air raids. This was much worse. Entire blocks were leveled. Piles of bricks with protruding, twisted rebar littered the landscape. It seemed that the Allied artillery and aerial bombardment had left no building or house undamaged. Many structures were reduced to crumbling facades. Some had been completely pulverized. Most of the once-paved streets were unrecognizable, now a wasteland of debris, remains of tanks, and dead German soldiers. The unforgettable, overpowering stench of burnt and decomposing corpses permeated the air.

Though the Allies had made it into Saint-Lo, they would not march through the city unabated. The bulk of the German force may have been destroyed or retreated, but pockets of resistance remained. And though many of the buildings still standing were in shambles, it made them perfect nests for snipers. It was a frightening and nerve-wracking proposition. A single shot would ring through the air and simultaneously a random soldier would fall. The snipers were good and it was difficult to tell from where they were shooting. But each one had to be eradicated.

On the second day, while marching through one of the rubble-filled streets, two infantrymen were shot by a sniper, one right after the other. A sergeant was able to ascertain that the shots had come from a factory down the block. A squad, including Frank, was ordered to enter the building and take out the sniper before the unit could move any further. Frank and three other riflemen scurried down an adjacent side street so they'd be hidden from the factory. When they got there, they realized it had been hit by at least one bomb. Its entire back facade was torn open as if a giant had ripped it right off. Part of its four concrete floors and contents were exposed.

"Okay," whispered the sergeant, as the squad took cover behind the westward wall. "We'll enter right over there," he said, pointing to a doorway. "The shots came from an opening on the second floor, but the sniper probably moved by now, so be careful. Make sure you have each other's backs." With that the four men cautiously entered the unstable building.

Being quiet as possible and using only hand gestures, the group cleared each room on the first floor. Then they moved to the second. As they approached the back area of the building, which was completely exposed to the elements, Frank was waiting for the floor to collapse, but fortunately it didn't. There were many rooms and even more hiding places and the search for the elusive sniper was becoming long, tedious, and fretful. In the tension-filled silence, Frank went to look behind an industrial sewing machine.

"Bam!" A thunderous shot rang through the silence, right by Frank's head. He was sure he had been hit. With everything now in slow motion, Frank looked to the right and saw one of his men pointing a rifle passed his head. He then looked to the left and saw a German soldier, bleeding on the ground, not more than six feet away.

"He lunged from behind that column at you, with a knife in his hand."

His heart racing uncontrollably, Frank fought to breathe. "Thanks, Roy," he sputtered with bated breath. "You saved my life."

Roy Tolson, who Frank knew fairly well, smiled as though it was just another day at the office. "No problem. Just buy me a beer when we get back to the States."

Just then one of the other men thrust his bayonet into the German's chest. "He was still breathing," he whispered. "And look Sarge, it's got a scope on it," he added, pointing at the rifle still slung across the soldier's back. "You think that Jerry is our sniper?"

"Very well could be," the sergeant replied in a low voice. "But either way, it doesn't mean he's alone. And if he's got friends, they sure as hell know we're here now. So let's hurry up and finish clearing this building."

The squad did not find any more Germans in the building. They eventually returned to the rest of their platoon and were able to march onward. But the sniper hunts were repeated over and over in other buildings, houses, and churches. There was also the occasional firefight with German positions.

Frank's unit stayed in Saint-Lo for several days, fighting to snuff out the remaining German elements. Once another company relieved them, they left the city, marching south towards the port city of Brest. Once there, they were to knock out a German garrison, which was fighting to protect a submarine base, and secure the port. The fighting lasted from August 24th to September 18th, when the remaining Germans surrendered.

It had been more than three, long, hard-fought months since D-Day. Frank had never been so exhausted. But at the same time, he was also becoming ever so accustomed to living in the middle of a battlefield. But, though Frank still found time to write letters home, he never divulged the details of his experiences. How could he write to Mary or his mother about seeing his friends killed, about watching a man get literally blown apart, about trying to pull someone to safety and realizing that he has no legs, about shooting someone in the face, or about the smell and sight of fields of rotting corpses? The person at home who Frank knew could relate to the horrors of battle was his father, who had served in World War I. But he knew that if he sent a letter home, his mother would read it. So, without being able to divulge his exact whereabouts or mission, and not wanting to write any details about what he was witnessing, Frank's letters became shorter and shorter in context. Nevertheless, the feeling of having contact with the "outside world," a world without war, helped him keep his sanity.

A day after the German surrender at Brest, Frank's unit marched through the city. They were looking for any lingering enemy resistance, but were greeted only by throngs of grateful locals, thanking the Americans for their liberation. As the columns of soldiers and trucks slowly inched their way down the streets, the sidewalks were jammed with men, women, and children applauding and offering food, cigarettes, and wine. It was a welcome change from being greeted by gunfire and artillery.

Frank was in the back of an uncovered truck, sitting next to Roy, the man who had saved his life.

"Hey, look at her over there," Roy said with a grand smile.

Frank looked in the direction in which Roy was pointing. It was a beautiful French woman, with long flowing, black hair and voluptuous breasts. She was holding a bottle of wine. "Oh my God!" Frank piped up.

Just then, the truck came to a stop and the woman ran up and extended the bottle to Frank. "Merci! Merci!"

Frank grabbed the wine and thanked her.

"What's your name?" Roy excitedly intervened.

"Valerie."

Before the conversation could continue, the truck started rolling again. "Oh, come on driver!" Roy hollered. "I was about to get lucky!"

"Hey guys, look over there!" A soldier yelled to Frank and Roy while pointing to another beautiful woman.

"Goddamn! These women are almost worth gettin' shot at for!" Roy proclaimed.

"Gettin shot at? Hell, I'd take one in the arm if I could spend *one* night with one of these girls!"

Several of the men laughed, including Frank. It was the first time he had laughed since stepping foot on Omaha Beach.

That night, the celebrations continued. Men were getting drunk, playing cards, horsing around, and for the first time in ages, eating real food. It was a raucous bunch, but most of the officers let them slide. Their men had fought hard and suffered many losses. Omaha Beach, the Battle of Hedgerows, Saint-Lo, Brest—the enlisted men of the 29th Infantry Division deserved at least one night to put the war aside and blow off some steam. They deserved much more than one night, but that was not to be. A few days later the entire division was on a train, heading across France and then Belgium, to a position in Holland near the German border.


Fall had given way to the bitterness of winter. Then, by the end of March, Frank's unit had fought its way into Germany. Inside the Deutschland, and with news and rumors of the greater war swirling around, the men of Frank's division could sense that the Third Reich was in its death throes. They were right. Hitler's last major offensive of the war, which would come to be called the Battle of the Bulge, had failed. On the Eastern Front, the Soviets were capturing city after city and forging towards Berlin. In the air campaign, the Allies had completely destroyed the German city of Dresden. It appeared only a matter of time now before the Allies were victorious. The only questions were: When would it end and how many more people would die?

By April 13th, news reached the troops that Roosevelt had died. At first, many of the men did not believe that their president was dead, instead thinking it was a rumor spread by the Nazis as a desperate, psychological ploy. But the truth soon became apparent. It was both devastating and a shock. More than a few men cried. For most of them, Roosevelt, having served nearly thirteen years in the White House, had been the only president they had really known. Moreover, hardly anyone realized how sick he had actually been. Roosevelt had led the United States through its darkest days and most Americans took for granted that he would be there to welcome home the troops and guide the nation into a brighter future. Though the men on the front were in a state of disbelief about Roosevelt's death, there was still fighting to be done.

April 17th marked Frank's twenty-first birthday. But instead of a celebration that day, he was hit by a large, hot piece of shrapnel in his right chest. It easily tore right through his thick jacket and left a deep, four-inch long gash. Luckily, it did not go deep enough to puncture his lung, but the wound required twenty-six stitches. It did not keep him from combat.

A week later Frank's unit had reached the Elbe River. By this time, the 29th Division had captured numerous German cities and towns, and captured thousands of prisoners of war. Word had spread that the Soviets had reached Berlin. Rather than join the fight for Berlin, Frank's division was ordered to stay at the Elbe. More than ever, the men could sense that the war was in its last weeks, if not days.

On May 1st, a brigadier general gathered his troops along the Elbe River. Frank, like many of the other men, figured it was to hear their new orders.

"Men," the general spoke in a loud, stern voice, "I have learned that the Soviets have taken Berlin and stormed the Chancellery." The crowd started to cheer, but the general motioned them to silence. "And there are reports, though still unconfirmed, that Hitler is dead."

Now nothing could stop his audience from erupting in a nearly five-minute-long cheer.

"Sometime tomorrow," the general finally went on, "a division of Soviet forces will be meeting us at our position to represent the joining of the Western and Eastern Allies. This is an important, historic event. I want each and every one of you to be shaved and looking and acting your best. It looks like this war is finally going to be over."

The men cheered once again.

The next day, as announced, Soviet troops met the 29th Division on the banks of the Elbe. It seemed more of a photo-op than anything else. Some men were chosen to personally greet their Russian allies, shake their hands and pose with them in front of the camera. Frank did not get to mingle with any of his eastern counterparts, but had great respect for the Soviet troops. Though he did not know the details, he knew how hard they had fought the same enemy, and that many more Soviet soldiers had died than Americans. He also was well aware that unlike America, the Soviets fought to expel the Third Reich from their own homeland, and that scores of Russian civilians had been killed. At that time Frank, as did many of his fellow Americans, saw the Soviet Union and its leader, Joseph Stalin, in a great light. But like most of his fellow citizens, Frank had no idea that during his reign Stalin caused the deaths of more people than did Hitler. And the warm sentiments towards the Soviet Union would quickly turn to bitter cold.

On May 7th, the same brigadier general gave yet another speech. "Men, this afternoon, in General Eisenhower's headquarters in Reims, France, the German High Command signed an unconditional surrender to the Allies. The war in Europe is officially over."

Every single man in the audience hollered and applauded with all of their might. The writing may have been on the wall, but the official finality of it was something that many of them feared they would never live to see.

That evening the camp was abuzz with electricity. The outpouring of happiness was more than any of the men had ever felt before. But even more than joy, there was a great, collective sense of relief that they were not going to die. The men knew now that they would make it home alive.

That night, Frank was by a campfire with Roy and about six other men when a captain joined them. As always, they all snapped to attention. "At ease men," the captain said, with a never-before-seen smile. "You deserve it." He then sat on a rock and huddled with his soldiers. "I just want you to know, each and every one of you, that it's been an honor and a privilege to serve with you."

"Thank you, Captain."

"Yes, thank you, Skipper."

"It's been a privilege to serve with you too, sir."

The captain continued: "You boys…boys, God knows none of you are boys anymore. You men made America, made the whole free world proud. We've been through a lot of shit!"

The men laughed and agreed.

"And we lost a lot of good men."

Now they just bowed their heads.

"But the Twenty-Ninth persevered against all odds."

"To the Twenty-Ninth!" a soldier cheered. Everyone followed suit.

The captain sat with the group for another fifteen or so minutes. Inevitably the conversation turned to Hitler and his still unconfirmed death.

"I don't think we'll know for some time, the true extent of the Third Reich's tyranny," the captain said in a strong, but somber voice. "A few weeks ago the Third Army liberated two prison camps. Last week, the Seventh Army came across another one called Dachau. They said there were thousands of bodies just stacked up in piles. And the survivors that they did find, many of them were naked and were so skinny their skin was hanging off their bones."

The men shook their heads. There had been rumors of death camps for some time and stories about Nazi murder squads rounding up and executing Jews for years, but there never seemed to be any concrete evidence or details.

"I know that you're all glad that you'll be going home soon," the captain added. "And you can't wait to finally find out again what a piece of ass feels like…"

The men cheered.

"Except you Roy. I still think you're a virgin," he said jokingly.

Roy just laughed.

"But don't ever forget that you played a part in putting an end to the greatest tyranny this world has ever seen. Who knows how many people have died at the hands of the Nazi regime? But only God knows how many people have been saved because of your and our allies' efforts. And we saw to it that our friends that are no longer with us did not die in vain. And don't you ever forget that."

After a moment of silence, Frank raised his canteen. "To freedom!"

"To freedom!" The men cheered in unison.

A few days later, Frank's unit was on the move again, this time to the German port of Bremerhaven. It was there, in early June, that Frank boarded a transport ship back to the United States. Frank was on his way home.

# 8

# HOME

On June 3, 1945, under a hazy morning sky, Frank boarded a ship, along with thousands of other servicemen, bound for New York. As they filed through the seaport and eventually across the gangway to the ship's deck, most men were quiet, each alone in their own thoughts.

In his Army fatigues, the only thing he could picture himself wearing, Frank leaned forward on the railing of the outside deck, watching as the ship started to pull away. There were hundreds of men alongside him, staring at the slowly, fading port, but few said anything. None of them could believe that they were leaving Europe for good, leaving the battlefields, the ruins—and a lot of fallen comrades.

After many of the men had dispersed, Frank remained by the railing, gazing silently at the disappearing German shoreline. It had been nearly three years since he had been home. But it seemed like a lifetime ago. And perhaps it was, for he was now a different person. Naturally, Frank was happy about going home and he thanked God that he had Mary and his parents waiting for him. But for the first time, Frank began feeling apprehensive about his return. For the first time, he wondered how he would cope with a life without war. Certainly, he was elated the war was over. But he had seen and done things over the last year that civilians could never truly understand. He had watched friends die in agony; young men with the rest of their lives ahead of them lying in pools of blood, calling out to their loved ones, a world away, with their last painful breaths. He had seen the charred remains of children, even babies. He had watched people literally get blown apart, close enough for their blood and guts to spray him. He had killed men, looked into their eyes and shot them dead. He had lived with the nonstop sound of bombs, gunfire, and tormented screams. He had lived under the constant thought that any minute could be his last on Earth. Were all these things going to haunt him? Was every time Frank heard a backfire, firecracker, or any loud noise going to make him duck for cover? What was he going to say to Mary if she asked about the war? What was he going to say if a child asked him about the war? Was he going to be able to flip a switch and return back to "normal"? Frank asked himself all these questions—but did not have the answer to any of them. Mentally exhausted, he finally adjourned to his cramped quarters.

Most of the trip Frank spent reflecting on the war. Surprisingly, they were not all bad thoughts. They say that the worst of times brings out the best in some men. Frank knew this to be true. Frank had witnessed selflessness and heroism on a scale that he could have never imagined possible before the war. He had seen men willfully run into a line of fire to rescue a wounded buddy, even a stranger. He had seen men carry out their duties when most people would have ran for their lives. He had watched medics kneel down with shells exploding all around them and administer aid to a dying soldier. He had watched men, without a second thought literally give up their life in order to save another. But it was not just men. Frank thought of all the women who served as nurses in MASH units, working day and night, doing everything they possibly could to save lives. And they did save many. And even those they couldn't save, they provided perhaps some sense of comfort.

It was not only the bravery of others that Frank pondered. He also looked upon himself, how he had reacted and performed during battle. Frank had worried that he would be so paralyzed by fear, that he would not be able to perform and let his fellow troops down. Frank had wondered that when the time came, if he would be a coward. He had passed the test. In fact, Frank even surprised himself by his courage and conduct. Sure, there was always a sense of fear, but he was able to overcome those fears. He never hesitated when given an order. And when the time came, Frank was willing to sacrifice his life to save another.

Despite the great valor and benevolence Frank had witnessed, they could not make amends for the horrors of war. Frank thought about not only his own nightmarish experiences, but of the greater conflict. He tried with immense anguish to wrap his head around the total number that lay dead across Europe. He thought of all those who had suffered and perished in the Nazi death camps. Frank closed his eyes and envisioned tens of thousands of corpses piled on top of each other as if they were rotted pieces of wood. He tried to imagine the unthinkable torment that must have gone on in the camps; people starved, tortured, and even killed just because they did not fit into the Third Reich's mold. How could such evil live in the world, Frank pondered? As heinous as Hitler was, what about all those who willfully carried out his wrathful orders? How could so many people be so evil as to murder defenseless women and children, wipe entire families off the face of the Earth? Even seeing what he had seen, Frank could not comprehend such things.

Frank also thought about the Pacific war. Although Germany had been defeated and the war in Europe was finally over, there was still the Empire of Japan. After all, it was Japan that had attacked the United States. It was Pearl Harbor that made Frank volunteer for service. Perhaps Britain, France, and the rest of Europe could tally their dead and take solace that the fighting was finally over. But Frank realized that in the Pacific, U.S, troops were still dying everyday and the fighting seemed far from over. Frank also realized that it took a concerted effort from America, Britain, and the

Soviet Union to take down the Nazis. In the Pacific, the United States was basically on her own. What was going to become of that war, Frank wondered? Would he soon be landing in some small Pacific island, or even the Japanese mainland?

Frank was awoken in his small bunk bed by the sound of the ship's loudspeaker. "Rise and shine. We are heading into New York harbor. In a few minutes, if you go on deck, you will be able to see the Statue of Liberty." Frank looked at his watch; it was 6:38 a.m. Used to being awoken at any time, he climbed down his bunk. Dozens of other men in his quarters were doing the same thing. While yawning, he was hit on the back. "Let's go! Can you believe we're actually here?" Frank groggily turned around to see an animated Roy.

"We gotta go, it's gonna be a mad rush," Collin, one of their friends, added.

Frank, Roy and Collin followed the line of other men topside, like ants working their way up to the surface of an ant farm. The whole ship was abuzz.

"Come on!"

"Move it, get out of the way!"

"Lets go, lets go!"

Finally, the trio made their way to the deck. Frank somehow forced his way through the logjam of people to a port railway. As the sun gradually illuminated a clear June sky, Lady Liberty shone in the morning light like a colossal beckoning sign of freedom. In an instant, every negative thought, every soul-searching reflection of the war, vanished from Frank's mind. As he stood there staring at the Statue of Liberty rising like a Phoenix from the earth, her torch seemingly reaching into the heavens, he was brought to silent tears of joy. As the ship gracefully glided along her passageway, Frank knew he was home—and at that moment, nothing else mattered. He had known for some time that he was going to make it back home, had been on a ship for over a week, headed for New

York. But none of that prepared him for standing on that deck, watching Lady Liberty slowly roll by.

As the ship reached the dock, it was greeted by countless civilians, four rows deep, waving, holding handmade signs, and welcoming the boys back home. Those servicemen who lived in New York, Frank included, searched the crowd for relatives and loved ones. Unlike when they boarded the ship silently, each in their own thoughts, the men were now all joking around, hollering at the awaiting crowd, and pulsating with energy.

Frank walked down the plank behind Roy. As they approached the dock, he could see a fellow, a few men in front down, kneel down and kiss the ground. After him, each man did the same. With a thirty-pound duffle bag and a smile from ear-to-ear, Frank was more than happy to follow suit. After almost four years, Frank Keller was back in New York.

While searching the crowd of civilians that were quartered off, Frank followed the deluge of other soldiers through the maze of signs. The main terminal was partitioned into makeshift rooms and each one had a paper sign out front with letters. Frank went to the section that was labeled *H-K*. Not thinking much of it, he followed the line of men to a long table, behind which were several people handing out manila envelopes and shaking hands. When Frank reached the table a woman asked his name. The man next to her then thumbed through myriad files in a cardboard box atop the table. After a few seconds, he pulled out a thick envelope and handed it to Frank. "Here you go, thank you for your service," he said before shaking his hand.

Frank was still wondering what had just happened as he was forced down the line and greeted by yet another man shaking his hand. "Thank you for your service. Transportation information is available in Terminal C."

Frank felt a firm hand on his shoulder. He turned around to face an unknown soldier. "Can you believe it?"

"Believe what?" Frank asked.

The tall, unshaven young man laughed. "We've been processed. We're free to go home."

*Free to go home.* Those words hung in the air and filtered through every molecule of Frank's body, as he stood there, oblivious to the world around him. He had naturally thought they would all be shipped back to some base where the slow, methodical process of de-enlistment would take place. But there he was, standing in a New York Harbor terminal, with his papers in hand, free to go wherever he wanted. It was almost too much to wrap his head around.

Frank spent the next half hour walking around the harbor, looking for his parents or Mary. They had no way of knowing exactly when his ship was coming in, but then again, there were hundreds of other civilians there. Sometimes, he would see a slim, young woman with long, straight black hair, waiting for her to turn around and be Mary. But it never was. However, after a while, Frank did run into Roy.

"All I know is by the end of tonight I'm going to have a shower, hamburger, and a blowjob," was the first thing Roy said.

Frank laughed. "Well, I'd say you deserve it!"

Roy readily agreed.

"So how are you gettin home?" Frank asked, knowing that Roy lived in Boston.

"Well I could go to Terminal C," Roy said with a sarcastic tone, "and let the Army figure out how I should get home. But I think I'm done listening to them. I'm gonna walk over to Grand Central Station and take a train." Roy paused. "But first, I'm goin to see if some folks will buy this soldier a few drinks along the way." Roy paused again and his demeanor changed. "Take care of yourself Frank," he said in a slow, serious voice.

"Roy, I can never repay you for saving my life."

Roy smiled. "That again." He put his hand on Frank's shoulder. "I'm just glad you made it home with me."

The two, who had already exchanged numbers and information before they boarded the ship, promised they would keep in touch. Then, Roy walked away and disappeared into the crowd.

Frank asked someone to point him in the direction of the subway. Then, lugging his giant duffle bag, he walked down the streets of Manhattan. But after several blocks, a taxi pulled up next to him. "Hey mister, you need a ride?"

"Nah, that's okay, I'm going to take the subway. Thanks anyway."

"Where you goin?"

"Bayside, Queens."

"No, no. No subway for you. Get in. It's free of charge soldier. It's the least that I can do. Please."

Frank asked if he was sure and the driver insisted. Frank thanked him and climbed in the backseat. He then uttered words he had not spoken, had not even thought about in a long, long time: His address.

The taxi dropped Frank off in front of his house. For a few minutes, he just stood there staring at it. Through all the gunfire, all the bombs, all the death, he could not believe that he was actually standing in front of it. Frank made a mental note how the front yard and house looked exactly the same. But of course, in reality, he had not been away for that long. Feeling surreal, he slowly walked the brick pathway up to the front door and rang the bell. Frank's heart was racing with excitement as the wooden door slowly opened. In the entranceway stood his mother, wearing an apron, probably doing some routine chores around the house. "Oh my God!" She gasped before putting both hands over her quivering mouth. For a moment, time seemed to stand still as she just looked her son over, in disbelief.

"I'm home," Frank said with a smile.

"Oh, Frank!" Margaret exploded with joy as she threw her arms around him. "Oh, Frank, I feared this day would never come. I prayed for you every night. For all you boys. I can't believe you're really here."

For what felt like twenty minutes the two just stood on the porch in a tight embrace. Frank was overjoyed to see his mother and it felt so good to hug her, but he was afraid that she was never going to let go. "Well, aren't you going to let me in?"

Mrs. Keller finally pulled away and dried her eyes. "Of course. Welcome home, Frank," she said with a glowing smile as she led him into the house.

Almost in a trance, he looked around soaking up the sight, the feel, the smell.

"I have to call your father at the store. Wait until I tell him!"

After getting off the phone, Mrs. Keller insisted on immediately getting to work on cooking her son a home-cooked meal. And she was not going to take "no" for an answer. As she scrambled around the kitchen, Frank sat at the table and asked her about things back home. He had received letters throughout the war, but they had been few and far between.

After about twenty minutes the front door burst opened. "Where is he?" Mr. Keller's voice bellowed through the house before he appeared in the kitchen. "Frank!"

Frank stood up. "Dad!"

The son and father embraced.

"I'm so glad your home," he said, still holding Frank tight. "And I'm so proud of you, son. We're all so proud of you."

For the next hour, the three sat around the dining room table, catching up. It was nearing noon and the Kellers did not usually have a big lunch. But his mother made Frank eggs, bacon, sausage, and toast. At one point, as Harold and Frank talked, she just stared at her son, not believing how much he had grown since the last time she had seen him. Frank was not taller, or broader. But he just had the look of a grown man. It was in his face, in his eyes, in the way he talked.

"So, does Mary know you're back?" His father asked.

Frank took a moment before answering. Just the mere mention of her name drew a sharp image in his mind. "No, not yet. I wanted to come home first. But if you don't mind, I'd like to take a shower and go see her."

His father smiled and put his hand on his son's forearm. "Of course," he said in a slow voice. "She's been waiting for this day as long as we have. She loves you very much."

Frank smiled. "I know. I love her, too."

For the first time in recent memory Frank could take as long as he wanted in the shower—and he did. It was also nice not having to shower with a dozen other men. By the time he was finished, it felt like years of grime had been washed away. After drying himself, Frank went to his old bedroom, where a set of clean clothes had been laid out for him on the bed. With a smile of gratitude, he tried them on. They were a little loose on him, but the length still fit perfectly. After putting on his shoes, Frank looked at himself in the mirror. It was a strange, almost surreal sight. He could not remember the last time he had worn civilian clothes. But he loved the way they looked and felt.

After telling his parents he would see them later on that evening, Frank set out on foot to Mary's house. The whole way there his heart was bursting with excitement. He had envisioned the moment of reuniting with Mary every single day while he was away. Now, against all odds, that moment was about to come to fruition.

Frank was met by Mrs. Capelli, who greeted him with a hug and a kiss. Mary, she told him, was at work in the metalwork factory, about five miles away. Frank stayed and chatted for a few minutes and then went on his way to surprise Mary.

While walking to the bus stop, Frank passed a florist, where he stopped and bought half a dozen red roses. After a short ride, he arrived at the factory, which was abuzz with noise and activity. He had no idea where exactly he would find Mary, so he walked up to someone who appeared to be a foreman. Frank explained the situation to the hefty, middle-aged man. "Not a problem at all," he readily replied. "But first I'd like to shake your hand soldier and thank you for serving in the war."

Frank shook the man's hand. "Well, you're welcome. But you know, we wouldn't have been able to win the war over there if it wasn't for all these factories and the people working in them. We couldn't fight without guns and tanks and bombs and ships."

"Well thank you. I appreciate that. I really do. Now come on, let's go find your girl."

With that, Frank eagerly followed the stranger around the noisy, factory floor.

At one point, the foreman stopped to ask a woman where he could find Mary Capelli. As he did, Frank scanned the bustling area. His eyes caught a slender woman turning around from her post. It was her! It was Mary! She was standing there with a white, elastic cap over her pulled-up hair and a black, rubber apron, but to Frank she looked like the most beautiful sight he had ever seen. With nothing but a few yards of open space between them, her eyes caught his. At first, her jaw just dropped in utter disbelief. But then she threw open her arms and ran towards him. "Frank!"

With flowers still in hand, Frank gladly met her ebullient embrace.

"Oh Frank," she cried, "I can't believe it's you!"

Suddenly the entire floor erupted in cheers. Women and men alike stood and clapped. It did not matter that Frank was wearing civilian clothes. Everyone realized what they were witnessing and a few of them even started to cry.

After a long, tight hug the two reunited lovers finally let go of each other. "Here, these are for you," Frank said with a smile from ear to ear as he handed her the flowers.

Just then Mary's supervisor walked over and put her hand on her shoulder. "Why don't you take the rest of the day off."

Mary wiped away some tears with her sleeve. "Are you sure?"

"Yes. It's okay, really. It's only a few hours anyway."

"Thank you, Mrs. Pettison." She then officially introduced Frank. Mrs. Pettison shook his hand and thanked him for his service.

Hand-in-hand Frank and Mary walked out into the hot June air. But as soon as they passed the factory gates, Mary stopped and threw herself at Frank, this time with a long, passionate kiss. Frank had waited over three years to oblige. The rest of the world melted away, the two stood there for nearly five minutes, caressing each other with hands and lips.

Mary put her slender, soft hands on Frank's cheeks and looked straight into his eyes. "I've waited so long for this day Frank," she whispered, as tears began to swell in her eyes.

"So have I. The thought of you, the picture of you, your letters, they helped me get through everyday. All I thought about was that

I had to get home to you."

Now Mary's tears were flowing freely. "Oh, Frank, I thought about you every second of every day, too. I was so worried about you," she cried before burrowing her head in his chest.

Frank petted her long, silky black hair. "It's okay. I'm home now. And we can be together." He paused. "I'm just glad you waited for me," he said jokingly.

Mary lifted her head and playfully punched him in the arm. "I told you that I would wait for you no matter how long it took."

Frank smiled as he stared at Mary. "God, you look so beautiful."

Mary wiped her eyes. "And you look even more handsome than the day you left." She paused, soaking up the moment. "Come on," she said with a devilish grin, "I have a surprise for you."

"Surprise? You couldn't even have had any idea I was coming home today. What kind of surprise could you have?"

Mary flashed Frank an even bigger grin and took him by the hand. "You're going to have to wait."

Frank and Mary took the bus back to the old neighborhood. But instead of walking towards Mary's house, she started leading him down a different street. "Where are we going?"

"You'll see."

After four blocks they arrived at a strange house. "Whose house is this?"

"It's one of my parents' friends," Mary replied walking up to the front door. "One of their sons was also in Europe," she went on as she pulled a set of keys from her purse and unlocked the door with them. "He's in the Air Force, but he just got back to his base in Georgia. The whole family went there to meet him and bring him back home," she said while leading Frank inside and closing the door behind them. "Anyway, they asked if I could look after the house while they're gone. Water the plants and such." Mary turned so that she was facing Frank, mere inches apart. "So what I'm tryin' to say is that we have the house all to ourselves."

Frank smiled. He was certainly not expecting this. Before he could say or do anything, Mary started kissing him and unbuttoning his shirt. Percolating with euphoria, he began to undress her as feverishly as she was undressing him. God, her skin felt so good on his hands.

Suddenly Mary stopped and rubbed her hands over the scar on his chest. "What is this?"

"It's nothing. I got hit by some shrapnel. I didn't want to tell you about it in my letters because I didn't want you to worry about it."

"But it's by your heart," Mary said, still staring at the wound. "What if…"

"But it didn't," Frank interjected. "All it required was some stitches. It's nothing, really. Don't worry, it's not goin' to affect anything in the bedroom," he said with a smile to break the ice.

Mary looked up at him and smiled back. They then resumed ravishing each other. They made love on the living room couch. They had sex on the carpeted floor. They had sex in the upstairs bedroom, which was where they finally ended up, naked in the bed.

As they lay there under the sheets, Mary rested her head on Frank's chest, listening to the beating of his heart. Every time she had heard news of the war, had overheard in the community that some young man had died in combat, she found herself a corner and cried, overcome with fear and sorrow that Frank would not make it back alive. Now here he was, holding her. Silently, she thanked the Lord for bringing him back home.

Frank too, was overcome with gratefulness. There had been times when he had felt guilty for surviving when so many others had died. But not at that moment. Lying there with Mary's head on his chest, her long, soft hair feathered out on his skin, Frank blocked everything else out. For a moment, it was as if the war had never happened. For the moment, nothing existed but him and Mary, lying on that bed. And he could have laid there forever.

It had been a long, but glorious day, a day that would forever be etched in Frank's memory as one of the best of his life. He had made it home from Europe alive. He had held his mother and father. He had been reunited with Mary and had made long, passionate love to her. He had even eaten real food for the first time in many moons. But late that night, as Frank lay awake in his own bed, his thoughts turned to the immediate future. The war in Europe might have been over, but the Pacific war raged on. Was he going to be reactivated to take part in the invasion of Japan? He knew that in the end he would serve whatever duty that called, but the thought of leaving Mary again ate at him. Regardless of the training and the many brave men that fought beside him, Frank knew that he was lucky to survive Europe. Could he be so lucky twice?

# 9

# IN LIMBO

The day after returning home, Frank called Bob. Bob knew through letters that Frank knew what happened to him, about his injuries. Bob also knew that Frank had made it through to the surrender of Germany. For old time's sake, the two best friends agreed to meet at the American Horse ranch.

It was a clear, but muggy June day. Frank took great pleasure in walking to the ranch, strolling through the neighborhood. He was freshly showered, wearing comfortable shorts and a shirt and had just eaten a delicious home-cooked breakfast. He arrived at the vast ranch first and like he had so many times before the war, walked up to and leaned on the wooden fence and gazed at the horses in the nearby distance. Everything seemed so quiet and peaceful. For a while he just stood there with a smile on his face, soaking up the friendly scenery.

"Who let you back into town?" A voice rang out.

Frank turned around to see a smiling Bob walking towards him. "I used to meet my friend here. A sarcastic little son-of-a-bitch with a chip the size of Nebraska on his shoulder."

"Yeah well, look where that got me."

The boyhood friends hugged each other, something they had never before done.

"Damn it's good to see you, Bob."

"Same here buddy. Same here."

Nearly four years earlier, before Pearl Harbor, the two friends congregated at that same spot, overlooking the ranch, pondering if America would eventually be dragged into the war in Europe and if they would be called to duty. Now veterans, still young men by age, but old to the things they had witnessed, they leaned against that faded fence telling their war stories.

"So, can you believe you made it through the whole war over there? I mean it must've been a crazy scene. I can't believe I didn't even make it through a day."

Frank put his hand on his friend's shoulder. "You did make it. Just thank God you didn't die over there on that beach."

A doleful silence filled the air as Bob shook his head. "You're right," he finally said in a low, fading voice.

"Speaking of which, so let me see," Frank said in an animated tone, changing the mood.

"See what?"

"Your scar."

Bob readily lifted up his shirt, revealing a thick, long, jagged scar going from his left shoulder down his arm, then another smaller scar midway down the same arm. "At least it's not my beautiful face, right?" He said jokingly, pulling his shirt back down.

"Nah, I think it mighta' helped your looks."

The two laughed.

"I also have a little loss of hearing in my left ear, but nothing too bad. My parents think I'm deaf; they keep shouting at me. So what about you?"

Frank slowly pulled up his shirt. "I'm almost embarrassed to show you. Just twenty-six stitches."

"Well, I'm glad you made it home in one piece."

"Me too," Frank exclaimed.

Over the next half hour, Frank told Bob about his experiences. He gave him an abridged version of Saint-Lo, Brest, and their march to the Elbe River. Frank also had the misfortune of telling him about John Harrison's death and Fish's wound. "I don't know if he made it or not," Frank somberly explained. As for their friend Vincent, the last time either man had seen or heard of him was when he was shipped off to Sicily. They only hoped he had survived the war.

As Frank and Bob talked, Old Man Baxter approached from the stable.

"Hey Mr. Baxter!" They both excitedly greeted him.

"How you boys doin'?" He yelled back as he continued to walk towards them. "Haven't seen either of you in a long time."

"Well we've been in Europe, helpin' rid the world of Nazis," Frank replied in an almost joking manner.

Baxter, now right on the other side of the fence, looked at Frank and Bob and shook his head, as if with approval. "Well I'm damn glad you made it home."

Bob smiled. "We were just sayin' the same thing."

Mr. Baxter's thin, weathered face looked as serious as a nail. "We're all proud of you boys." He then extended his wrinkled, but firm hand over the fence. "And I want to personally thank you."

Frank and Bob looked at each other, then back at Baxter and took turns shaking his hand.

"Listen, if you boys have a few, I'd like to invite you into the house for a bit."

On different occasions throughout the years Baxter had invited the friends onto the ranch and even let them ride the horses. But he had never invited them into his actual house. They gladly accepted his polite offer.

Frank and Bob followed Baxter across the ranch and into his home. "I remember you boys when you were just wee high," he said, putting his hand about four feet from the ground. Now you're men. Men putting your lives on the line for our country."

For the next hour or so, the two best friends sat, talked and even shared a drink with the man whom during their childhood seemed almost mythical. He asked them about their experiences and thanked them over and over again for their service. But upon questioning, Baxter also opened up about his own life. His wife, Matilda, had died of polio fifteen years earlier, but he had never remarried. He lived by himself and ran American Horse with some part-time ranch hands. The horses, he explained, were his life. "A horse will keep you young at heart," he said with a rare smile. "Matilda used to love horses."

Upon volunteering for the Army and even while in combat, Frank never expected to be thanked or shown such an intimate level of respect for his service. He enlisted not to be showered by gratitude, but rather out of duty, because he felt that it was the right thing to do. He was somewhat surprised even, that a man like Baxter would talk to him like an equal, if not more. But it did feel good. It filled him with a sense of self-pride. He was also grateful to have the opportunity to be a man amongst men.


Over the next month, Frank tried to settle back into civilian life, though with one ear always towards what was going on in the Pacific and with the knowledge that his service might be once again called upon. Around town and in the hardware store, where he was back helping his father, people treated Frank like a hero, which at times made him feel uncomfortable. A thank you and show of respect was one thing, but Frank did not want to be put up on some pedestal. He wanted to be treated like any other twenty-one-year old. He also felt a sense of guilt whenever he came in contact with someone from the community that had lost their son in the war, or whose son was permanently disabled. In fact, he started having nightmares about men torturously dying on the battlefield, crying out for help with their last painful breaths. Some nights, he would dream about what happened to John Harrison, covered in blood, dying in his arms. It seemed the more time that passed, the more guilt and anguish he felt for his fellow men.

The only time Frank was completely free from guilt and mourning was when he was with Mary. Whenever he was with her, nothing else mattered. It was as if she brought with her a shield that refused to let in anything negative.

One day a man, who looked to be in his late twenties, came into the hardware store on crutches, his right leg amputated below the knee. Frank watched as the man walked over to his father and the two started talking. It was not long before Harold pointed to his son.

"Frank, why don't you come over here," he said proudly.

Somewhat reluctantly, Frank put down the box he was stocking and walked down the aisle.

"This is my son," Harold told the man with a great sense of pride. "Frank, meet Lieutenant Kowalski. He also landed on Normandy on D-Day."

"Well, we parachuted behind the beach. Eighty-Second Airborne," he said with a smile, extending his hand towards Frank, while still leaning on his crutches.

At first, years of protocol told Frank to salute, but when he saw the man's extended hand, he shook it. "Pleased to meet you, Lieutenant."

"Please, this isn't a base or battlefield. Just call me Paul. So, your father told me you were with the Twenty-Ninth."

Frank nodded. "Yes sir."

"Hell of a division. It must've been something making that first landing."

"You can say that," Frank replied almost uncomfortably, trying not to look at the lieutenant's dangling limb.

Just then a woman called out for Harold. "Excuse me. It was a pleasure meeting you," he said before giving the lieutenant a firm handshake.

"So, you must have seen a lot of action with the Twenty-Ninth."

"Yes sir. But the Eighty-Second didn't exactly sit on the sidelines and play cards. Not only D-Day, but I heard you guys were involved in the Ardennes offensive," Frank said, referring to what would become known as the Battle of The Bulge, Hitler's last major offensive and one of the fiercest battles of World War II.

The lieutenant paused and shook his head. "Yes. That's where I lost my leg. German sniper."

Frank felt ashamed and looked away. "I'm sorry. I...I..." Frank didn't know what to say.

"It's okay," Kowalski replied with an upbeat demeanor. "I'm alive."

"Still, I mean I just feel bad. And all those guys that didn't make it home. I mean and here I am, made it through the whole war with barely a scratch."

The lieutenant firmly put his right hand on Frank's shoulder. "Now, I want you to listen to me Frank," he said in a calm but stern voice as he looked him straight in the eyes. "First of all, you did your duty. You put your ass on the line every day. I know all about the Twenty-Ninth. So don't you ever, ever feel ashamed or guilty about making it back home in one piece. You should be thankful."

Frank looked into Lieutenant Kowalski's eyes. "I am thankful, believe me. It's just—"

"You hear me, don't you ever feel guilty. You can mourn. We all do. We all lost friends. But don't you ever feel guilty. If you do, it's almost like all those men died for nothing. If you don't live every single day to the fullest, if you don't enjoy every moment from here on out, then you might as well have died on that beach too. The good Lord spared your life, spared my life, for a reason. And though we may not know now exactly what that reason is, it sure isn't to sit around and feel guilty."

The lieutenant paused and took his hand off Frank's shoulder. "And you know as well as I do Frank," he went on in a softer tone, "that those friends of ours that died, if they're looking down on us right now, which I'm sure they are, they're saying 'Live. Live every day like it's a gift.' Because it is."

Frank would never see Lieutenant Kowalski again. But his words had been an epiphany. It was as if a tremendous weight had been lifted from his shoulders. No more did he suffer from guilt. Gone were the recurring nightmares. No longer did he feel uncomfortable around disabled veterans. In fact, soon Frank would volunteer his time, and later money, helping soldiers wounded in the war.

It was a Monday, August 6th. Frank had finished helping his father close the shop for the day and was meeting Bob and a fellow soldier, who he had met from the community, for a quick drink at a local tavern, before rendezvousing with Mary. As he approached the bar, he saw Bob and Francis, one of their old high school friends, walking towards him in a hurried fashion. "Have you heard the news?" Bob asked excitedly.

"What news?"

"We dropped some new super bomb on Japan!"

"Truman called it some kind of 'atomic bomb,'" Francis added. "Supposedly we've been building it in complete secrecy. It's equal to something like twenty thousand tons of TNT. And Truman said that if Japan doesn't surrender, they're going to drop more of these bombs on other cities."

Taken completely off guard, Frank tried to digest what he had just heard. "So what'd it destroy an entire city or something? What the hell is an atom bomb?"

"Supposedly it uses the same energy as the sun," Bob replied. "We dropped it on some base in a place called Hiroshima. It sounds like it wiped out most of the city. I'm not sure. Let's go inside, I'm sure they have the radio on."

With that, the three veterans walked into the darkened tavern. As Bob suggested, everyone, including the bartender, was intently listening to the broadcast, which was a replay of President Truman's initial address. Frank, Bob, and Francis quietly found stools at the bar and sat down. Besides Truman's crackled, stoic voice, the otherwise noisy establishment was dead silent. The more Frank listened, the more he began to realize the magnitude of this new super-weapon. More importantly, he realized—he hoped—that this could mean the invasion of Japan, which would have been larger and bloodier than D-Day, would not be necessary.

After the broadcast, everyone talked at once, sharing their sentiments.

"We should drop ten more of those bombs on those yellow, rat bastards!"

"Do you really think the Japanese will surrender?"

"You know how many of our boys will die if we have to invade Japan?"

"Do you think the war will really be over?"

"We should drop one of those bombs right on the emperor!"


Three days later, on August 9th, a lone B-29 Superfortress called Bockscar dropped a second atomic bomb on the industrial city of Nagasaki. An estimated fifty thousand Japanese were killed instantly. Thousands more would die in the coming days, weeks, and even years.


On August 14th, instead of working at the hardware store, Frank adorned his Army greens and volunteered at the hospital, helping wounded servicemen. Mostly, he would take them for a walk, push them in their wheelchairs, maybe take them outside for some fresh air. They all seemed to like Frank. Though he was not suffering like them, they respected and could relate to him, because he had seen extensive combat. Frank's guilt might have been alleviated, but he still naturally felt horrible for these men, some younger than he was. Some had missing limbs, were paralyzed from the waist down, blinded, or hanging onto life by a thread. But he tried to stay positive, always spreading Lieutenant Kowalski's uplifting message.

Finished at the hospital, Frank decided to surprise Mary at the factory after work and take her out to dinner. When she walked out the factory gates, along with a stream of other people, she was excited to see Frank and greeted him with a big hug and kiss on the cheek. The two then went back to their neck of the woods to a local restaurant.

Frank and Mary were just about to walk into the eatery when up and down the main street, they could hear cheering. People began running out of the stores all excited, and the cheering grew into a roar.

"I wonder what that's all about?" Mary asked, as Frank opened the door to the restaurant.

But before they could enter, a middle-aged man ran out, practically floating on air. At first he passed right between Frank and Mary, almost knocking into them. But then he turned around to face them. "Can you believe it soldier!" He yelled excitedly, with a giant smile, as more people poured out of the establishment. "The war's over!"

As Frank stood there, still clutching the handle of the door, he began to hear other people echoing the same sentiment. Mary asked the stranger what he meant—though it could mean only one thing.

"Truman just announced it! The Japs surrendered! The war is over!" With that, the man ran off.

Frank let go of the restaurant door and faced Mary. For a second, they just stood there staring at each other, as the sound of cheering continued to grow in the background. *The war is over.* Those words hung in the air and swirled through their minds. They both knew what it meant. Not only would no more young American men have to die in the Pacific, but Frank would not be called back to duty. He was home now, for good. Finally, they fell into each other's arms, in a tight embrace.

"I can't believe it's actually over," Mary happily cried into his shoulder. "The whole darn thing!"

"Thank God for the bomb!" Frank replied, knowing that if it was for the atomic bomb the invasion of the Japanese mainland would have been a certainty.

Just then a couple, two strangers, came over to them. "Can you believe it?" The man said with his arm draped over the good-looking woman. "I already did a tour in the Pacific. Fought in Guadalcanal and Leyte. I thought I was goin back for sure!"

The woman then grabbed the man by the cheeks and gave him a passionate kiss, right there in front of Frank and Mary.

When they came up for air, the man put his hand on Frank's shoulder. "No more dodgin' bullets for us fella." He then threw his hand in the air and cheered before running off with his partner.

Frank and Mary looked at each other and laughed. A crowd was beginning to form on the sidewalks and even in the streets. Though early evening, the August sun was still shining bright on the revelers. People were hugging and kissing each other, drinking Champagne straight from the bottle, climbing lampposts and yelling that the war was over. It was not a time for mourning and remembrance. There would be plenty of time for that. On this night, it was a collective burst of jubilation. It was a celebration no one had planned, but every person had been waiting for, for years.

Suddenly a bell went off in Frank's head. "Come on," he said dragging Mary into the restaurant. Once inside he went up to the counter. "Excuse me, do you think we can use your phone? We have to call our parents," he excitedly asked a young woman behind the counter.

At first she looked like she was going to say no, but then realizing the situation, quickly changed her demeanor. "Sure," she said with a smile.

Frank dialed his parents, but it was to no avail; all circuits were busy. Under the circumstances, everyone must have been trying to use the phones. Frank thanked the young woman and left with Mary.

At first, Mary and Frank were going to go to each of their homes together, to celebrate with their parents, but before even getting one block they were caught up in the festivities. By this time the streets were wall-to-wall people of all shapes and sizes, men and women, the elderly and young, all partying like they never had before. Strangers were going up to each other everywhere, and because Frank happened to be wearing his uniform, endless people kept coming up to him.

"Can you believe it, soldier?"

"It's over! It's really over!"

"Thank you! Thank you so much!"

"Well we made it!" Said another serviceman in uniform.

"Can I get a kiss?" Yelled a young, pretty woman.

Mary gently put her arm out and proclaimed that they were together. But Mary couldn't get mad. How could anyone be mad at such a time?

At one point, a young man, who appeared to be Frank's age, and was wearing an Army uniform with a First Infantry Division patch, came over with two bottles of Champagne in one hand. "Twenty-Ninth, huh?" He said looking at Frank's patch.

Frank nodded.

"Well here's to Normandy brother!" He yelled over the crowd, while handing Frank one of the bottles of Champagne. Then, without saying another word, he turned around and disappeared into the sea of people.

Frank popped open the bottle, the cork flying into the air and white foam overflowing in streams, onto his hand. "Well I know you would never normally drink out of the bottle, but this is no ordinary day."

Just as the last word left his mouth, Mary grabbed the bottle from him and took a big gulp, Champagne spilling on her chin.

Frank laughed and took his turn. Then, right in the middle of the crowded street, the two locked into a long, sensual kiss. When their lips finally separated, Frank held onto Mary's arms and stared at her. She looked so beautiful. "Let's get married!"

Even over the crowd, Mary heard what Frank said, but couldn't believe it. "What did you say?"

"Will you marry me? I'm sorry. I know it's not how you imagined me proposing, but—"

"Of course I'll marry you." She then thrust herself back on Frank and gave him another passionate kiss.

Still in Frank's arms, Mary looked at her one and only love. "Oh Frank, I've been waiting for you to ask me that since you came back from Europe. I don't need some big wedding or some fancy ring. I just want to spend the rest of my life with you. I just want to be Mrs. Keller."

As the boisterous crowd of thousands celebrated the ending of the worst war history had ever known, Frank and Mary held each other tight. Frank was right. He had always envisioned getting permission from Mary's father first, then in some romantic setting falling down to one knee with a ring in his hand. But usually, the best moments in life are not ones that are previously conceptualized, imagined in one's mind in detail; they are born out of spontaneity, moments not planned, but forever remembered.

Later than night, when Frank arrived back home he was embraced by his mother and father. They, of course, were as happy as anyone that the war was over, that Frank would not be called upon to join in the invasion of Japan. Frank explained that he and Mary had been celebrating in the streets with everyone else. Then, he told them of his proposal and Mary's acceptance.

Margaret put her hands over her mouth and started crying. "Oh, can this day get any better?"

Harold put his hand on Frank's shoulder. "Congratulations son. Mary's a fine girl."

"Thank you, but you can't tell anyone yet until I talk to Mr. Capelli. I swore Mary not to even tell her parents until I talk to him first. I mean I always planned on asking Mary to marry me after the war ended. But I didn't want to do it before Japan surrendered in case I was called into duty again." Frank caught his breath. "I always meant to ask Mary's father's permission first and give her a ring. But when I heard that the war was over and saw all those people celebrating and looked at Mary…I just couldn't help myself…I just got caught up in the moment. I mean, I love her so much and when I realized that I wasn't goin' to Japan, I…I mean…"

"It's okay," his father said with a smile. "I understand."

"So when are you planning on talking to Mr. Capelli?" Asked Margaret.

Frank looked at his parents and let out a deep breath. "Well I guess I can't wait too long. If you don't mind Dad, I guess I'll take tomorrow off too, and go looking for a ring. Then I'll go talk to Mr. Capelli."

Harold laughed. "Of course son. Of course."

"Oh, what an amazing day," added Mrs. Keller. "First the war, now this."

"You're right!" Mr. Keller proclaimed. "Marge, don't we have anything to celebrate with?"

Mrs. Keller thought for a moment. "Well I think we have a bottle of brandy in the cabinet."

"That'll do!"

Margaret excitedly fetched the bottle and three of their best glasses. Then, around the living room table, they toasted to both the end of the war and Frank's engagement. It was a perfect ending to a perfect day—and one they would cherish for the rest of their lives.

# 10

# A LIFE WITHOUT WAR

The next morning, Frank went to Macy's in the city to buy Mary an engagement ring with money he had saved up. After going back and forth, looking at dozens of diamonds, he settled on a nice but modest ring. After purchasing it, when the salesman gave him the box, Frank could feel a tingling sensation working down his body. *This is for real*, he thought. After all they had been through, after the separation that war brought, he was finally going to get to marry the only girl he had ever truly loved.

That evening, with ring in pocket, Frank went to Mary's house to talk to her father. He knew how much Mr. and Mrs. Capelli admired him. But that did not stop him from being nervous. Frank always dressed proper, but on that night he put on a suit.

When Mr. Capelli answered the door, he figured that Frank and Mary were just going somewhere nice. Mr. Capelli shook Frank's hand and excitedly started talking about the war being over. Frank went along for a few minutes, but found it near impossible to concentrate on anything but the task at hand. Finally, he mustered up enough nerve to tell Mr. Capelli that he needed to talk to him about a personal matter. Mr. Capelli graciously led Frank into the living room. Mrs. Capelli, who had come out to welcome Frank, adjourned to the kitchen. Mary, knowing what the visit was about, was still upstairs.

Frank told Mr. Capelli the truth; that he had already asked Mary to marry him the day before, but wanted his blessing. "I'm sorry I didn't ask for your blessing first."

Mr. Capelli jumped up from the couch. "Nonsense! This is wonderful! Of course you have my blessing! I know how good you are to Mary and how much you two love each other. And it will be an honor to call you son," he said extending his hand.

Frank let out a smile and a gasp of relief. "Thank you, Mr. Capelli," he said while firmly shaking his hand.

"Come here," Mary's father said, as he pulled Frank closer and gave him a big hug.

Frank was going to show Mary's father the ring, but before having the chance, Mr. Capelli called out for his wife. "Teresa, get in here! I have wonderful news!"

She rushed in from the kitchen.

"Frank proposed to Mary. They're getting married!"

Teresa Capelli let out a scream of jubilation that was probably heard by the neighbors. "Finally! This is magnificent!" She gave Frank a giant hug and kiss on the cheek.

At that moment, Frank and Mr. Capelli's eyes caught Mary, standing halfway up the staircase, peering over the rail with a giant smile. "Mary, get down here!" Her father bellowed.

Before Mary could even get into the room, her mother ran over and embraced her. "Oh honey, congratulations!"

"Thank you Mom." Mary started to cry.

Next, Mr. Capelli went over and hugged his daughter, kissing her on the forehead.

As Frank watched Mary and her parents, he realized how lucky he was. Some people didn't even have a family; he had two.

Three months later, Frank and Mary were married in a Catholic church. Mary's sister, Mildred, was her maid of honor. Frank's best man, of course, was Bob. The ceremony, which included a full Mass, was exactly how Frank had envisioned it in his head all those years, all those godforsaken nights holed up in a foxhole, praying that he would live to see the day. And when that day finally came to fruition, he was filled not so much with nerves, but adrenalin. As Frank stood at the altar, staring into Mary's pale, blue eyes, he knew without a scintilla of doubt that he had made the right decision. In fact, as he stood there, mesmerized by how beautiful Mary looked in her flowing, white gown, strands of her long silk hair resting perfectly on her shoulders, Frank could only think how fortunate he was.

After the ceremony, the reception was at the Capelli residence. At one point, Mr. Capelli called for everyone to be silent. "I'd like to give a little speech if I may," he said proudly as he raised his glass of Champagne in the air. "Today me and my wife Teresa are blessed. Although we have considered Frank a son for some time, we are blessed today to officially welcome him into the family. And to also welcome in his wonderful parents, Harold and Margaret. Harry, Marge, you raised an outstanding man, one that I am proud to call son. Frank, may you and Mary live out the rest of your days in health and happiness. You deserve it. And may God always watch over you. So here is to you Frank, Mary. Salute!"

With that, everyone cheered in unison, before taking a drink.

After taking hers, Mary turned to her new husband. "This is the happiest day of my life," she whispered with a smile.

"Me too," replied Frank. "Me too."


Frank and Mary did not go on a honeymoon. Instead, they moved into a one-bedroom apartment in Bayside. They quickly settled into their new place and Frank continued to work with his father at the hardware store. It may not have been a glamorous life to some, but it was good living. With Frank's income they were able to pay their rent, have three square meals a day, and even put some money aside. Having been a boy during the Great Depression and having survived D-Day and other truculent battles, Frank was more than grateful for his situation.

Frank and Mary had talked about having children. Back then, if you were married, starting a family was obligatory. But they did not want kids merely because it was a societal rite of passage. Though he would have been happy with a daughter, for some time he had envisioned himself raising a son, teaching him as his father had taught him. He imagined playing ball with him and even taking him to the American Horse ranch. Mary had her own visions, but with a daughter, playing house with her, taking her to buy clothes. However, neither of them saw a need to rush to have children. They were just getting started on their own. If Mary was to get pregnant it would be a welcomed surprise, but time was on their side.

Besides working at the hardware store, Frank continued to volunteer at the veterans' hospital and also would occasionally hang out at the veterans' hall. Not only did he feel comfortable around other military men, but more importantly felt the need to help the wounded, not only physically, but also mentally. He was no psychiatrist, nor pretended to be, but those that had seen combat could relate to Frank and perhaps he could at least lend an open ear and consolation. Once again, he always carried with him and perpetuated Lieutenant Kowalski's message of hope.

As for Bob, he decided to go to college at St. John's, majoring in engineering. He had always been good at math and his father convinced him, rightfully so, that with all the new technology that the war had brought, engineering would soon become a booming career. Bob also started dating again, an attractive twenty-year-old named Dorothy, whom he met in school. The two quickly became serious and it was not long before they started hanging with Frank and Mary. Dorothy was not only easy on the eyes and smart, but she had a sunny, outgoing disposition. Frank was happy for his best friend and so was Mary. In fact, she forged her own separate bond with Dorothy. As for Annette, she had all but faded into memory. Not even Mary heard from her anymore.

As the dark days of war drifted further into the rearview mirror, America, which had emerged stronger than ever, continued her bright path to superpowerdom. The economy was once again churning, the factories building. Across the vast land roads and highways were being paved, connecting cities to new, sprawling suburbs. The American pie was expanding and more and more of its citizens were being able to have their very own piece.

One Saturday afternoon in May, 1947, Frank stopped by his parents for lunch. He had called that morning so they were expecting him. His mother greeted him at the front door with a hug and a kiss on the cheek and then led him into the kitchen where his father awaited.

"Hey Pop," he said with a smile.

Frank noticed his father looked somewhat serious.

"Frank, your mother and I have to talk to you about something."

Frank's heart sank. His father looked serious and no good news usually followed the words: *we have to talk*. But then Frank looked over at his mother standing by the kitchen counter and saw her smiling. *Okay, it can't be that bad of news*, he realized. "What is it Pop?"

"Have you heard about a place called Levittown?"

Frank thought about it for a second. "No, can't say I have."

"Well it's a new community being built on Long Island. They're building it especially for veterans who returned from the war and want to start a family, want to have a house and backyard of their own. They're about to break ground there and once they do, they expect to build several houses a week, almost like an assembly line. It's a new way of building." Mr. Keller paused. "Well, anyway, your mother and I think you and Mary should move there. It's time for you to start a family, make your own mark."

Frank took a moment to digest his father's words. "Well Pop, that sounds great, but how am I going to afford a house? And what am I going to do there? Besides, I have to help you out with the shop."

"Don't worry about the shop. What do you think I did the three and a half years you were gone? Now listen, I know I told you to do whatever you wanted in life. And I still feel that way. I mean it, whatever you want to do, you earned that right and your mother and I will support you. But I was thinking, what if you were to open your own hardware store in Levittown? I mean a brand new community, new houses. People are going to need hardware supplies and you know everything there is to know about the business." Harold stopped for a moment and gently exhaled. "Now I'm not talking about going in business with me," he continued in a slower voice. "This would be your own store completely. I'm always here to help and give advice, but this would be all yours."

"It's a golden opportunity Frank," Mrs. Keller, still standing by the counter, chimed in.

Frank leaned back and let out a fleeting laugh. "I'm sorry, I don't mean to laugh. I mean all that sounds like a dream come true. But a new house, now a store—what did you guys find, a big bag of money on the street?"

Mr. and Mrs. Keller looked at each other. Then, Harold pulled an envelope from his back pocket and extended it towards his son. "Here," he said in a matter-of-fact tone.

Bewildered, Frank slowly took the envelope and opened it. Inside was a check for $4,600. Shocked, Frank looked at his parents. "I don't get it? Did you guys really find a bag of money?"

Harold and Margaret laughed. "No, that would be nice," Mr. Keller replied. "We've been saving it up."

Frank immediately threw the check on the kitchen table. "No way! I mean thank you, but there is no way I am taking your life savings."

"Don't worry, Frank," said his mother. "We still have some more. We're not gonna starve."

Frank shook his head. "Forget it. I'm your son, I know you're not rich. This had to be most of everything you've saved up over the years. Everything you worked for, Dad. I'm not gonna take your money."

Mr. Keller leaned forward and put his stern hand on his son's. "Now I want you to listen to me," he said dead seriously, staring straight into Frank's eyes. "That money means nothing to me. It's true, I worked for it over the years. But every hour I worked, everything I've ever done, I did for you. A man's—a parent's—only wish is that their children will have a better life than they did. And one day you're going to have a child—maybe three or four children—and you're going to do everything in your power to see to it that they have a better life than you."

Mrs. Keller walked over to the table and put her hand on her son's shoulder. "We love you Frank. And we love Mary. And to see you two in a nice house and start a family of your own, have children and raise them in a good town…that will bring your father and me more happiness than all the money in the world ever could."

Frank bowed his head, not wanting his parents see him start to cry. "But…" he said, trying to inconspicuously wipe his eyes.

"The money from this check, along with some of the money you earned from the GI Bill should be enough to get started. I will co-sign a loan for the rest. In a few years you'll have that hardware store booming."

Frank looked up at his parents. "I…I don't know what to say."

His mother looked at him, tears starting to swell in her eyes. "Just say yes."

"Thank you so much."

Before his last word could even float into the air, Margaret leapt forward and wrapped her arms around him. "Oh Frank, I'm so happy."

Next Frank turned to his father. "Thank you so much, Pop. I promise I'll pay you back."

Harold gave his son a firm handshake, while grabbing his arm with his other hand. "The only repayment we need is to see you and Mary live a happy and prosperous life."

For a moment time seemed to freeze as Frank stared at his smiling parents. He had always known how much they loved him, how much they had done for him. But he was amazed just how selfless they were. "I hope that when Mary and I have children," he said, fighting not to cry, "we can be half the parents you've been to me."

"You're going to make a great father," Mr. Keller proudly replied with a smile. "And I know Mary is going to make a wonderful mother."

That evening, Frank went home and told Mary the news. At first, she had the same initial reaction that Frank had; they could not take his parents savings. But after he explained their emphaticalness and how much it meant to them, she relented. Once she did, Mary realized the reality of the news and was overcome by a euphoric feeling. She had married her high school sweetheart, her only true love, and now they were going to have their very own house, where they could start a family. Mary threw her arms around her husband. "Oh Frank! I can't believe it! It's like a dream come true!"

# 11

# LEVITTOWN

That August, Mary and Frank moved into their newly built home. There were two types of houses in Levittown: A cape and a ranch. Theirs was a ranch. It was two-stories with two bedrooms upstairs and a small backyard. By modern standards it was a diminutive space. If someone from the twenty-first century looked at it they would consider it a dollhouse. In fact, by the turn of the century there would be hardly any original Levitts left. All but a few had been extended and dormered, all having their own unique personality. But at the time, the cookie-cutter boxlike homes designed by William Levitt were revolutionary and an affordable gateway to the American dream.

When Frank and Mary moved, Levittown was still a fledging community. Blocks and plots of land were active assembly lines for more and more houses as people from the boroughs continued to arrive in troves. But unlike so many other perennial communities, this one's residents were young upstarts, families forged by those returned from World War II. It was one of the birthplaces specifically developed for, and claimed by, what would come to be known as the Greatest Generation.

Thirty-five miles from New York City, Levittown seemed a world away from the congestion and clamor of even the most rural areas of the five boroughs. Not far to the east were woods and in some areas vast potato fields. However, newly built parkways connected them to the rest of the world. And being on the south shore of Long Island, it was only a quick ride to Jones and other beaches.

Frank wasted little time in starting his own hardware store. On a small strip of commercial property he was able to lease a sufficient space and within three months had the store up and running. Immediately, the customers started pouring in. His father had great perspicacity in realizing that a brand-new community would need a place from which to buy tools, paint, and other home improvement items. In a strike of luck, timing or both, Frank's store was the first in the area—and quickly became a staple.

Perhaps in part because of the business, Frank became acquainted with many of the town's residents and he and Mary assimilated well into the community. In a time when everyone knew, or at the least was cordial with, their neighbors the Kellers were no exception. They also made friends from church, which they attended every Sunday. Furthermore, especially in the early days, Levittown was a close-knit community because many of the men had served in World War II and thus shared a unique bond.

Though Frank hired help, he was always at the hardware store while it was open for business. This busy schedule and logistics meant that he could no longer spend time volunteering at the veterans' hospital in Queens. However, helping his fellow veterans was extremely important to Frank, so whenever he could find the time, he volunteered at a closer hospital and also stopped by the local veterans hall.

He and Mary did miss spending time with Bob and Dorothy. But Dorothy's parents, who were wealthy, had bought her a new 1947 Chevrolet Fleetmaster Coupe and they would come down sometimes on a Sunday and spend the afternoon. Bob finished his two-year degree that June and had started working for the city doing mechanical engineering.

One day, in late September, Bob called up his old friend to tell him that he and Dorothy had gotten engaged. The wedding was set for that January. Frank and Mary could not have been happier for them. The following weekend, Bob and Dorothy came out to Levittown and the four of them celebrated. It was a joyous occasion.

Bob was not done with the surprise news. A month later, he called Frank again, this time telling him that he had just been offered and accepted a job at Northrop Grumman at their plant near Levittown. He had already put a small down payment on a house. The two best friends would soon be reunited. It was almost as if it had to be, as if it was fate.

In a time when a woman and a man living together without being married was still considered sacrilege, Bob and Dorothy moved up their wedding date to the second week in November. Bob was due to start his new job at the beginning of December and thus wanted to be moved into the new house by then.

Frank was Bob's best man, as Bob had been his. It was a proud moment for Frank. He could not have been closer, not have cared more for Bob if they had shared the same blood. Though Bob kept it to himself, Frank knew how crushed he must have been when Annette left him for another man. But now he had Dorothy and the two could not have seemed happier. He was starting an exceptional job and would be moving into a new house. It seemed only fitting that the two best friends would be paving their way into that bright, prosperous future together. They had both made it through the war. They had both married. And after everything, just like when they were kids, they would live within walking distance from each other.

A week before Thanksgiving, Bob and Dorothy moved into their new house, a mere five blocks from Frank and Mary. For the first time since opening the store, Frank took the afternoon off to help with the move. Mary, happy that she and Dorothy could spend more time together, also assisted.

When most of the heavy lifting was done, Dorothy turned to Bob, with the look of a child about to open presents on Christmas morning. "So, can I tell them?" She asked her husband in an excited voice, her hands clasped in front of her waist.

Bob smiled. "Go ahead."

Frank and Mary looked puzzledly at each other, then at Dorothy.

"I'm pregnant! I just went to the doctor's the other day."

"Oh my God!" Mary grabbed her new, but dear friend's hands. "Congratulations!"

"Thank you. We figured this would be the best time to tell you."

Now the two women locked in a jovial hug. "I'm so happy for you! This is such good news!"

Frank turned to Bob with a look of utter proudness. "Congratulations!"

Bob smiled and nodded his head. "Thank you, buddy." The two shook hands and embraced.

Frank then said his congratulations to Dorothy and Mary to Bob.

"Heck, I feel like we need some Champagne, have a toast," Frank proclaimed.

"Well, it's funny you should say that," Bob replied. "We were thinking the same thing. That's why I bought a bottle of Champagne. Honey, can you get it from the car, it's in the back seat."

Almost floating on air, Dorothy went to retrieve the bottle.

"I can't think of two people I'd rather drink to the occasion with."

Mary grabbed hold of Frank's arm. "Oh Bob, that's so sweet."

It was thirty-eight degrees out and even sitting in the car for hours, the Champagne was cold. Bob ceremoniously popped the cork and poured four glasses.

"If I may," Frank spoke up, "I'd like to say something."

"Of course."

Frank raised his glass to his chest. "Bob, I've known you all my life. And I couldn't be prouder to call you my best friend. More than a best friend, a brother. And Dorothy, though I have not had the privilege of knowing you as long, I know you are a fine woman. And I know I speak for Mary as well when I say that you will both make the best parents. And we wish you and the baby all the happiness and health in the world. Cheers!"

With that, everyone clanged their glasses together and took a sip of Champagne.

After a little while, the men and women found themselves in separate groups. Dorothy was telling Mary how she was forgoing the rest of her schooling to become a housemother. In the living room, over a second glass of Champagne, Frank and Bob talked amongst themselves.

"So, Papa Davenport, huh?" Frank said to his old friend.

"How does it sound?"

"It sounds like a restaurant. 'Come to Papa Davenport's! We make only the best home-cooked meals.'" The two laughed. "Hey you know you're gonna have to watch that sewer mouth of yours around the kid," Frank joked.

"Me?"

"I still remember when your mother washed your mouth out with that bar of soap when you dropped your father's hammer on your foot and yelled out 'Shit!'"

Bob cracked up. "Oh man, that sucked. For a whole week everything I ate tasted like soap. I can still picture the look on my mother's face—like I had just burned down the house or something. And you—you just ran off."

"Hey, I thought she was going to wash my mouth out just for being there."

The two chuckled some more about the childhood memory.

"Hey, really though," Frank said, "all kidding aside, I'm really happy for you and Dorothy."

Bob nodded. "Thank you buddy, that means a lot. Really."

"I meant what I said before, you're going to make a great father and Dorothy is going to be a great mother."

Bob put his hand on Frank's shoulder. "I'm sure the day's coming for you and Mary soon, too. Then we can raise our kids together. Just like it was always supposed to be."

Frank smiled. "That would be something."

Bob raised his glass. "To the future."

"To the future." With that, they toasted.

That Thanksgiving, Mary and Frank spent half the day with Frank's parents and the other half with Mary's. Mary bragged about how well the hardware store was doing and though outwardly Frank displayed modesty, inside he was filled with pride. Frank was especially proud to show Mr. and Mrs. Capelli how well he could take care of their daughter. But her parents never had any doubt.

It was a festive day of eating and spending time with family. But there was a certain, unique comfort of returning to their own home.

"Next Thanksgiving, let's have it at our house," Mary said.

Frank happily agreed.


As Christmas approached, the hardware store was doing better than ever. Not only were new residents to the area coming in all the time, but with a long, arduous winter upon them, people were buying up shovels and rock salt. Like in his father's store, Frank also decided to sell indoor and outdoor Christmas lights, which were flying off the shelves.

Two weeks before Christmas, Mary came down with what she thought was some kind of bug. She had no fever, nor did she have a sore throat. But she had become sporadically nauseous, so much so that she would sometimes throw up. After two days, Frank began to worry—much more so than Mary. He urged her to call a doctor, who during that time, still made house calls. But Mary, always strong-willed, told him it was nothing serious, that it would go away on its own. But by the fifth day, when she realized that she was always sickest in the morning, Mary started to figure out what could be going on. Keeping her suspicions to herself, she made an appointment with a local doctor and asked Frank to take her.

"Why don't you have him come to the house?" Frank asked. "This way you don't have to exert yourself."

Mary brushed him off. "It's not like I'm bedridden. I'm able to walk around. Besides, when I called, his assistant said that the doctor could see me sooner if I went to the office."

Not thinking anymore of it, Frank took Mary to her appointment.

The doctor confirmed it. Mary was pregnant. Frank had never felt so high after hearing the news. He was going to be a father! As for Mary, she was every bit as ecstatic as her husband.

Bursting with excitement the first phone call they made was to Mary's parents. Frank put his ear next to hers so he could listen in on the receiver. "Mom, I have great news!" Mary blurted with jubilation. "I'm pregnant!"

"Oh my God! Sal, come here! Come here!"

Next it was Frank's parents' turn. They took the news just as proudly and elated as the Capelli's. As Frank talked to his mother, Mary was actually brought to tears seeing his face, how happy and excited he looked. *He's going to be a great father*, she thought.

After telling their parents, Frank and Mary called Bob and Dorothy. It was 7:00 p.m., so they were both home. Bob and Dorothy said how happy they were for them.

A half-hour later, trying to come down from all the excitement, the doorbell rang. Not expecting anyone, Frank went to see who it was. Standing on the porch were Bob and Dorothy—and Bob was holding up a bottle of Champagne. "Hey, it's tradition now!"

In an almost surreal moment, the four friends toasted to a new edition to their circle for the second time in a month. Dorothy and Mary talked about how great it was going to be to go through pregnancy together; Dorothy was expecting in early May, Mary in late June. Frank and Bob talked about being fathers together. "I guess you were right when you said we'd have our own child soon, too," Frank said laughing.

Though Mary was less than three months along, Frank went out of his way to pamper her; getting her whatever she needed, drawing her a bath, even massaging her feet. He began to take more time off of work, leaving the store in the hands of his employees. Mary would tell him that his coddling was unnecessary, but secretly she basked in it. She had always been strong, able to stand on her own two feet, but what woman doesn't like to be pampered from time to time.

That Christmas was no doubt a special one. It was the first in their new home and now they had a baby on the way. As they had done for Thanksgiving, Mary and Frank visited their respective parents on Christmas Eve. But Christmas, they decided to spend in Levittown. Bob and Dorothy stopped by for a while and exchanged gifts, but for most of the day it was just the two of them. Mary cooked a turkey with stuffing and mashed potatoes. They talked about how next Christmas would be the baby's first.

Christmas in 1947 was on a Thursday. Late the next evening the first snowstorm of the winter arrived in New York. When Frank woke up early that Saturday morning, he looked out his bedroom window to see everything covered in a thick blanket of pristine white; the sidewalks, roads, parked cars, front yards. Frank usually tried not to make too much noise and wake Mary up, especially now that she was pregnant. But on that Saturday morning, he could not help himself. "Mary, Mary, wake up!"

Mary groggily opened one eye. "What is it?" She moaned.

"You've gotta see this," Frank replied while still holding the curtain and looking out the window. "There must be at least a foot and a half of snow out there." He was like a little kid.

Slowly, Mary pulled off the covers, rolled out of bed and in her nightgown, sauntered over to the window. Frank pulled the curtain more open and Mary peered down at the white landscape. "Oh Frank, it's so pretty," she said, while snuggling up close and holding her husband's hand. "It's like a Norman Rockwell painting."

"Yeah. It looks different than in Queens. So peaceful."

Mary tugged at his hand. "I want to build a snowman!"

Frank turned to face his wife and let out a fleeting laugh. "Snowman? Aren't we a little too old for that?"

"You're never too old to build a snowman," Mary excitedly pleaded.

"But it's Saturday. I have to open the shop."

Mary, now fully awake, still held onto Frank's hand. "Look at it out there. No place is going to be open today. Come on!"

"People are going to need shovels and salt." Frank saw the disappointed look on his wife's face. "Look, I'll tell you what, I'll go downstairs and shovel the sidewalk and the walkway. Then I'll go to the store and I'll see how business is. I have to at least shovel in front of the store. But if it's a real slow day I'll close early and I'll come back and we'll build a snowman. We'll see how it goes. But tomorrow's Sunday and the snow's not gonna melt before that. So I promise, either today or tomorrow, we'll build that snowman."

Mary jumped as if she was still ten-years-old. "Oh Frank, thank you!"

Frank wasted no time in getting dressed and going out front to shovel. By this time a few neighbors were also outside doing the same and they exchanged pleasantries. It was a laborious task. The snowstorm had dumped seventeen inches on the south shore of Long Island. But though Frank did not work out like he used to, he was still in good shape. And he never shied away from manual labor. After about an hour of continuous shoveling, just like he always did, Frank walked the five blocks to the hardware store.

Most of the sidewalks remained unshoveled and the streets unplowed. Every step Frank took, his feet dug deep into the snow. But he had boots and had been through much worse. Arriving at the store, he was greeted by the man who owned the candy store next door. He was already busy shoveling the sidewalk. They said good morning to each other and chatted about the snow for a while. Then Frank opened the hardware store and joined his business neighbor cleaning up the sidewalk.

As Mary predicted, business was slow. The storm had been forecast and most people had already bought their snow shovels and salt. By 1:30 p.m., only two customers had come into the store. Frank decided to let the one employee working with him that day go home and close shop early. As Frank was closing up, who walked in but Bob, who had every Saturday and Sunday off work.

"Hey, what are you doing here?"

"Well I shoveled all morning and Dorothy's taking a nap. I was getting cabin fever just sitting around the house. Especially with all the snow, makes me feel like I should be out. So I figured I'd stop by." Bob looked at Frank, who had keys in his hand and was standing by the light switch. "You closing early?"

Frank said he was.

"Hey, let's go get a beer!"

Frank thought about it for a moment. "I promised Mary that if I closed the shop early I would come home and help her build a snowman."

Bob looked strangely at his friend, before letting out a short laugh. "A snowman?"

Frank realized how weird it sounded and also laughed. "She wants to build a snowman. What can I say?" He said shrugging his shoulders. "I don't know, I guess the snow makes her feel like a kid again."

"I'll tell you what," Bob said while looking at his watch, "it's not even two o'clock. Let's go have two beers. The tavern's right on the next block. We'll be out of there by three. Then I'll even go home and ask Dorothy if she wants to help you guys build a snowman."

Frank thought about it. "Okay. Yeah. Mary would love that."

Frank finished closing up the store and he and Bob walked the short distance to Lucky's, a neighborhood tavern. As soon as they walked into the dimly lit establishment, a middle-aged bartender greeted them. They acknowledged him and continued towards the long, oak bar. There were only two other patrons sitting there and one of them lifted his head from his drink and called them over. "Hey Frank," he said in an upbeat voice.

Frank led Bob towards the man, a slender, but fit fellow with perfectly slicked-back, thick black hair. "Hey Peter, how are you?"

"Very well," he said, arising from his stool to greet his guests. "Eleanor took Charles to her parents' house in Connecticut for the weekend. So I'm home alone for a few days," he said with a smile. "Figured good as time as any to hang out at the bar without her busting my chops."

Bob and Frank laughed.

"Bob, this is Peter Mullen. He lives down the block from me."

"Pleased to meet you," Bob said before shaking his iron-like hand.

"Peter here is a flyboy. He flew bombing missions over Germany during the war."

The three veterans sat down together and chatted over some beers. The conversation started out mundane, about the snow, but inevitably turned to the war. Bob asked Peter what it was like to take part in the bombing raids.

"I know you guys had a tough time of it on the ground, but let me tell you, being in the air was no picnic. We lost a lot of good men up there. Especially early on, we took on heavy losses from the Luftwaffe and anti-aircraft artillery," he said in a clear, but somber voice, before taking a big gulp of his beer. "It was like being inside a tin can in front of a firing range. Fifty planes would take off and only forty or thirty-five would come back. And every time you went on a mission you wondered, when is it going to be my time? Is this the mission that my plane will be one of the ones not making it back?" Peter took another drink.

"Did you ever get hit?" Asked Bob.

"Oh yeah, a few times. One time we lost our tail gunner and navigator on the same mission." Peter paused. "But by the time Dresden came around we had already achieved air supremacy. We were still taking on some fire from artillery, but the Luftwaffe had been decimated."

"You were part of the Dresden raid?" Bob asked with enthusiasm.

Peter polished off his beer and shook his head. "Yep. We lit up the entire city. From up in the air, looking down, it was like looking down at hell. All you saw were giant flames for miles. Everything was ablaze."

"Well it had to be done," Bob responded in a fading voice.

Just then the bartender, who had been listening to the conversation, brought over another round. "This one's on the house fellas."

They all thanked him.

Peter swiveled in his barstool to face Frank and Bob and raised his beer. "Well guys, this is to the war being over."

"Amen," said Bob.

"Here, here," added Frank as the three young men clanked their mugs together.

"It's funny, I can't believe it's been over two years now since the war." Peter said in an almost lighthearted tone.

Frank let out a sigh. "I don't know, in some ways it seems like it was just yesterday, but in others it feels like a lot longer."

Peter shook his head. "I know what you mean. My son's already a year and a half old."

Bob raised his beer. "Congratulations."

Frank put his hand on Bob's shoulder. "Bob here and his wife are expecting their own baby."

"Well than, congratulations to you," Peter said while clanking Bob's mug with his own. Peter already knew that Mary was pregnant. "I'll tell ya, it's nice having a weekend to myself, but being married and being a father, I wouldn't change it for the world. I get goose bumps just thinking about my son. You fellas will see. I can't wait to teach him how to play baseball and take him fishing. Go camping together."

Now Frank raised his glass. "To fatherhood!"

"To fatherhood!" Peter and Bob replied in unison as they all cheered.

"And let me tell you," Peter went on, "Levittown is going to be a great place to raise a family."

Frank and Bob stayed for one more round, mostly listening to Peter proudly go on about his son. When they departed, Bob felt like he had a new friend.

It was 3:20 p.m. Bob went home and said he would ask Dorothy if she wanted to come over and help build a snowman. Now, with a few beers in him, the plan sounded much more fun. Frank hurried home himself. The gray, winter sky would soon start to darken, but Frank was determined to grant his wife her wish. When he walked through the door, Mary was on the phone. Bob had already arrived home and called to say that Dorothy was feeling under the weather and they would not be coming over. Undeterred, Frank urged Mary to put on her boots and coat.

Like two kids, Frank and Mary built their snowman in the front yard, for all to see. Perhaps inevitably, an impromptu snowball fight broke out. As they finished their creation, Frank replayed Peter's words about parenthood in his head. He envisioned a time not far away when he and Mary would be building a snowman with their son or daughter.

# 12

# THE PATH IS NOT ALWAYS SMOOTH

One afternoon Frank was in the stockroom of the hardware store when he heard a commotion. Instinctively he went out to see what was going on. Down one of the aisles, he saw a black gentleman being confronted by two teenage males. The man looked not a day over thirty, but was holding a cane.

"Listen, I told you I don't want any problems," the man said in an obsequious voice.

"We told you we don't want any niggers in this town. Now you want us to make you leave?" One of the teens barked, inches from the man's face.

"Okay, okay," he replied, while raising the hand not being propped up by the cane, by his chest signaling he was giving up.

Frank knew both the teens, but neither one worked in the store. "Wait a minute," Frank shouted as he rushed down.

The stranger had already one foot out the door when he turned back to look at Frank. "Listen mister, I told them I was leaving. I won't come back. I didn't mean for any problems."

By this time, Frank was between the man and the teenagers.

Freddy, a sixteen-year-old who worked at the store, was now also at the scene, though at this point just observing. "Well I own this store and I didn't say you have to leave."

"Mr. Keller, we were just keepin this riffraff out of the store for ya," said the main aggressor.

Frank shot him a stern look. "This is my store, Billy!"

"Listen, there's no need for this. I'm leavin."

Just then Frank realized that he recognized the black man. "Do I know you?"

The stranger looked towards the ground, seemingly ashamed to answer the question.

But then it came to Frank. He had seen the man before while volunteering at the veterans hospital in Queens. The two had never spoken, but Frank was certain it was him. "I've seen you at the vet hospital, haven't I?" He then extended his hand towards the man. "I volunteered there. My name is Frank Keller. I was in the Twenty-Ninth Division."

The man let the door close in back of him, as he stood in the entranceway looking down at Frank's extended hand. It seemed like a minute went by before he finally felt comfortable enough to shake it. "Yes, I've seen you there. My name is Hubert Whittaker. I was in the Ninety-Second Infantry Division."

In World War II, all black soldiers were segregated into their own "colored" divisions. Nicknamed the Buffalo Soldiers, the Ninety-Second saw heavy combat in Europe during the war. Mostly in Italy, they fought numerous battles and took large casualties.

"You know this nigger?"

Frank instantly turned and grabbed the teen by the lapel. "You ever address this man again, you will address him as Mr. Whittaker! This brave man was wounded fighting the same enemy that all of us white soldiers were fighting. His division suffered over three thousand casualties. This man is a hero."

The boy that Frank was holding and reprimanding shook his head submissively and looked like he was about to pee in his pants. But his friend wasn't lying down. "I'm gonna tell my father about this!"

Frank crouched down and looked him square in the eyes. "You

tell your father. You tell him everything I said. Now you both get the hell out of my store!"

Wasting no time, the two hoodlums opened the door and scampered down the block.

Frank then turned his attention back to the man he now knew as Hubert. "You're welcome in my store any time, sir."

"Thank you Mr. Keller. I appreciate it. I really do. But I don't want to cause any friction between you and any of the folks in town."

"Please call me Frank. And don't worry about those ignorant kids. Or any other ignorant bastards." Frank paused as he looked Hubert over. "It is an honor to formally meet you."

Hubert shook his head. "Believe me, the honor is all mine."

With that, Freddy went back to work and Frank escorted Hubert to the counter, where the two talked for a while. As several customers came and went the two veterans exchanged war stories. Hubert told how he had been shot in the leg, thus the cane. However, he explained, the reason he frequented the veterans hospital was to visit a good friend, who had to have both his legs amputated just below the kneecaps, due to a grenade. Hubert asked about Frank's experience, specifically about D-Day. After about a half hour, Frank helped his new friend find the wrench for which he had originally come into the store. Then, with a firm handshake, the two parted ways, but promised to run into each other again around town and have a drink together.

When Frank arrived home after work that evening, Mary could instantly tell that something was bothering him. Even after a long day at the store, he usually came through the door in a good mood, with a smile on his face and greeted Mary with a big hug and kiss. This day there was no kiss or hug, just an obligatory hello.

"I made pot roast tonight," Mary said with a smile. "I know how much you love it."

"Okay. I'm gonna go change first," he grumbled.

Instead of giving Frank his space, Mary followed him into the bedroom. Not even acknowledging her presence, Frank angrily unbuttoned his shirt and then whipped off his belt.

"Did something happen at work today?" Mary hesitantly asked.

Frank threw his wallet on the bed. "This man came into the store today. This colored man, and these two kids confronted him. Started calling him a nigger and told him that he was not welcome. I recognized him from the vet hospital. Turns out he fought and was wounded over in Europe. I mean, what the hell is wrong with the people in this country?" He lamented. "We treat them like animals. But still, they go over there and fight and die and hold their own as much as any white man. And what do they come home to? Jim Crow. It's bullshit!"

Frank had never before cussed in front of Mary. "But Frank, what can you do about it? I hear what you're saying, but that's just the way it is."

"Don't you understand Mary? How many young American and Allied men died in Europe fighting the Nazis in the name of democracy? In the name of freedom. So the world didn't have to live under oppression and fascism. And we celebrate winning the war. But where's the democracy and equality for the Negros? Their own bars, their own restaurants, their own water fountains…their own schools. Hell, isn't that exactly what the Nazis did to the Jews? What's next, are we going to start putting them all into concentration camps and gassing them?"

Mary didn't know what to say. She had never really thought much about the subject. But to her, everything Frank said made sense. In fact, it was almost like an epiphany. Unfortunately, she had no answers.

Later that night Frank apologized to his wife for blowing up. He had never before done that in front of her. However, Mary explained that he had every right to be upset. Furthermore, she was glad that he had stuck up for the black soldier. In fact she asked about him—and Frank was more than happy to tell his story. He also told of what little he knew about the mighty Buffalo Soldiers.

Over the weeks and months Frank did run into Hubert again and the two became friends. And as an extension, Hubert also became friends with Bob. Not everyone in the town approved of their friendship and from time to time words were exchanged and on a few occasions it nearly came to fisticuffs. But there were also those, mainly veterans, who stood by Frank and Hubert.

It was the first week in February. Frank was at the hardware store and had just finished helping a customer when the phone rang. Expecting a routine call, he picked up the receiver while asking his employee to straighten out one of the shelves. But before Frank could even start his usual greeting, a sobbing, frantic voice came through the other end. It was Mary. "Frank..." she cried, trying to get out each word, "the baby..."

A cold rush shot through Frank's body. "What? What's the matter?" His voice quaked.

"Just come home. It's the baby."

Mary was not the type of person to exaggerate or panic because she was not feeling well. And she was hysterical. Frank knew immediately that something was terribly wrong. "Okay honey, I'm coming right now," he replied with bated breath.

Frank did not even hang up the phone; he just left it dangling as he dashed out of the store. On his way, he told Freddy to watch the store. Alarmed, his young employee asked what happened, but there was no answer. Before the last word left his mouth, Frank was already out the door. Freddy was much more concerned about his boss and mentor than taking care of the store. He had never seen Frank act like that and knew something bad had happened.

As fast as he could, Frank flew down the uncongested sidewalks towards his house. As he did myriad of thoughts raced through his head. *Did something happen to the baby? Had something happened to Mary? Did someone break into the house? Should he have called an ambulance or the police? Were they already at the house?*

Still processing all these thoughts, Frank arrived at the house. At least from the outside, all seemed to be quiet. Out of breath, he opened the front door and burst inside. Mary was sitting by the kitchen table crying. She did not even lift her head to look at her husband. Mary was wearing a robe and as Frank approached, he noticed blood smeared on her legs.

"Mary," he uttered, his heart pounding, "what happened?"

Mary stood up and wrapped her arms around her husband. "Oh Frank," she cried into his shoulder. "I had a miscarriage. We lost the baby."

Frank felt like he was going to blackout as his knees began to buckle. The whole house seemed like it was spinning. The reality of the moment overcame him. But knowing that there was no escaping it, that it was no mistake or dream, was almost too much to take in. Time moved in slow motion. Seconds were measured in minutes. Finally he stroked his disconsolate wife's hair. "What happened? When did it…"

"About a half hour ago. I was taking a shower upstairs and all of a sudden I felt strange. Then it happened. It's in the tub," she cried.

Tears were streaking down Frank's face. Mary's words burned a horrific image in his mind and he fought not to vomit. There was no way he was going up there to look. He just couldn't. Just the thought of it decimated him.

After Frank tried to compartmentalize his own pain and console Mary, he called the hospital. An ambulance came and paramedics took care of the fetus. Frank could not bring himself to watch. They then took Mary to the hospital to make sure she was okay. Frank rode in the back of the transport, all the time holding his wife's hand.

Mary was not physically harmed during the miscarriage. But the mental strain was just beginning for her and Frank. Of course, Frank was devastated by the loss of the baby. But he tried to be strong for his wife. He explained that they were both young and had plenty of time to try again.

"But what if the same thing happens?" She would say. "I can't go through this again."

"But the doctors said that there's nothing wrong with you. That you should be able to deliver a healthy baby."

"But they also said that they can't guarantee that I won't have another miscarriage again."

There seemed to be nothing Frank could say to comfort his wife. But he made sure she was comfortable. For the first week and a half he left the hardware store to his most trusted employee. He would sometimes walk over and check on the store. But most of the time he spent by Mary's side, bringing her food in bed, drawing her baths, and just being there for her.

Of course, Frank and Mary had to let their family and friends know what happened. Besides Mary's parents, who she told, Frank took this grievous task upon himself. Everyone wanted to help, but at the same time was helpless. Dorothy felt a special kind of anguish. She and Mary were supposed to go through pregnancy together. Mary's eyes would light up when they talked about it and looked forward to not just delivering close to each other, but raising their children together. She felt such immense sorrow for her friend and for Frank. But also, a part of her could not help but think, what if it happens to me, too?

A week after the miscarriage, another substantial snowfall blanketed Long Island. It started coming down on Sunday morning. Mary was not feeling well so Frank said they would skip church that day. As Mary slept, Frank stared out the kitchen window, sipping a hot cup of coffee. He watched in silence as thick flakes of snow slowly fell to the ground. It seemed just like the other day that he and Mary avidly gazed down at the snow from the bedroom window and then later played in it. He remembered how alive it made them feel and how beautiful it looked. Now, it looked so gelid and somber. The thick, cloudy sky cast a shadow on every tree, every yard, every house. It's strange, Frank thought, how the same view could look and feel so effervescent one day and another day so bleak.


As the weeks pressed on, Frank became more concerned about Mary's mental state. She had always been so strong and full of life. Now she seemed so frangible, lethargic, and was sleeping for nine, ten hours a night, taking naps during the day, never smiling, and not wanting to indulge in conversation.

In the 1940s and fifties there was a stigma attached to going to a psychologist or even therapist. But it was routine, even encouraged, in difficult times to seek guidance from your parish priest, pastor or rabbi. Frank suggested to Mary that they should talk to their priest, Father Mallard, about what happened. They were both practicing Catholics and perhaps turning to the church and God was the answer. Secretly, Mary was angry at God for what happened. But after some inner struggle she decided to go. She was sick of feeling despondent and was not getting better on her own. And despite her husband's best efforts, he was not able to lift her spirits.

That next week, Frank and Mary met with Father Mallard, a cherub-looking fifty-three-year-old with thick gray hair and rosy cheeks. Until then, they had only talked to him after Mass, but nevertheless felt comfortable around him and part of his flock. The priest seemed sincerely heartfelt to hear about the miscarriage. Also, he could immediately tell how distressed Frank and Mary were.

"I just don't understand, Father," Mary opened up, almost in tears. "Everything was going so well. Frank survived the war—and in one piece. We got married, were able to get our own house in Levittown. Frank opened up his own store and it's doing extremely well. Then we were blessed with this baby. It was like we were on this road to all our dreams coming true, and all of a sudden this happens. Why? Why would the Lord bless us with this baby only to take it away?"

With his hands clasped together on his neat, oak desk, Father Mallard leaned forward. "The path is not always smooth," he said in a slow voice. "Sometimes there is a detour, a pitfall, a tragedy. But rest assured that God is always with you on that path. And God will be there to lead you back to better days." The priest raised his still clasped hands to below his chin. "As for why God does the things he does…well, some things are beyond the understanding of man. But that is where faith comes in. And it is in that faith where God grants us strength, promise, redemption, healing."

# 13

# THOMAS

Father Mallard's words were not a magic wand. Mary did not leave the church that day and immediately feel her old self. But more and more she started to think about what he had said. Of course, time is also the great healer. And day-by-day, week-by-week, Mary slowly came out of her lugubrious state. As she did, Frank started spending more and more time back at the hardware store, until he returned to being there Monday through Saturday.

As time pressed on, Dorothy drew closer to her due date. Mary harbored no jealousy or resentment towards her friend. To the contrary, she was as happy as she always had been for her. However, it was Dorothy who started to feel a touch uncomfortable talking to Mary about her pregnancy. She could not help it. She almost felt a sense of guilt; why did fate take Mary's baby away and not hers? Dorothy felt so happy about expecting a child, but Mary could feel no such joy. Mary could sense her friend's discomfort, as if she was restraining her gaiety when they talked. In an almost reversal of roles, she would go out of her way to make Dorothy feel comfortable and after time, she did.

On May 3, 1948, Bob and Dorothy gave birth to a healthy baby girl. They named her Diana. They asked Frank and Mary to be the godparents, to which they proudly accepted.

Seeing little Diana, and how blissful Bob and Dorothy were made Mary start thinking for the first time about trying to get pregnant again. But she could not get over the fear of having another miscarriage. She and Frank had yet to make love again. Frank did not even think about pressing Mary, whether it be for trying to have a baby or just the pleasure of sex. *She'll let me know when she's ready*, he told himself. He was just glad to see her starting to resume a normal life again.

That summer Frank received more bad news, learning that his father had lymphoma. He was going for treatment and was living at home, still stubbornly going to work. But in those days any type of cancer seemed a certain death sentence. The only question was how long? The news crushed Frank. He had always been close to his father, his sole role model. Growing up he had always seemed so indestructible, somehow beyond the bounds of mortality.

Now it was Mary's turn to console her husband. She knew how much his father meant to him and how she would feel if something happened to her father. Of course, she also loved Harold and felt horrible for him. But she knew that her pain and sorrow, however sincere, paled in comparison to what Frank must have been feeling.

The man of the house, Frank tried to put on a stoic front for his wife. But inside he was torn. He not only thought about his father, but also his mother. What was this going to do to her? How was she going to be able to take care of him? Should he and Mary move back with his parents in order to help care for his father? But that wouldn't be fair to Mary. But what about his father? He owed him—and his mother—at least that. Frank didn't know what to do. But on a weekend visit to his parents, both his mother and father set him straight.

"Don't you even think about it," Harold said angrily upon hearing his son's thoughts about possibly moving back home.

"Whatever your father needs, I can take care of it," Margaret added in a robust tone.

Frank, who was standing against the living room cabinet, bowed his head.

Harold appreciated how much his son cared and put his hand on his shoulder. "Do you remember that talk the three of us had when I told you about Levittown?" He asked in a gentle, but sincere voice. "How I said that nothing would bring as much meaning to our lives than to see you and Mary happy."

"I know, but…"

"You listen to me, Frank," his father said in an almost whisper. "I know you have the best intentions. And that means the world to me. It really does. But it would break my heart—it would break your mother's heart—if you abandoned the life you and Mary are living to take care of me."

Mrs. Keller stepped closer to her son. "Your father's right Frank. I know you're just trying to help, but your father has good doctors. And when he's home it's my job to take care of him, not yours. Your place is with Mary—in Levittown."

"Listen son," his father went on. "Your mother and I feel terrible about what happened. But I know you and Mary will get another chance. And this time, you'll have a healthy son or daughter. And perhaps more after that. I know in my heart it will happen for you two. And like your mother said, that's where you belong."

Frank simply nodded.


Inevitably, months tore themselves from the calendar. Summer gave way to fall, then winter, then a new year. Frank seemed to have little time for leisure. The business was booming. In fact, he started contemplating opening another store in the next town. Also, almost every Sunday after church, he and Mary now went into Queens. He wanted to keep checking up on his father, and in addition it became a perfect opportunity for Mary to spend more time with her parents. Frank also still tried to find the time to volunteer at the veterans' hospital.

For Mary, though she loved Levittown, the days were becoming long and solitary. She tried to occupy her time cooking and going over to Dorothy's to chat and help her with Diana. But there were still too many hours left. Both having too much time on her hands and being around Diana made Mary realize that perhaps the time was right. She let Frank know that she was ready to try and get pregnant again. Frank was ecstatic. Not only did he want a child, but it had been a long time without any sex. Now however, it became a nightly ritual.


August 30, 1949. As he did every morning before work, Frank went outside to get the newspaper. The headline: *Soviets Test Atomic Bomb*. The world had changed.

Mary was usually still asleep by the time Frank went off to work. But on that morning she happened to be up and in her robe and came downstairs to find her husband sitting at the kitchen table, locked into the newspaper. "Anything interesting?" She asked lightheartedly.

Frank hesitated. He folded back the paper and showed her the front page.

Mary gasped. "Oh my God!" Then, after a few seconds of digesting the headline, she asked, "What does that mean?"

Frank swiveled in the chair and looked up at his wife. "It means that we no longer have the upper hand. It means that the Russians might try to get bolder."

Mary put her quivering hand by her mouth. "Do you think there will be war?"

The last thing Frank wanted to do was alarm his wife. He stood up and put his hand on her arm. "No, no, nothing like that. It just means that it may be more difficult to negotiate with them. Believe me, they don't want war with the United States."

Mary shook her head. "I just don't understand. I mean they were our allies against Germany."

"It was a partnership born out of necessity, out of survival. They were being overrun by the Nazis. Besides, a lot changed with Yalta and Potsdam. We were so concerned about the war still going on in the Pacific and the possible invasion of Japan that we gave those darn Reds nearly half of Europe."

Mary sighed. "I don't know. It's such a mixed up, crazy world."

Frank assured her again not to worry. Then he gave her a kiss and said he had to go open the store.

When Frank arrived home from work, he saw Peter Mullen talking to his next-door neighbor Nick, a Marine who saw action in the Pacific. He walked over and said hello.

"So, I guess you heard about the Commies getting the bomb," Peter said to Frank.

Frank nodded. "Yeah. They're the last people you want having the bomb."

"You know it's only a matter of time before they try to spread their tentacles, try to take over even more land," Nick said with the look of disdain.

"They're like the goddamn Roman Empire, trying to conquer as much land as possible and spread their Commie way of life," Peter added.

Frank had been thinking about the news and its implications all day. "I don't know. I mean they'll try to be bullies, but you really think they want to risk war again? Their army was decimated."

"That's why they have the bomb," Peter quickly replied. "You know how crazy those Russians are, how crazy Stalin is."

Frank exhaled and a cold, thin white cloud floated from his mouth. "I think of how we stopped at the Elbe River. We should've marched right into Berlin. What, just to appease the Russians? Truman let them get away with murder, giving nearly half of Europe to them."

Peter and Nick nodded agreement.

The neighbors talked for about another fifteen minutes before they dispersed.

Life went on, despite the new Soviet threat. And in October, Mary learned that she was pregnant again. Her due date was May 1st. At first, she and Frank celebrated the news with unrestrained ebullience. But it was not long before their excitement was tempered just a touch by the fear of what happened last time—and if it would happen again. Of course, Mary and Frank never shared this uneasiness with each other. Instead, each wrestled with it internally, trying to eradicate the thought from their minds. Unbeknownst to each other, both separately prayed daily that there would not be a miscarriage, that the baby would be born healthy. Openly though, they showed nothing but optimism and exhilaration.

Bob and Dorothy were much like Frank and Mary. Outwardly, when around their friends, they showered them with merriment. But behind closed doors, they had the same fear of Mary losing the baby again. Dorothy would sometimes sit with her rosary and ask God to look after her friend and see that the baby be born healthy. "She deserves it Lord," Dorothy would whisper. "She is a good, caring person. And a good Catholic. Please Lord."

Dorothy and Mary started spending even more time together. Not only did they enjoy each other's company, but going through childbirth and now having a year-and-a-half-old baby, Dorothy could provide much appreciated advice. But in January, life, as it always does, gave another twist when Dorothy found out she was pregnant again. She was due in late July. Now, not only could she provide company and advice to Mary, but the two once again had the opportunity to go through pregnancy together.

It was not until Mary entered her third trimester and was given a clear bill of health that she and Frank relinquished their inner fears about a miscarriage. It was during this time that they first started discussing names. They were not aware of the baby's sex, which was accustomed for the day. After much discussion, they decided that if it was a girl, they would name her Eileen. Mary suggested that if she had a boy they name him Frank Junior But Frank was quick to shoot down the idea. "No, I want my son to have his own identity. He's going to grow up to be his own man."

Mary smiled and agreed.


On May 12, 1950, Thomas Michael Keller was born, weighing seven pounds and by all account, perfectly healthy.

When the doctor first handed the baby to Mary, quiet tears of joy flowed down her cheeks. Cradled in her tired arms was a flesh-and-bones life that she and Frank had created. A life that she and her husband were now proudly responsible for. She looked at Thomas, so beautiful, and a long string of events flashed through her head that had led to this point: Meeting Frank for the first time; him going off to war; him coming home; getting married; her and Frank moving to Levittown; the miscarriage; getting a second chance. But she knew and relished in the idea that there was so much more to come than had already passed. She knew, looking at her baby, that a new life had just begun—not just for Thomas, but also for her and Frank.

Frank too, was moved to tears in the delivery room. He had never in his life felt such bliss. His entire body felt light and was overcome with a sense of blessing and gratefulness. Standing there, he silently thanked God for the amazing gift that he had just received.

Once outside the delivery room, his tears wiped away, Frank stuck his chest out and pranced around like the proud father that he was. In the waiting room were both his and Mary's parents. Before even spreading the news that the baby had been born and was healthy they could all tell by the giant smile bursting on his face. There was a round of hugs and congratulations. But Frank became particularly emotional when hugging his father.

"Congratulations son, I'm so happy for you and Mary," Harold said.

Frank grabbed his father tight. "I'm so glad you're here to be a part of it," he whispered in his ear. "I just hope I can be half the father that you have been to me."

That evening Bob and Dorothy came to the hospital. Mary was sleeping, but they were able to look through the glass of the nursery at little Thomas. Dorothy was so elated for both of them, but especially Mary. They shared a bond now, a bond only two mothers could understand.

Bob wasted no time taking his friend outside for a celebratory cigar. "I'm so happy for you," he said while patting his friend on the back.

A thick cloud of cigar smoke spewed into the night air from Frank's mouth. "Thank you. I still can't believe it. I mean standing there in the delivery room...and then holding him for the first time."

"I know. It's something you have to go through to understand." Bob paused. "Of course, we had the easy job."

They laughed.

"Seriously though. I'm glad you and Dorothy are in Levittown. It's going to be great, raising our families together."

Bob shook his head. "Yeah. Who woulda' thought it'd be like this? Seems like just yesterday we were fifteen-years-old, leaning on the fence of the horse ranch thinking about what we were going to do for the weekend. Now here we are, both fathers. I wouldn't change it for the world. I'll tell ya', I really lucked out when I found Dorothy."

"Yeah, she's a great woman."

"Yes she is." Bob took a puff of his cigar and exhaled. "Hey, but this night is all about you and Mary," he said in an upbeat voice. "You guys are going to make great parents. And yes, I'm glad the girls are so close and we're going to have the opportunity to raise our children together." Bob took another puff. "But no offense, I'm tellin' you right now that I don't want your son going out with my daughter," he joked.

Frank laughed. "Hey, who says your daughter is going to be good enough for my son?"

Bob smiled. "Come here you," he said before giving his friend a big, bear hug. "Congratulations."

# 14

# A NEW CONFLICT

Over the next few weeks, friends and neighbors stopped by the Kellers to bring well wishes and see the new arrival. One day Hubert Whittaker stopped by with his wife and flowers for Mary. Frank was pleasantly surprised to see him and welcomed them into the house. Though she had heard about him from her husband, it was the first time Mary was formally introduced. Likewise, it was the first time Frank had met Mrs. Whittaker. At Mary's insistence, the four sat around the kitchen table and got to know each other better over coffee and cake.

"I have to tell you Mrs. Keller," Hubert said in a gentle voice, "I can't tell you how kind your husband has been to me, sticking up for me. He's a good man."

Mary just smiled and nodded. She knew about the confrontation at the hardware store. Mary was proud of Frank, of his values and will to always stand up for them. She also appreciated how he had opened her eyes to the injustice of segregation and racism. She had never been a bigot, really had never given race relations much thought. But she knew her husband had been right; how could someone go to war, lay their life on the line and fight with honor, only to come home and be subject to ridicule and Jim Crow, just because they were a different color?

For the first few weeks after the birth of Thomas, Frank spent little time at the hardware store. Instead, he stayed home, catering to Mary and the baby. In a state of constant euphoria, he was always bouncing around the house with a permanent smile. And he could not get enough of his son. Even when Thomas was sleeping in his crib, Frank would just stand there and watch him. But Frank would also imagine all the things they could do together once Thomas was older.

Eventually, Frank returned to running the store. While he was at work, Dorothy would come over to the house with Diana. Dorothy was due in less than two months and she and Mary talked about if she had a boy too, he and Thomas could grow up together as best friends. By this time, Mary and Dorothy were as close as Frank and Bob.

On the first Friday of July, Frank came home after work and asked Mary if she was all right with him going to the veterans hall for a while. Mary told him to go and stay as long as he wanted, she would be fine. Mary knew how much Frank liked spending time with his military brethren and had been unable to lately because of the pregnancy. She also knew that Frank was eager to talk to the men about current events. For there was a new conflict brewing.

In the waning days of World War II, at the Yalta Conference, despite signed documents to the contrary expressing veiled references to free elections and democracy regarding Poland, Roosevelt struck a now infamous side deal with Stalin, basically giving Poland to the Soviets in exchange for their help defeating Japan. Though Roosevelt knew about the Manhattan Project, having given the go-ahead, the creation of the atomic bomb, even at that late stage, was far from a certainty. The United States was already making plans for the invasion of the Japanese mainland, an invasion that would dwarf the landings at Normandy. Stalin agreed to assist his ally.

A day after the first atomic bomb was dropped on Hiroshima the Soviet Union declared war on Japan. But it was a farce. Under the ruse of maneuvering troops to attack Japan, they marched into Manchuria in order to accumulate more territory. They quickly made their way into North Korea, where they sealed off a border at the thirty-eighth parallel, as U.S. troops were already occupying the territory to the south. This went against the agreement made at the Potsdam Conference that Korea would gain its own independence. But by this time the frail alliance between the Soviet Union and the United States had already turned into a schism.

In 1948, North Korea proclaimed itself the Democratic People's Republic of Korea—though there was nothing democratic about it—and Stalin handpicked Kim Il Sung as its supreme leader.

On June 25, 1950, communist North Korea invaded the south in a surprise attack. A few days later President Truman ordered the Seventh Fleet to the area. Then, on July 1st, under the umbrella of the newly formed United Nations the first American troops entered the conflict.

When Frank arrived at the local veterans hall, it was abuzz with various men cordoned-off in their own groups, talking, drinking, and smoking. Most of the men were relatively young, in their twenties or early thirties, but there were some old-timers mixed in as well. The separate conversations melded into a general white noise that swirled around the main, square room. Smoke from cigarettes, cigars, and pipes hung in the air like stale clouds.

Frank was immediately greeted at the door by Francis Scalia, a paratrooper who saw action in Europe. Francis knew Frank from the neighborhood but had not seen him since the birth of Thomas. He congratulated Frank on his son and escorted him towards the bar. Along the way, Frank said hellos to some men sitting at one of the round tables. Someone from one of the other tables also waved to him.

The bar, which was only about seven feet long, was full with men of different shapes and sizes, all standing and conversing in several different fractions. Francis brought Frank over to Peter Mullen and two other familiar faces. They all said their hellos and Frank ordered a round of Shclitz for himself and the fellows.

"So, whaddaya think of what's goin' on in Korea?" One of the guys wasted no time in asking Frank.

The jovial expression on Frank's face quickly morphed into a serious one. "It's bad news. Very bad. You know they're hell-bent on kickin' us out of the south and taking control of the entire peninsula."

"To hell with them," Dave, the youngest one in the group, interjected. "We'll wipe the floor with them and then we'll control all of Korea."

Peter shook his head and smirked. "You think it's gonna be that easy? It's only a matter of time before those damn Chinese get involved…if they aren't already."

Francis took a healthy gulp of beer from his mug. "Not just the Chinese. What about the Soviets? You know Stalin's behind this."

"Yeah, and now that the Russians have the bomb, you can't really use that as a deterrent." Peter took a puff off his half-smoked cigar. "You don't want to start Armageddon."

Frank, leaning against the bar, took a drink. "Just think of it. Japan invades China. So during the war, we're friends with China against the Japs. And we're allies with Russia against Hitler. Now both Russia and China are our enemies—and the Japanese are supposed to be our friends."

The men all shook their heads and let out a laugh.

"It's a crazy world," added Francis.

Peter raised his oversized hand, already holding a beer, and pointed to the others. "And don't forget that at one time Japan had invaded Korea. It's like everything has come full circle."

Dave took a drag of his cigarette and blew it up into the already smoke-filled air. "So whaddaya think is going to happen?"

"I don't know," replied Peter. "Even if we kick the North regime out of Korea, it's only a matter of time before Stalin and Mao try to spread their communism somewhere else."

"And there's no guarantee that we're just going to go in there and expel Kim Il Sung from the peninsula like we're taking out the trash." Frank took another drink, then added: "Like you said, what if the Chinese send a couple hundred thousand troops into the area. Hell, they have more people than the rest of the world combined."

Peter let out a slow swirl of smoke from his almost finished cigar. "I'm just waiting to get my call-up."

The others all looked at him with somber faces.

"You really think?" Asked Dave.

"I'm still on active duty. But if this thing gets out of hand, half the guys in this place could get called-up. Reserves…who knows."

It was something all of them secretly feared and none of them wanted to hear.

Frank stayed for another two hours. Eventually, after several more rounds of drinks, the conversation turned more lighthearted. Frank and Dave, infantrymen, egged on Peter about the Air Force, which in return he joked how they wouldn't be standing there if it wasn't for his bombing raids. Meanwhile, Francis adamantly insisted that the paratroopers were superior to everyone. After about an hour Bob showed up and obviously took sides with Frank and Dave. By the end of the night they were all play wrestling and fighting. Other groups joined in on the fun.


On July 17th, Dorothy gave birth to a healthy baby boy, which she and Bob named Billy. From the time he was born, Frank and Bob could not stop talking about how great it was going to be having their sons grow up together. They discussed all the things they were going to do as a foursome and how Thomas and Billy would become best friends, just like they were. It was as if someone had written a perfect script. Frank and Bob had been like brothers since grade school. As kids they were inseparable and now in adulthood they were just as close, if not closer. They were certain, and grateful, that their sons would share the same bond.

Dorothy and Mary were just as happy. After a few days, when

Bob returned to work, the two women now best friends themselves, spent nearly everyday together. Mary would bring Thomas over to Dorothy's and soon Dorothy would bring Billy and Diana over to Mary's. They would spend hours together while the men were at work. They helped each other out with the children, went to the store together, shared wisdom and advice. But they also enjoyed just chatting and laughing together. A phone call and a few blocks away, neither ever had to feel like they were alone, carrying a burden by themselves. Of course, Frank and Bob were happy and extremely appreciative that their wives were so close and able to lean on each other.

The Kellers and Davenports had become one family. When Thomas was old enough to talk he referred to Bob as Uncle Bob and Dorothy as Aunt Dorothy. Likewise, Diana and Billy would call Mary and Frank Aunt and Uncle.

On some Sundays, Frank and Mary would take Thomas to visit his grandparents. They would spend time at Mary's parents and then move on to Frank's. Of course, Frank was delighted that his mother was able to spend time with Thomas. But it was particularly important to Frank that his father spend time with him. Harold's cancer was progressing. He had closed the hardware store, and though the doctors had not yet given him a specific timeframe, there was no denying that his days were numbered.

Frank was torn between immense sorrow and pain for his father, but at the same time gratefulness that he was able to spend time with his grandchild before passing away. It was difficult to see his father, who had always been stalwart and full of vigor, now so frail and moribund. But Frank could not help but smile knowing how much joy his father derived from playing with little Thomas; bouncing him on his knees or making funny faces at him. However, Frank never let his inner turmoil get the better of him in front of his parents or Mary. Each time they visited he always put on a buoyant face, no matter what he was feeling inside.

One Sunday the Kellers accepted a gracious invitation by Mary's parents to have dinner at their house. It was a nice, rare opportunity to have everyone together. It was a jovial affair. There was a lot of laughter and showering of attention on their grandson. Both sets of parents were extremely proud of Frank and Mary and the life they were making for themselves.

After dinner Mary, Teresa, and Margaret cleaned dishes in the kitchen and talked, mostly about pregnancy and both the joy and travail of raising an infant. In the den, the men sat around sipping on cognac and chatted about fatherhood, Levittown, and the mighty New York Yankees once again rolling through the American League, and to a probable second straight World Series appearance. Also in the den was Thomas, comfortably asleep in his stroller.


In late September, U.S. troops had recaptured Seoul back from the North Korean Peoples Army (NKPA) and had the enemy on the run. By mid October, U.S. led forces had pushed their way to Pyongyang, the North's capital. Not only had the North's advances been thwarted, but it seemed like the communists might be eradicated from the peninsula altogether. However, all that quickly changed on November 1st, when a massive contingent of Chinese troops entered the war with a surprise attack on American positions. In great numbers, better trained than the NKPA, and hardened by years of fighting the Nationalists, the Chinese Communist Forces (CCF) started to push back the U.S. and South Korean armies. In less than two months, the communists once again captured Seoul. And they were not stopping there. General MacArthur's November mantra to have U.S. troops home by Christmas had turned into a forgotten pipe dream. Now, not only did the war seem far from over, but it was feared the United States and the democratic government of the South just might be the ones expelled from the peninsula.

Back in the States, the rapidly worsening conflict in Asia was of course being reported daily by the newspapers, radio, and television news. The majority of Americans, still hungover from the immense casualties and destruction of World War II, were opposed to their country's involvement in another war a world away. Others, realizing the spreading threat communism was bringing to the entire globe, bought into the government's stance that if South Korea fell to the communists other countries would soon follow suit, the so-called "domino effect". And they certainly did not want the red menace knocking on their backyard, perhaps in Central America, the Caribbean, or even Mexico. But, however engaged the American populous was, the news updates brought nowhere near the communal fervor that even the lead-up to World War II had brought. Unless someone had a son or a brother in Korea, daily life went on as usual across the U.S.

For Frank and his military brethren, however, and those that were more in tune with world affairs, the concern with what was happening in Korea was exasperatedly growing, like a freight train gaining momentum down a slope without brakes. Would they once again find themselves on the frontline? Many saw it as an increasing possibility. They also knew that this was not merely about two armies clashing on some peninsula half a world away. It was a war of proxy, being fought by the most powerful countries in a new, dangerous atomic world. Their concerns were not only about what was happening in Korea, but the possibility of the conflict spreading into another global war. This was exacerbated when General MacArthur boldly suggested dropping multiple A-bombs on the Chinese troops and in China. This extreme stance, as well as his already strained relationship with Truman, would soon lead the President to relieve MacArthur from his duties as the supreme commander in the conflict and replace him with General Matthew Ridgway.

Frank's civilian life continued to be routine. He ran the hardware store, came home to Mary, and reveled in the time he spent with his son. But the intensifying war in Korea never left his mind. How escalated was this new war going to become, he wondered? Would it spread into China? Would the Soviets get directly involved? Would there be an exchange of atomic weapons? Would there be a draft? Would he be called to serve, leaving Mary and Thomas?

Also, beyond the current situation, Frank pondered the precarious world in which his son would be growing up. Even if the Korean War came to some quick, miraculous ending, how long would it be before another conflict arose? Was it only a matter of time before the Soviet Union and the United States exchanged the ultimate of weapons? Frank knew continued world peace was too much to ask for, but at least prayed that Thomas could grow up without the constant threat of Armageddon or knowing such horrors and ravages as those endured in the World War II.

# 15

# HAROLD & SON

In August of 1951, Frank decided the time was right to expand his business and open another store in neighboring East Meadow. Up until the end of World War II, East Meadow had been mostly a rural, farming community. However, it was expanding as more and more people were leaving the boroughs of New York for the space and calmness of suburbia. Frank knew that East Meadow was still just beginning its residential boom and that he should strike while the iron was hot, before others cornered the local hardware market.

Frank had no doubt that if he acted swiftly, his new store would be a success. But that did not mean he had no reservations. Thomas was only a little more than a year old and he wanted to spend more time with his son, not less. Of course, he also wanted to be around to help out Mary. But Frank realized that the more money he made, the better off the whole family would be. Yes, Frank looked upon his own childhood with great fondness and though his father was successful by the day's standards, he was by no means rich. Still, Frank wanted his son—and if he had more children—to be better off than he had been. And he wanted Mary never have to worry about money again, never have to agonize over bills the way his parents had.

One night, while having dinner, Frank broached the subject with Mary for the first time. Before Mary even had a chance to respond, he started rattling off a litany of pros. "I know you have your hands full with Thomas and I should be around even more, but once the store is up and running, I'll hire someone else to manage it. I won't need to be there for the day-to-day. In fact, I also want to start having one of the employees manage this store more, too, so I don't even have to be there as much. It's the right time. If I don't get in there soon, other people will open up and corner the market. I know it will be successful. It will be a great thing for us, for Thomas. I know I'm already making good money with this store, but this can really catapult us to a different level. I don't ever want you to have to worry about money. I want us to be able to have nice things and go on vacation."

Mary sat across from her husband, digesting every word. When it seemed he finally ran out of breath she responded. "I'm happy now. I don't need fancy things. As long as I have you and Thomas, that's all I need. But if you want to do this, if you think it's a good idea, then I'll support you and I think you should do it. And I know it will be successful." Mary could see a perplexed expression grow on Frank's face. She knew what he was thinking: *Okay, thanks for the confidence, but is she for it or against it?* She also knew that Frank *did* want to do it. Mary reached across the table and put her hand on his. "I think you should go for it," she said with a smile. "And don't worry about Thomas. I can handle him, and I always have Dorothy to help out if I need it."

By the next day, Frank was already putting plans in motion. Before the end of the month he had found a space for the new store and secured a loan from the bank.


One Sunday in mid-September, Frank and Mary were with Thomas at Mass when Father Mallard made an announcement that no one was expecting.

"Unfortunately, yesterday I learned that our parish has suffered an immense loss. Peter Mullen, a great man and a great pilot, who fought in Europe during World War Two, and was just recently called back to active duty to fight in Korea, was shot down and killed the other day. He leaves behind his wife, Linda, and four-year-old son, Peter Junior. Our hearts and prayers go out…"

Frank could no longer hear Father Mallard's words. In fact, everything went completely silent. As his body went numb, his mind tried to grasp the news. He knew Peter had shipped to Korea that summer. But hearing he'd died felt like a bomb out of the clear blue sky. As he sat there frozen, Frank could picture Peter's face, chiseled chin, and perfectly slicked-back black hair, with a luminous smile. It was as if he was standing right there about to say, "Hey Frank, let's go for a beer."

It was not supposed to end like this. Peter was still so young. He had made it through countless bombing raids over Europe, as planes all around him were shot down, taking on the best the Third Reich had to offer. Now he was in the prime of his life, happily married with a young son. Frank had not once been around Peter when he did not mention his wife and son. Oh, what sorrow Frank felt for them. Linda was now a widow and Peter Jr., only four-years-old, would never really know his father. There would be no playing ball, no fishing or camping trips, no father-son talks. For little Peter, the only evidence that his father ever even existed would be family photos and stories passed down.

For the first time, Frank finally realized that Mary was clutching onto his arm, quietly crying into a handkerchief. She also knew Peter and his wife, Linda. Frank was sure that she was having many of the same thoughts.

A few days later Frank and Mary attended Peter's funeral. Mary's mother came down from Queens to watch Thomas. Dorothy and Bob, who also knew the Mullens were at the service as well. In fact, in such a tight-knit community of mostly military families, it appeared as though half the neighborhood was there. Peter and Linda also both had big families. It was of course, a somber occasion. There seemed not a dry eye.

Mary knew and liked Peter and mourned his loss. But for her, the hardest part of the day—the most difficult moment since hearing the news—was when she had to go up to Linda to give her condolences. By her side was little Peter Jr., dressed in a black suit, eyes red from crying. Mary could not imagine what each of them must have been feeling. She felt so awful for them. But adding to her dismay and sorrow was the fact that a part of her could not help but think what if she was standing in Linda's shoes? What if something suddenly happened to Frank? Not only would she lose the love of her life, her soul mate, but she would be left to raise Thomas by herself. Could she do it? It was almost too overpowering to even fathom.

As usually happens in life, bad news comes in waves. Harold's cancer had metastasized and he was rapidly spiraling downhill. In early October, Frank went to the hospital to visit his father in what was now his deathbed. Margaret was always there, hardly ever leaving her husband's side. But after staying there for a little while with Frank she went home, wanting to give the father and son some time alone. She knew it could very well be the last time they would have the chance.

Harold was confined to his bed and constantly taking morphine for the pain. But he was coherent enough to not only know Frank was in the room, but also have a lucid conversation with him. It was hard for Frank to see his father lying there, a shadow of his former self, hooked up to tubes and machines and utterly helpless. But he tried to hold it together.

"Hey Pop," he said with a forced smile, before kissing his father on the forehead and then sitting down on a chair beside the bed.

Mr. Keller gingerly moved his arm and placed his frail, brittle hand on his son's wrist. "Hey son," he said in a weak voice. "How is Mary and Thomas?"

"They're fine. They're doing just fine, Pop."

"You tell them that I said hello. And that I'm always thinking of them." Harold painfully tried to clear his throat. "Mary's a good woman. Some people live their entire lives without ever finding someone like that. You take good care of her. And of Thomas."

"I will Dad. I will." Frank could not hold it in anymore; tears escaped from his swelling eyes.

His father tried to sit up more. "What's wrong? Is something going on with you and Mary? Is something wrong with Thomas?"

Frank quickly wiped away his tears. "No, no. Not at all. Just seeing you like this…knowing…I'm just going to miss you so much."

Using all his might, Harold sat straight up and leaned towards his son. "I know you will. But don't cry for me, Frank. There's no need. This may not be the best way to go, but I've had a blessed life." He inched even closer to his son. "You hear me, a blessed life. I married your mother, one of the finest, most caring people to ever walk this Earth, and we had many years together. I had a wonderful son, who turned into a man that any father would be proud of. I've got to watch you marry the love of your life, someone who I'm proud to consider a daughter. And I've got to see my grandchild. I've had more fortune than all the money in the world could ever bring."

That was his father, even in the face of death, a paragon of gratitude and benevolence. He knew his father had seen the roughest of times: The Great Depression, the loss of his daughter at only eleven months old. Now Frank put his hand on his father's arm. "You're a great man, Dad. A great father. You always put me and Mom before yourself."

"I just did what any man worth his salt would have done." Harold coughed and Frank could see that it caused great pain, but he said nothing. "Yes, I've had a good life. But one regret I have is that we were not able to spend more time together. I mean outside of the store. I just wish—"

Frank cut his father off. "I had a great childhood, Pop. Yeah, you worked a lot, but only so you could provide a good life for me and Mom. Everything you did, you did for us. And make no mistake about it, you taught me everything I know. You taught me how to stand up for what I believe in, taught me about the things that are really important in life: Family, integrity, loyalty. You were…you are the greatest father anyone could ever have."

Suddenly, a nurse came in announcing she had to perform some daily tests on Harold. Not wanting for his son to see him get stripped down and prodded, he asked the nurse if she could come back in a few minutes so he could say goodbye to his son. She obliged.

Frank stood up and bent over to give his father another kiss on the forehead. "I love you, Pop."

"I love you too, Son," Harold replied, fighting back tears.

"I'll come visit again real soon."

With that, Frank started to walk across the room. But before he could get to the door his father called out to him. Frank turned around. "Yeah Dad?"

"You're doing a good thing with the business and providing for your family," he said, straining his coarse voice. "But you spend as much time with Mary and Thomas as you can, you hear? You cherish them every single day, because life is short."

Frank nodded. "I will, Pop. I will." With that, he turned around and walked out of the room.

Those were the last words Frank would ever hear his father speak. Harold Dustin Keller passed away early the next morning. Even though the writing had been on the wall for quite some time, Frank could not believe that he was gone. No longer could he even visit him in the hospital. There was such finality to it. But in his heart, Frank was sure that his father was in a better place. His final months had been mired in pain, a pain from which he was now released.

Frank's main concern shifted to his widowed mother. He talked to Mary about the possibility of her coming to live with them. Mary agreed without objection. However, when Frank brought up the idea to his mother, she quickly shot it down, insisting that she would be fine and was very capable of taking care of herself. Margaret was a strong woman, but more than anything, she did not want to intrude on Frank and Mary. Margaret let her son and Mary know that the issue was not open for debate. But almost every weekend Frank visited his mother and called her nearly every day to check in on her.

By mid October Frank had opened his new store. But instead of giving it the same name as the store in Levittown, he renamed both stores Harold & Son Hardware, in tribute to his father.

Frank was bent on keeping his promise of not letting the new store consume all of his time and keep him away from Mary and Thomas. Instead of running every nuance of the day-to-day activities, he looked to hire a manager to run the new store and let his most trusted employee take more responsibility taking care of the Levittown store.

Frank already had several loyal employees working with him in the original store. The one most sensible to be bumped up the ladder was the eldest, Simon Janovich, an eager twenty-one-year-old who seemed to embrace responsibility. When Frank sat him down and told him his idea Simon thanked his boss for the opportunity.

The new store in East Meadow was a different situation. Though only twenty-one, Simon was a known commodity to Frank. Also, the store in Levittown had already been turned into a well-oiled machine. For the new store, Frank would have to interview people he had never met, relying on references and resumes. And no matter how impressive the references and resumes, it is no equivalent for really knowing someone.

Frank interviewed five people for the new managerial position before meeting Walter Rubenstein. At thirty years of age, Walter was a tall, slender man with thick, curly black hair and marble-like black eyes. He spoke with confidence and stood with his back straight and head high. Walter had escaped Nazi Germany with his mother, sister, and younger brother during Kristallnacht. But his father, who stayed behind to look after their residence and his business, was eventually sent to Auschwitz, where he died, along with Walter's aunt, uncle, and several cousins. This story immediately struck a chord with Frank. He felt for Walter and at the same time admired his resilience to forge ahead. Of course, he could also relate to losing a father.

But no matter how touching Walter's story, Frank could not let his emotions dictate the hiring of the man who would run his new store. However, Walter also had qualifications. Though he had never worked in a hardware store before, Walter had a Bachelor's Degree in business. Even more impressive, he had spent the last three years managing and doing the books for a five-and-dime store. Unfortunately for Walter—but luckily for Frank—the owner had recently sold the store and the new owner replaced nearly the entire staff.

Frank offered Walter the job on the spot, but with a caveat. He wanted to make clear in no uncertain terms that it was his store, and he would take care of the bookkeeping and have final say on all of the decision-making. Frank may not have had a college degree, but when it came to the hardware business, it was in his blood. Walter eagerly and gratuitously accepted the offer, insisting that he knew that Frank was the boss.


In early November, the Keller household received surprise news. Mary was pregnant again. Thomas was only seventeen months old so, although Frank and Mary had been having sex, another pregnancy was unexpected so soon. Nevertheless, it was greeted with jubilation.

Frank's excitement however, was tempered by his decision to open the new store. Even though he had hired Walter to manage the store, for the first several months at least, Frank would have to be there with him, teaching him the hardware business and ensuring that everything was running smoothly. Frank's goal was to ultimately turn over much of the day-to-day operations of both stores to Simon and Walter, but in the short-term he would have to spend *more* time at work. But now Mary was pregnant, and had

Thomas to take care of. Yet he had invested too much money to turn back now and shut down the new location. Frank told Mary his concern. Mary told her husband not to worry, that she could handle it. Frank promised not to work too many hours and to have Walter trained and the new store running efficiently soon. Mary smiled and told him not to overdo it and reiterated that she would be fine.

Since Simon had been working with Frank for several years and had already learned most of the nuances of running the store—and had run it before by himself in his boss' intermittent absences—Frank spent most of his time at the new location, training Walter and making sure the business was off to a strong and steady start. He was pleased to see that his new manager was a fast learner.

When he wasn't at one of the stores Frank was home, spending time with Thomas and coddling his wife. But he still made time to visit his mother every Sunday, if only for an hour or two. When Frank was not around, just as when she was pregnant with Thomas, Dorothy helped out. Not only did Frank genuinely like Dorothy, but saw her as a godsend. He really appreciated all her help.

Almost immediately the new store turned into a cash cow. But it was not just the new location. By 1952, Levittown was expanding exponentially and the original hardware store was bringing in more and more profits. In fact, two different people asked Frank if he was interested in selling both stores, but he would not even entertain an offer.

By March 1952, Simon and Walter were taking charge of their managerial roles in their respective stores. Though Frank made sure to know and be on top of the end of each day's till, ordering, and expenses, as planned, he was able to curtail his daily involvement. No longer did he have to stand behind the register all day or help each customer. Still, the customers in the old store, many of whom had come to know him, appreciated his presence. They didn't need for him to help them or ring them up; they just knew that as long as he was in charge of the ship they would be treated with honesty, care, and respect. Frank had forged a great adulation in Levittown as a war hero and a man of utmost integrity. That reputation followed him to the new store. And in those days reputation was everything.

On June 5th, Mary gave birth to a healthy baby girl, Eileen Teresa Keller. Though Mary loved Thomas with every fiber of her being, she had always dreamt about having a daughter. However, Eileen would soon become daddy's little girl.

Frank wished that his father could have been alive to witness the occasion. But he did not let that damper his exultation. His mother had come to the hospital, as of course did Mary's parents. Her sister Mildred, who had moved to Chicago some time ago, was also in town. Without her husband and own three children, who had stayed at home in Chicago, Mildred spent several days at Frank's and Mary's.

Frank spent as much time at home as possible over the next few weeks, helping Mary with their now two infants. Where Thomas was a well-behaved baby, sleeping much of the night, Eileen was a seemingly nocturnal crier. And sometimes when Dorothy came over with Diana and Billy, it was a full house. But sleepless nights and sporadic bouts of crying were well worth the joy and blessing that Frank and Mary felt.

# 16

# A DIFFERENT
# KIND OF WAR

The weeks and months seemed to fly by. From Monday to Saturday, Frank would routinely work five hours a day, splitting his time between the Levittown and East Meadow stores. This gave him more time to spend at home with Mary, Thomas, and Eileen. On Sundays, after church, he would go visit his mother. Sometimes, Mary and the kids would go along into Queens and they would visit her parents. On occasion, Bob and Dorothy would come by the house with their children—or Frank and Mary would go to their house—and they would have dinner together. But it had been a long time since Frank had gone out with just Bob or the fellas.

During the holidays, Frank and Bob went to the veterans hall. As much as they loved spending time with their families, it felt good to hang out with the boys again. There were rounds of drinks, laughing and banter. But inevitably, the conversation turned to a more serious matter, the ongoing war in Korea.

The conflict had been going on now for two and a half years and there seemed to be no conclusion in sight. All the men at the hall, as did many other people, realized that this was a different kind of war. The American Revolution, the War of 1812, the Civil War, World War I, World War II—in all of these wars the objective, though arduous and bloody to achieve, was clear. And on June 25, 1950, when North Korea invaded the south, the objective seemed straightforward as well: End the North's advance and push them back across the thirty-eighth parallel, the pre-war de-facto border. And in fact, the U.S. and its allies quickly achieved this goal. But then, for a brief time it appeared that the U.S. might be able to eradicate Kim Il Sung's communist regime from the entire peninsula. However, when the Chinese entered the conflict, that objective became ephemeral. Then, in July of 1951, truce talks commenced between the parties. But here it was, more than a year later, and the fighting raged on, scores of men on both sides getting killed every day.

Another thing most previous wars, especially those fought by the United States, had in common was the mantra of winning at all costs. Whatever it took, America had to defeat the British in the War of 1812, the Spanish in the Spanish-American War, Germany and Japan in World War II. But this was a different situation. It was a war deemed worth the lives of the hundreds of thousands of young men sent into battle. But it was not worth provoking the Soviet Union, or further provoking China, into a broader war. The men in the veterans hall could understand not wanting to start World War III, but that did nothing to alleviate their mounting frustration.

"I don't understand, either a war's worth fighting or it's not," someone angrily put it.

Frank, sitting at one of the tables, slammed down his mug of beer. "I'll tell you what they're doing! The White House and the Russians, they're playing a game of chess—and our soldiers and airmen are the pawns!"

"You can add China to that," Bob said in a disgruntled tone. "It's not just Stalin we're afraid of, it's Mao. I wouldn't be surprised if the Soviets already gave China the bomb."

One of the men at the table leaned forward. "Well then, what the hell are we doing over there? I mean I get that we don't want communism to spread to other places. God knows I hate those commie motherfuckers. But right now we're just fightin' over tiny scraps of land and hilltops."

For some time, while the on-again-off-again truce talks among the U.S., South Korea, North Korea, and China dragged on, the men on the ground were mired in a seemingly un-strategic, fatuous battlefield. Armies fought fiercely over splotches of land and hills. In some instances U.S. forces were ordered to take a hilltop, only to abandon it to the enemy, then retake it again. Infamous battles such as Heartbreak Ridge, Bloody Ridge, and Pork Chop Hill saw thousands of American troops die for what appeared to be meaningless parcels of real estate. And these were just the most notorious of many similar campaigns. It seemed as though both sides kept fighting, just because no one had told them to stop.

"Well thank God Eisenhower is going to take office next month," proclaimed Bob. "He'll do something about this. Unlike Truman, he knows what it's like to be in battle."

"Hey, Truman did drop the bomb on the Japs. Twice."

One of the men raised his mug. "I'll give 'em that."

"He also gave Stalin half of Europe," added someone else.

Bob lit up a cigarette. "Hey, that was mostly Roosevelt. I mean I loved FDR, but I'm just sayin'."

All the men in the hall had great respect for the newly elected incoming president, who they knew as General Dwight D. Eisenhower. And they had great promise for him. Eisenhower's valor, strategy, and tenacity during the war in Europe had put him on a pedestal reserved for only the greatest of heroes. But some still openly questioned what he could do to bring the war in Korea to an end. However, most Americans agreed on what they wanted to happen. Though no one wanted the spread of communism, at this point everyone just wanted to bring the boys back home. The nation had seen enough war.

Despite the war in Korea, for most Americans, their lives went on without interruption. At this point, the fear of the war expanding had been abated.

In March, Bob received a big promotion at Grumman, where he worked. To celebrate, Bob and Dorothy decided to go out to dinner in Manhattan with Frank and Mary. Not wanting to ask one person to babysit four small children, Dorothy dropped her kids off at her parents, and Mary dropped Thomas and Eileen off at her parents for the night. It had been a long time since the four of them had gotten together without the children.

That afternoon, while finishing getting ready, Frank stopped to look at Mary, standing at the mirror, gracefully putting on a pearl necklace. For what seemed like minutes, Frank just stood there mesmerized, examining every strand of Mary's long, flowing black hair, every iota of her soft, flawlessly made face, every curve of her body, every motion she made. She looked so elegant, draped perfectly in a sheer, black dress. Finally, just as Mary finished clasping the necklace, Frank crept closer until he was right in back of her. "You look so beautiful," he said in a gentle voice a he placed his hands on her bare arms.

Mary looked at Frank through the mirror, a smile gleaming on her face. "Thank you." She then tilted her head backwards, resting it on Frank's shoulder. "That feels so good," she said euphorically as he tenderly stroked her arms.

Through the mirror, Frank gazed at Mary's majestic, pale blue eyes; the same eyes that made him melt the first time he ever saw them. "I'm so lucky to have you."

"Oh Frank, stop it. I'm lucky to have you."

Frank's hands gently moved from Mary's arms to her midsection, gliding along the soft silk. Mary began to breathe heavy. As his hands then worked their way up to her breasts, she clutched onto her husband's legs. "Oh Frank," she moaned. In one motion Frank spun her around. Without exchanging another word their lips interlocked. Before long Frank started to unzip Mary's dress. Reluctantly, Mary pushed away. "Oh Frank we can't," she said with bated breath. "We're late. Bob and Dorothy are waiting for us."

"But…" Frank was all worked up.

"Believe me, I want to, too. But we have to go." Mary sounded as disappointed as her husband. "When we get back tonight." she said with a sinful smile.

By 7:30 p.m., the four best friends found themselves at Delmonico's Steak House in Manhattan. It was a Saturday night and the atmosphere was electric. The maître d greeted them as if they were royalty and after having someone check their coats, led them across the bustling restaurant to their booth. On their way, laughter and dozens of separate animated conversations melded together into an energetic mumble. The smell of garlic and butter wafted through the smoky air.

"Your waiter, Maurice, will be with you shortly," the maître d assured. "And if there is anything else I can do for you, please let me know."

Frank and Bob thanked him.

"This is so exciting," Dorothy proclaimed.

"I've always wanted to eat at Delmonico's," added Mary. "Did you see that sizzling steak?"

Just then, a tall, debonair, middle-aged waiter came over to the table and introduced himself. After handing them menus and explaining the night's specials, he took their drink orders.

Bob leaned forward across the table. "I'll tell ya', I love my kids and I know you guys love yours, but it sure is nice getting a break once in a while."

"Yeah," Mary agreed. "And it's so nice that the four of us could get together."

As the two couples conversed, the waiter came back with their drinks: A screwdriver for Frank, highball for Bob, cosmopolitan for Dorothy, and for Mary a red wine.

As soon as the waiter left, Frank raised his glass in the air. "Well I'd like to make a toast."

Everyone else raised their drinks as well.

"To Bob. Congratulations on your promotion. You deserve it."

With that, everyone clanked their glasses together and gave their own congratulations.

Steaks and other dinners kept passing the table and the smells were tantalizing. But none of them were in a rush to get the main course. They were having too much fun laughing and talking, enjoying being out and about. The drinks were flowing. The conversation was mellifluous. There was no talk of war or work. There were no crying children to tend to. There was nothing anyone had to do but have fun.

"Hey, you remember the time we were playin' stick ball and broke Old Man Mindelton's car window?" Bob asked Frank in an excited voice.

Frank finished taking a gulp of his screwdriver. "Me? You were the one who hit the ball. And for some reason he thought I did it. He chased me for three blocks."

Bob busted up, slapping his hand on the table. "I thought he was either going to kill you or have a heart attack chasing you."

"Why'd he think you did it?" Asked Dorothy.

With drink in hand, Bob leaned towards his wife. "This guy always had it in for Frank. I don't know why. But he never liked him."

"Yeah, I remember him," Mary said. "I just think he hated kids. He used to look through his apartment window—he was on the first floor—and any time he saw kids playing near his place he would shoo them away. He would come out waving this stick he had like a crazy man."

Frank and Bob started cracking up. "Yeah, what the hell was that thing anyway, a broom handle?"

"Didn't any of the other parents say anything?" Dorothy asked with a smile.

"Nah. I mean I don't think he ever actually whacked anyone."

Dorothy took a drink of her second, almost finished, cosmopolitan. "So what happened when you broke his window?"

"So your husband here is up to bat. I throw him the ball and he plants it right through Mindelton's rear window. Now you gotta remember, this is like thirty-five, thirty-six. Not many people had a car. But Mindelton had just bought this brand new Cadillac Fleetwood. The thing was beautiful. It was his baby." Frank took another drink. "Anyway, I guess Mindelton heard the glass break and came running out of his apartment building."

"You should've seen his face. I thought his head was gonna pop off his shoulders." Bob thought it was hysterical. "Then he turns and sees me and Frank standing there. We were just frozen, didn't know what to do. But I had dropped the bat and for whatever reason, Mindelton fixated on Frank. He started chasing him and screaming at the top of his lungs. Frank just took off running as fast as he could."

Filled with liquor, everyone at the table was now laughing.

"So what happened?" Dorothy asked. "Did he ever catch you? Did you have to pay for the window?"

"He never did catch Frank," Bob answered. "But he went to his father's hardware store. Mr. Keller went to everyone's parents who had been playing the stick ball game and had everyone chip in money to replace the window. He…"

At that moment, the waiter arrived with their dinner.

"Hey, the foods here," Bob proclaimed, already forgetting about the last subject.

"Oh, that looks delicious," Mary added.

Frank chimed in as the waiter placed the plate with his sizzling New York strip in front of him. "Oh boy, will ya' look at that! Come to Poppa."

After the waiter was finished putting all the plates on the table Bob ordered another round of drinks. Then, everyone enthusiastically dug into their meals. Moans of ecstasy followed, with everyone saying how amazing their food was.

"Oh Frank, you have to try this lobster," Mary said.

"You have to try this steak," he replied. "It's perfect."

"This filet mignon is to die for," Dorothy added.

"This rib eye is out of this world," exclaimed Bob.

Over the next hour the two couples indulged in their main course, had some more drinks, conversed about a multitude of subjects, laughed, and then had dessert. When the check came, Frank and Bob fought over it. "No way," Bob asserted. "Don't even think about it."

"This is for your promotion. Let me pick it up."

Bob put up his hand. "No way, it's too much. Besides, we invited you."

"It's okay, really."

The women let the men squabble, staying out of it. Finally, Frank was able to win the argument, but with the stipulation that next time they all went out Bob would pay.

By the time Frank and Mary arrived at her parents to pick up the kids it was 10:20 p.m. Though he had had a cup of coffee and it had been over an hour since his last drink Frank should not have been driving. But unfortunately, in 1953, drinking and driving was not looked upon as serious and criminal as it is today. It was just a different world. And unless someone was visibly impaired, stumbling around and slurring their words, getting behind the wheel after a night of drinking was almost accepted. Thankfully, Frank made it back to Levittown without any incidents.

As soon as they arrived home, Frank and Mary put Thomas and Eileen to sleep. It was late and had been a long day. But Frank and Mary were still buzzing with the excitement of the night.

In the bedroom, Mary grabbed her husband by his lapel and pulled him close. "So, are you ready to finish what we started earlier?" She asked in a low, seductive voice.

"God, you're so sexy," Frank replied as a tingling sensation ran down his spine.

Still holding onto his lapel, Mary inched closer, until her lips met his. Frank slowly unzipped the back of her long dress.

Mary moved from Frank's lips to his ear. "I want you so bad," she whispered. As the words left her mouth, her dress slid off. Mary began to undress her husband.

Falling onto the bed the foreplay continued as Frank and Mary caressed nearly every part of each other's bodies. Then, as the night ticked away, they made love. It was a perfect ending to a perfect evening.

On July 27, 1953, delegates from the United Nations, China, and North Korea signed an armistice, bringing a halt to the war. An actual peace treaty was never signed. After thirty-seven months of intense fighting the peninsula was divided in half by the thirty-eighth parallel, exactly where it had been divided before the war. In the end, nothing had changed—that is except for the staggering number of people who had been wounded or lost their lives. In all, it is estimated that the war caused a total of four million military and civilian casualties. Over 36,000 of them were American servicemen. Despite that fact, in America the conflict is most commonly referred to as "The Forgotten War".

The end of the Korean War did usher in a long period of peace for America. But with the omnipresent threat of the Soviet Union starting a nuclear Apocalypse, it was a tenuous peace. A tension was always there that at anytime the "button" could be pressed. But even with the title of the Cold War, there were no real battles. American servicemen, though always on high alert, were not dying.

Like everyone else, Frank was happy that the Korean War was finally over. He grieved for those lost, especially his friend Peter Mullen, and the families left behind. But he felt, even with the propaganda of the Cold War, a cloud had been lifted over the country. And he hoped that there would be no more "real" war for a long time to come.


That Christmas Frank invited Mary's parents and his mother to the house to celebrate. Also, he surprised Mary with her own new car, a 1953 Chevy Bel Air. Mary couldn't believe it. Frank took a picture of her shocked, speechless face. Mary's parents and Frank's mother were equally taken aback.

"You must be doing real well for yourself," Mr. Capelli proudly said.

"Yes. Actually things are going great. Both stores are booming. And with people still flooding into Levittown and East Meadow, things should only get better. In fact I've even been toying with the idea of opening another store."

Margaret grabbed Frank by the cheeks. "My son, the business-man."

"I always knew you would be successful, Frank," added Mr. Capelli.

It was a joyous occasion. The family was together. Mr. Capelli was playing with Thomas, chasing him around. The two grand-mothers were ogling over little Eileen. Mary was going on about her new car. Frank kept going in the kitchen, and when no one else was looking, flirted with and groped his wife. Everyone was in a jovial mood. There was plenty of good, home-cooked food. Though Eileen was still too young to know what was going on, when presents were exchanged Thomas feverishly unwrapped his and at the sight of each toy, jumped around in excitement the way only a child on Christmas could.

# 17

# ONLY IN AMERICA

On April 17, 1954, Frank Keller turned thirty-years-old. At thirty, he was already a highly successful entrepreneur, owning two highly profitable hardware stores. Financially well off, he had over $50,000 in the bank, at that time a small fortune. He was also already into his ninth year of an exceedingly successful marriage, with now two wonderful children. He was a pillar in the community. He had survived numerous harrowing and infamous battles in the World War II. At only thirty, Frank had experienced and succeeded more than many men do in fifty, sixty years. But for him, the road ahead still seemed much longer than what he had already traveled.

April 17th fell on a Saturday that year. For his birthday, Mary threw a surprise party at the house. As he usually did every Saturday, Frank checked on both his stores in the morning. So not to come home too early, Mary had Bob meet him at the East Meadow store. Bob said that he happened to be in the area and stopped by to take Frank out to lunch for his birthday. At first Frank said he wanted to get home to spend the rest of the day with Mary and the kids, but invited Bob and Dorothy to the house. However, with strict instructions from Mary, Bob would not take "no" for an answer.

"Come on. We'll go to Donavan's for quick sandwich and beer. I have to buy you a beer for your thirtieth birthday."

Frank looked at his best friend and quickly relented. "Okay, why not," he replied with a smile. "I guess it's only one o'clock. Just let me call Mary and let her know."

Of course, Mary told him to take his time; she was taking the kids over to Dorothy's for a little while anyway.

Frank and Bob went to Donavan's, a local bar that had food. Over lunch and a few beers, they talked about turning thirty, as Bob's birthday was fast approaching.

"Look at us," Frank said proudly, sitting across the table from Bob. "I own two successful stores. You're making great money, being an engineer at Grumman. We both own a house. Only in America."

Bob raised his mug. "Amen to that."

"Really, think about it. If we lived somewhere else we would never be able to have the things we have. If we lived in the Soviet Union or China we could work twice as hard as we do now and still not own our own house."

Bob nodded. "Our own house? We couldn't even go to the store and buy what we wanted to buy, watch what we wanted to watch on television."

"Even if we lived in Mexico or South America, we could never lead the lives we're living now." Frank took a swig of beer. "I mean I always tell myself how grateful I am to have Mary and Thomas and Eileen. And I'd love them no matter what. But even with hard work, the only reason I can provide them with the things I can is because we live in the United States of America."

A contemplative look washed over Bob's face as he digested his friend's words. "It's true. And you know I feel the same way. I mean I may not agree with everything that goes on here, with some of the things the government does, but I'd give my life for this country."

"You almost did," Frank quickly replied with a smile.

Both he and Bob let out a fleeting laugh.

"You know, when I was about ten," Frank went on in a more se-rious tone, "in the depths of the Depression and I first started really realizing what was going on—all the soup lines, troves of men wandering the streets looking for work, people in the neighbor-hood having to leave their houses and apartments, seeing how hard my father was struggling—I asked him what was going to happen to us. I asked him if we were going to have to pack up and move? If things were ever going to get better?" Frank took a breath and leaned forward. "He told me that times were tough, but that better days were on the horizon. He told me that the strife hands of history had given the country its best shots before, but the peo-ple had always gotten back up and persevered. 'You know why?' I can hear him say. 'Because we're Americans.'"

Bob smiled and raised his mug. "Here's to being American!"

Frank proudly met his glass with his own. "To the greatest coun-try in the world!"

"And for all those who sacrificed their lives—going back to the Revolution—to protect our freedom and way of life."

"Here, here!"

Frank and Bob were at Donavan's for about an hour and a half. On their way out, Bob stopped to use the pay phone. After a brief conversation, he hung up and said that Dorothy and Mary were go-ing back to Frank's house. "I'll follow you there," Bob said casually.

Frank didn't think anything of it. After a few beers and stimulat-ing conversation, suspicion about his wife throwing a surprise par-ty was the furthest thing from his mind.

Mary had told anyone who was driving not to park in front of the house, so not to rouse suspicion. The plan was perfectly exe-cuted. Frank was in shock when he opened the front door to a bombardment of "Surprise!" and "Happy Birthday!"

The first person he turned to was Bob, who had walked into the house with him. "You," was all he said with a smile.

Before anyone else could get to Frank, Mary ran over and em-braced him. "Happy birthday honey," she said into his ear. "Are you surprised?"

"I didn't have a clue. Thank you."

Next came a chorus line of friends, family and neighbors congratulating the blushing birthday boy. Of course, Dorothy gave him a big hug. His neighbor Nick was there, as were some other men from the veterans' hall. His mother had come in from Queens, as had Mary's parents. Charlie, an eighteen-year-old who had worked for Frank for three years, was also there. Mary had invited Hubert Whittaker and his wife, but he was in Massachusetts tending to his gravely sick mother.

As Frank was shaking hands and talking to his guests, little Thomas ran up to him. Frank looked down at his son, who was holding something in his hand.

"Happy birthday, Daddy. I made you card," he said in a four-year-old's voice as he reached out his little arms holding the folded piece of cardboard paper.

"Ahhh," the people standing around said in unison.

Frank knelt down to his son's level and retrieved the card. "Thank you Tommy." On the front was a stick figure with a big, almost round head with a smile. Above the figure, in a small child's uneven scroll it said *Daddy*.

"Mommy helped me with the inside of the card," he said as Frank folded it open. It read *Happy Birthday*, in an adult's handwriting and under it, Thomas' own scribbled signature.

"Well that's a great job Tommy. Thank you very much. Do I get a hug?" Thomas tried to wrap his arms around his father's waist. Frank grabbed him and picked him up. "Look what Tommy did," he said proudly, showing the card to the people who were standing there.

Frank had a good time mingling, especially with the people he did not get to see every day. More than anything though, he was happy to see his mother there. Finding a moment when the two of them were alone, he thanked her for raising him right and always being there for him. Margaret said how happy she was that he turned out to be such a fine man and loving husband and father.

At one point, Frank walked out back by himself. It was an extra warm day for mid April and the sky was bright blue, speckled only with a few, small transparent clouds, rolling peacefully by. Frank took in a deep breath of fresh spring air and thought how lucky he was to have such wonderful and caring friends and family.

He was about to walk back inside when Charlie came out of the back door. "Hey, Mr. Keller." He had already wished him a happy birthday.

"Hey, Charlie. It's a beautiful day, isn't it," he said, looking back to the sky.

"It sure is. I can't wait for summer." Charlie paused. "Speaking of which," he continued in a more staid voice, "you know that this summer I'm graduating."

Frank shook his head.

"Well…" Charlie's sentence trailed off. Frank turned and faced the teen. "What is it Charlie?"

"Well…I don't know if this is a good time to tell you, but I got accepted into St. John's Law School and—"

"That's great Charlie! Congratulations!"

"Well thank you. But that means…well, I'm going to move to the campus in the fall and I won't…well, I won't be able to work at the hardware store anymore."

Frank could tell that it pained Charlie to break the news. He put his hand on the teen's broad, fettle shoulder. "Listen Charlie, I couldn't ask for a better employee. But don't you worry for a second about the store. You've done everything I ever asked of you—and more. I've been proud to work with you. But I've been even prouder to see you develop into a fine young man. And believe me when I tell you that I couldn't be happier for you. You're gonna be a damn fine lawyer."

Charlie's face lit up as he smiled. "Thank you, Mr. Keller. That means a lot to me. It really does. You know you've kinda been like a role model to me. And I appreciate everything you've done for me, including all the advice you've given me."

Now Frank smiled. "Thank you."

"You know, I'll still be able to work until August."

"Whenever you need to leave you just tell me. And I want you to stay in touch with me, let me know how you're doing."

Just then Nick came walking out of the backdoor. "Hey there he is," he said to Frank. "I've been looking for you."

The two war veterans and the high school senior stayed in the backyard talking for a little while before other people came out and joined them.

Once all the guests left, Mary walked over to Frank and draped her arms around his neck. She asked him if he had had a good time, to which he responded, "Of course." He then thanked her again for the party and helped her clean up.


A few weeks after his birthday, on a Saturday afternoon, Mary went to visit her parents. Dorothy went to visit her parents, too, who also lived in Queens. Since they were both near the old neighborhood, Frank and Bob decided to take the kids to the American Horse ranch, which was still there. They parked a few blocks away and then, just like when they were young, walked up to the wooden fence that encircled its perimeter. Only this time, they had their own children with them.

It was a sun-soaked day with a slight, May breeze.

"Your uncle and I used to come here all the time," Bob said to Diana, who was holding his hand.

"We used to dream about owning our own ranch one day," Frank added as he pushed Eileen in a stroller, Thomas by his side.

As they walked up to the fence, Eileen leaned forward and pointed. "Horsey!"

Frank leaned down. "Yes honey, it's a horsey."

Though Frank and Bob frequently visited the old neighborhood to visit their respective parents, neither one had been to the ranch in a long time. At first, in unison, they walked right up to the aged wooden fence and just stared at the vast, serene landscape. One horse aimlessly pranced about in the long, green grass, her mane subtly blowing in the breeze. Another two stood closer to the barn, busy feeding from the trough. Frank and Bob had brought the kids there so they could see it, but it was them who seemed the most mesmerized, as if gazing at a living, breathing picture of their past.

After about ten minutes a ranch hand appeared. Bob called him over and asked if Mr. Baxter still owned the ranch.

He did, the young man replied.

Bob then asked if he could tell him to come out, that they were from the neighborhood and used to know him.

The ranch hand asked their names.

"Frank and Bob," Frank replied, "but he probably won't remember the names. But he'll definitely remember us. We won't take up too much of his time."

The young man seemed bothered by the request, but after looking at the kids shook his head. "He's not well, but I will go in and tell him."

Frank and Bob looked at each other, each one wondering how bad off was Mr. Baxter. He had been old when they were kids. Though they did not know his age, he must have now been at least in his late seventies, maybe even eighties.

Frank and Bob entertained the kids, pointing to the horses through the rails of the fence, while the ranch hand walked back to the main house. He returned about ten minutes later and told them to meet him by the side gate; he would show them into the house to meet Baxter. The children seemed excited to be actually going into the ranch. Frank and Bob were also enthusiastic, but at the same time a little apprehensive about seeing Old Man Baxter.

Frank and Bob walked with the kids along the fence until they came to the side gate. There, the stranger led them inside the ranch, towards the main building. On a concrete patio adjacent to the building, by a table and some chairs, was Baxter in a wheelchair. He appeared hoary, with a blanket over his lap. As they slowly approached, he leaned forward and inspected them through his thick, metal-framed glasses. As his wrinkled, weathered face switched between Frank and Bob they wondered if he would remember them. They also could not believe how much he had aged.

Bob was about to explain who they were when a cracked smile rose from Baxter's face. "Frankie and Bobby! My two brave soldiers.

I haven't seen you since after the war. Look at you both. And who are these little ones?" He asked in buoyant voice.

Frank and Bob were relieved that not only did he recognize them, but still seemed to have his facilities.

"Mr. Baxter, it's so good to see you," Frank said with a smile. "These are our children."

He and Bob then introduced each of them. Baxter asked his hand to show Diana, Thomas, and Billy around the ranch. Eileen, who was still in the stroller, stayed behind. At Baxter's request, Frank and Bob briefly caught him up on their lives and careers. He seemed genuinely gratified that they were both doing so well. Then it was the old rancher's turn, and despite his smile and upbeat demeanor, it was not good news. He was suffering from emphysema. In addition, he was getting increasing and continuous pressure to sell the ranch.

"There's no room for ranches in New York anymore," he said in a crackled voice. "Pretty soon the whole damn state will look like Manhattan."

"What are you gonna do?" Asked Bob.

For the first time since seeing them, the smile disappeared from Baxter's face. "I don't know," he said, looking down, shaking his head. "I guess I'll hold out for as long as I can. I'm too old and sick to restart somewhere else." Baxter looked towards the field. "It's not just about the land. It's those horses—they're my life. I dunno what I'd do without them."

Frank and Bob felt terrible. "Is there anything we can do?" Frank asked, knowing the answer.

Baxter turned his head back to face his guests. The last thing he wanted was to make Frank and Bob feel bad. "It's okay. I've had a good run," he said almost sarcastically, with a smile. "Everything comes to an end. The world belongs to the young—as it should. And when I look at you two, at least I know it's in good hands. Really, I couldn't be prouder of you boys."

Just then the ranch hand returned with the kids. Thomas came running up to Frank. "Daddy, Daddy, you should see the horses!"

"One of the horses ate from my hand!" Diana excitedly blurted to her father.

Baxter laughed and appeared amused at the children's enthusiasm.

Frank, Bob, and the children bid Baxter farewell. The kids thanked him for letting them see the ranch. Frank and Bob said how good it had been to see him. Baxter reciprocated in kind.

They would never see Old Man Baxter again.


November 2, 1955, marked Frank's and Mary's tenth wedding anniversary. Frank surprised his wife with a trip to Hawaii. Expecting just flowers and dinner, maybe earrings, she was completely swept off her feet. Moreover, they were leaving that weekend. Frank had already made all the arrangements. His mother had volunteered to stay at the house and watch Thomas and Eileen. Frank also let his managers and other employees know that he would be away for five days.

Mary barely had time to pack and come down from her shock before that Saturday morning came and they were getting a ride to Idlewild Airport. Frank was also excited. He had never been to Hawaii and was looking forward to getting away and spending alone time with his wife by the beach. But for Mary it was joyfully overwhelming. She had never before even been on a plane.

When the plane was taxing on the runway, Mary's bliss turned to nerves. Clutching Frank's arm, she asked if they were going to be okay. He assured her that everything would be fine, that flying was completely safe. Mary apprehensively shook her head and pretended to calm down. But as the 707 tilted up its nose and lifted into the air, she again clutched onto Frank's forearm, this time practically digging her nails into his flesh. Her other arm was locked in a death grip on the opposite handrail. Propelled back in her seat, Mary looked as if she knew they were going to die.

"It's okay, it's okay. It's going to level off and be smooth once we reach cruising altitude," Frank tried to soothe his terrified wife. But for some reason there was a part of him that secretly found it funny.

It was a long flight and they had a one-hour layover in Los Angeles. Fortunately, Mary was able to sleep much of the time to California. Because of the time difference, when they arrived in Honolulu the local time was only 2:30 p.m. When de-boarding the plane, Frank and Mary were greeted by a man and woman, both in grass skirts, who placed the ceremonious lei around their necks.

Mary turned to Frank with a bursting smile. "I can't believe we're actually in Hawaii."

Frank reciprocated with his own smile. "I know, it's wild, huh?"

Mary grabbed onto his arm and nestled close. "Thank you so much. I still can't believe you did this."

After retrieving their bags, Frank and Mary went outside to hail a taxi to take them to the hotel. They were immediately hit by sun and warmth. When they left New York that morning it was cloudy and thirty-eight degrees—the high for the day was supposed to be forty-seven.

On the cab ride from the airport to the hotel Mary and Frank looked out the backseat windows in amazement at the rolling landscape and sky. Everything was so vibrant and picturesque. Towering palm trees reached into the infinite, azure sky. Statuesque mountains formed a majestic backdrop. Tall fields met the long, open road. Mary pointed to a large hut, abuzz with people. She and Frank felt like strangers in a strange land. But what a beautiful and wondrous land it was.

If Frank and Mary were enthralled by the taxi ride, when they arrived and checked into the hotel they were in complete awe. The hotel itself, which looked new, was expansive and modeled in pulchritude, down to the last detail. The foyer was grand and open, letting sunlight pour in. By the front desk stood a huge, polished brass cage with a giant, brightly colored bird with long-flowing tail feathers. The guest room was also charming and spacious, with its own balcony with a spectacular view. The grounds of the resort were capacious, with brick walkways, lush gardens, outdoor bar, and two swimming pools. The staff walked around carrying drinks and taking orders. But none of that could compare to the main attraction: The vast, white sand beach on which the resort was situated. It was in one word, Paradise. It looked so pure, sprawling as far as the eye could see, washed by an endless blue ocean. The only beaches Mary had ever been to were Jones Beach and the Rockaways. Even while in Europe during the war, Frank had never seen anything like it. Sure, both had seen pictures, but it was absolutely nothing like standing there, absorbing it with all of their senses.

Frank and Mary had the time of their lives in Hawaii. The days were long and sun-soaked and they took turns relaxing on the beach, sightseeing, and going into town. It was strange for both of them not having Thomas and Eileen around. They had never been away from them for even a day. But both knew that they were in good hands. Besides, this was their time.

As if the landscape and resort was not enough, Frank made sure Mary was thoroughly pampered. He booked her an hour-long massage and patiently tagged along when she went into all the souvenir shops. That's not to say Frank was also not taking full advantage. There was sex every night, sometimes several times a day. There was room service with breakfast in bed. Frank also loved just laying on a lounge chair facing the ocean with an exotic drink in his hand, then going in the water.

On the third night of their vacation, Frank treated Mary to a romantic dinner on the beach. The night sky was clear and speckled with countless, flickering stars. By their intimate table, two tiki torches added an enchanting glow. Though other tables adorned the beach, they were far enough away for Frank and Mary to feel as if they had the night to themselves. Besides the occasional visit from the waiter, no other voices but their own could be heard, only the sound of waves slapping gently on the shore.

Frank ordered a bottle of red wine, recommended by the waiter. The white-dressed server elegantly uncorked the bottle and poured Frank a sample. Frank had a taste and then gave him the okay.

Once the waiter disappeared into the background Frank raised his glass. "Mary," he said, his tranquil voice floating into the night air, "we've been married for ten years. And I can't imagine living a life without you. I look into your eyes and realize that I'm the luckiest man alive. I've always loved you and I will never stop loving you."

Mary started to put her glass down as tears swelled in her eyes. "Oh Frank."

"I don't want you to cry."

Mary wiped a tear from her eye. "Oh Frank, I'm the one who is lucky. And I can't imagine living a day without you. You're the greatest husband, greatest friend anyone could ever ask for."

Frank was moved by her words. He raised his glass once more. "Well here's to us."

Mary met his glass with her own. "Forever."


Frank and Mary had a magnificent and memorable time in Hawaii. But it was not all relaxation and romance. On their last full day in Oahu, Frank visited Pearl Harbor. It would be another seven years until the USS Arizona Memorial was established. But Frank just wanted to see with his own eyes where that infamous December day in 1941, took place. Standing at the pier, looking out at the ships, he tried to imagine what it was like that fateful morning. He was standing on the spot of history, a watershed moment not only for America, but the entire world. Of course, he thought of all the people who lost their lives in the entire war, but mostly at Pearl Harbor. As he gazed into the water, he realized that underneath lay the final resting places of many young men.

There was a chapel on the base and Frank and Mary went in to say a prayer for the fallen. They exchanged no words verbally. There was no need. They spoke loudly with their souls and hearts.

# 18

# THE CATSKILLS

The year was 1960. After the first-ever televised presidential debates, Massachusetts senator and World War II veteran, John Fitzgerald Kennedy beat incumbent Vice-President Richard Nixon to become the thirty-fifth President of the United States (President Eisenhower had already been elected to two terms, thus his ineligibility to run again). At the age of forty-three, he was the youngest man ever elected to the office. Kennedy had his hands full abroad. The Cold War between the Soviet Union and United States was as tense as ever, and would soon reach an apex.

Cuba, which had been a lively and exotic vacation spot for the affluent, with its beaches, expansive posh resorts and casinos, and tropical climate, had been taken over by communist guerrillas led by Fidel Castro. By 1960, he had become, for all intents and purposes, its dictator. More alarming, he was forging a close alliance with the Soviet Union. Having a communist regime halfway around the world, in China and North Korea, was one thing, but Cuba was right at the United States' doorstep.

Despite the Cold War and what was happening in Cuba, in 1960, America was seeing a time of relative calm and prosperity. Though the civil rights movement was gaining ground, it had yet to reach its explosive and polarizing boiling point. Most Americans were living better than ever. More people owned their own home than ever before. Wages were at an all-time high. Perhaps most importantly, though always on high alert, American servicemen were not fighting in foreign lands, losing their lives.

Frank's generation grew of age during the bloodiest war in the history of the world. Before that, an entire generation spent their adolescence in the throes of the Great Depression and the Dust Bowl. Now, the main worries for teenagers and young adults seemed to be where to hang out and what to do on a Friday night. Only twenty years ago, cars were reserved for the wealthy, but now they were being driven and owned by seventeen-year-olds. It was more of a status symbol than ever. It was the time of hotrods. Everyone wanted to prove that his car was the best looking, the meanest, the fastest. Though iconic James Dean had died at the early age of twenty-four in 1955 in a car accident, it did not stop every young man from wanting to be him, drag-racing for bragging rights. When they weren't racing, the youth of the time could probably be found hanging out at the drive-in diners, showing off their cars, socializing and hooking up. And of course, listening to rock-and-roll.

In 1960, Elvis Presley returned from his two-year stint with the Army and released *Elvis Is Back*. Artists like Chuck Berry and Chubby Checker were not only electrifying young American audiences, but were taking their raucous rhythm overseas, inspiring scores of British musicians who would soon invade the States.

In the theaters, Alfred Hithcock's thriller Psycho was released, starring a young Anthony Perkins.

By 1960, the exodus of Americans out of the inner cities and into suburban communities was still continuing. From New York to California, new housing developments were being built. In Long Island, the potato farms and open land were disappearing. In their place, neighborhoods, strip malls, industry, and roadways. But the balance was to build without overbuilding. People wanted a life away from overcrowding and the rat race. People wanted to live in a peaceful neighborhood, where they could raise their children. They wanted the convenience of nearby stores, but not a bodega or bar on every corner. They wanted sufficient businesses to make the community viable, but not rows of office buildings. They wanted to live in an area with trees, not skyscrapers; houses, not apartment complexes; front lawns, not congested sidewalks; open roads, not traffic; quiet, not the constant sounds of honking horns or yelling. People wanted to be away from the city, but still close enough to commute there.

In 1960, like many Americans, life for Frank and Mary was good. Two years earlier Walter Rubenstein had talked Frank into opening a third Harold & Son. He also talked Frank into letting his cousin manage the new location. Like the other two stores, it was an immediate success. Though Walter had developed into a well-capable manager, Frank split his time between all three locations, making sure everything was in order, going over things with his managers, and also schmoozing with the customers. Though Frank felt his customers were in good hands, he still enjoyed and knew it was important, meeting and talking to people, making sure they were happy with the service they were getting.

Despite still splitting time between the stores, Frank was home every weeknight by 6:00 p.m. Thomas, now ten and Eileen eight, would eagerly wait like clockwork for their father to walk through the door and bombard him with hugs. The whole family would sit down for dinner together every night. Then afterwards, they would always watch an hour of television together. Tom's favorite show was *Gunsmoke*. But he also loved *Rawhide* and *The Rifleman*, anything western. Like many boys at the time, Thomas wanted to be a cowboy.

Unless something specific came up, Frank no longer went to work on Saturdays, wanting to spend more time with his family. He loved teaching Thomas how to play baseball. Sometimes the father and son would team up with Bob and Billy for an impromptu game. As their fathers had hoped for, Thomas and Billy had already become best friends.

But of course, Frank also loved spending time with daddy's little girl. And for Eileen, at age eight, her father was almost God-like.

Every Sunday the family would go to church. Afterwards, they would sometimes go to Queens to visit Frank's mother and Mary's parents.

Dorothy and Bob had a new addition to their family in 1957, with the birth to their second son, Michael.


In June of 1960, the Kellers and Davenports went up to the Catskills together for a week. In upstate New York, the Catskills at the time was a prime vacationing spot, with lakes, woodland and mountains, and camp-like resorts with activities for both adults and kids. The two families rented adjacent lakeside cabins. In all there were eighteen cabins and a main lodge, but spread over a large enough area so as not to feel on top of each other.

For the adults it was a nice getaway. The vast, sprawling timberland terrain, with its capacious, open lake made it feel like they were in the middle of nature. The kids also loved the natural playground. But even more, they loved the manmade playground. They also loved going in the pool and running into the lake. Frank realized it was a perfect opportunity to teach both Thomas and Eileen how to swim. They quickly caught on.

The resort provided ample canoes. Though everyone enjoyed going out on them, Frank seemed to enjoy it the most. Not a day went by when he didn't take at least one trip out on the lake. One time just he and Mary went out, while Bob and Dorothy watched the kids. It was romantic. They were gone for over an hour, Frank gleefully rowing, taking them to secluded enclaves, seemingly adrift in their own private world, surrounded by calm water with the backdrop of trees and mountains, nothing to be heard but their own voices and the occasional squawking of birds.

Of course, the children also loved going out on the canoe. A few times Frank took Thomas and Eileen out together. Other times he would take just one or the other. On a few occasions he and Thomas, or he Thomas and Eileen, would race Bob, Billy, and Diana in another canoe. It was fun, but being natural competitors Frank and Bob really tried to beat each other out.

One morning Frank took the canoe out with just Thomas. It was early, about 8:00 a.m. and serene mist hung over the lake.

"Wow, it looks cool," Thomas said, looking around at the light fog.

"Yeah, huh," Frank replied as he lightly rowed towards the middle of the lake. "You almost can't see where you're goin'. I hope we don't get lost."

Wearing his orange life vest, Thomas leaned forward, his eyes bulging. "I don't wanna get lost. Maybe we should head back."

Frank let out a brief laugh. "I'm just kidding, we won't get lost. Besides, the fog will probably be dissipating soon."

"Dissipating?"

"It means it'll be disappearing, going away."

Frank continued to row the boat, the oar cutting into the water, the only sound to be heard.

"Hey Dad, can I ask you something?"

"Sure."

"What was it like being in the war? Did you have to kill anybody?"

It was a question Frank was not at all expecting. He brought the wooden paddle out of the water and placed it across his lap. "Well Tommy, I'll just say this: War is a horrible thing. Horrible. Many people get hurt and even die. And believe me, I wish to God that we lived in a world where wars never had to be fought. But sometimes, as a last resort, it's necessary."

"Why?"

"Because not every place is like America. In some countries people aren't free. In some countries people can't own their own houses or cars or even toys. In some places people have to do whatever the government tells them and you can get thrown in jail just for speaking your mind."

Thomas listened intently, hanging on every word.

"We're lucky here in America, because we have freedom. But sometimes we have to fight for that freedom." Frank paused. "And sometimes America has to stand up and fight for other peoples freedom around the world as well." Frank took the oar off his lap and began paddling again. "As for what I did during the war, what it was like exactly, that's a story for another time, when you're older."

Thomas looked disappointed.

"So, how do you like it up here?" Frank asked, changing the subject. "You and Billy having fun?"

Thomas' face lit up. "Oh yeah! We met this boy Eddie. He's real neat. He's teaching us how to play basketball. Then we were playin' cowboys and Indians and hide and seek with him and some of the other kids. Later on today we're supposed to have this big water gun fight. I really like it here."

Frank smiled. "I'm glad."

Almost every evening the adults and kids would all get together in one of the cabins to play Monopoly or Life. Besides some meals, it was the only time they were all together. Though Thomas and Billy were inseparable, Eileen didn't usually hang out with the boys, and at thirteen, Diana had made her own friends. Of course, Michael was only three and always had to be by at least one of the adults. Sometimes Mary and Dorothy would take Eileen into town with them to have lunch or just browse through the few quaint stores on the main street.

One afternoon, Frank and Bob were lying on side-by-side lounge chairs on the water's edge, overlooking the lake. The wives were at the pool with Eileen and Michael. It was a beautiful day, a spotless blue sky, warm but not too hot or humid. Frank was sipping an ice tea, just taking in the fresh air and vast, beautiful scenery.

"That was fun earlier," Bob said, snapping Frank out of his trance, "playin' baseball with the boys."

Moving only his head, Frank looked over at Bob. "Yeah, it was. Especially that we whooped your team's ass."

Bob leaned forward in his lounge chair. "Hey, we had that Kevin kid and his father on our team. Dorothy and Diana would've done better."

They both laughed.

"Really, though, this is great."

Frank exhaled. "It sure is."

"It's perfect," Bob went on. "We can relax and the kids are occupied. And we do stuff with the kids, too, like playin' ball today. The women are havin' a good time. There's no work or anything to worry about. Plus it's beautiful out here, the lake, the mountains. We should do this every summer."

"That sounds like a plan. It's close enough and we can bring the whole family."

Bob stretched out in his lounge chair, putting his arms behind his head. "I'm tellin' ya, this is the life. I mean it's probably one, two in the afternoon, I don't even know, and we don't have anything to do for the rest of the day. Hell, why don't we have beers in our hands?"

Frank looked over. "Hey, that don't sound like a bad idea."

Just then Diana burst upon the scene. "Hey Daddy. Hey Uncle Frank."

They both greeted her.

"Dad, Julie's parents are having a picnic and asked if I could join them."

Bob looked over at his daughter, wearing a swimsuit and shorts. "I don't see why not. But you sure it's okay with Julie's parents? I should talk to them first."

"Dad, it's only lunch," Diana whined. "Besides, it's right over there by the picnic tables."

Bob thought about it for a second. "Okay, sure."

Diana hugged her father's neck. "Thanks, Dad, you're the best." With that, she excitedly ran off to be with her newly made friend.

"She's a good kid," said Frank as he watched her scamper away.

Bob also watched his daughter. "Yeah she is," he said in a proud voice. He then turned to his friend. "I just can't believe how fast she's grown. I mean it seems like just yesterday I could fit her in my arm. Now she's thirteen."

"What are you going to do when she starts wanting to date?"

Bob sat up in his seat. "Oh, hell no! She's not dating till she's twenty. Even then I'll be waiting on the front porch with a shotgun when she gets home."

Frank laughed. "I know what you mean. I know Eileen's still young, but I'm already worried about the day she starts talking about boys. I don't know what I'm gonna do."

"Get the shotgun ready."

They laughed again.

"Hey, what about those beers? Let's go to the bar and have a drink. Then I'll kick your ass in shuffleboard."

Frank sprang up. "You're on!"

The two families lucked out with the weather. For the most part it was warm, sunny and beautiful. But one evening a heavy rainstorm passed through. Thomas and Billy were in the recreation room hanging out and playing table tennis and foosball. Mary was taking a rare nap. Frank was on the couch reading a newspaper when Eileen walked up with a sad look on her face.

"What's the matter?"

"Daddy, I'm bored," she whined in her eight-year-old voice.

Frank smiled and put down the paper. "Come here, Pumpkin." He patted the spot on the sofa next to him.

Eileen climbed onto the couch and plaintively rested her head on her father's shoulder.

Frank combed his hand through her long, black hair. "You want me to read you a story?"

"I wanna go do something."

"Well it's raining outside Pumpkin."

"Tommy's out doin' somethin."

Frank smiled, continuing to caress his daughter's hair. "Tommy's with Billy, but they're inside, too. But I don't think it's supposed to rain tomorrow. How about tomorrow me and you go on a canoe ride, just the two of us."

Eileen lifted her head and looked at her father. "Promise?"

"Of course. I wouldn't lie to my Pumpkin. We'll have a great time."

Eileen smiled.

"Now how about I read you *Cat In The Hat*?"

"Okay."

Everyone had a wonderful time at the Catskills, but every vacation must come to an end. And every summer must turn to fall, then inevitably to winter. There is no doubt that winters in New York are long and cold. That year, an above average snowfall befell the Tri-state. But although snow can be a burden for adults, for kids it is a welcome playground. Over Christmas break, when the largest blizzard of the year hit New York, Frank and Mary excitedly made a snowman with the kids and then had a half hour-long snowball fight. But of course, no major snowfall was complete without sleigh riding. That Saturday the Kellers and Davenports took the kids to nearby Wantagh Park to join a plethora of other families sliding down large hills and playing in the snow. It was the rite of passage for any young boy or girl.

That Christmas was also a joyous occasion. Thomas and Eileen were old enough to really enjoy it. Frank was doing extremely well so there were plenty of presents. Mary's parents and Frank's mother had come over. Even Mary's sister and husband were in town. There were no wars to weigh on the adults' minds. Things seemed to be getting only better.

# 19

# IS THIS HOW IT ENDS?

The tense situation in Cuba had been ratcheting up. Unbeknownst to the public at the time, the CIA had secretly greenlighted failed and often-bizarre assassination attempts on Fidel Castro. One plan actually called for an exploding cigar, but supposedly no operatives could get close enough to Castro to plant it. But the CIA's most hopeful and realistic scheme was the training and arming of anti-revolutionary Cuban exiles for a planned invasion of Cuba and overthrow of the Castro regime. On April 17, 1961, that invasion, the infamous Bay of Pigs, was commenced. It was a complete failure and utter embarrassment for the United States. When the news came out the Kennedy administration, only in its third month in office, was publicly slammed by both sides: Those who thought Kennedy should have done more to assist the exiles, such as using the Air force; and those furious at him for approving the operation at all. One thing most people agreed on though was that Cuba was a serious problem. However, no one, including the government, could have foreseen what was coming next.

In mid-October 1962, President Kennedy was on a campaign trip that would take him to Ohio, Illinois, and other western states. On October 20th, his press secretary abruptly announced that the President would be canceling the rest of his trip due to an "upper respiratory infection" and returning to Washington. At the time of the announcement, though, the press, always suspicious and biting at the bit for a big story, felt something was up. Over the next two days, as news from the White House fell eerily silent, the rumor mill started to churn. Some people thought it was some sort of political ploy. Others believed it was something more serious, perhaps something to do with the Soviets. Still others were convinced that Kennedy was gravely ill. So when the announcement came on Monday, October 22nd that the President would address the nation that evening, everyone tuned in to watch.

Frank, Mary, and the kids were huddled around the television in the den. Frank really had no idea what the President was going to say, but insisted that Thomas and Eileen watch. He realized the importance of mathematics, English, and science. But he also wanted to make sure his children knew and understood what was going on in the world.

The President started:

*Good evening, my fellow citizens. This government, as promised, has maintained the closest surveillance of the Soviet military buildup on the island of Cuba. Within the past week, unmistakable evidence has established the fact that a series of offensive missile sites is now in preparation on that imprisoned island. The purpose of these bases can be none other than to provide a nuclear strike capability against the Western Hemisphere.*

Frank and Mary, sitting side-by-side on the couch, looked at each other. As the President went on, Mary took hold of her husband's hand.

*The characteristics of these new missile sites indicate two distinct types of installations. Several of them include medium-range ballistic missiles capable of carrying a nuclear warhead for a distance of more than one thousand nautical miles. Each of these missiles, in short, is capable of striking Washington, D.C., the Panama Canal, Cape Canaveral, Mexico City, or any other city in the southeastern part of the United States, in Central America, or in the Caribbean area.*

Eileen, who was sitting Indian-style on the floor in front of the couch, looked back at her parents. "What does that mean?"

Mary placed her hand on Eileen's shoulder and shushed her.

As Frank and Mary watched and listened to the address, they absorbed the seriousness of the situation. That seriousness was especially hammered home when Kennedy laid out his seven edicts, including a blockade around Cuban waters by the U.S. Navy to stop and inspect any inbound ships—of course, this was directed at Soviet ships. But perhaps it was his third directive that portended the gravity of the situation:

*It shall be the policy of this nation to regard any nuclear missile launched from Cuba, against any nation in the Western Hemisphere, as an attack by the Soviet Union on the United States, requiring a full retaliatory response upon the Soviet Union.*

As soon as the speech was over Eileen turned back to her parents. "What does all that mean Daddy?"

"It means we're going to war," Thomas replied.

"Thomas, don't even say such a thing," Mary snapped. "Are you trying to frighten your sister?" She then turned to Eileen. "Honey, it just means…" She was at a loss for words. "Frank?"

Frank cleared his throat. "It'll be okay, Pumpkin. President Kennedy is going to call the Soviet Union's leader and they're goin' to work it out."

"But what if they don't work it out?" Replied Eileen.

"They will Pumpkin, they will."

Mary sprung up from the couch. "Come on, it's time to get ready for bed." She clapped her hands.

"But it's not even eight o'clock yet," Thomas whined.

Mary looked at the clock. "I know, I know. But at least get ready. Come on, change into your PJs and brush your teeth."

Eileen and Thomas whined some more, but Mary persisted.

Just then the phone rang. Frank picked it up; it was Bob. The two men talked a few minutes about the President's speech. But Frank did not want to talk too loud, did not want to say anything that Mary or the kids could overhear that would frighten them. After telling Bob they would talk more tomorrow, he hung up and wandered into the kitchen. Mary was standing by the sink, facing him, her hand over her mouth. Tears were swelling.

"Oh Frank, what does all this mean?" She asked in a quivering voice. "What is going to happen? Do you really think...do you think they'll..." She could not even bring herself to say it.

Frank stepped up to his wife and caressed her arm. "Come on now, it'll be okay," he said in a soft voice so the kids wouldn't hear. "It's all posturing. The Soviets just want to see how much they can get away with. They don't really want a nuclear war. They know they couldn't win. And we're certainly not going to start it."

Mary put her head on her husband's shoulder and cried into it. "Oh Frank, I hope you're right. I'm just so scared."

Frank was able to calm Mary's nerves for the moment. But once in bed, both unable to sleep, they talked more about the situation. Though Mary was no longer crying, she was understandably distressed. Frank was also concerned, but he kept repeating his belief that the Soviets were not foolish enough to launch any kind of nuclear strike on the United States. And Frank really did believe that. Even in 1962, the Soviets and Americans had enough combined nuclear weapons to destroy the entire world. In fact, at the time, there was a race between the two superpowers to build the most devastating, highest-yield bombs. In 1960, the United States created the Mk/B-41, the single most powerful nuclear bomb ever deployed by America. It's yield: Fifteen megatons. The Soviets had developed and tested the Tsar Bomba ("King of Bombs"), reportedly yielding an inconceivable fifty megatons. In retrospect, the atomic bomb dropped on Hiroshima had a yield of sixteen *kilotons*. If it came down to it, there was almost no chance that one or two nuclear weapons would be exchanged. If the Soviet Union launched a nuclear attack on the United States, there was a high probability that America would respond with an all-out nuclear assault of its own. All the available bombs in each country's arsenal would be used, resulting in what would come to be known as Mutually Assured Destruction.

Getting little sleep, the next morning Frank went to work as he did every weekday. He first stopped at the Levittown hardware store. Of course, the crisis in Cuba was all anyone could talk about. Panic was already starting to set in.

"It's finally going to happen, World War Three."

"You'll see, those commies are going to try to launch a surprise attack on us!"

"This can't be happening!"

"Whadya think the Russians are gonna do when we try to stop and board one of their ships?"

"Maybe Khrushchev will blink."

"Kennedy should've taken care of Castro when he had the chance."

"I just started a family."

"The Ruskies are goin' to make a move on West Germany, you'll see!"

Frank had gotten so entrenched in the plethora of conversations at his first stop that he never did make it to the other two stores. Instead, he just called his managers to check in. But, of course, all they wanted to talk about was what was going on in Cuba. Frank found it near impossible to concentrate on work anyway.

Besides talking to customers and his employees, Frank had the radio turned on in the store, trying to listen to any updates on the situation. There were no new developments, but plenty of verbosity. There was talk of being prepared in the event of a nuclear detonation, making sure you had sufficient supplies, and knew where the closest shelter was. By 1962, in response to the parlousness of the Cold War, many Americans had built bomb shelters in their cellars or even fortified underground bunkers in their backyards. Houses in Levittown did not have basements and the yards were too small, and the ground too hard to feasibly build bunkers. But more than one person in the store pointed out that there was a bomb shelter in the high school. However, another person replied that it was not big enough to hold everyone.

Larry, an ex-paratrooper, who Frank knew and happened to be in the store, laughed. "You think any of that stuff is going to save you anyway? All that stuff that they teach kids in school about hiding under desks and telling people they'll be safe in their basements or some handmade bunker. If a nuclear bomb drops on your head it's gonna create a crater a hundred feet deep and a quarter-mile long—and it's gonna obliterate everything within five miles."

"But what if it's not a direct hit?" Asked one of Frank's young employees.

Larry shook his head. "Son, you ever hear of fallout? One big bomb hits Long Island, or even near it, and from Queens to Montauk will be contaminated for years."

"I was thinking about going out to the country," a middle-aged customer responded. "Maybe the Midwest."

Soon, Frank and Larry found themselves in their own private discussion. Frank explained his belief that the Soviets were not foolish or impetuous enough to start a nuclear war. Larry actually agreed, but expressed his major concern was a minor incident escalating into all-out war.

"What if a captain of one of those ships or a pilot gets trigger happy? Or what if a Soviet ship heads straight for the blockade, what do we do? How do we make them stop? It has to be by force. What if they fire on one of our ships? What do we do? And I'm sure our birds are on alert, some of them already in the air. What if the Soviets shoot one of them down?" Larry paused and shook his head in dismay. "I don't know… there's just too many things that can go wrong. It's like a big pool of gasoline; all it takes is one little match to set the whole thing off."

Unfortunately, Frank could not disagree with him.

Just then a new patron came in the door, saying how he was just at the grocery store and the shelves were becoming bare. Hordes of people, fearing the worst, were buying up all the food. After further discussion, Frank announced that he was going home early.

On the way home Frank stopped at the local grocery store. The man had been right; it was packed with people, filling up their carts with food. As Frank was looking at the refrigerated section, a young employee that knew him walked up.

"Don't worry Mr. Keller, we're supposed to be getting another shipment of goods tomorrow morning. But I would suggest comin' in early. As soon as we start stocking the stuff it'll start flyin' off the shelves."

Frank thanked him and finished his shopping, before waiting on one of the long cash register lines.

Mary was gladly surprised to see Frank home early. So were the kids, who had just arrived back from school. With two bags of groceries in his hand, he was greeted by Eileen.

"Daddy, in school all the kids were saying that there's going to be a nuclear war."

Mary, who had just heard the same thing from her daughter, gave her husband a look.

Frank handed the bags to his wife and crouched down. "There's not going to be any war," he said with a calm voice, patting Eileen on the head.

"You promise?"

Frank was not expecting that. He had never before lied to his daughter and had planned to never lie to her. And he hoped to God, and truly still believed, that in the end war would be avoided. But he also knew there was a chance the worst could happen. Certainly, he was in no position to promise something completely out of his control. However, what was he supposed to say to his ten-year-old daughter? *I can't promise that honey, because there is a chance that there will be war and that we're all going to die.* Frank exhaled. "I promise, Pumpkin," he said with a lump in his throat. That seemed to be all Eileen needed to hear.

After dinner, the family gathered in the den and turned on the news. They were reporting that the U.S. Navy ships had moved into place around Cuba. The anchor then started going into a commentary on how everyone should be prepared for the worst-case scenario, making sure they had adequate supplies and knew where the nearest bomb shelter was.

Eileen started crying. "See, there is going to be a nuclear war."

Before Mary or Frank had time to respond, Thomas, who was sitting right next to Eileen on the floor, put his arm around her. "It's going to be okay Eileen," he said as her head fell onto his shoulder. "They have to say that on the news. You know they've been saying that stuff even before all this happened. But like Dad said, there isn't going to be any war. You'll see. There's no need to be afraid."

Eileen lifted her head and looked up at her older brother. "Are you sure? We're gonna be okay?"

Thomas smiled. "Yes. We're gonna be just fine. I would never let anything happen to you."

Mary and Frank looked at each other and even in such a parlous moment their hearts filled with warmth, seeing Thomas, who was only twelve, comfort his little sister. They had always gotten along, with only the occasional, minor squabbles. But now their relationship seemed to be entering another stage. Thomas, even at his young age, was becoming her protector.

Later that evening, Frank went into Thomas' room to wish him good night, just as he always did. Frank told his son how proud he was for him comforting Eileen.

"I didn't want to scare her," he whispered, tucked tight in his bed. "But what if we do go to war with Russia? What if it does happen? I don't want to die."

Frank fought back tears. It is wrenching for any father to hear his young son speak about dying. "No one's going to die, Tommy. The Soviets know that they can't win a full-scale war with America. This will come to a peaceful solution, believe me. President Kennedy will get us out of this. Now you go to sleep and I'll see you in the morning." With that Frank kissed Thomas on the head and went on his way.

At 3:00 a.m., Frank shot up in bed, breathing as if he had just run a marathon and coated in sweat.

The commotion was enough to wakeup Mary. "What...what is it? Are you okay?"

Frank tried to slow down his breathing. "Yeah…yeah, I'm fine. I think it was just some kind of bad dream. Crazy huh?" He said letting out a forced chuckle. "It's nothing, really. Just go back to bed."

Internally however, Frank was still shaken by the nightmare, which he remembered well. He had dreamt that he, Mary, Thomas, and Eileen were standing in the backyard when all of a sudden there was a bright, blinding flash of light. Then, in the distance, an enormous mushroom cloud began to form, reaching high into the red sky. As Frank stared at the fiery, expanding cloud, Eileen and Thomas grabbed his hands. Then, before any words could be exchanged, there was another, even brighter flash, followed by a deafening, thunderous boom. A few, brief petrified moments later he watched in agonizing horror as a shockwave, spreading faster than any jet, knocked down trees, buildings, and houses. He watched in slowed motion as the unrestrained wave approached their backyard. Then, suddenly everything just turned white and Frank woke violently.

Since Frank had spent the previous day solely at the Levittown store, he decided to split his time between the other two locations. Just as the day before, people were coming in talking about the crisis. That was all the employees wanted to talk about as well. Frank understood, but he just didn't even want to discuss it anymore. At one point he told Walter that he was going to take a walk down to the deli. The fact was he just wanted to get away and clear his head.

The dense clouds of the previous two days had dissipated, leaving a clear, pale October sky. It was brisk but clam, no wind nor breeze. Wishing to find ephemeral refuge from all the hysteria, Frank sauntered down a residential block towards a nearby park. Alone with his thoughts, he suddenly started thinking about his father, wishing he was there. Frank knew that even his father would not be able to solve the current situation. But somehow his father always knew what to say, how to comfort him. Sure, Frank had Mary and the kids, but with them it was his job to be the guardian. Frank needed someone putting their hand on his shoulder, assuring that everything would be okay. Then, the more Frank thought about it, the more he realized how much he just missed his father.

As Frank continued to stroll down the sidewalk, hands in his coat pockets, one thought flowed into another. He might have evaded the conversation about what was going on, but his mind could not escape the reality of the situation. He thought about his nightmare, about Mary and the kids, about what the end game was, about life and death. Before he knew it, Frank had arrived at the park. It was quiet, not even the sound of chirping birds could be heard. Frank looked up at the clear, tranquil sky and wondered: *Is this how it is going to end? If the worst happens will there even be any warning? Will people just be walking down the street, going on their way and be vaporized before they even know what hit them? Will the clear sky turn into a blinding flash, signaling the end of the World as we know it?*

When Frank arrived back at the store he went into the back room and phoned his mother. He wanted to check in with her, but also just hear her voice. Always stoic, she assured her son that she was okay. But at the end of the conversation Margaret announced that she was going to church. "We all need to pray Frank."

After getting off the phone Frank told Walter that he was going home. It was 1:15 p.m. when he arrived home. Upon entering the door he announced to Mary that they were going to church. On the drive home, Frank had weighed whether or not to bring Eileen and Thomas. He did not want to alarm them. But in the end, he came to the conclusion that it was more important that they go along. Mary agreed. After getting home from school their parents gave them the news.

"But it's not Sunday," Eileen said in a puzzled voice.

Mary crouched down so they were face to face. "Your father and I just think that it's important to go to the house of the Lord and pray for President Kennedy," she said in a gentle voice. "So that he is able to put an end to what's going on."

Eileen looked concerned, but nodded in agreement.

Thomas didn't say anything.

When they arrived at the church, it was already full. There was no Mass going on; everyone was just sitting or kneeling at the pews, praying silently. Some had rosaries in their hands. Quietly, Mary found a half-open row and ushered in her family. Each of them knelt down and prayed in their own unspoken words, but all for the same thing. Frank and Mary had passed their strong faith down to Eileen and Thomas at the earliest age, just as many Americans had done at the time. And whether you are a fifty-five-year-old scholar of religion, a twelve-year-old attending Sunday school, or a seven-year-old just opening your virgin eyes to the world, a prayer is a prayer.

For the next three days the Kellers, along with the entire world, waited with maximum apprehension—for either a peaceful resolution, or the Apocalypse. Across America, citizens stayed glued to the radio or television. The hysteria, however, abated. A person can stay in a state of panic only for so long. Whatever was going to happen was going to happen. People had readied their shelters, headed for what they thought was safe ground, stockpiled their supplies, and said their payers. Now they sat atop pins and needles, unable to concentrate on anything else but their fears and the next news report.

On Sunday, October 28, President Kennedy issued a statement that Soviet Premier Khrushchev had agreed to dismantle the nuclear weapons in Cuba and return them to the Soviet Union. In return the Unites States pledged not to invade Cuba. The crisis was over. The world was spared annihilation. Though not known to the public at the time, the United States also secretly agreed to remove its nuclear missiles from Turkey.

Some people celebrated with jubilation, but many were just overcome with an enormous sense of relief.

Frank was sitting on the couch watching the television when the news broke. He immediately sprung up. "Mary, Mary get in here!"

Mary, who was in the kitchen, could tell right away from her husband's ecstatic tone that it was nothing bad. Before she had time to process what it could be, she scurried into the den.

"It's over! The Soviets are going to dismantle their nukes and ship them back to Russia."

Mary just stood there in disbelief. "What? What happened? Are you sure?"

Frank faced his wife and put both hands on her upper arms. "Yes. They just read a press release from the President," he said in a quiet, drawn-out voice. "Khrushchev has agreed to take back all the nuclear missiles. It's over."

Mary fell into her husband's outstretched arms, burrowed her head in his shoulder, and started to cry. But these were no tears of fear or sadness.

Just then Eileen walked down from the hallway. "What's going on?"

Her parents blithely broke the news.

A smile glowed on her ten-year-old face. "Does that mean there's going to be no war?"

"Yes, Pumpkin," Frank replied with a smile of his own. "There's not going to be any war. It's all over with."

Eileen hugged her father's leg. "I'm so glad."

As the three of them stood there in one embrace the front door burst open and in ran Thomas. "Did you hear the news?"

Frank, who already had Mary and Eileen attached to him, stretched out his left arm. "Come here."

With that, the entire family joined in a hug.

"I think we should all pray and thank the Lord for this peaceful outcome," suggested Mary.

"I think that's a good idea," Frank replied.

# 20

# DEALEY PLAZA

I n a time before Nixon and Watergate, and long before people
burned later presidents in effigy, the public might not have
always agreed with the politics and initiatives of the President,
but nearly every citizen respected the office. It was to most a sacred office, which represented the People and the United States
abroad. Disapprovals with the President were usually reserved for
other politicians, voting, and the occasional op-ed pieces. When
Kennedy took office, even being the youngest man to ever do so at
that point, he was bestowed this public respect. But when the Cuban Missile Crisis ended the way it did, he was exalted to a hero. At
the time, most Americans did not care about what had happened
behind the scenes, or who played what supporting role. In the end,
John F. Kennedy was at the helm and had steered the country
through its most treacherous waters, without a scratch.

A week after the crisis, Thomas met his father at the front door
when he came home from work, just as always. But this day he was
waving a paper. "Dad, Mr. Resner had us all write a letter to the
President today," he said enthusiastically.

"Ah, that's very good," Frank said as he was greeted by an agog Eileen, grabbing hold of his waist. "Hey, Pumpkin," he said, patting her on the head."

He turned his attention back to Thomas. "Let me take off my coat and settle in and then I'll read it."

As they sat down for dinner, Frank asked for the letter, which Thomas eagerly produced. It read:

> *Dear Mr. President,*
>
> *I want to thank you for putting an end to the Cuban crisis and making the Russians take back their nuclear missiles. My father, mother, little sister Eileen, and I all went to church and prayed for you.*
>
> *I know you have said ask not what your country can do for you, but rather what you can do for your country. Like you, my father fought in World War II. He landed in Normandy on D-Day. And when I grow up I also want to serve my country by joining the army.*
>
> *Sincerely,*
>
> *Thomas Keller*

Frank put down the letter and smiled. "Very good Tommy. So you want to become a soldier too, huh?"

"Oh yeah! I want to be just like you and President Kennedy. Well, I know he was in the Navy, but I think I'd rather be in the Army."

Mary looked at her husband. She did not like the idea of her son enlisting in the military. Neither did Frank. However, they figured it was just the daydream of a twelve-year-old boy. At some point every young boy imagines himself a warrior, heroically landing on a beach, fighting in a fierce battle, parachuting from a plane with rifle in hand, or engaging in a dogfight. Besides, Frank was honored that Thomas had such admiration for him.

One Friday during the holidays, Frank went with Bob to the veterans' hall. It had been a while since either had been there. Once a community almost solely for military families, as Levittown expanded and the years went on, it was seeing more and more non-military families move in. Still, there was a large active and veteran contingent. Frank and Bob were happy to see many of the same old faces waiting for them. It was also great to gather with the guys and just be able to enjoy the time, without having to talk about ongoing wars or crises. There was certainly no world peace and the Cold War still loomed, but after the World War II, Korea, and most recently the brink of nuclear annihilation, for at least the moment, things seemed almost like milk and honey.

The vociferous hall was filled with men drinking and smoking, laughing and engaged in banter. It being the holidays also added to the festive atmosphere. Frank and Bob mingled, hanging out with different groups throughout the night. At some point an arm-wrestling contest broke out. Frank beat four different guys before finally falling to the would-be champion, a 6'4" Marine who looked like he had been sculpted out of stone. Still, Frank was extremely proud of himself for doing so well. Of course, he also had to rub it into the faces of a few of the men he had beaten. Bob won one match and lost the next to a formidable opponent; still, not enough to boast.

It was not all badinage and machoism. The men talked about their families, getting each other up to speed on whose kids were how old and what they were doing. Photos were pulled from wallets and shown. They also talked about their wives and careers. Some of the guys asked Frank about how the hardware business was going. Bob had an in-depth conversation with someone about working at Grumman.

As they left, three sheets to the wind, Frank and Bob made a pact to start going to the hall more often again.

On May 12, 1963, Thomas turned thirteen. That weekend Mary and Frank had a birthday party for him at the house. That morning, the proud parents discussed their disbelief that their son was now a teenager. It seemed like just yesterday, they agreed, that he was learning to walk.

Frank knew that there was nothing he could do about the perseverance of time. Instead, he looked forward to spending even more time with his son and doing the things they could not do together when he was younger: Helping him make the high school football team; giving him advice about girls; teaching him how to shoot, maybe even go hunting together; soon, teaching him how to drive. Frank looked forward to helping his boy become a man.

That summer, the Kellers and Davenports once again went up to the Catskills for several days. Only this time, they did so over the Fourth of July.

Of course, Thomas and Billy were joined at the hip the whole time. Diana, who had just turned sixteen, was allowed to bring a friend with her. Bob, who was doing extremely well at Grumman, rented a large, three-bedroom cabin.

Mary had been concerned about Eileen having someone her own age to play with. But this time Eileen quickly made friends with two girls whose families were staying at the resort. She was not exactly an extrovert, but neither was she shy. Now eleven-years-old, Eileen had a sunny disposition and never had a problem fitting in at school or on the playground.

The families arrived in the Catskills on the morning of Independence Day. That evening there was a fireworks display by the lake. The Kellers and Davenports, along with every other guest at the resort, set up camp at the picnic area and by the shoreline. People were laying in lounge chairs and folding chairs, some laid on blankets. All the picnic tables were taken. Some people brought wicker baskets with snacks and coolers. It was a clear night and there was electricity in the air. Everyone was excited.

The display itself was spectacular; a plethora of multi-colored trails streaming high into the sky, bursting into an assortment of red, blue, silver, and green bouquets, stars, and chrysanthemums. The night came alive with glimmering and shooting colors and roaring and crackling sounds. In a reclining wooden chair next to his wife and with Eileen on his lap, Frank marveled at the continuous barrage. The vivid rising and falling colored lights were a spectacle to his eyes; the whistling and exploding noise, euphonious to his ears. But it was not just the fireworks themselves; it was what they represented. A patriot, Frank was always proud and grateful to be an American, but the celebrations on the Fourth of July reminded him of the country's tumultuous, but grandiose beginning, of a government and people born out of the right and struggle for freedom.

Of course, Frank also took pleasure in the kids' excitement of the fireworks. Eileen, sitting on his lap, would animatedly point to the sky. "Daddy, look at that one! Did you see that one, it's a star!" Thomas and Billy, sitting next to each other, would do much the same, oohing and awing. Even Mary was mesmerized.

One of the days they were at the Catskills, Frank and Bob rented a small boat and took Thomas and Billy out fishing. It was a good bonding experience. They were out on the lake for about four hours. Frank caught four trout, though two of them had to be thrown back. Billy also caught a trout and a yellow perch. Bob wound up hooking a small-mouth bass. Thomas seemed to be enjoying himself, but Frank knew he had to be disappointed that he had yet to catch anything. But then, just as they were about to head back, he reeled in a trout and it was a keeper. After the fish was in the boat he threw his arms up in the air in victory and was unable to remove his smile. In a stroke of fortune they had all caught fish. They had also enjoyed just being on the lake. But it was difficult to tell who enjoyed themselves more, Frank and Bob, or the boys.

Once back at the resort, Billy and Thomas sought out their mothers to show off their prizes. That night, the families had a barbecue and grilled some of the trout and the bass. They also cooked hamburgers and hotdogs, as Eileen, Diana and her friend were not touching the fish.

Another day, Frank and Bob took the boys to the retreat's archery range. While there, Diana came over with her friend and asked if they could join. Bob looked at his daughter, ready to say no, but then realized it was a good opportunity for them to bond as well. Besides, the girls were sixteen.

It was a fun-filled vacation. No one complained about being bored. No one argued with each other. The fact was that neither the adults nor the kids wanted to go home. But life isn't always a vacation.


On July 17th, it was Billy's turn to celebrate his thirteenth birthday. Bob and Dorothy threw him a small birthday party at the house. Of course, the Keller clan was there.

Frank and Mary presented Billy with his present, a fishing rod and tackle box. "Now we can go fishing more often," Frank said with a smile.

Billy hugged each of them. "It's great! Thank you, Uncle Frank. Thank you, Aunt Mary."

Not only where Frank and Mary his godparents in name, but Billy had become a second son to them. Of course, they also loved Diana and Michael, and had promised to take care of them if, God forbid, anything happened to Bob and Dorothy. But Billy was different. He had become inseparable from Thomas and thus was always around, and Frank and Mary enjoyed having him around. Frank would ask him the same things he would ask his own son, talked to him the same way he talked to Thomas. Frank also related to the special bond his son and Billy had together, because he and Bob had shared that same bond since childhood.


On August 28, 1963, at the Lincoln Memorial in Washington D.C., in front of a massive crowd, Martin Luther King Jr. gave his historic *I Have a Dream* speech. The following day, while in the back office of his Levittown store, Frank read the text of the speech in one of the newspapers. Frank had known about King, but had only followed him loosely in the news. However, reading the speech moved him greatly. Since returning from the war, Frank had empathized with the black man's plight, feeling it a crime that they did not have the same rights as whites, simply because of the color of their skin. But never before had he heard that plight put both so eloquently and powerful.

Frank read the entire speech, but it was its awe-inspiring end that touched him the most:

> This will be the day when all of God's children will be able to sing with a new meaning, 'My country, 'tis of thee, sweet land of liberty, of thee I sing. Land where my fathers died, land of the pilgrim's pride, from every mountainside, let freedom ring.'
>
> And if America is to be a great nation this must become true. So let freedom ring from the prodigious hilltops of New Hampshire. Let freedom ring from the mighty mountains of New York. Let freedom ring from the heightening Alleghenies of Pennsylvania! Let freedom ring from the snowcapped Rockies of Colorado! Let freedom ring from the curvaceous slopes of California!
>
> But not only that; let freedom ring from Stone Mountain of Georgia! Let freedom ring from Lookout Mountain of Tennessee! Let freedom ring from every hill and molehill of Mississippi. From every mountainside, let freedom ring.
>
> When we allow freedom to ring, when we let it ring from every village and every hamlet, from every state and every city, we will be able to speed up that day when all of God's children, black men and white men, Jews and Gentiles, Protestants and Catholics, will be able to join hands and sing in the words of the old Negro spiritual, Free at last! Free at last! Thank God Almighty, we are free at last!

Frank could not stand in the shoes of the black man. He never had to endure their struggles. But he knew what it meant to fight and be ready to lay your life down for freedom. And in Europe, he had bared witness to the other side of freedom.

However, Frank did not come away with a bleak vision of the future after reading the speech. To the contrary, like King himself, he felt America on the cusp of a great day.

That evening, he asked Thomas if he had learned about Martin Luther King Jr. in school. Thomas replied that he had not. Frank explained to him who he was and shared some of his speech.

Frank truly believed that America was about to see its brightest days. He could not have been more wrong.

It was Friday, November 22, 1963. Frank was at his East Meadow store, routinely going over some numbers with his manager, Walter. Part of his thoughts were on going to Queens with Mary and the kids the next day to visit his mother and Mary's parents. The two men were in the back room looking over a ledger when they heard the employee out front yell, "No! No!" They both went to see what the commotion was about.

Behind the counter, the seventeen-year-old employee was crying and a frequent, male customer was standing on the other side, ashen-faced.

"What? What's the matter?" Frank apprehensively asked.

The employee pointed to the customer. "He said that the President's been shot."

Frank's jaw dropped. "What? What are you talking about?"

"I was just walkin' down the block to come to the store and everyone was talking about it," the middle-aged man said, choking back tears. "It must have just happened. Do you have a radio?"

Frank could feel his heart racing. "Walter, turn on the radio."

Walter went to the back room and returned with a portable radio, which he quickly plugged in and turned on.

*…Once again, for those of you just tuning in, it has been confirmed that President Kennedy and Texas Governor John Connally were shot while the President's motorcade was driving through downtown Dallas.*

*The President has been taken to Parkland Hospital. His condition at this time remains unknown.*

Frank combed his hand through his hair. Time seemed to stand still. "I can't believe this. This has to be some bad dream."

"Maybe it just grazed him or hit him in the shoulder," the customer said wishfully. "I'm sure they have the best doctors in the country working on him."

Frank shushed everyone as the radio report continued. The phone at the store rang, but no one answered. After about fifteen minutes, unconfirmed reports were coming in that Kennedy had died. Frank slammed his fist on the counter.

Walter put his head in his hands repeating over and over, "It can't be, it can't be."

The employee and customer were just standing there in disbelief, shaking their heads.

"Walter, I'm going home," Frank announced in an exasperated voice. "I have to be with my wife."

Five minutes later, Frank was in his car heading home, racing to get there. He had the radio on and halfway into the drive the report broke over the airwaves.

"Ladies and gentleman," said a direly somber voice, "I…I don't know how else to say this, but it has been confirmed. The President is dead. Repeat, President Kennedy is dead."

Frank punched the dashboard, fighting back tears. After a few deep breaths, he got out of the car.

Frank entered the house to see Mary standing in front of the television, her hand over her mouth, tears streaming down her face. She turned to Frank, but did not move from the TV. "Oh, Frank, you've heard the news?"

Frank walked over to his wife. "Yes," was all he said in a tombstone voice as Mary fell into his arms.

Just then the front door opened. It was Eileen. Mary was usually there at the bus stop on the corner to meet her. "Mommy, Mommy, they said the President was killed," she cried, running to her parents.

While Frank and Mary were trying to console their daughter the door opened once again. This time it was Thomas. "Is it true?" One look at his parents gave him the answer.

"Come here," Mary said as she opened up her arms.

All four of them embraced.

"Let us say a prayer for Mrs. Kennedy and their family—and for the country."

The entire family stayed in the den, glued to the television the rest of the afternoon and evening, only stopping to eat something that Mary had quickly whipped up. They watched as the news showed video of bystanders still congregating around Dealey Plaza, crying and in disbelief. The eyewitnesses that were not being interviewed by reporters were speechless, trying to come to grips with what had happened. The news also showed live footage of the Trade Mart, where President Kennedy had been headed to give a speech. Grown men dressed in suits and women adorned in formal wear were walking around their long tables like zombies. The camera locked in on a lone black server, silently wiping his tears away with a handkerchief, shaking his head. But the people at the Trade Mart and around Dealey Plaza were just a microcosm of the entire nation, entranced in a somber shock.

Early on, the authorities had found the rifle suspected of killing Kennedy and there were several reports of different people being detained for questioning. But then some man named, Lee Harvey Oswald, was arrested at a movie theater. The news was saying that besides being a suspect in the President's assassination, Oswald had allegedly also shot and killed a policeman in a Dallas neighborhood. So much information was coming out that it was not only hard to keep up, but decipher fact from rumor.

Before long, Frank and Mary, along with the whole nation, had their first chance to see Oswald when he was taken to a chaotic Dallas police station. It was hard to see him because of the mob of reporters, policemen, and federal agents. But for a brief moment, his entire body and face was shown. He was an unimposing lanky man with short hair and a smug face.

"I'd like to get my hands on that bastard," Frank spewed.

Eventually, reports started coming out that Oswald had been in the Marines. But much more alarming was the news that he was a communist, who was married to a Russian national.

"You think the Soviets had something to do with this?" Mary asked with trepidation.

Thomas and Eileen looked at their father.

"It…it's probably just some lone nut," he replied to not alarm his children. Internally, he hoped to God he was right.

"But Dad, they said he was a communist," Thomas pushed on. "What if the Russians are behind it?"


Everyone was understandably spellbound by the assassination, mourning for the President, and trying to find what exactly had transpired. But there was also the paramount business of leading the nation. Not too long after Kennedy was assassinated, his vice-president, Lyndon Baines Johnson, was sworn-in aboard Air Force One. Upon landing in Washington, right on the tarmac, Johnson gave his first speech as President of the United States. In the short address, a solemn Johnson famously promised: "I will do my best. That's all I can do." It did not exactly invoke confidence in Frank or Mary—or the rest of the nation.

The next day, Frank canceled the family's trip to Queens, though he did spend time talking to his mother on the phone about what happened. He and Mary spent the day once again plastered to the television. Reports were already coming out from eyewitnesses that they had heard shots coming from a grassy knoll along the parade route. A few had even stated seeing a suspicious man fleeing from the area. The question was already being asked: Was there a second gunman? As Oswald was being led to another room in the police station, he told a hall full of reporters that not only did he not shoot the President, but he still did not even know what he was being charged with.

"Of course he's going to say that," Frank scoffed. "You think he's gonna say he did it?"

"But what if he wasn't alone?" Mary asked. "What if he was part of a bigger plot? You really think it was just him?"

Frank took a moment to process the question. "I don't know," he answered truthfully.

The following day, November 24th, the Kellers went to morning Mass like they did every Sunday. Father Mallard talked about the assassination and asked his parishioners to say a prayer for Kennedy, Governor Connally—who had survived but was still in critical condition—their respective families, now-President Johnson, and for the entire nation.

After church the family returned home. Thomas went to hang out with Billy and some other friends. Eileen went to a friend's house nearby. At one point, Frank was in the kitchen talking on the phone to Bob when he heard Mary scream. With the phone cord stretched as far as it could go, he peered into the den where his wife was standing in front of the television. "What is it?"

"Oswald, they just shot him!"

"What are you talking about?" He asked with the phone still in his hand. "Shot him? Who shot him?"

Mary pointed to the TV. "I don't know," she said in a shaky voice. "Some man. It just happened. They were getting ready to transport Oswald and someone came up to him and shot him."

"Someone just shot Oswald," Frank told Bob. "Turn on the TV. I gotta go. I'll call you back later." He then hung up and joined his wife in front on the television.

History knows that Lee Harvey Oswald was killed by a single gunshot to the abdomen. The shooter was a Dallas nightclub owner named Jack Ruby, who no one but locals had ever heard of. Until his death in 1967, Ruby claimed he shot Oswald out of self-patriotic revenge for the assassination of Kennedy and that no one else was involved. But rumors already spreading that Oswald had not acted alone now turned to full-blown conspiracy theories. One thing was for certain: Oswald would never go to trial and divulge what really happened that day at Dealey Plaza and the Texas School Book Depository.

# 21

# THE WORLD'S FAIR

Life went on after President Kennedy's death. It had to. But the country was left not only in mourning, but adrift in a dark sea of suspicion. A week after the assassination President Johnson established what would come to be known as the Warren Commission to investigate and get to the bottom of what exactly happened. The commission would submit its final report in September of 1964, finding that Lee Harvey Oswald had acted entirely alone. The report would only add fuel to the plethora of conspiracy theories.

But even long before the commission came to its final conclusion, many in the public did not believe the lone gunman theory. The list seemed to grow every day of who wanted Kennedy dead and why. And myriad group of people quickly began to smell a government cover up. In fact, many say that after Kennedy's assassination the public's faith and trust in the government would never be the same. Of course, soon there would be even more reasons for that distrust.

In January of 1964, Frank and Mary's focused shifted from Kennedy's assassination to their sick daughter. During the second week in January, Eileen came down with what her parents thought was the flu or a bad cold. At first, they just had her stay home from school, lie in bed, and fed her chicken soup and ginger ale. However, by the fourth day, when her symptoms had not improved Mary made an appointment for her to see the doctor. He diagnosed her with an upper-respiratory infection and prescribed penicillin. A few days later Eileen seemed to improve. She was still weak and lethargic, but was able to move around and eat more and was not coughing as much. She also no longer had a fever. By this time Eileen had been out of school for a week and was eager to get back, mostly missing being with her friends. Frank and Mary also didn't want her to miss too many classes, even if it was only the sixth grade. After consulting with the doctor, that Monday they sent her back to school.

Two days later, Mary received a call from the school nurse. Eileen was not feeling well and was running a slight fever. Mary picked her up and put her in bed. Later that night, as her mother intermittently checked up on her, Eileen's fever reached 103 and she was coughing constantly. The next morning Mary scheduled another doctor's appointment, but the doctor could not see her until the following day. In the meantime, he suggested to give Eileen children's aspirin and plenty of fluids and not to worry.

The next morning, before going to work, Frank went into Eileen's bedroom to check on her. Though bundled in blankets, she was covered in a thick layer of sweat. Frank felt her head; it was burning up.

"Da... Daddy, I feel really sick," she said in a listless voice before going into a violent coughing fit.

Frank called for Mary to bring the thermometer. As soon as Mary saw Eileen, she knew she had taken a turn for the worse. Then came the temperature reading: 104.5. "Are you sure that's right?" Frank asked in a tremulous voice.

"Frank, look at her," Mary replied in her own distressed tone.

Eileen began to cough some more, straining her entire body.

"I'll call the doctor again."

Frank looked at his daughter, coughing, pale and soaking wet. "To hell with that! We're taking her to the emergency room."

At the hospital Eileen was diagnosed with bacterial pneumonia. The doctor on call explained that they were giving her antibiotics intravenously and that "should do the trick."

"What do you mean *should*?" Frank barked.

Mary put her hand on his chest, to calm him down.

The doctor understood Frank's concern. "Listen, Mr. Keller," he said in a subdued voice, "it's not like the old days. Pneumonia is very treatable now, unless the patient is elderly or has some pre-existing condition that weakens their immune system. A lot of times we're able to treat bacterial pneumonia with oral antibiotics. But because of her high fever we've given her antibiotics intravenously. I'm sure that's going to take care of it." The doctor paused. "But just as a precaution, until the fever goes down, she might have to stay overnight."

Eileen did wind up staying overnight. So did Frank and Mary. Mary phoned Dorothy and asked if she could pick up Thomas and have him spend the night. Of course, it was no problem.

Early evening, Frank went back to the house to pick up Eileen's favorite stuffed bear. He then stopped at Bob's and Dorothy's to check on Thomas. Bob and Dorothy asked about Eileen, greatly concerned, and both gave Frank their own optimistic speech. And they truly were optimistic, figuring Eileen would be out of the hospital the next day and feeling herself after a week. Thirteen-year-old Thomas however, was frightened.

"Dad, is Eileen going to be okay? Why is she in the hospital if she's not that sick? What if something happens to her?" He asked on the verge of tears.

Frank consoled his son and assured him that she would be better in a few days.

Frank and Mary spent the night in Eileen's hospital room, camped out on two metal chairs, getting hardly any sleep. The next morning, when a nurse came to read Eileen's vital signs she called for a doctor. Frank and Mary could immediately tell that something was not right. The new doctor on call explained that Eileen's fever had barely gone down; it was still near 103. He called for a stronger dose of antibiotics and a round of new tests. Fear and panic started to take hold of Mary and Frank.

For most of that day, the Kellers waited with heavy hearts and tormented minds for Eileen's condition to improve. They went to the hospital's chapel and prayed. Around 2:30 p.m., Mary went to Dorothy's to check on Thomas.

Frank remained in the room. Eileen was getting some much-needed rest. As she slept, Frank stood over her. It was gut-wrenching to see his daughter lying in a hospital bed, with an oxygen tube in her nose and two IVs in her arm. Since the day before, time had seemed to lose its form. He did not know how long he was standing there, watching her, but eventually Eileen opened her eyes.

Frank bent over and kissed her forehead. "Hey, Pumpkin," he said with a forced smile. "How you feelin'?"

Eileen took hold of her father's hand. "Daddy, I'm scared. Am I going to be okay?"

Frank could feel his heart breaking as he tried his hardest to fight back tears. It's something that no father should hear from his child. He felt so helpless. He was supposed to be there to protect his daughter, to pick her up when she was down, to help her feel better when she was sick. But this was out of his hands—and that killed him. Still, he had to put on a reassuring front for Eileen. "Oh honey, they just need to give you stronger medicine, that's all," he said still trying to hold back tears. "I'm sorry, I know this really stinks, but you'll be home and better soon."

Eileen looked up at her father with exhausted eyes. "You promise?"

"I promise." What else could he say?

Eileen went back to sleep, with Frank right by her side. Then, after a short while a nurse came in and announced that the doctor had asked her to take Eileen for a new set of X-rays on her lungs.

With his daughter out of the room, Frank went outside to get some fresh air. By the front entrance, he stood there in the cold of

January, his exasperated breath forming white clouds in the air. He had slept maybe two and a half hours the night before and forced down only half a sandwich since the prior morning. Visions of Eileen lying in that hospital bed, along with various memories of happier times they had spent together, swirled in his head. He felt helpless, he felt angry, he felt heartbroken.

As Frank was standing there, lost in his thoughts, Mary walked up from the parking lot with Thomas. "Where's Eileen? I want to see her," he said right away.

Frank explained that she was taking some x-rays, but would be back soon.

"Thomas, why don't you go inside, it's cold out here. I want to talk to your father for a minute."

Reluctantly, he did what his mother asked.

"I had to bring him," she said to Frank once Thomas was gone. "He's understandably very upset. Dorothy said he was crying last night." Frank just shook his head.

"So she's gone for more x-rays? How is she? Did the doctor say anything?"

"I haven't seen him."

Mary fell into her husband's arms and started crying. "Oh Frank, what if something happens to her? She's our baby."

Frank stroked her hair. "Shhh, don't even say that. She'll be okay."

When Frank, Mary, and Thomas went up to the room, Eileen was just getting back. She was happy to see Thomas and actually even smiled. Her brother promised that when she was better he would take her to the soda shop and buy her all the ice cream she could eat.

That evening Eileen's fever started to go down. Though still weak, she was released from the hospital the following afternoon. After several more days of rest at home, she started returning to normal, and even began complaining about being bored. Within a week Eileen was back to her old self. Frank and Mary breathed the biggest sigh of relief they had ever breathed in their lives. They went to pray, thanking God for their daughter's recovery—and to never have to go through anything like that again. That first Saturday Eileen was out and about, Thomas asked his father for some money and took his little sister to the soda shop.

That April, of 1964, Frank turned forty. Mary had a big party for him at the house. She also bought him a nice watch. But Mary had a much more important surprise and present in store for him. She had tracked down Roy Tolson, his old Army buddy. He had still been living in Boston. Mary knew about him from the letters Frank had sent during the war. Frank was shocked to see Roy. The two men embraced in a manly hug.

"Man, I can't believe it," Frank said, looking his old friend over. "Last time I saw you was at the dock when we came in from Europe."

"Can you believe that was nineteen years ago already?"

Frank shook his head in disbelief. "Man, I guess so." Frank rubbed his hand on Roy's head. "At least I still have all of my hair. Wow, you goin' bald already?" Even being separated by nearly two decades, there was nothing like some razzing between two buddies.

Amidst a full house, Frank and Roy caught up. Roy was married with three children. In fact his wife, Rosalie, had come with him. Roy introduced her to the Kellers. Roy explained that he was now selling cars for a Chevrolet dealership; "a pretty good gig" was how he put it. Frank gave him an abridged version of his life and introduced Roy and Rosalie to Thomas and Eileen.

It was Frank's fortieth birthday party and the house was filled with friends and family. So he could not spend his entire time with Roy. However, later on in the evening, the two comrades were able to find some time together in the backyard, just the two of them.

"I'm so glad you came," Frank said.

"Well you have your wife to thank for that. I should've tried to get in touch with you over the years but…well, you know."

"Yeah I know, it's crazy how the years pass by. Anyway, I could've tried to get a hold of you, too."

"Well hell, we're both here now," Roy proclaimed as he raised his bottle of beer.

"I'll drink to that!"

"I'm glad you're doing so well. You have a beautiful wife and children."

Frank smiled. "Thank you. Rosalie is very nice."

"Yeah, I guess we both got lucky." Roy took a swig of beer and grabbed Frank's shoulder. "We went through some crazy shit together, my friend."

Frank thought about it for a second before answering, as he looked back in his mind's eye. "Yeah, we sure did."

Roy took another drink from his bottle. "It's crazy, it all seems like it was some other world, a lifetime ago—yet I remember every last detail."

Just then Thomas walked out. "Dad, Mom's looking for you."

"Okay, I'll be in in a second." Thomas was about to go back inside, but Frank patted the patio chair next to him. "Come here, have a seat for a second."

Thomas looked puzzled, but sat down.

"You know, Mr. Tolson over here saved your old man's life."

Thomas looked at Roy with a dropped jaw and wide eyes.

"It's true. We were in the midst of a firefight. A German soldier had me dead in his sights and Roy here took him out. I never even saw the guy. If Mr. Tolson hadn't been there and did what he did I never would've made it home from the war—and you woulda never been born."

Thomas couldn't believe what he was hearing. First, his father never talked to him about the war. Secondly, it brought home how close his father had come to death. "Is that true?" He asked Roy, suddenly in awe of this new man.

Roy smiled and waved his hand. "It was nothing. We all saved each other's lives. And don't let your old man fool you, he didn't get the Silver Star and Purple Heart for nothing. Your old man was a real tough son-of-a-bitch."

Thomas looked at his father. "Wow, you never told me you got medals! What did you get them for?"

Frank thought about it and then told his son. He was old enough to hear about what happened during the war, though his father still spared him the graphic details.

That night, after all the guests had left, Frank thanked Mary once again for the gift and the party, but most of all for finding and inviting Roy and his wife. "We're definitely going to stay in touch now," he said with assurance.

After turning off the lights, Frank lay in bed next to Mary and thought about the war—he thought about it more than he had in a very long time.

Just a few days after Frank's birthday, on April 22nd, the much-anticipated World's Fair opened in Flushing Queens. Spanning an enormous area, the fair would last a total of 360 days, from April 22 to October 18, 1964 and then from April 21 to October 17, 1965.

The following weekend, Frank, Mary, Bob, Dorothy, and all the kids went to the fair for the first time. It was a sprawling ground, seemingly as big as a city, filled with various small and massive pavilions and numerous villages of the world, represented by such countries as Mexico, Ireland, Japan, Spain, Belgium, Greece, India, and Africa.

Many U.S. states also had their own areas. The pavilions, villages, and other attractions were all connected by wide walkways. The families arrived early on a Saturday and the fair was already bustling with tens of thousands of people. There was so much to see, so much to experience.

The kids loved the two-acre United States Space Park sponsored by NASA. It contained both the real Atlas and Titan II rockets, massive in size, standing upright like tubular skyscrapers. The park also contained the Mercury and Gemini capsules, as well as pieces of other rockets.

Most of the pavilions, however, were sponsored by American companies and housed elaborate displays, shows, even rides. The giant dome-shaped General Electric pavilion presented a show called Progessland, depicting the history of electricity, which brought the audience members through several separate auditoriums, each representing different evolutionary stages, starting with the Big Bang. The last stage was a large circular enclosure with a giant, clear bubble in its center demonstrating nuclear fusion.

General Motors' pavilion held Futurama, a massive display of what the future would look like, with computer-guided cars and trucks gliding along seemingly endless, elevated highways. There was also a city on the moon, as well as Futurama's Undersea City, with bubble-like houses and workplaces, even a resort called Atlantis. People would be ferried to the surface by submarine trains and ride about the ocean floor on personalized "aqua-scooters."

Ford's pavilion housed the most elaborate and expansive attraction: The Magic Skyway. Up to six visitors would pile into a mock Ford convertible that would autonomously glide along an extensive conveyer belt. Along the way, the car would take the riders through Earth's past, from an expansive exhibit of giant, moving dinosaurs, to a time of cavemen, and finally to the City of Tomorrow. This city was filled with glass-bubbled buildings, massive, clear rectangular and cylinder-shaped skyscrapers, and jet-powered vehicles suspended in the air. Everyone enjoyed the Magic Skyway, which was Eileen's favorite. She wanted to go again and again. Of course, she loved the dinosaurs—what kid wouldn't? Then, in awe of the City of Tomorrow, she would ask her parents if that's what it was really going to be like.

There were many other companies with their own pavilions and exhibits. Bell Systems displayed a Pitcurephone, the phone of the future, where two people could not only hear and talk, but also see each other. Avis offered a ride in scale models of different antique cars that took visitors on a slow ride through an old-fashioned country setting. IBM, American Express, Westinghouse, and other mainstays also had their own sections. Then there were the foreign country exhibits, which ranged from single buildings or pavilions, to sprawling mock villages and cities. Perhaps the largest of these mock towns was the Belgium Village. Spanning nearly four acres, it contained cobblestone roads, numerous houses, a church, a city hall, carousel, and a flowing canal. However, perhaps the most memorial attraction of the Belgium Village was a mostly unknown, but soon to become popular, treat being served up by the street-side cafes: Belgian waffles. As word spread throughout the fair, soon every kid had to have one.

There was way too much to see and experience at the fair in just one day or weekend. Many people went back numerous times; this included the Kellers and Davenports. By the fair's end in October of 1965, Thomas would brag that he had been there a total of fourteen times, with his parents, friends, and even school. Eileen also went once with her school on a field trip—which was not uncommon—as well as other times with her parents and friends. As for Mary and Frank, they not only had fun taking the kids there, but also enjoyed it themselves. Twice they went with Bob and Dorothy and all the kids and once with just Eileen and Thomas. By then, the adults and kids would separate for a while. Frank and Mary would walk around and experience the attractions and food by themselves, as if they were on a date. Especially in the summer of 1964, it was a welcome escape from the Kennedy assassination and Eileen's illness. In fact, it made them feel like everything was all right with the world again. Little did they know that storm clouds were on the horizon—and in the storm's aftermath, things would never again be the same again.

# 22

# A PLACE CALLED VIETNAM

On January 4, 1965, in his State of the Union address, President Johnson outlined his ambitious goal of achieving what he dubbed the "Great Society." It was a vast program aimed at tackling an ever-expanding population and a diminishing of the country's land, resources, and according to him, values. Johnson stated that "For once the battle is lost, once our natural splendor is destroyed, it can never be recaptured."

In the speech, he pushed for education reform, explaining that classrooms were overcrowded, teachers underpaid, and not nearly enough Americans attending, let alone graduating college, because they could not afford it. Johnson also spoke on civil rights, stating: "So, will you join in the battle to give every citizen the full equality which God enjoins and the law requires, whatever his belief, or race, or the color of his skin?"

In the end, despite a presidency which would be marred by historic domestic unrest and a violent and unpopular foreign war, Johnson did more to advance the civil rights movement perhaps more than any other president since Lincoln. Carrying the torch of his predecessor, Johnson signed the Civil Rights Act of 1964 into law, changing forever the face of America. Among other provisions, it established that all public accommodations must be open to all Americans regardless of their race, color, religion, or national origin. In March of 1965, Johnson ordered a full investigation into the Klu Klux Klan. Then in August of 1965, he signed into law the Voting Rights Act of 1965, which he had pushed for some time, banning literacy and other eligibility tests that had been aimed at preventing minorities from voting.

Like most American families at the time, the Kellers sat around the table together during dinner and conversed. Now that the kids were getting older, those discussions often took on a more adult tone, frequently about current events.

"So," Thomas said as he cut a piece of his meatloaf, "Mr. Archibald was telling us today that President Johnson ordered bombing raids over North Vietnam."

Frank looked over at his son, seemingly disgruntled by the topic.

"Where's Vietnam?" Asked Eileen.

"It's in Asia, right below China," Thomas eagerly replied.

"Why are we bombing Vietnam?"

"Because the commies are trying to take it over." Thomas then looked to his father. "Right dad?"

Frank nodded in acknowledgement.

"Mr. Archibald said that it's only a matter of time before we send ground forces there. What do you think, Dad?"

Frank finished chewing his piece of meat and put down his fork. "I don't know son. I hope not. Having advisors there is one thing, but bombing, sending in troops..." Frank paused and looked at his wife. "We don't need to get involved with someone else's mess."

"But isn't that what they said about Europe when the Nazis started taking over countries and killing everybody—that we shouldn't get involved? And aren't you always saying that communism has to be stopped from spreading?"

Frank felt like he was having a flashback to one of the many dinner conversations he had with his father leading up to Pearl Harbor. "This is different Tommy. Look what happened in Korea."

"What happened in Korea, Daddy?" Eileen asked.

Frank looked at his daughter. He wanted to explain it to her, but without going into a fifteen-minute diatribe about how he really felt. After all, she was only twelve. "Haven't you learned anything about the Korean War in school?"

"Yes." She strained to remember the facts. "That we helped part of Korea, because the communists wanted to take it over. But what did you mean when you said 'Look what happened in Korea?'"

"Well, that's right, that is what happened. Only…well, you see, before the war the communists controlled the north part of the country and the south was a democracy, it was free. Then the North invaded the South, so America helped them fight off the communists. But after a long and bloody war the North and the South wound up exactly where they started."

Eileen looked puzzled. "So we did get the commies out of the South?"

"Well yes, but…" Frank looked at Mary as if for guidance. "Well you see, the U.S. forces pushed the communists back to the North very early on in the war…but everyone kept on fighting. For a long time, no one knew exactly how to end the war."

Eileen looked even more puzzled.

"Hey, did I say that I made banana cream pie for dessert?" Mary announced with a smile. She did not mind discussing current events and intellectual topics at the dinner table—in fact, she encouraged it—but she loathed even the mention of war. She had already seen two in her lifetime and was not ready for another.


A few days after the Kellers' dinner conversation, on March 8th, the first U.S. combat troops arrived in Vietnam as 3,500 Marines landed on a beach to defend an American airbase in Da Nang. They joined the 23,000 American "military advisors" already in Vietnam.

Despite Mary's disapproval, the growing conflict in Vietnam

would become a regular topic at the dinner table. It was also quickly becoming a polarizing issue across the entire nation. As early as April 17, 1965, an estimated 15,000 students staged an anti-war protest in Washington D.C. It would be far from the last.

When Thomas finished freshman year in high school, during the summer of '65, he would sometimes work at the Levittown hardware store, just as Frank had worked with his father growing up. There was no need for Thomas to have a job; the family was well off financially. Frank just wanted his son to learn responsibility and work ethic. And Thomas was actually eager to learn, and of course earn some money of his own.

With Billy turning fifteen that summer as well, Bob also wanted his son to get work experience. Bob had mentioned to Frank that Billy had tried to get a job at Sears and J.C. Penny but had yet to hear back from either of them. Frank suggested that he could put Billy to work part time in one of the stores—but not the same store as Thomas, to keep the best friends from goofing off together. Bob thanked him and Billy gratefully accepted.

Thomas and Billy proved to be hard workers and fast learners. But although Frank thought of Billy as a son, he taught Thomas more about the business end. However, he had absolutely no intentions of driving his son to one day take hold of the hardware baton.

"This business is here for you," Frank would tell Thomas. "If one day you decide you want to run one of the stores or eventually help me run the entire business, this is your birthright. But that does not mean it's your destiny. I want you to think long and hard about what you want to do with your life and leave all the options open. And whatever you choose, your mother and I will stand by you and support you."

During the last weekend in July, Mary and Dorothy decided to have a rare women's night out. Dorothy had asked Diana to watch Michael. Thomas and Billy had plans to go see a movie that evening,

*The Great Race*, starring Jack Lemmon, Tony Curtis, and Natalie Wood. Eileen happened to be having a sleepover at a friend's house. So Frank and Bob saw it as the perfect opportunity to also go out. After eating an early supper at a diner, they moved on to a local bar.

Sitting at the bar, over cold beers, Bob once again thanked his friend for giving Billy a job and showing him the ropes. And once again Frank said that it was no big deal and that Billy was a hard worker.

After a few rounds, the conversation turned to Vietnam.

"So, what did you think of the President's speech?" Bob asked in a sarcastic tone. A few days earlier, Johnson had announced that he was sending an additional 44 combat battalions to Vietnam, increasing America's military presence there to 125,000 men. He also stated that monthly draft calls would be doubled.

Frank became agitated. "I think it's gonna be another Korea, end in another stalemate. We were too afraid of the Chinese back then to go all out and win the war…and that was before Mao had the bomb." In October of 1964, China tested their own atomic bomb.

"Yeah, I'm with ya. You know me, I hate those commie bastards as much as the next guy, but I'm not ready to have our boys come back in body bags over Vietnam. To hell with the domino effect. If the reds want South Vietnam so bad they can have it for all I care."

"Exactly."

Bob polished off his beer and signaled for the bartender to bring another round. "What worries me is this draft thing. You think they'll bring back the lottery again?"

The elderly bartender brought over two more mugs of beer.

"I don't think so," Frank replied to Bob's question after thanking the bartender. "I mean they didn't implement the lottery during Korea, and look how many troops went there and how long that lasted."

Bob nodded. "That's true. It's just that, I mean, before you know it our sons will be eligible."

Frank nearly spit out his beer. "I don't even want to think about that. Besides, Bob, they just turned fifteen. What are the odds that we'll still be in Vietnam three years from now?"

Late that August Eileen started her freshman year. Now both she and Thomas were in high school. A week into the school year, Mary let Frank know when he came home from work that the principal wanted to see them the next day. Thomas had gotten into trouble. Upon hearing the news, his father asked him what happened.

"Right after school I saw these two juniors picking on Eileen by the parking lot," he said with bated breath. "So I went over there and told them to quit it. The one kid, Jeremy, asked me what I was going to do about it and then he pushed me. So I pushed him back. Then he took a swing at me, but I moved back and he missed. So I punched him back—but I didn't miss. I was just defending myself."

"What happened to him?" Mary asked.

Thomas looked at his parents and hesitated before answering. "I gave him a bloody nose…I…I think I might have broke it."

Frank smiled and let out a fleeting laugh.

"You think this is funny?" Mary scolded her husband. "This is a very serious offense. What if they suspend him for this?"

"For what, defending himself? What was he supposed to do, just stand there and get hit?"

"See Mom, Dad understands."

Mary looked like steam was going to come out of her head. "Thomas, go to your room, I want to talk to your father."

Mary did not get angry often, but Frank could tell that she was pissed. "Listen, I know what you're going say," he said in a submissive voice. "I know we need a united front and you know the last thing I would ever do is try to undermine you. But really, you have to look at this from his point of view. He didn't go looking for trouble. All he tried to do was stick up for his little sister—our daughter. And when the kid shoved him and took a swing at him, what was he supposed to do? Don't we want our son to stick up for himself? We certainly don't want him to be a coward."

Mary thought about it. "I guess. I mean he is a good kid. He's never been in trouble at school before."

Frank was able to soothe his wife. He knew that Mary definitely didn't want Thomas to be a coward. Frank always thought that his son would stand up for himself and others and now he had proof. Inside, Frank could not have been more proud of Thomas. He had come to the aid of his little sister and took on two older kids without hesitation.

The next morning Frank and Mary went to the school and met with the principal. Mr. Dinowski knew Frank from the hardware store and he also knew and liked Thomas. Frank and Mary started off by saying they realized that fighting had no place on school grounds, but also stated their case that their son was only defending himself. After talking to the parties involved, as well as other students who witnessed the event, inside Mr. Dinowski wholeheartedly agreed with them, that Thomas was just defending himself and was in the right. But as principal of the school, he could not downplay the incident. He also had the other boy's parents to deal with. He gave the party line that no matter who started it, fighting in school could not be tolerated and that Thomas should have called for a teacher instead of trying to handle the situation himself.

"Look," Dinowski went on, "I know Thomas isn't a troublemaker. He's a good kid. And I also know that in the end, boys will be boys. That's why I'm not going to suspend him. But I am going to give him detention after school for a week. I just can't let him go Scott free. That would set a very bad example. He could've really hurt that kid."

Frank wanted to smile, but didn't.

"But what about the other two boys?" Asked Mary. "They were calling my daughter names and she felt threatened. And Thomas might have gotten the best of that boy, but that boy did push my son and take a swing at him."

Now Frank wanted to pat his wife on the back and say "that a girl," but he refrained from that as well.

"They will also get detention. I want you both to know that picking on other students, calling them names, won't be tolerated here either."

Frank and Mary agreed with the punishment. Thomas would also take his punishment without any argument.

Eileen had always looked up to her brother, but now he became a hero to her. As for being picked on, no one ever messed with her at school again—or Thomas.

That October, Frank received a call at work with devastating news: His mother had a massive stroke. She died in the ambulance. He never even had a chance to say goodbye. The last time Frank had seen her was two weeks earlier, during a routine visit to Queens— and she seemed fine.

Just as when his father died, Frank could not imagine a life without his mother. Her teachings, her words, her unyielding support had been woven into the every fiber of his being since his birth. And their love for each other was without bounds. Of course, Frank always realized that one day his mother would not be around, but the end came so sudden, so out of the blue. But Mary helped ease his pain.

"You have to think of the time you were able to spend with her," she would say, with her own heavy heart. "She was able to watch you grow into a successful man and loving husband. She was able to experience Thomas and Eileen grow-up. Never did a whole month go by that you didn't see her. She was able to spend Christmases and other holidays with us and the kids. And unlike your father, God rest his soul, she never suffered."

Frank knew his wife was right—about everything.

Frank deeply missed his mother and she would always be in his thoughts. But with Mary's support and the love of his children, he was able to deal with the grief.

# 23

# LAST CHRISTMAS

By 1967, the war in Vietnam was only escalating. By the start of the year U.S. troop levels were nearing 400,000. There had already been over five 5,000 combat deaths and over 30,000 wounded. Also growing was the anti-war movement, the likes of which had never been seen before in America. There had been opposition and even protests during Korea, the World War I, and even during World War II, before Pear Harbor, but never on such a large and organized scale.

On October 16, 1965, coordinated anti-war rallies occurred in forty American cities as well as international locations such as London and Rome. In March of 1966, other massive, concerted protests were held in New York, Washington, Chicago, Philadelphia, Boston, and San Francisco. But smaller protests were becoming a routine scene in the nation's capital, New York, and San Francisco.

Frank did not approve of the war in Vietnam, based mostly on how the Korean War unfolded. And at first, he had no problems with the anti-war rallies. After all, the pillar of democracy was the freedom of citizens to voice their opinions. However, by 1967, the face and message of the Vietnam protests had changed and so did Frank's feelings about them. In the beginning the overall message was against America's involvement in Southeast Asia. People held up signs like: *Stay out of Vietnam; No More Troops in Vietnam; Don't let our Sons Die for Nothing*. But by 1967, some protesters were already changing their opposition from the war itself to the soldiers fighting it. More signs now read: *Stop the Murders in Vietnam; No Money for Bombing and Burning*; and *Stop America's Atrocities*. Some of the protests were even turning violent. Frank soon began to find these rallies as an assault on the morale of American troops.

Not only were many young citizens protesting the war, but soon the burning of draft cards became commonplace at the rallies. This angered Frank, as well as many of his and the older generation. Also, it was not just citizens who were railing against Vietnam; celebrities and major newspapers were voicing their fierce opposition. But perhaps the biggest rallying cry of the times was in music. Anti-war songs like Country Joe's *I Feel Like I'm Fixin To Die Rag* with the chorus of "And it's one, two, three what are we fighting for? Don't ask me, I don't give a damn, next stop is Vietnam" became forever woven into the country's culture.

Escalating and intertwined with Vietnam and its protests was the civil rights movement. Many blacks were refusing to fight a "white man's war." Heavyweight champion Muhammad Ali refused to serve in the Army during the war, famously stating "I ain't got no quarrel with the Vietcong. No Vietcong ever called me a nigger." In 1966, the militant Black Panther Party was formed.

It was of course, also the time of the hippie revolution, with their mantras of "Make Love Not War" and "Drop Acid Not Bombs." Timothy Leary, psychologist and vocal advocate of LSD, famously told an entire nation to "Turn on, tune in and drop out." The hippies not only listened, but also took it to heart. They had their own music, long hair, open drug use, and swap-meet-like sex lives. It was in 1967, when the hippies would reach their zenith as throngs of them made the pilgrimage to Haight Ashbury for what would come to be known as The Summer of Love.

Frank never thought of himself as prude or close-minded. He enjoyed having drinks with the guys every now and then. Like some of his peers, he didn't mind rock music. In fact, he owned several Beatles and Elvis albums. He had no problem with boys growing their hair past their ears. But Frank did have a problem with guys growing hair down to their ass and looking like women. He certainly had a problem with the growing drug culture. Frank accepted that no matter the generation, youth were always going to rebel in their own way. But he also expected them to have respect. Frank looked at the hippies and saw the disintegration of morals, the imploding of society. Unlike his generation—and all the generations that came before—they had no work ethics. Many of them didn't work at all. They just gathered in parks and fields, smoked pot and took a smorgasbord of other drugs, and listened to music all day. They had no veneration for relationships, let alone marriage, openly flaunting having multiple partners, even orgies. And as Frank saw it, they had absolutely no allegiance to the country; in fact, they reviled it.

One Saturday in March, Frank was at his East Meadow store. Billy was also working that day and Frank decided to take him out to lunch. They went to a nearby diner. Frank said hello to the manager and a server that he knew from going there and then he and Billy grabbed a booth by the front.

"Thanks, Uncle Frank, I wasn't expecting this."

"It's okay," Frank replied with a smile. "You're a hard worker. I figured it'd be nice for us to grab some lunch and shoot the breeze."

Frank looked across the table at the sixteen-year-old he considered his own son. He was fit, with naturally broad shoulders and short, thick blonde hair. His cut chin and face looked like his father's, but his wide, bright hazel eyes resembled Dorothy's.

"So, you have any luck getting a date with Elizabeth?" Frank asked with a smirk.

Billy sighed and put down his menu. "I don't know, Uncle Frank. She's so beautiful. Every time I try to get up the nerve to ask her out, I get so nervous and stumble over my words. I feel like an idiot. Then finally, the other day after class, I went up to her and asked what she was doing Friday night. She said that it was her brother's birthday and she had to get home." Lowering his shoulders and head, Billy looked like a deflated balloon. "I think she was just sayin' that. I think she's just out of my league."

"Don't say that, Billy. You're a fine looking kid. You're smart, built, funny. You get along with everybody."

"Thanks, Uncle Frank," he replied in a defeated voice. "But Elizabeth, she's like…she's one of the prettiest, most popular girls in school."

Frank crossed his arms. "Yet she doesn't have a boyfriend."

Billy looked up at Frank and thought about it for a second. "I don't think she has a boyfriend, but maybe she does. How can she not?"

Frank smiled. "Billy, she's a teenager in high school. If she was going with someone you and everybody else in school would know about it." Billy nodded.

"Well, what did she say when you asked her about Friday? She just said she had to be home for her brother's birthday and then just walked away?"

"Well, she said it was her brother's birthday and she had to be home and then two of her friends walked up and started talking to her. I just said I'd see her later and walked away."

Frank leaned forward across the table. "So maybe it was her brother's birthday. For all you know, she was going to tell you that she could do something on Saturday, but you walked away. You have to ask her out again."

"Oh, I don't know Uncle Frank. I—"

"Listen, girls love confidence and they can sense if a boy or a man is confident. You have to walk up to her with your head held high and ask her out on a date. And be specific, like 'would you like to go out with me Friday night to see a movie?' And if she says she has something to do that night ask her about Saturday night."

Just then their attention was taken away by a ruckus a few

booths over. A waiter and manager were arguing with three young hippies sitting at the table. It appeared to be a dispute over the bill.

"Look at those guys," Billy said with disgust. "Look how long their hair is. They look like they haven't showered in weeks."

The argument quickly became more heated and now everyone else in the diner was looking over.

"You wait here," Frank said to Billy in a stone-cold voice as he stood up. But just as he did, the three hippies also got up and the manager announced to the customers that everything was okay.

On their way out, one of the young men muttered something about the manager being a fascist. Frank took a few steps towards the man, but was intercepted by the manager. "It's okay, Frank," he said in a calm voice. "It's not worth it. Just let 'em go."

Frank sat back down. Billy smiled.

"Uncle Frank, you were gonna kick their butts."

"No."

"Yes you were. I've never seen you so mad. I don't blame you. Those hippies are a cancer on society."

Frank looked across at Billy, who seemed years beyond his age of sixteen. "Just promise me that you and Tommy are never going to turn out like that."

"No way. I like not smelling or looking like a girl. And only losers do drugs." Billy paused. "And what kind of person badmouths his own country? You don't ever have to worry about me turnin' into some hippie…or Tommy."

Frank smiled. "You're a good kid, Billy. A real good kid."


One of the things Frank had looked forward to once Thomas grew up was teaching him how to drive. Now, he was finally old enough. Before the first lesson, Frank promised himself not to be too aggressive or lose his patients. But there was no need; Thomas turned out to be a quick learner.

When Thomas passed the test and received his license, Frank was excited for him. It had now become a rite of passage for a boy to be able to drive. Also, Thomas could now borrow one of the cars to take out his new girlfriend, Alice.

Alice Bouldin was an attractive sixteen-year-old who Thomas had met in his English class. She had thick, long blonde hair and big, brown eyes. Both Frank and Mary approved of her. She was polite, but at the same time had a warm, outgoing personality.

Billy had taken Frank's advice and asked Elizabeth out again. She accepted and before long the two were going steady. Though Elizabeth and Alice had not really known each other before, Billy and Thomas introduced them and soon the four began going out on double dates. For Frank and Bob, it naturally brought back memories.

In early April, the Kellers sat down together for dinner as they did every weeknight.

"So Dad, we were talking in school today about Martin Luther King's speech about Vietnam the other day."

"Well son, you know I've always had respect for King," Frank replied as he scooped some mashed potatoes onto his plate. He then looked up, across the table at Thomas. "But he's way out of line on this one. From what I read of the speech, he's basically taking sides with the communists and saying we're the bad guys. I couldn't believe what I was reading."

"Yeah, it really portrays America in a bad light," Thomas said.

"I want to read it," Eileen enthusiastically chimed in. "Do you have a copy?" She asked her brother.

Thomas thought about it for a second. "Yeah, Mr. Phelps handed out copies of it so we could discuss it. But you don't want to read it—it's pretty long. Besides, it's just him blasting America and what we're doing over in Vietnam."

"I do want to read it," Eileen shot back. "Besides, I agree with him. What's happening in Vietnam is wrong."

Frank and Mary looked at each other and then back at their daughter.

"What do you know about what's going on in Vietnam?" Asked Thomas.

"I know that we're bombing entire villages and killing civilians."

Mary gasped. "Who told you that? Is that what they're teaching you in school? Frank."

"I'm not ten-years-old Mom; I'll be fifteen in June. I'll be a sophomore next year. I'm old enough to know and understand what's going on in the world. I mean you and Dad are the ones that've always told me I need to know what's going on. Ever since I can remember you guys have been talking to me about current affairs."

Frank looked at Mary and then back at his daughter. "Yes, I know Eileen. And it is very important that you understand what's going on in the world. But we're not sending you to school so they can fill your head up with liberal, hippie propaganda."

"I don't understand, Dad. You've said yourself that you were against the war."

Frank took a moment to gather his thoughts. "There's a difference between being against the war and calling our brave men fighting over there murderers." Frank paused. "Believe me honey, I don't like war anymore than you do. But if we didn't have brave young men like the ones that are fighting over in Vietnam, willing to risk their own lives, then we wouldn't have all the freedoms that we have now. If it wasn't for our military we would have been taken over a long time ago."

"If it wasn't for brave men like your father," Mary said as she put her hand on Frank's forearm, "the Nazis would've taken over the world and who knows how many more millions of people would have been slaughtered or sent to the gas chambers."

"I know. And I appreciate that. But this isn't Hitler and the Nazis."

Mary looked at her daughter. "Communism is every bit as evil as Nazism," she said in a calm, but strong voice. "That's what all these protesters don't understand—we're trying to help the South Vietnamese, save them from communism. We're trying to save the whole world from the spread of communism."

That June, Eileen turned fifteen. Frank knew what to say or how to act when Thomas grew older, what advice to give him. He knew how to handle the problems of being a teenage boy. But Eileen was a different story. Frank had never been a teenage girl. He and Eileen had always been very close and he wanted to make sure that continued. So he set aside time for just the two of them to hang out together, even if it was once a week or once every two weeks. Sometimes they would go out for lunch on a weekend, go to the park, or go to the movies.

Eileen loved her father and knew how hard he was trying to maintain their relationship. But if both parents are around, a girl's bond naturally slips more towards her mother as she gets older. There are just some things that a teenage girl feels more comfortable doing and talking about with her mother, like going clothes shopping or discussing her development. Still, Eileen appreciated and enjoyed the time she spent with her father.

Eileen had always been a well-behaved child and always did well in school. But she was now fifteen. Certain frictions did arise and not uncommonly, it mostly had to do with boys. She was head-over-heels for a boy in her class, but her parents told her she was too young to date. Mary and Frank agreed on this point, but it was Frank that took the brunt of being the "bad one." Eileen would give the standard teenage "it's not fair."

"I'm sorry Pumpkin, but fifteen is just too young."

"You have to stop treating me like I'm a little kid," she demanded. "You still think I'm ten! I mean you still call me Pumpkin. I'm too old for that, Dad! Like it or not, I'm growing up—and you can't do anything about it."

Eileen was fifteen and her parents could still lay down the law and give her rules to follow and dish out the appropriate punishment if she disobeyed. But she was right about one thing: Neither Mary nor Frank could stop her from growing up. On one hand, Frank was sure that Eileen would grow into a wonderful woman and looked forward to the day she would find a loving husband and start a family of her own. On the other hand, just the thought of his daughter with someone of the opposite sex made his blood boil. Eventually, Eileen would be able to date and against Frank's wishful thinking, it would be before she turned twenty. Frank was conflicted between the hope that she would be her own person and the fatherly instinct that wanted to keep her his little girl.

During the last week of August 1967, Eileen entered her sophomore year in high school, and Thomas, his senior. Neither Mary nor Frank could believe how fast time had gone. In May, Thomas would turn eighteen and a month later, graduate. Though they would have preferred time to have slowed, the proud parents were thankful that both their children had turned into well-behaved, courteous, bright, and healthy teenagers. Both Eileen and Thomas did well in school and stayed out of trouble. In fact, the time Thomas stood up for his sister and wound up getting into a fight was the only incident the school called home for either of them. Like Frank, Mary looked at the hippie movement spreading across the nation and thought: *Thank God my son didn't turn out like that.*

That Christmas, of 1967, the Kellers insulated themselves from the turbulence of the outside world. They had each other, they had their health, and they had good fortune. It was a time to pause from the daily grind, pray for an end of the division and strife that was encompassing the nation and beyond, but also to realize and be grateful for what they had. And it was a cheerful occasion. Mary's parents came over for Christmas dinner. Bob, Dorothy, and the kids stopped by to exchange presents. Thomas' girlfriend, Alice, came by for a while.

After everyone else left, Mary and Frank snuggled on the couch in front of the crackling fireplace. The voices of Thomas and Eileen, playfully horsing around with each other in the other room carried through the house.

"It was a good Christmas," Mary said in a fading voice as she laid her head on her husband's shoulder.

Frank smiled. "Yes. Yes it was."

Neither of them could have imagined at the time that it would be the last Christmas the four of them would ever spend together.

# 24

# LIKE FATHER,
# LIKE SON

The Lunar New Year has always been a sacred holiday for the people of Vietnam. And ever since America's military involvement, there had always been an unspoken truce, or little fighting, during the several-days-long celebration. But on January 31, 1968, during the first day of the New Year, or Tet, the Vietcong and North Vietnamese Army launched a massive surprise attack, simultaneously hitting multiple American and South Vietnamese targets. Although the communists did not achieve their initial objective of completely overrunning the South Vietnamese and American positions, the prolonged and now infamous "Tet Offensive" would mark a tangible turning point in the war. In some locations, American television news crews observed the battles and their aftermaths and although initially labeled a failure for the communists, grim and disturbing images were broadcast back home. Furthermore, because of the Tet Offensive, General Westmoreland would soon request an additional 200,000 U.S. troops and an activation of the reserves.

On the evening of February 27th, the Kellers—like many families across America—sat down together to watch Walter Cronkite on the CBS news. Unlike today, there was no CNN, MSNBC, Fox News, or the Internet or blogs. In 1968, there was only three television networks: CBS, ABC, and NBC. As such, there was only a handful of news anchors. But no reporter was, or ever has been to this day, more revered than Walter Cronkite. For nearly two decades he acted not only as America's newsman, but its counselor. His credibility was beyond reproach. So when on February 27th Cronkite, freshly returned from Vietnam, laid out his assessment of the Tet Offensive, the entire nation tuned in. His now historic address was not what anyone wanted to hear. Of his broadcast that night it was three sentences that resonated the most with the American public:

*To say that we are closer to victory today is to believe, in the face of the evidence, the optimists who have been wrong in the past. To suggest we are on the edge of defeat is to yield to unreasonable pessimism. To say that we are mired in stalemate seems the only realistic, yet unsatisfactory, conclusion.*

That night, while lying in bed, Frank and Mary discussed Cronkite's assessment of the war, as well as their own opinions. For Frank, his worst fear had come true: Vietnam had turned into another Korea. Time would tell him that it would be even worse.

"Thomas is going to be eighteen in May," Mary said in a distressed voice, as she lay propped-up in bed, underneath the covers. "What if they initiate the lottery and he's drafted?"

Frank turned and looked at his wife. "Don't even think like that."

"I'm just so sick of war," Mary lamented.

Frank let out a deep sigh. "Me too."

"Hopefully, Kennedy will wind up running for president and be elected and stop the war."

It was widely speculated that Robert F. Kennedy, then a senator from New York, would seek and win the Democratic Party's nomination for president, over sitting President Johnson. Though it was under his late brother's watch that America became entangled in Vietnam, Kennedy had become a strongly outspoken critic of the war. Many believed that if elected he would put a quick end to the already long and bloody conflict.

Frank chewed on his wife's words. "Yeah, I think he will run. And I think he will win—and get us out of Vietnam. Johnson sure doesn't sound like he has any plans to."

Regardless of who the Republican candidate turned out to be, Frank knew he would vote for Kennedy in the general election if he wound up winning the primary. Frank wanted out of Vietnam as soon as possible. But there was another factor that endeared him, and many others, to young Bobby Kennedy. He reminded them of his brother—and John F. Kennedy, almost regardless of his politics, reminded people of a simpler time, a more innocent and sound time. A time of promise.

A few weeks later, on March 16th, Robert Kennedy officially announced his bid for president. Then, at the end of the month, on March 31st, Lyndon Johnson shocked the nation by proclaiming that he would not seek, nor would he accept, his party's nomination for another term as President. There seemed little doubt now that Kennedy would win the necessary Democratic primaries. In a tumultuous sea of division, chaos, and strife, an island of hope appeared. Perhaps Kennedy could put an end to Vietnam and bring the country back together, as he promised. Unfortunately, he would never get a chance. The country was soon to plunge into even further contention and see perhaps its darkest days since the Civil War.

It was Thursday, April 4th. Frank had just arrived home from work when he heard the news: Martin Luther King Jr. had been struck down by an assassin's bullet. He went into the small liquor cabinet they used only for special occasions and poured a glass of scotch, which he took out to the backyard. There, under a cold and breezy April evening he sat alone at the patio table, sipping his drink. He didn't feel like talking to anyone, even Mary, who came outside but was politely waved away.

Staring aimlessly at the backdrop of a darkening sky, Frank thought not about King's recent Vietnam speech, but rather his historic *I Have A Dream* speech. Frank respected King as a man and what he had done—and was trying to do—for the civil rights movement. But that speech in particular had always held a special place in Frank's heart. So eloquently and powerfully put, it was about freedom, equality, and most of all, hope. Sipping his scotch, a biting breeze blowing in his face, Frank remembered reading that speech for the first time. He remembered feeling that the country was on the verge of a new greatness, that King's dream would indeed soon come to fruition. Now that dream, that greatness, seemed lost. Now the entire country seemed lost.

If Frank was disconcerted with the news of King's assassination he, along with millions of others, grew even more troubled by the events of the ensuing days and weeks. Early on signs pointed not to a lone, crazed gunman, but rather a conspiracy. A fingerprint on the rifle that was found, the signature for the boarding room where the sniper took his shot, and the registration of the supposed getaway car pointed to three different individuals. However, it would later be determined that it was all the same man, James Earl Ray, using aliases.

However, even if early evidence hadn't pointed to three separate individuals, many people, especially in the black community, were immediately convinced that their own government was involved in the silencing of King. Devastating riots broke out in several cities; stores and buildings burned. Clashes with police and even the National Guard exploded throughout the country.

That May 12, of 1968, was Thomas Keller's eighteenth birthday. The previous afternoon, he sat his parents and sister down at the kitchen table. Neither Frank nor Mary knew what it was about, but they did not have a good feeling. Their son had never before done such a thing. But the news was worse than they could have even imagined as Thomas announced to the family that he and Billy were enlisting in the Army as soon as Billy turned eighteen in July, with the hope of being sent to Vietnam. Frank and Mary were speechless. They could tell that this was no fleeting, teenage idea. Thomas was dead serious and had thought it out for a while. Frank had a flashback to when he sat down his parents and told them he was enlisting, but with very different feelings.

"You can't go," Mary finally blurted out, breaking the tension-filled silence.

"What do you mean I can't go? I'll be eighteen tomorrow and I'll be out of high school. I know this isn't what you want to hear, but you can't stop me."

Frank stood up from the table. "Listen son," he said, trying to maintain a calm voice, "we're asking you, please think about what you're doing."

"I have. And I've made up my mind—and I'm not going to change it."

The fact that Frank could not stop his son frustrated him to no end. He could not help himself from yelling. "Dammit Tommy, you had talked about going to college after school. Why the hell would you want to join the Army to fight some war in a place you've never heard about five years ago?"

Thomas stood up to his father, looking him square in the eyes. "Why did you join the Army during the war, Dad?"

"Because the Japanese attacked Pearl Harbor," he replied without hesitation.

"So if the Japs would've never attacked us you wouldn't have joined the military? You would've stood by as Hitler and the Nazis swallowed Europe and tried to take over the whole world. You would've kept standing by as the Nazis killed millions of innocent people?"

Frank let out a deep breath. He knew that Thomas was just trying to do the right thing. "Son, Ho Chi Minh might be a bad guy, but he's not Hitler," he said in a subdued tone. "And the North Vietnamese are not going to take over the world."

Thomas shook his head. "So Ho Chi Minh has to kill as many people as Hitler?" He said in a slow, but deliberate voice. "How many people have to be killed before it's an atrocity? And the communists aren't trying to take over the world? You taught me better than that, Dad."

As Frank tried to find a response and Mary sat at the table, her head in her hands, Eileen stood up. "Tommy, you can't go to Vietnam. The Army is killing innocent people over there. Is that what you want to be a part of?"

This infuriated her brother. "You don't know what you're talking about! We're saving the South Vietnamese people from communism! Do you have any idea what communism is like?"

"Oh please, our government doesn't give a damn about the South Vietnamese!" Eileen shot back. "This war is an atrocity!"

"You watch what you're saying!" Frank intervened.

Eileen turned to her father. "What are you talking about, Dad? You don't agree with this war either. You were just telling Tom that it was wrong to go. You want him to help our government bomb villages and kill families?"

Now Mary finally sprung from the table. "How dare you!" She yelled at her daughter, in a tone she almost never used. "Is that what's on your mind? Is that what you're thinking about? You're more concerned with the Vietnamese than your own brother being injured or killed?"

"Mary!" Frank yelled.

"I'm not going to get killed, Mom." Thomas then turned back to his sister. "You should thank God every time you go to sleep for the U.S. military!"

Eileen got right into her older brother's face. "Are you kidding me? It's an atrocity what they're doing over there!"

Frank got between them. "You don't know what you're talking about! Who's feeding your head with this bullshit?"

"No one! I can think for myself!"

"Stop it!" Mary's scream rose above all others. "I can't take this anymore!" In tears, she stormed out of the kitchen.

Frank glared at Eileen. "Look what you did to your mother!"

Eileen's head looked as though it was going to explode.

"Aarrgghh!" Then she stormed out, finally exiting through the front door, towards who knew where.

That left Frank and Thomas. Frank took a deep breath and fought to compose himself. "Listen son," he said in calm voice as he put his hands on Thomas' shoulders, "please don't do this. For me…and your mother."

"Dad, I knew you wouldn't be happy about this, but at the same time, I figured you of all people would understand. I thought you would be proud of me." With that Thomas left the kitchen, leaving his father by himself.

Frank stood there, his head bowed towards the floor. Was this how his father felt when he told him about joining the Army, Frank wondered? Was this his payback, the wheels of fate coming full circle? There was no doubt that Vietnam was different than World War II, but his son held the same ideals as he had, over twenty years ago.


The next day was a Saturday and Thomas' birthday. The family had already planned a small party at the house that afternoon. As difficult as it was, they tried to enjoy the occasion. At least for the time, fences were mended. Eileen, though not backing off her strong and growing opposition for the war, apologized to her brother, saying that she loved him, and that she would be devastated if anything was to happen to him. Frank told Thomas that though he still did not want him to go, he was proud of him. Even Mary put on a forced smile.

Bob and Dorothy came over with Billy. As soon as they entered, a silent tension permeated through the house. At first, Billy thought about addressing the obvious, but then decided against it. However, after only a few minutes Frank and Bob went out back together to discuss their sons' decision. Both men were of the same mindset. They commended their sons' patriotism, but were dead-set against them enlisting to fight in Vietnam. Moreover, they saw little chance that Thomas or Billy would enlist and not be shipped to Southeast Asia.

Inside the house, in the kitchen, in low voices, Mary and Dorothy were having a similar conversation. Dorothy explained that she had been crying all night and morning and almost didn't come.

Soon a few other people stopped by the house and the two sets of parents tried to push their worry aside. It was, after all, supposed to be a celebration.


That next week, while Billy was working at the hardware store, he and the man he called Uncle Frank, finally talked one-on-one about the decision to enlist. Frank took Billy out to lunch and explained that it was very admirable what he and Thomas were doing, but tried to talk him out of it. It was to no avail. Though in an always-respectful manner, Billy stood his ground.

Frank and Mary also took Alice aside one evening when she came by the house and tried to get her to convince Thomas not to enlist. While Thomas was in the bedroom getting ready, Mary went as far as to suggest that Alice give him an ultimatum: If he enlisted, she would not be there waiting when he came back.

Alice was taken aback by the suggestion. "Mrs. Keller, I'm devastated about Thomas' decision. I can't even sleep at night, thinking about if he's shipped to Vietnam. But I just can't do that. I love Thomas and I want him to know that I will be here waiting for him when he gets back."

"You're right honey," Mary said with a sense of guilt. "I'm sorry. I should have never said such a thing." Mary could not help but think of when Frank went overseas. She could not imagine giving him such an ultimatum, whether she was serious or not.

As the days peeled off the calendar, Frank and Mary realized that there was no stopping Thomas from enlisting, and the only real hope that he would not wind up in Vietnam was if the war was to end, or at least no new troops be called upon. As they lay in bed on the night of June 4th, they agreed that the best chance of that happening was if Robert Kennedy was elected President that November.

The next morning, as Frank woke up to go to work the phone

rang. No one ever called that early. Curious, but not really worried, he picked it up.

It was Mary's mother. "Oh Frank, have you heard the news?"

Mrs. Capelli sounded like she was crying, and Frank immediately feared that something terrible had happened to Mary's father. "No, what is it?" He asked in an apprehensive voice.

"Turn on the TV. Robert Kennedy...he was assassinated."

Frank nearly dropped the phone. "What?"

"Kennedy, he's been killed," she repeated through tears. "It happened just after midnight, last night."

Frank felt as if all the blood had been drained from his body. "I've got to go. I'll have Mary call you later."

Just as Frank was hanging up the phone Mary groggily propped herself up in the bed. "Who was that?" She asked with a just-awoken voice. "What's going on?"

Frank looked at his wife, her innocent blue eyes fresh from a deep sleep, gazing back at him. Time seemed to stand still. He felt like telling her to go back to sleep, go back to the safety of a dream. "That..." It was hard for him to even say it. "That was your mother. She... she said..."

Now wide awake, Mary's tired face morphed into one of great concern. "What is it? Did something happen to my father?"

"No, she told me to turn on the TV. Bobby Kennedy's been assassinated."

That was the furthest thought from Mary's mind—and it hit her like a metal pipe in the face.

"Come on honey," Frank said as he took hold of her limp hand. "Lets go in the den and turn on the television." They did not have a TV set in their bedroom.

As Frank and Mary went out to the living room, they ran into Thomas, getting ready for school. He could tell right away by their ashen faces that something was wrong. "What? What is it?"

Just then Eileen came out of her bedroom, dressed and ready for a normal day of classes.

"We have to turn on the TV," Frank said in a solemn voice. "Your

Grandmother called to tell us that Robert Kennedy was assassinated late last night."

Thomas and Eileen were dumbstruck. Like their parents, they could not believe what they were hearing.

Frank turned on the television and the whole family stood in front of the set. It was a special news report. The unthinkable was true: Robert Francis Kennedy, age forty-two, had been murdered. Mary and Eileen stood there crying, tears streaming down their faces.

"The government wanted him dead," Eileen lamented. "Just like Martin Luther King. They knew he would be elected and get us out of Vietnam!"

Frank put his hand on Eileen's shoulder. "Honey, don't say that."

Eileen pushed her father's hand away and ran back into her bedroom to cry alone.

"I can't believe this," Thomas said. "What is going on in this country?"

Frank shook his head. "I don't know, Son. I don't know."

Thomas wound up going to school, though late. More than anything, he wanted to talk about what had happened with Alice and his friends. Eileen however, stayed home. Her parents were not going to make her go to school. She spent most of the morning locked in her room sobbing. She then planted herself in front of the television. But she was convinced it was a conspiracy, mainly to keep America in Vietnam.

After watching about a half hour of the news report, Frank and Mary went back in their bedroom. There, Mary fell into her husband's arms.

"Oh Frank, what is going on?" She cried into his shoulder. "First JFK, then King, now Bobby. Who's next? Is the whole world going to hell?"

Frank caressed Mary's hair. "I don't know. I don't know what the hell is going on." He wished that he could tell her that everything was going to be all right, but in light of recent events who would believe that?

As Frank continued to console Mary, his own mind wandered down a dark, dolorous corridor. Kennedy's assassination went beyond his hopes of an end to the Vietnam War. It was another, perhaps the final nail in the coffin of humanity and innocence. It was not just Robert Kennedy's assassination, or King's assassination, or Vietnam, or the race riots. It was all of those things. Starting with the murder of John F. Kennedy, it seemed an evanescence of the very fabric of the United States. However, with the spread of communism, the Cold War and the threat of nuclear annihilation always overhead, swinging like the Sword of Damocles, not only America, but the entire world appeared to be plunging into twilight. Was this the end of days, Frank wondered?

That evening, Frank and Mary took the kids to church to pray for Robert Kennedy, his family, the nation, and the entire world. They were far from alone. Across the country that night people, some who had never even been to church, prayed to God to bring them out of the chaos—and show them that there was still hope.

# 25

# 1<sup>ST</sup> CAVALRY

Towards the end of June, Thomas and Billy graduated high school. It was only fitting that they celebrated together. The following day, which was a Saturday, Bob and Dorothy threw a party at their house. It was a warm, sun-soaked June day, perfect for a barbecue. The backyard was packed with smiling faces. Bob's parents were there as was Dorothy's father. Her mother had passed away several years earlier. Mary's parents were also in attendance. There was extended family as well as plenty of friends of both sets of parents and graduates. People were laughing and conversing, eating and drinking. Thomas' and Billy's girlfriends were joking around with each other. But behind it all was a well-hidden trepidation. Thomas and Billy were still adamant about enlisting the day Billy turned eighteen.

By now everyone in attendance, family and friends alike, knew of the boys' intentions. No one wanted to see them go through with it. But everyone realized that it was now basically etched in stone; they were going to join the Army and more than likely end up in Vietnam. However, for at least one day, everyone put aside their concerns. Thomas and Billy had graduated high school and with excellent grades. It was time to brush everything that was going on in the world under the rug and celebrate.

With only one week left until Billy turned eighteen and he and Thomas enlisted, Frank took his son out, just the two of them. The drinking age was still eighteen and although Frank had never seen his son drink, let alone share a beer with him, he decided to take him to a neighborhood tavern. Not wanting to be disturbed by anyone that he might know, Frank picked a table in the corner and ordered two Schaefers.

Thomas squirmed in his seat. Though glad to spend time alone with his father, he was also a bit uncomfortable. "This is kinda strange, huh?" He said with a half-smile. "I mean I know I'm eighteen, but it just feels weird having a beer with my father."

Just then the server came by and placed two cold bottles on the table. Frank thanked him and he went off to the next table.

"Well, you shouldn't feel weird. You're a man now. You're old enough to go off to war, you're old enough to have a beer with your Old Man." Frank grabbed his bottle as Thomas took hold of his. "Now you sure I can't talk you out of enlisting?"

A look of disappointment grew on Thomas' face. "Dad, if you brought me here for that… I told you before…"

Frank put up his hand. "Whoa, whoa, whoa. Relax. I just figured I'd try one last time." With his elbow still on the table, Frank raised his beer. "Listen Tommy, this may not be what your mother and I wanted for you, but I want you to know…and this is important…that I'm proud of you. We're both proud of you."

Thomas smiled. "Thanks Dad, that means a lot to me."

Frank raised his bottle even higher. "So here's to you joining the Army, becoming the best damn soldier they've ever seen, and returning home safely."

With that, the father and son clanked their beers and then took a drink.

"So, did Grandpa have a drink with you before you enlisted?"

Frank laughed and then took another chug. "Well, right after I finished basic training. The same thing—I had never had a drink before with my old man. But he knew I was on my way to Europe. He took me to this bar by the base and we got drunk together." As the words left his mouth, Frank re-lived the memory as if it was yesterday. *God, was it really twenty-six years ago?*

"Hey just think, with me it'll be three straight generations of Kellers joining the military."

Frank gave a half-smile. "Well, no one could ever call us unpatriotic."

The father and son stayed in the bar for another two hours. They talked a lot about basic training. Thomas asked what it would be like and Frank told him what to expect. Trying to keep the conversation light, Frank told him some funny stories. They also talked about Alice, Billy and Elizabeth, and even some baseball.

Thomas had consumed alcohol only a few times before and after a barrage of continuous rounds of beer he was inebriated. Though Frank was nowhere near as drunk as his son, he did have a heavy buzz going. But that did not stop him from driving them home. Fortunately, they made it home without incident.

It was just after 10:00 p.m. and Mary was awake, watching television in the living room when Frank and Thomas stumbled in the front door. Mary knew Frank was taking their son to the bar. She did not approve at first, but then thought that it would be a good bonding experience. But when she saw Thomas drunk out of his mind, being propped up by Frank she was livid.

"Hey Mom!" Her son said with a crooked smile, waving wildly at her.

"Look at him!" She blasted her husband. "He can't even stand up on his own."

"Relax, he's fine."

Suddenly Thomas' cheeks puffed up and he put his hand over his mouth. "I think I'm gonna be sick."

Frank and Mary quickly took their son into the bathroom and just in the nick of time. As soon as his head was over the toilet he began to throw up.

Eileen, who had been in her room, came to see what was going on. "Oh gross!" She looked as though she was ready to vomit. "What's wrong with him?"

"He's drunk," Mary replied in an incensed voice. "Just go back in your room."

Once Thomas was done his parents put him to bed. Then, in the confines of their bedroom, Mary read her husband the riot act. "Is this the kind of example you want to set? Why couldn't you two have just gone out to dinner together? Why'd you have to sit at a bar until he couldn't even stand? Why'd you let him get so drunk? And now Eileen had to see this! What if she thinks it's okay to start drinking?"

Frank was trying not to laugh. He would never mock Mary, but perhaps because of the alcohol, he found the whole ordeal funny.

"I'm sorry. I guess we got carried away. But it's tradition. My father took me out to get drunk after I graduated from basic training. In fact after I left him, I snuck into your hotel room and spent the night—remember? Besides, he's eighteen, he's allowed to drink."

Mary didn't even hear his last sentence. Suddenly she was remembering vividly that night so long ago—and she could not help but smile about it.

"What are you smiling about? Wait," Frank said with a grin of his own, "you're thinking about that night you came up and saw me with my folks. You know, that was the last time I had sex for a long, long time."

"Well me too," Mary replied with a stern look. "You know you're the only man I've ever been with."

"And you're the only woman I've been with. You're too sexy and good in bed. It'd all be downhill from you."

Mary adorned an even wider smile. "Frank Keller, that is so sweet." She then picked up a pillow and hit him with it. "But I'm still mad at you." However, she was not. The steam had all been let out. "So what did you two talk about?" She asked calmly.

"It was great," Frank replied before detailing the conversation.

A week later, on July 17th, Billy Davenport's eighteenth birthday, he and Thomas enlisted in the United States Army. Then, in late August, in seemingly a blink of an eye, the day came for them to leave for basic training. The Keller and Davenport families drove Billy and Thomas to John F. Kennedy International Airport, where they were to board a plane to Fort Hood, in Texas.

Frank and Mary tried to put on a strong front for their son, but inside their hearts were breaking and minds unable to focus. Once inside the airport, by the gate—back in a time before only ticketed passengers were allowed past security checkpoints—they were surrounded by other families saying farewell to their loved ones. Mary looked around at the recruits and realized that just like her son, they were all still only children, none looking more than twenty-one-years-old. She then wondered how many of them would wind up in Vietnam and never make it back home. She hoped and prayed with every fiber of her being that Thomas would not be one of them. She wished her son the best and told him she loved him. Thomas reciprocated as they locked into a tight embrace. Mary promised herself that she would not cry, but could not help it. But even with tears escaping from her eyes, she smiled.

Frank felt a surreal sense of deja vu. Only this *had* happened before, though he had been in Thomas' shoes and his father in his. After all the years Frank finally truly understood just how his father must have felt that long-ago day when he went off to basic training, destined to fight in World War II. Sure, it was a different kind of war, with different circumstances. But battle was battle. The risk of being wounded or even killed was the same.

Like his father had done, Frank remained stalwart for his son. He shook his hand then gave him a hug. "Make sure you write. Let me know how it's going. And just do everything your drill sergeant tells you to do."

"I will," Thomas replied with a smile. "Thanks for everything, Dad."

Frank put his hand on Thomas' shoulder. "You take care of yourself son, you hear." With that, the two hugged again. "I love you, Son," Frank whispered in his ear.

"I love you too, Dad."

Next it was Eileen's turn to say goodbye. She threw her arms around her older brother, her head coming up to his chest. "Take care of yourself," she said as the tears started to flow. "I'm going to miss you."

Eileen did not agree with the war in Vietnam, nor did she agree with her brother's desire to take part in that war. But Thomas was her brother and the two had always been close. Thomas had always looked out for her and she did love him with all of her heart. In fact, as she stood there in the airport, just the thought of something happening to him was almost too much to take.

Thomas stroked his sister's hair. "I'm gonna miss you, too. But don't you worry about me, I'll be all right." As the two relinquished their embrace, Thomas wiped a streak of tears from Eileen's cheek. "You look after Mom and Dad—and stay away from those boys," he said with a smile.

Next, Alice, who had gone with the family to the airport, said goodbye to her boyfriend. It was difficult for her to let Thomas go and it was hard for him to leave. They were teenagers in love and assumed that they would always be together. They had not spent more than a few days apart since first dating. Still, it was one thing to be separated for a couple of months while Thomas went through basic training; but like everyone else gathered around that morning, Alice felt certain in her heart that right after graduation he would be shipped off to Vietnam.

As Alice said goodbye to Thomas, Frank went over and wished good luck to Billy. After all, both he and Mary thought of him as their own son. They had been caught up worrying and praying for Thomas, but Billy also weighed heavy on their hearts and minds. It was the same with Bob and Dorothy and Thomas. They were all one big family.

"You take care of yourself, you hear. And you and Tommy take care of each other." Frank remembered his father telling Bob very much the same thing.

"I will, Uncle Frank. I will."

Mary also said farewell to Billy, and Bob and Dorothy did the same with Thomas.

Both families and Alice and Elizabeth watched as the plane tax-ied down the runway and lifted off into the great, blue sky. More tears were shed. It was not the fact of going off to basic training that weighed on them—it was what waited afterwards.


Two days later, Eileen started her junior year in high school. Though there was a palpable absence in the house, Frank and Mary had agreed that they did not want Eileen to feel as if all their thoughts and energy were solely on Thomas. "We have a daughter, too and she's right here, and she needs our attention," Mary put it. "This is a very important time for a girl of her age."

Frank agreed, but was almost insulted that Mary even brought it up. Of course, this did not mean that they never discussed their son. Once in a while they would receive a letter from Thomas. Ei-leen was always eager to hear from her brother as well, so when-ever a letter was received from him Frank would read it aloud to them. Thomas, who had been assigned to the Army's 1st Cavalry, joked about his experiences in basic training, wrote about the people he had met, how Billy was doing, and always asked about things back home.

A few times Eileen and Thomas had exchanged their own, pri-vate letters. They were always short and lighthearted, but it meant a great deal to both of them. While he was in basic training, Eileen, who was growing even more disenchanted with the war, had completely separated her brother from Vietnam.

Even in the most tumultuous of times, the world inevitably ro-tates and life goes on. Frank was busy running his business. Eileen pleaded with her parents to let her go out with a new boy she was interested in. Mary argued to Frank on her behalf. Eileen also start-ed nagging her parents about learning how to drive and getting her learner's permit. As often happens, a week turns into a month and a month into two, almost unnoticed. Soon, the cornucopia of trees in Long Island had gone bare and the long, cold was settling in. The changing of the season would bring with it no miracles, especially with respect to the war. By year's end Thomas and Billy would be in Vietnam.

# 26

# THE DOWNWARD
# SPIRAL

On January 20, 1969, Richard M. Nixon, who had won the election, was inaugurated as the thirty-seventh President of the United States. With respect to Vietnam, he campaigned on a promise of "peace with honor," though no one could quite understand exactly what that meant.

Before month's end peace talks opened in Paris among the United States, South Vietnam, North Vietnam, and the Viet Cong. At first, many people were guardedly optimistic. But that thinly held optimism soon crumbled when in late February communists attacked 110 targets throughout South Vietnam, including Saigon. The television footage and printed reports and photographs told that the war was as deadly and volatile as ever. In fact, U.S. troop levels in Vietnam would soon peak at over 500,000, with over 33,000 American casualties—and growing.

With their sons in Vietnam, Mary and Dorothy turned to each other for support. Not a day went by when they didn't talk, and more often than not they did so in person. Likewise, Frank had Bob confided in each other; not only were they best friends, but they had also been through war together. They knew what it was like, knew the nightmarish truth of being in combat. But Frank, consumed with the thought of Thomas mired in the jungles of Vietnam, and being shot at from every direction, also started to turn to the bottle. He had never been a big drinker, but that was about to quickly change. In fact, Frank was about to begin a crapulous journey into the abyss.

As Frank began to spend more and more time at the bar, he started neglecting his business, just going into the stores from time to time to check in, sometimes while drunk. Fortunately, Frank had a good, trustworthy manager taking care of the Levittown store and still had Walter Rubenstein, who was now capably managing the other two locations.

Walter, who had now worked for Frank for some time, offered to buy all three stores from his boss for $275,000. He and his brother pooled enough money and could get a loan for the rest. Walter certainly knew enough about the business.

Frank immediately and vehemently turned down the offer. "This business is for my son!" Frank shouted. "You hear me? He can do whatever he wants to do, be a doctor, a lawyer, the President of the United States," he drunkenly ranted. "But when he comes back from Vietnam, Harold and Son will be here for him if he wants to take it over. This is his birthright! So don't you ever bring it up again! This isn't for you to take or buy! You Jews can't have everything!"

The two men would never look at each other, or treat each other, the same way again. Frank had felt like firing Walter for even making the offer, but thought the better of it. Especially since he was spending less and less time at the stores, he needed Walter. As for Walter, feeling disrespected and sure he could make more money somewhere else, he wanted to quit. However, his brother talked him out of it, saying that Frank was in a downward spiral and it was only a matter of time before he lost all control and had to sell the business. Besides, he said, there was a good chance that Thomas wouldn't make it home from Vietnam.

Walter scolded his brother, telling him not to say such a thing about "the boy." He also disagreed with his brother, insisting that even if Thomas had no desire to take over his father's business, Frank would never sell the stores. Even if he did, Walter argued, he would find another suitor. However, after much debate, Walter told his brother that he would stay managing the stores for the time being.

Mary grew concerned about her husband. She would smell the alcohol on his breath when he came home from "work." Sometimes he outwardly acted drunk, stumbling around the house and slurring his words. In addition, Frank would think nothing of having a few beers or even a glass of whiskey before dinner or late at night. In the past he had drank only at home once in a blue moon. At first, she thought it was the initial news of Thomas' deployment to Vietnam that drove him to drink and it would soon pass. But after a few weeks Frank was drinking more and more, so she confronted him about it.

"Listen Frank, I know that Thomas being sent to Vietnam is stressful on all of us," Mary said one Friday evening when Eileen was out of the house. "But I'm really concerned about your drinking. It's not like you, drinking during the week, coming home from work with alcohol on your breath."

Frank had just arrived home from the bar, though Mary thought he had been at work. A lecture on drinking was the last thing he wanted to hear. "It's nothing for you to worry about." He waved his wife off, trying not to make eye contact. "It's no big deal. Sometimes I have a few beers at lunch. It's not like I need to be at the stores every minute. Everything is just fine."

"I'm not stupid Frank," she said in a louder, sterner voice. "It's not just a few beers at lunch. You've been coming home drunk—and then drinking at home almost every night. You think that sets a good example for our daughter? You think it's good for her to see her father drunk all the time?"

Feeling backed into a corner, Frank snapped. "What do you want from me? Last time I checked, I was the one working to pay for the nice house we live in, the food we eat, the car that you drive!" Frank was looking straight into his wife's eyes. "I put this business together all by myself and turned it into a cash cow. So if I want to have a few drinks now and then, I think I deserve it. So why don't you just get off my back!"

Mary was shocked, furious, troubled, and hurt. Unable to put into words how she was feeling, she just stood there and started to cry.

It immediately hit Frank like a hundred-pound weight of guilt. "I'm sorry," he said, putting his hand on her hair.

Mary pushed away his hand. "Just get away from me," she lashed-out, before scampering out of the room, still crying.

For a while after that confrontation, Frank didn't slow down his drinking, but tried to conceal it better. Before coming home he would chew on breath mints. He also scaled back his drinking at home, although he now went out more. Mary was not buying it, but she tried to avoid any further conflicts. However, once in a while it was unavoidable.

Mary was concerned about her husband, but she was also mad at him. She had always appreciated Frank's hard work and the good life he had provided for her and the kids. But now it seemed as if he was holding it against her, using it as leverage and made it appear that what she did was unimportant and without any hardship. Mary was also mad because Thomas was her son, too. Him being in Vietnam was agonizing for her as well, but she did not turn to alcohol. Furthermore, she felt as though Frank was not there for her, to help her through this difficult time. They should have been able to lean on each other.

Some days, however, Mary thought that she was being too hard on Frank. After all, where would she be without him? Everything he had ever done, he had done for her and the family. Also, although Thomas being in Vietnam had not drove her to drink, she did not have the added stress of running a business. She also had never been in combat; she didn't know what it was truly like.

But even if some days were better than others, there was an omnipresent strain on their marriage that had never before been there.

Fortunately, Mary always had Dorothy to confide in. She never held anything back from her friend and Frank's habitual drinking was certainly no exception. However, Mary made Dorothy promise not to say anything to Bob. He knew that if Bob confronted Frank about it he would know where it had come from and all hell would break loose.

As for Bob, he too was dealing with his son being in Vietnam, but although it weighed heavily and constantly on his mind, he did not take the same path as Frank. He also didn't know how deep his friend was getting, because they usually didn't see each other during the week. When they did see each other, it had never been unusual for them to knock down some beers together.

Frank had lost his luster. He was rarely happy anymore and always on edge. The only time he was in high spirits was when a letter arrived from Thomas. Of course, the whole family looked forward to his letters. The first since he had been deployed came three weeks after he had landed in Vietnam. Frank, Mary, and Eileen gathered around the kitchen table as Mary read it out loud.

*Dear Dad, Mom and Eileen,*

*I hope everyone is doing well. Sorry it took so long for me to write once I got to Vietnam, but I am fine. I am somewhere in Saigon, but as you probably already know, I can't say exactly where. The funny thing is that Vietnam, or at least what I've seen of it so far, is really a beautiful country. Too many mosquitoes and other nasty bugs, but the countryside is carved with wide hills and valleys and lush with dense green. Other areas are sprawling with vast rice fields. Even the town by us seems exotic, like a different world.*

*Perhaps I would have a different view of the jungle if I was trekking through it. But I am not. I've actually been assigned to be a helicopter door gunner. It's really neat. I couldn't have asked for a better post. Not only do I get to see much of Saigon and other places from above, but also our main mission is to serve as ground support and even rescue at times the troops down below. It really makes me feel like I'm making a contribution. Unfortunately, Bob was assigned to a different unit so I haven't seen him. But I'm sure he's doing fine.*

*The guys in my outfit and base are good people. They're from all over America. I even met one fellow from Arizona. Anyway, please don't worry about me. I'm in good hands. But I do miss you all dearly.*

*Your loving son and brother,*

*Thomas*

Even though Frank found pleasure in receiving his son's letters, almost immediately after reading the joy would disappear and Frank would go into a depression. He was always reading between the lines and imagining what his son was not saying. Even with Thomas' first letter, Frank knew that being a helicopter gunner meant his son would be seeing a lot of action, flying into extreme hotspots. Then the letters, though still innocuous, began being less cheery. Frank thought back to when he sent letters home; he would never write how things really were, so as not to alarm his parents or Mary. Frank never fought in a jungle or rode in a helicopter, but he sure as hell knew the horrors of war. He knew the gruesome sights Thomas was witnessing, the fear he was feeling, the death that was never further than a few feet away.

One Friday evening in late May, Frank and Bob decided to make a long-overdue trip to the veterans hall. For no reason other than the passage of time, they had not been there in several years. On the short ride there, the two best friends talked about their respective sons' letters. Frank was always thinking of Billy, and Bob of Thomas.

In the past, the hall would be bustling on a Friday night. But many of the old-timers had stopped coming—Frank and Bob included. Of course, some of them had been replaced by newer faces, veterans of Korea and even Vietnam. Frank and Bob were surprised to see only a handful of men there, mostly by the small bar.

However, they did run into two familiar faces. One of them was an ex-paratrooper, Wally Polinski, and he was talking to a young man in an Army-green uniform with crutches and his left leg missing below its knee. Wally and the other old-timer were excited to see Frank and Bob. The men greeted each other with handshakes and smiles and said how long it had been.

"Frank, Bob, this is my son, Garrett," Wally proudly announced.

"Pleased to meet you," the tall, slender young man said in a strong voice, then shook hands all around.

"Garrett here just got back from Vietnam last week."

Both Frank's and Bob's stomachs sank below their feet. Each man looked at Garrett's amputated lower leg and wondered: *Is this is what's going to happen to my son?*

It felt like a minute had passed as Bob just stared at Garrett.

"My son Billy is in Vietnam right now," he finally said, breaking the heavy silence. "So is Frank's boy."

The look on Wally's and his son's faces immediately changed. Garrett suddenly seemed at a loss for words.

Eventually, the five of them ponied up by the bar and shared some drinks. Frank and Bob asked about what it was really like in Vietnam, even though they had seen endless news footage, and were also afraid of the answer. Knowing that their sons were there, Garrett tiptoed around every question, giving them some information but either avoiding the gory details or evading the truth all together. He knew by now that both men had landed at Normandy and were well aware of the brutality of combat, but he was not about to start talking about seeing his buddy's decapitated body, witnessing his sergeant step on a landmine, the burnt corpses of children, or women blowing themselves up as suicide bombers.

Frank did not need to meet Garrett that night in order to fear the worse about his son. But sometimes when he sat alone at the bar drowning in his drink, he would think about Garrett and envision opening the front door and seeing Thomas with one leg, or in a wheelchair, or without arms. Of course, he still also dreaded the worse. Every morning Frank wondered if this was going to be the day a messenger would bring that telegram telling him his had been killed. By now, Thomas was on his second tour of duty. Since his unit needed him, he stayed in Vietnam and gave up any brief leave home.

Frank continued his drinking and neglect of his business. Mary had seemingly thrown in the towel and rarely confronted her husband anymore, and there was always a sense of tension and negativity in the house. Then, on one Friday afternoon in late June, the combustible atmosphere ignited.

After stopping at the Levittown hardware store and then having several rounds of drinks at the local bar, Frank arrived home earlier than usual. It was just past two, but that had not stopped him from already being half-drunk. When he walked through the front door, Frank announced his arrival. There was no response. Thinking that Mary was out and Eileen had not yet come home from school, he figured he would pour himself another drink. But when he walked into the kitchen he found Mary sitting at the table with an open bottle of wine and an almost empty glass.

"Drinking wine in the afternoon?" He said, thinking it was odd, but not reading too much into it.

Mary lifted up her head, streaks of tears dried on her face.

Frank's heart stopped. "What's wrong? Did something happen? Did you get a letter or a phone call?"

"No Frank, nothing happened," she replied in a weary, slurred voice. "I just figured I might as well start drinking, too. Come, pull up a chair, have a glass of wine—though I don't think there's much left."

Frank didn't know how to respond. Clearly something was deeply bothering his wife. Apprehensively, he walked over and took a seat at the table. "Mary, what's going on? You don't just drink in the middle of the afternoon by yourself."

Out of nowhere Mary exploded. "What? You're the only one who can get drunk?" She yelled at the top of her lungs. She then sprang up from the seat and slapped away the wine glass, shattering it on the floor.

Frank was in shock.

"He's my son, too you know!"

Actually frightened, Frank stood up. "What are you talking about?" He moved closer to Mary.

"You think you're the only one that worries about him? You think you're the only one who stays up at night or lives with the fear of hearing that knock on the door? He's my son, too Frank! But while you're out getting wasted, I'm here at home taking care of Eileen, looking after the house, being the good mother and wife! Well no more, Frank! I can't take this anymore!"

Then suddenly, the anger ran away from her face, replaced by one of dread. Her eyes passed right through Frank and he immediately turned to see what she was looking at. Standing in the entrance to the kitchen was Eileen.

"Honey," Mary said in a trembling voice.

"Look at you two!" Eileen yelled, fighting back tears.

"Honey, I didn't mean...you know we love you so much...it's just..." Mary stuttered for words.

Eileen shook her head in disgust. "Look what this war has done to you! Now you can both be drunks. I don't need either of you."

"Don't you talk to us like that!" Frank shot back.

"Whatever!" With that Eileen scurried away.

"Wait, Eileen." Mary went to run after her.

Frank tried to stop Mary, taking hold of her arm. "Just let her go. She just needs time to cool down."

Mary shoved Frank's arm away and gave chase. However, it was to no avail. Eileen had run out the front door and was already halfway down the block. After watching her disappear into the distance, Mary walked back into the kitchen and collapsed into her husband's chest. "Oh Frank, what's happening to us?" She cried.

The following day Mary went to church by herself, without telling Frank. The family no longer went to Mass together, and it was Saturday, but Mary wanted to speak privately to Father Mallard, to explain her situation and ask for spiritual guidance. Father Mallard was not there, but a younger priest, whom she recognized, sat down wit her. At this point, as Mary explained, she just didn't know who else to turn to. A theme he had heard many times before, the priest said that God never turns his back on someone in need and though it sometimes seems that he is not there, he always is. He told her to pray and bring Frank and Eileen back with her so that he or Father Mallard could talk to all of them together.

"It is more important than ever, when times seem at their darkest, that you not lose your faith—as individuals and as a family. With God's help, and each other's love, you will get through this. But it's also important for everyone's voice to be heard, and I or Father Mallard will be here to help you through the process."

Mary had always been religious, a devoted Catholic, both ideologically and how she lived her life. And she was going to take the priest's advice. But she was skeptical that it would work.

Mary apprehensively approached Frank with the idea of the whole family going to the church for guidance. To her surprise he agreed. Frank's faith, once so strong and ingrained in his fiber, had been eroded the last couple of years. He agreed to go, not because he thought that some priest or even prayer could wave a magic wand, but rather to appease his wife. The fact was that Frank felt terrible about Mary's breakdown the previous day, as well as Eileen's witnessing it. Immediately afterwards, he started to think long and hard about the path he was on and how it was affecting his wife and teenage daughter.

Unbeknownst to her parents, Eileen had not only lost her faith but had become severally cynical of not only Catholicism, which she had been brought up on, but all religions. However, like her father, she agreed to go for the sake of trying to mend the deep wound that was infecting her family. She did want things to return to the way they had once been.

Frank, Mary, and Eileen met with Father Mallard twice. However, perhaps more than anything it was Frank's decision to cut back on his drinking that brought peace back to the Keller household. It was certainly no nirvana. They could not shield themselves from the seemingly unstoppable chaos of the outside world. Thomas being in Vietnam still weighed on them and there was still the occasional argument, mostly involving Eileen. But the atmosphere surrounding the family had ameliorated.


On July 20, 1969, Frank, Mary, and Eileen, along with the rest of the nation, huddled around the television set to witness history. Even two decades earlier, thought the idea of pure science fiction, Apollo 11 was about to land on the moon. For one afternoon, at least in the living rooms of millions of households across America, there was no Vietnam, no protests, no riots.

On the same couch, Frank, Mary, and Eileen sat squeezed together, all on the edge of their seats, mesmerized by the grainy, black-and-white images of the lunar module approaching the desolate, rocky alien surface. Tears swelled in Mary's eyes. "I can't believe that's really the moon. I can't believe we're actually going to do it."

Frank put his arm around his wife's shoulder. "I know. I know."

"The Eagle has landed." With those fuzzy words, President Kennedy's goal of landing on the moon had been fulfilled. It had been less than ten years earlier, in 1961, that the first man—a Russian—had gone into orbit, and a mere twelve years since the first satellite. The fact that a manmade craft was now on the lunar surface, witnessed on TV, seemed an unimaginable feat. But that was just the appetizer.

Sitting in the middle, Frank had his arms around Mary and Eileen. Using every morsel of focus, they watched in surreal awe as Neil Armstrong climbed out of the lunar module and almost floated down to the awaiting, rugged surface. "That's one small step for man, one giant leap for mankind," his crackled voice carried from millions of miles away, right to their living room.

Eileen gasped and put her hand over her mouth, astonished by what she was seeing.

Mary excitedly pointed to the TV. "We did it! He's on the moon! He's actually on the moon!"

Frank just stared and smiled from ear to ear.

Something that not so long ago seemed unattainable had come to fruition. Man had stepped foot on the moon. But not just any man—an American. Soon, Neil Armstrong, and fellow astronaut Buzz Aldrin, with the eyes of the nation and world still upon them, planted that historic American flag on the lunar surface. For at least a moment anything seemed possible. For a moment, the triumph and greatness of mankind—and specifically a nation—shined bright. For a moment, America was no longer divided, but stood together.

It was a snapshot, a moment in time never to be forgotten. But unfortunately neither the Kellers nor the nation would get to stay there for long. For soon, both would return back to Earth—and the reality of the times.

# 27

# MISERY LOVES COMPANY

During the second week of January 1970, Bob and Dorothy learned that Billy had been taken prisoner by the North Vietnamese. It was bad enough to be held captive, but for some time horror stories had abound about how the communists treated their prisoners of war. Understandably, Bob and Dorothy were devastated, as were Michael and Diana. Frank and Mary felt terrible and rushed to their friends' side. They were there for moral support, trying to put a positive spin on a horrendous situation, saying that the important thing was Billy was alive and not to believe everything they heard about the North Vietnamese's draconian treatment of prisoners. But it was a helpless feeling. All they could really do was hope and pray.

Dorothy was a nervous wreck, going from depressed to more depressed. Mary, who had her own son to think about, was worried about her best friend and tried to spend as much time with her during the day as possible. Dorothy did appreciate it. She knew that without Mary, she probably would have lost her mind.

Unlike his wife, Bob had a busy and integral work schedule to occupy his mind. But usually always focused, he found himself drifting on the job. For the first time, he started making repeated mistakes. That was not good for an engineer. However, Bob's boss knew about Billy and cut him some slack. But after another crucial mistake, his boss told Bob to take a week off to clear his head.

"Don't worry, your job is safe. It'll be here when you come back. I think you just need a week off—with pay of course."

At first Bob fought the idea, saying that he wouldn't make any more errors, but he quickly realized that the hiatus was not merely a suggestion.

Bob had seemingly held it together better than Frank when their sons were deployed to Vietnam. But now with the news of Billy's capture, Bob, too, turned to the bottle. At first it was just on the weekends and a few evenings, hanging out at the bar with his old friend, who himself was starting to drink more again. Then, once Bob was told to stay home for a week, he and Frank began hitting every bar every day, sometimes being drunk by noon.

Dorothy and Mary were furious at their husbands and felt abandoned by them. Dorothy was also mad at Frank, feeling that Bob would not have become a drunk without his friend's influence. However, she never said anything to Mary, nor did she hold it against her. It was not her fault; they were both in the same boat.

When Frank first found out that Bob was forced to take time off work, a part of him was actually excited. Frank did not want his friend to lose his job, but he knew it was only for a week. So he was just grateful to maybe have a full-time drinking buddy for the next five days. As the old adage goes, misery loves company.

Frank happened to be at the Levittown hardware store that Monday morning, spending as little time as possible at the East Meadow store because he could no longer stand the sight of Walter. Sure enough, around 11:30 a.m. Bob stopped by.

"I just had to get out of the house," Bob said in a distressed voice. "Dorothy thought it'd be nice for us to stay home together. Nothing against Dorothy, but I was going stir crazy—and it was only eleven. I'm used to working, doing something. I can't just sit around."

Frank smiled. "I know what you mean. Hey, you wanna go to lunch? We can go to O'Brien's."

"Aren't you working? I mean I don't want to…"

"That's one of the perks of having your own business. C'mon, it'll be fun."

Frank and Bob walked a few blocks to O'Brien's, a local pub. They had agreed to go have lunch, but both of them instinctively knew there would be drinking involved. On the walk there, they ran into a woman who Frank did not recognize, but it was obvious that she and Bob knew each other. Frank could sense this strange interaction between the two. She kept fiddling with her hair and kept changing between looking at Bob's eyes and the ground. Bob seemed almost nervous and spoke in a sped-up voice. The conversation was mundane, yet was speckled with a certain tension. The woman, who was pretty and blonde and looked to be in her early thirties, explained that she was just out running some errands.

Finally, filled with curiosity, Frank butted in. "Aren't you going to introduce me?" He asked to his friend with an almost sarcastic smile.

"Oh, I'm sorry, Frank this is Betty. Betty, this is my friend, Frank."

"Nice to meet you," she said in a sheepish voice, shaking hands.

"Same here."

Bob and Betty exchanged a few more words before they parted ways. Frank waited until they were at O'Brien's and on their fourth beer before he asked about the mysterious woman. "So, what's with you and that dame we ran into?"

Bob took a big swig of his beer. "Whaddaya mean?"

"C'mon Bob, it's me. We've known each other ever since I was old enough to remember. We've been through hell and back together."

Bob slammed the rest of his beer and then motioned the bartender for another round.

"Okay," he said lowly, leaning closer to Frank. "Her son is friends with Michael. One Saturday, I go over there to pick Mikey up. But she tells me that they went to the movies with another friend. I'm about to go back home but she tells me to come in and offers me a drink, says her husband is away for the weekend."

Just then the bartender brought over two more beers.

Bob quickly took a chug of his. He then combed his hand through his thick hair. "I don't know why I said yes. I mean she's always been a flirt. Anyway, we have a drink, talk, laugh a little, then she puts her hand on my arm." Bob looked around to see if anyone else was listening. "The next thing I know we're making out like two teenagers in heat."

Frank was taken aback. He thought Bob was just going to say that they had an innocent attraction for each other. "And then what?"

"Well, you know… we had sex."

"Holy shit," Frank said before gulping down nearly half his beer. "Just that one time?"

Bob took a drink. "Well we wound up doing it a few more times. We actually met in a motel twice. But I finally cut it off. I became so paranoid that Dorothy was going to find out. Or her husband." Bob inched even closer to Frank. "I love my wife. I know it sounds crazy, but I really do. She's the greatest. But I just couldn't fuckin' help myself. It was like that goddamn forbidden fruit. And did you see her? She's quite the looker…I mean not that Dorothy's not." Bob shook his head. "Believe me, I feel guilty about it."

Frank put his hand on his friend's shoulder. "Well it's over. Don't beat yourself up about it."

"I mean, I started going out with Annette when we were young, then we went to the war. And not long after we got back home I started going out with Dorothy—and I never cheated on her before this. I mean before Betty, I had only been with two other women in my entire life." Bob leaned back and looked at Frank with an almost puzzled look. "What about you? I mean you and Mary have been together forever. You're…she's…you never…you're not telling me that Mary's the only woman you've ever been with."

Frank took a swig of beer and then let out a sigh. "I know it sounds crazy, but yeah." He then laughed. "Can you believe that shit?"

"Hey, well, I mean Mary is a great woman. You're a lucky man."

Frank looked straight ahead and nodded. "Yes I am."

Even though he had never committed adultery, Frank knew he was in no position to judge his friend—nor did he want to. In fact, he never again brought up Betty and neither did Bob. However, Frank never quite looked at Dorothy the same. There was always a sense of guilt, but he hid it well.

Bob wound up meeting Frank every day that week except Wednesday, and that was only because he was too hungover to even get out of bed. Dorothy was constantly riding her husband's ass about becoming a drunk. Mary was once again doing the same to Frank. But their nagging only made the men stay away from their houses and their wives that much more.

Most of the time, Frank and Bob were just two, old life-long friends laughing and shooting the shit. But at any time, their blithe demeanor could change into animated anger or bitterness. All it took was someone mentioning something about Vietnam, a news report on the bar's television, or something they had heard the previous night. They could try to drink it away, but reality was always right there beside them.

One afternoon, while walking to the bar, they ran into several young adults holding up cardboard signs about Vietnam. One read: *Stop The Slaughter Of Innocent Vietnamese*; another *Nixon Is A War Criminal*. There were two males and three females. Though one of the girls looked like a hippie, the others were somewhat clean-cut.

When Frank and Bob came upon the scene there were already two older ladies confronting the protesters. "You should be ashamed of yourselves! Our young men are fighting for your freedom," one of them lambasted.

"What freedom?" One of the female protesters sharply replied. "They're killing innocent civilians! This is an unjust war and if you're too blind to see it, you're part of the problem!"

Before Frank could say anything Bob had already run over to the crowd, wedging himself between the youngsters and the two women. "You're in the wrong neighborhood you freaks!" He yelled, his strained face a mere inches from one of the males. "Why don't you go back to the city, or better yet hop a plane to San Francisco?"

Just then three middle-aged men came out of the store they were in front of and stood shoulder to shoulder with Frank.

"This is America man," the protester bravely barked back at Bob. "Have you ever heard of free speech, you fascist?"

Bob's veins extended from his neck and his face turned red. "Have you ever heard of an ass-kicking?" He pushed the young man and his sign onto the ground.

"You just assaulted him! You can't do that," raged one of the girls. "Someone call the cops."

There was now an even bigger crowd circling around the protesters. "Go ahead, call the police!" One of them yelled. "I'd love to see them use their batons on you."

The small mob cheered.

The young man, who had been pushed down, got back up and brushed himself off. He looked around and saw that he and his friends were becoming greatly outnumbered—and by some people who were much bigger than they were. "C'mon, lets just go."

At first, one of the girls stubbornly stood her ground. But he finally convinced her that it was best if they left.

The protesters were halfway down the block when Bob picked up a small rock and hurled it at them, hitting one of the males in the back. It didn't knock him down; it just made the group start running. Bob's stunt received a mixed reaction from the crowd. A few of the men laughed and applauded. But the women gasped with repulsion. One elderly lady even scolded Bob. But Bob was all smiles. He and Frank finished their trek to the bar and once there boasted about the escapade.

Though it seemed like it lasted for a while, that following Monday Bob went back to work. However, to his wife's dismay, he still met Frank at the bar sometimes after work or on the weekends.

One Saturday in mid-April, the two cohorts started drinking beer at 11:30 a.m. and switched to liquor by 3:00 p.m. They were joined by a couple of guys they knew from the neighborhood and wound up at a bar in Astoria, Queens. One of the guys they were with start-ed a fight with two other patrons. The whole clan was kicked out. They jumped in a buddy's car and drove to yet another bar.

Early the next morning Dorothy found her husband passed out cold on the front lawn. At first Dorothy thought he may be dead. Then, when she realized he wasn't, she wanted to kill him. Still half-drunk and disheveled, Bob had no recollection of how he made it back home. In fact, the whole previous evening was a complete blur. Dorothy had received one inebriated phone call from him around 6:00 p.m. But he was on a payphone somewhere crowded and noisy, probably a bar, and she could barely hear him. All she could make out was that he was out with the boys, would be back later, and something about moving to California. She was up wor-ried sick most of the night. Of course, Dorothy repeatedly called Mary, knowing that Bob was with Frank, but Mary was in the same boat. She stopped calling around 1:00 a.m., then passed out around 3:00 a.m. When she awoke at 7:30 a.m. and saw that Bob was not in bed, she called Mary again. Mary told her that Frank must have come home while she was sleeping and was passed out on the living room couch. Mary was on her way to wake Frank up to find out what happened to Bob when Dorothy, still on the phone, looked out the bedroom window and saw her husband sprawled out on the front lawn.

Dorothy read Bob the riot act, right there in the front yard. She knew she was probably going to cause a scene, but could not hold back. His entire body throbbing in pain, Bob did not even try to defend himself. As Dorothy was yelling at the top of her lungs, Di-ana and Michael came out of the house to see what the commo-tion was about. Neighbors were peering through their windows.

Later, during that week Bob called Frank at work and asked to meet him at a local diner that evening. At 6:00 p.m., as planned, Frank went to the diner, where his friend had just pulled up. They exchanged mundane pleasantries and then grabbed a booth.

"So, a diner," Frank said in a bantering manner. "I know, bar food is getting old. Don't worry they serve beer here. Then we can hit the bar."

Bob explained to Frank that there would be no more drinking for him, no more getting drunk in the middle of the day. "Listen Frank, you heard what happened the other day—I woke up on the fucking lawn," he said in a whisper, leaning over the table. "I don't even know how I got there."

Frank was about to answer, but Bob cut him off. "Listen, Dorothy was ready to pack her bags and leave me."

"C'mon. Okay, Mary wasn't too happy with me either that morning."

Bob shook his head. "It's not just that day Frank. I mean, don't get me wrong, I love us hanging out, but ever since we got the news about Billy, I've gone over the deep edge. This isn't me. I mean I've always enjoyed a good drink now and then, but..."

The waiter came over to take their order, but Bob politely waved him off, asking for another few minutes. "Listen Frank, my son and daughter saw me that morning, sprawled out on the lawn. Michael asked me about it. He's fifteen; he's not stupid. I told him I was just going through a rough time because of what happened to Billy. But it's too much." Bob bowed his head. "I worry so much about Billy that sometimes I think I'm gonna lose my mind. But I have another son and a daughter to think about—and Dorothy. They deserve better than this."

Listening intently, Frank wasn't sure what to say. "I understand," he replied almost perfunctorily.

"I mean they need me, too. Plus they all love and worry about Billy as much as I do. Hell, Dorothy gave birth to him. I can just imagine how she feels. But I've been so selfish it's almost like I never took that into account." Bob let out a deep, slow breath. "You know I was still so hungover sick from last Saturday that I had to take Monday off of work. And that's after being forced to take a week off because I was making so many mistakes. Look," Bob continued in a more subdued, drawn-out voice, "I can't lose my job. Like I said, I have Dorothy and Michael and Diana to think about—and Billy. I just can't go down this path anymore. I just can't"

As Frank listened, he felt as if he was having an out-of-the-body experience. He knew that Bob's words could be his own. He consoled his friend and told him he was doing the right thing by sobering up. That seemed to please Bob. Then, while trying not to preach or be too forward, Bob hinted that Frank should also do the same and at least cool it for a while.

"You're right my friend. I can't put Mary through this anymore. Maybe I have been overdoing it and should chill out for a while."

At the time Frank meant what he said. He was happy that Bob was straightening up and planned on doing the same. But Frank never did sober up, and after a short while, he felt as if Bob had abandoned him. Now, Frank was again left to drown in his sorrows all alone.

# 28

# POWDER KEG

The tension at the Keller home had reached an all-time high. Frank was continuing his drinking and neglect of the family. Mary was splitting her woe amongst her husband, daughter, and son. Eileen, who was in her senior year in high school, was rebelling against her parents, society, and most of all the war.

In late April, Mary had found a bag of marijuana in her daughter's jacket pocket. She confronted Eileen, who swore she was just holding it for a friend, but never told Frank in fear he would explode. The three of them seemed isolated, each in their own vacuumed worlds.

Frank did not know about the marijuana, but nevertheless his relationship with Eileen had become increasingly strained. Frank was home less and less and so was his daughter, and when they were around each other they were usually arguing about her new boyfriend, her curfew, what she was wearing, or the war. But sometimes they could argue over the most trivial of things like her leaving a dirty plate in the sink, or her talking on the phone too long, or watching the living room television when Frank wanted to see something. Now seventeen and full of vigor, Eileen was always ready to stand up for herself, but found it much easier to avoid confrontation with her father. Though she tried just to stay out of his way, some nights Mary, always trying to play the peacemaker, would still make the three of them sit down for dinner together.

On May 4th, during a massive protest at Kent State University, the Ohio National Guard was called in. The students were told to disperse, but instead, stood their ground and started shouting at the guardsmen. According to reports, some of the demonstrators started throwing rocks at them. The National Guardsmen opened fire, killing four students and wounding nine others.

That evening, as Mary was finishing up dinner, Eileen was watching the news about the shootings on TV. She was horrified and enraged. "Are you seeing this? Can you believe this? They just shot them dead!"

Mary, who had not yet heard the news, came running from the kitchen to see what in the world her daughter was yelling about. She, too, was aghast.

Frank came out of his bedroom, where he had been changing. He saw his wife and daughter standing directly in front of the television with the look of disbelief. Mary's eyes were swelling with tears.

"Yeah," was all he said as he saw what they were watching. Frank, who had already heard about the incident, did not know what else to say. He could not defend the guardsmen's actions. He had railed against the Vietnam protests—even thought he didn't agree with the war—but found nothing but disgust and outrage with United States troops opening fire on their own unarmed citizens. It reinforced his belief that the whole country, perhaps the entire world, was imploding.

"You see, Dad? This is what we're fighting against. The government is out of control!"

Before Frank had time to answer, the phone rang. Mary went to get it. It was Eileen's best friend, Helen.

Eventually, with a tense atmosphere hanging in the air, Frank, Mary and Eileen sat down to eat—though they had all lost their appetite. Eileen announced that she and Helen were going to join a sit-in at the high school the next day in protest over what happened at Kent State.

Frank put down his fork. "Like hell. You're not going to any sit-in or any protest."

"You can't stop me."

Frank sprung up from the table. "Are you kidding me? First of all, I'm your father, you live in this house, and you will do whatever I say! Secondly, did you just watch the news? You wanna get shot too?"

Eileen thought about her father's words. "So is that it, you're worried about me?"

"Of course your father worries about you. We both do."

"I wanna hear it from Dad," Eileen said, looking straight at her father.

Frank took a second to calm down. "Look, I know we haven't been on the best of terms lately, but you're my daughter and of course I worry about you."

Eileen smiled. Mary nearly came to tears. In that one moment it seemed that maybe a wound was about to heal, a fence mend. But some wounds run too deep.

"Thank you Dad. Really. I know you care about me. And I'll be fine. But I have to do this. It's up to the youth to protest this injustice."

Frank blew up. "Do you believe this shit? Here I am trying to be nice! You will not disobey my order!"

Eileen shot up from her seat. "This isn't the military, Dad! See, you're just part of the problem!"

With that Eileen stormed off. Frank went after her, but afraid what he was going to do, Mary threw herself in front of him. But as Eileen went out the door Frank pushed his wife aside.

"You get the fuck back here!" He yelled at his daughter to no avail. It was the first time he had ever used profanity towards her.

Once Mary was confident that Frank was not going to chase after Eileen, she locked herself in the bedroom and began to cry.

Later that night, while both of them were in bed, Mary tried to reason with her husband. "What happened to you and Eileen? She used to be Daddy's little girl. She used to wait for you to get home from work and then run to you as soon as you walked in the front door. You guys used to do things together."

Frank sighed. "That was a long time ago."

"But don't you want to have a relationship with her again? She's your daughter, Frank."

"We'll patch things up. She's just going through a rebellious phase right now." He paused. "The whole country is."

Of course, none of it was Frank's fault. Mary just gave up and tried to go to sleep.

On June 5, 1970, Eileen turned eighteen. It was a Friday. She asked her mother if instead of a party, she could go out with a few of her friends to Manhattan that evening. There was a concert they wanted to see. Mary agreed and also talked Frank into it, though it took some coaxing. But before she left for the city that evening, they had a quick, small celebration. Bob and Dorothy came over with Michael and Diana. They had a birthday cake and Eileen opened up her gifts. Her parents bought her a gold bracelet; Mary picked it out, Frank paid for it.

Everyone was able to get along for an hour. Frank even managed to smile, though most of the time he spent talking with Bob. However, when it was time for Eileen to leave, Frank gave her a hug and a kiss on the forehead and without lecturing or being argumentative, told her to be careful and have a good time.

A few weeks later Eileen was to graduate from high school. This time Mary was bent on throwing her daughter a big party. However, Eileen pleaded with her mother to just have a small celebration and that most of her friends would probably not come. At first she said it was because her friends had their own parties to attend. But Mary could sense there was more to the story. Finally Eileen explained that she did not want her father to embarrass her, either by getting drunk and doing something stupid, or having a confrontation with one or more of her friends.

"You know dad doesn't like any of my friends. He can't stand Jason," her boyfriend. "He'll get drunk and start lecturing them about the anti-war movement or how anyone that protests the war is a traitor."

Mary wanted to cry. But she promised Eileen she would make sure that her father would be on his best behavior.

"Mom, you can't control Dad." Eileen saw her mother fighting back tears and relented, saying she would invite *some* of her friends.

That evening Mary talked to Frank about Eileen's party. He happened to be sober at the time, though still a little hungover.

"What do you think I'm going do, strip search her friends when they walk in the door and then beat 'em with a rubber hose? Gee, Mary, what do you really think of me?"

"I'm just saying, this is a very important day for our daughter. She's graduating high school. And despite any differences you two have had recently, she went through school with all As and Bs and we should be very proud of her."

"I am, I am," Frank grumbled. "Just relax, everything will be fine. We'll have a barbecue. I'll get all the food and cook."

In what had become a rare occasion, Frank and Mary snuggled in front of the couch that night and watched television together. Then, after adjourning to the bedroom, they made love for the first time in nearly two months.


As planned, Frank picked up all the food for the party and also helped Mary with some other details. It was a blue-skied, sunny late June Saturday, a perfect day for a barbecue. Frank woke up clear-eyed and in a good mood. The graduation ceremony was flawless. Mary and Frank sat in the stands and cheered as their daughter accepted her diploma. It was as if all the turmoil that had surrounded them had been brushed aside and they were a normal happy family again.

After the ceremony, as Eileen hung out with her friends for a while, Mary and Frank rushed home to get the party ready. Bob and Dorothy, who had also been at the ceremony, arrived at the same time. Michael and Diana would be coming later. Dorothy helped Mary while the men started the grill. As soon as it was lit, Frank grabbed two cold beers from a nearby cooler and handed one of them to Bob. Bob had drastically cut down on his drinking, going sometimes weeks without having a drop of alcohol. He also knew that Frank still had a problem with the bottle. But it was a party. Also, he was certainly not going to tell his friend that he couldn't drink in his own house. Bob just figured they would have a few beers and Frank would behave himself because it was Eileen's graduation.

Mary was understandably not happy to see her husband drinking, but the last thing she wanted to do was start a confrontation with him during the party. One by one the guests arrived, including some of Eileen's friends. Eileen also had some trepidation about her father drinking, but knew he was not going to go through an entire party without having a beer, and was just happy so see him in a good mood. In fact, for most of the afternoon Frank was jovial, talking and laughing with his guests, serving hamburgers and hotdogs, chicken, even steaks.

By 6:00 p.m., Frank was feeling no pain, haven been chain-drinking beer for nearly three hours. But he was still being the merry host when several of Eileen's friends approached the grill.

"So, what'll it be?" He asked buoyantly, with a spatula in one hand and a beer in the other.

They all politely told him what they would like.

"So, Mr. Keller, Eileen says that her brother is in Vietnam," one of the guys added.

Frank looked at the teenager, wondering where his comment was leading. "Yeah, that's right."

"Well I wish him the best."

Frank smiled and thanked the young man.

"Hopefully he'll be home soon."

"It's an atrocity what we're doing over there," spewed one of the girls.

Before Frank reacted, one of the other guys jumped in. "They're just doing their job. It's not our troops' fault."

"Thank you," Frank said.

"Just doing their job? Isn't that what the Nazis said—just following orders?"

That was it. Frank was not going to let anyone compare U.S. troops to the Nazis. He unleashed on the girl in a tirade of spit and profanity. All the teens looked scared. Within seconds the entire backyard was staring at Frank, but he was undeterred. First, Bob ran over to try and calm his friend down. Then Mary, fuming, rushed upon the scene.

"What are you doing?" She said in her lowest yelling voice.

"Do you know what this little bitch said?" He hollered, pointing the spatula nearly into the girl's chest.

Just then a man ran over and put himself in front of the girl. "That is my daughter! What's the meaning of this?"

"I don't care whose daughter she is! You don't go comparing our boys to Nazis!" Frank looked like he was getting ready to hit the girl's father.

Eileen appeared. "Dad what are you doing? You're drunk." She then turned to her mother. "I knew this would happen!" She yelled, nearly in tears.

Now Frank was yelling at the girl, her father, Mary, and Eileen, causing an even bigger scene. In fact, he seemed to be getting more and more worked up. Eileen finally yelled that he was an embarrassment and stormed off with her friends in tow. Frank tried to run after her, but had to be physically restrained by Bob and another friend. In the end, Frank also left, saying "I don't need this shit!" Mary, in tears, was left to apologize to all her guests.

For the next several weeks the tension that filled the Keller home was so thick it could suffocate. Mary did not even want to look at her husband and neither did Eileen. Mary tried to make amends with her daughter, but Eileen did not want to have anything to do with either of her parents and avoided being home as much as possible. Frank, who was forced to sleep on the couch for several days after the graduation, and knew he had screwed up, also tried to stay away from the house. No longer did the family all sit down and eat dinner together. On Sundays, Mary went to church alone, praying for God to help put her broken family back together. When the three of them *were* near each other, there was this invisible fuse, always burning, always ready to ignite the powder keg.

On the first Friday in August, Frank went straight to his East Meadow store. After looking over the books for a while in the backroom he became convinced that Walter had been stealing from him. Frank confronted him about it and a screaming match ensued. It ended with Walter saying he quit and storming off. Frank turned to the only other employee in the store at the time and announced that he was now the manager. Then he went off to the nearest bar.

It was not even 11:00 a.m. when Frank entered the dark, smoke-filled bar. He sat down next to another regular and ordered a scotch on the rocks. The large, plump, balding man sitting next to him pointed to the television set hanging in the corner. "You believe this shit?"

Frank looked up at the TV, which was showing a preview of the news.

"These goddamn draft-dodging hippies are spitting on our troops when they arrive home. Actually spitting on them! Someone should stick them in the fucking jungle with a bunch of gooks shooting at them and see how they like it."

A younger man, the only other patron, sitting a few stools down, overheard his comments. "It's a crime what they're doing over there."

Frank and his drinking companion almost gave themselves whiplash, turning to look at the stranger. "Well what do we have here? Frank, I think we got ourselves a pansy-ass hippie."

"I'm no hippie, but at least the hippies don't go around killing innocent people. They live for peace. Maybe our soldiers could learn a thing or two from them."

The regular stood up, showing his full girth and height. "You little fucker!"

As Frank also stood up, the younger man realized that he was in over his head. "Listen, I don't want any problems," the man said while extending his arms. But it was too late; the older man charged over like a bull and with one, swift left-hook to the head, knocked the young guy to the floor. Smelling blood, Frank wanted in on the action and kicked the guy in the stomach while he was down. As Frank and his buddy hammered away, the bartender yelled that it was enough; they had proved their point. After a few more kicks, the beating stopped.

The bartender came to the other side of the bar, where the young stranger was curled in a fetal position on the dirty floor, with blood seeping from his face. "You better do something with him, Artie," the bartender whispered to his large regular. "I'm telling you right now, this shit ain't comin' back on me, you hear?"

"Don't worry, he's not hurt that bad," Artie replied. "Is that cab still out front?"

The bartender looked out the window and nodded. Artie knelt down and told the wounded man that if he went to the cops or told anyone what happened, he would find out where he lived and pay him a visit.

With the help of Frank, Artie got the man to his feet and the bartender gave them a hand towel to put over his face for the bleeding. Frank and Artie then walked him outside and put him in the cab. Of course, the cab driver was up in arms, but Artie handed him a ten-dollar bill and told him it was for the fare. Then Frank handed him another ten dollars and said it was his tip, a large amount for 1970. The driver was still somewhat reluctant, asked where the hell he should take him. Then the wounded man, ready to cut his losses and call it a day, told him where to go. With that, the driver took him away and Frank and Artie went back in the bar.

Artie assured the bartender, who was mopping up the floor, that everything was okay.

"Listen, you guys better take off anyway, just in case this guy calls the police." The gray-haired bartender, who was also the owner and a veteran of both World War II and Korea, looked at Frank and Artie. "Don't worry, on the off chance they do come here I'll cover for you guys." He then smiled. "That son-of-a-bitch did have it coming."

Frank and Artie piled into their respective cars and drove to another bar about a half-mile away. There, they continued drinking and laughed about what they had done. But before long, they were locked in a passionate conversation about the Vietnam protests and the treatment of U.S. soldiers by many in the public.

"It's bad enough what they have to go through over there," Artie ranted. "Then they come back here and get shit on? It just ain't right!" Of course, he was preaching to the choir. Frank's blood was boiling just thinking about it.

Frank arrived home by 3:15 p.m. But he was already completely shitfaced. Mary could tell her husband was drunk, but she set her disappointment and frustration aside for the moment.

"A letter came from Tommy today. I waited to open it till you came back."

At that moment, Eileen walked through the door.

"I was just telling your father that a letter came today from Tommy."

Mary retrieved the letter and then the embattled family gathered in the living room as she read it:

*I hope everything is well at home. I wish I was there with you all. It feels like I've been here for five years. But I know I'm needed and what we're doing is important—not saving the world from communism or helping the South Vietnamese, but flying into hot zones and extracting our men. You should see the guys' faces when they hear and see our choppers coming. It's as if they're seeing an angel. Of course, unfortunately we can't save them all. A lot of good men, boys really, with their whole lives ahead of them, lost their lives or lost limbs or have been paralyzed from the waist down. And more and more recently I've been asking myself what for? Sometimes it seems that the South Vietnamese don't want us here anymore than the North does. And most of the time it's nearly impossible to tell them apart anyway. When guys raid a village how are they supposed to know who's a friendly and who's not? It'd be easy if everyone was in a uniform, but they're not.*

*The other day, we landed in a village to extract some of our wounded. A sergeant told us that one of his men went to give a hurt Vietnamese woman some aid and she blew herself up, killing the soldier and wounding three others. Unfortunately, you hear stories like that all the time.*

*I know all this sounds grim and I probably shouldn't be telling you. But please don't worry about me. I'm doing fine. I'm surrounded by the bravest men I've ever known and like I've said, doing an important job. And I'd rather be flying in this chopper with an M-60 in my hand than on the ground.*

*Hopefully, this war will be over soon. My love to everyone. Can't wait to see you all again!*

"Do you know what those helicopters do?" Eileen said with disdain. "They fly into villages and shoot everyone on the ground."

Mary stared at her daughter with ice-cold eyes. "How can you say that? Didn't you hear what you're brother wrote? They're trying to help those villagers and what do our boys get in return—blown-up."

"Please Mom! What do you want them to do? They've seen their towns and villages burnt to the ground, their families slaughtered like cattle, by both the NVA and us."

"What the hell are you talking about?" Frank snapped, with rage bubbling in his face.

Eileen stood her ground. "You heard what he said, they can't tell who's supposed to be an enemy—so they kill them all. Like what happened in My Lai. We're committing atrocities over there!"

Frank could take no more. He reared back and with a clenched fist punched his daughter right in the face as if she was a full-grown man. Eileen immediately collapsed to the ground.

"Frank!" Mary yelled in horror.

"That's our son she's talking about!"

Mary went to help her daughter up, but Eileen pushed her away and staggered up on her own. "I hate you!" As she screamed at her father, blood spit from her already swollen mouth. "I'm packing my stuff and I'm leaving," she cried, tears streaming down her face. "I'm going to live with Victor—and I'm never coming back again!"

Mary, who was also now crying, slapped Frank as hard as she could with an open hand. Then she ran after Eileen, who had stormed into her bedroom. "Open the door honey, please," she pleaded, jiggling the door's handle.

When Eileen finally did appear again, after a few minutes, she was carrying a suitcase.

"Baby, please don't go!"

"You can't just leave!" Frank hollered.

Mary turned to her husband. "You shut up! You sicken me!"

Mary tried to physically stop Eileen from walking out the door, but it was no use.

"Don't worry, she'll be back. Where the hell does she think she's going to go? Who's this Victor, anyway?"

Mary explained that Victor was a new older boy Eileen had been seeing who she met at a protest. He lived in Queens and supposedly had his own apartment. Mary knew that her daughter would not be coming back—and she could not blame her. But Eileen was not the only one leaving.

"You've gone too far Frank," she said with tears pouring down her face. "You're not the person I married anymore. You've turned into this drunken, bitter, out-of-control monster. And I'm not going to live like this—not a day longer. I'm packing a bags and going to my parents." Mary raised her hand and pointed in Frank's face. "And don't you dare come after me!"

"Mary, I'm sorry. Please…"

"Sorry's not going to cut it this time," Mary cried as she went into their bedroom.

"Well when will you be back?"

Mary, who was already pulling out some of her clothes from the dresser, turned to look at her husband. "I don't know Frank…maybe never."

# 29

# GOODBYES

Frank did not try to stop Mary that afternoon. He knew he had gone too far. As angered as he had been over Eileen's diatribe, he could not believe that he had punched her. Frank had never raised a hand to her before, had never even spanked her when she was little. Alone in an empty house, Frank knew he had no one to blame but himself. That evening Frank went into the cabinet and pulled out a half-empty bottle of scotch. He drank right from the bottle, crying by himself about what had become of his life, until finally he passed out. He woke up the next afternoon on the living room floor, every part of his body aching, and realizing that it had not all been some bad dream.

Later that day, after hearing what happened from Dorothy, Bob went over to the house to find Frank lying on the couch, unshaven and disheveled, wearing sweat-shorts and a dirty T-shirt. Bob asked him what happened and Frank told him the truth, the same story he had already heard from Dorothy. Bob knew Frank had a problem with drinking and that there had been a growing friction between him and Eileen, mostly due to her views on the war, but

Bob could never have imagined it would come to Frank punching his daughter. But Bob completely believed his friend when he said how sorry he was that it happened. He knew Frank loved Eileen.

Bob sat down on the couch and had a heart-to-heart with his best friend. If anyone knew what Frank was going through it was Bob. After all, the North Vietnamese was still holding Billy as a prisoner of war. He said that the most important thing was that Thomas was alive and well and that despite Eileen's feelings towards the war, some of which Frank agreed with, she loved her brother.

"When Tommy gets back, he deserves to come back to the home he left. You guys deserve to be a family again. Don't let Vietnam destroy you. It's destroyed enough families already," Bob said. "Listen, give Mary some time and then give her a call and tell her how sorry you are. And beg her to come back…the same with Eileen. You can't blame her for her ideas. She didn't come up with them on her own. It's what they see and hear on the news and in the papers. It's propaganda that's everywhere. Forget your differences. Tell her how much you really love her—which you do—and tell her that the two of you will leave the politics at the door." Bob paused. "And Frank," he said in an uneasy, hesitant voice, "I say this as your best friend. You have to slow down on the drinking. And I'm not telling you anything you don't already know."

Frank looked at his friend and nodded. "I know. You're right."

Bob went out and picked up some food and brought it back to Frank, as he had not eaten all day. As they ate, they engaged in more lighthearted conversation. Then, before leaving for the night, Bob wished his buddy luck.

Frank took Bob's advice. Though it was not easy, he left Mary alone for a couple of days. Then on Tuesday he called her at her parents. Mrs. Capelli answered the phone and Frank had never felt so uncomfortable talking to her, knowing that she probably heard the whole story of what happened. But she did not preach; she said a few words in a strained tone and fetched Mary. Frank told his wife how sorry he was, how he was going to stop drinking, how she and Eileen meant everything, and pleaded with her to come back home. But to his utter dismay, Mary was steadfast, saying she had heard it all before. As for Eileen, Mary explained she had been in touch with her and she was okay.

"I'll pass your message onto her and if she wants to call you, well that's up to her."

Frank asked, practically begged, for the number where Eileen was staying, but Mary would not give it to him. This angered Frank but he bit his tongue. The last thing he wanted to do was become irate with his wife.

"Listen Frank," Mary said, "I just need to be alone right now. I just need some time to think things through. I'll give you a call in a few days to check on you and maybe we can talk some more."

Frustrated and dejected Frank told Mary he would respect her wishes. He did not want to push her away anymore than he already had. All he could do was reluctantly hang up the phone and hope that in a few days Mary would have a change of heart.


For the next several days Frank walked around like a zombie, spending time at each of his stores, but not really able to concentrate. The only time he was really forced to work was training his new manager. But even then his head was not in the game. After work he would come home, eat a frozen dinner and watch television until the programming went off the air and the national anthem came on. Feeling too strange to sleep in the bed without Mary, he would pass out on the living room couch.

For the rest of that week, Frank abstained from drinking. Then on Saturday, having not heard from Mary, he called her at her parents. He asked why she had not called him like she had said, but tried to restrain his agitation. She apologized, but said she was "still thinking things through." Frank did not know exactly what that meant and was afraid to find out. Once again, he pleaded for forgiveness and for her to come back home. However, although speaking with a calm voice, Mary let him know how distraught she still was.

"I just need some more time," she kept saying.

Frustrated, Frank changed the subject and asked if she had heard from Eileen.

"Yes, she's doing fine," Mary replied. "I told her what you said, that you were very sorry, but...I mean you can understand that she's still mad. She's living with Victor and they have another female roommate."

"Mary, I don't want to argue, but you can't possibly approve of our eighteen-year-old daughter shacking up with some guy."

"Of course I don't. I told her to come stay with me for a while, but she's not leaving. And there's nothing we can do about it."

"Yes there is. You can come home where you belong and so can she—and we can be a family again."

There was a few seconds of silence on the other end. "I don't like the idea of her living with this Victor guy either, but I can also understand why she won't go back home." Mary paused. "As for me, I don't know. Like I said, maybe I just need some more time." Mary then asked how Frank was doing.

He said he had not had a drop of alcohol. She wanted to believe him but didn't. Even if he was telling the truth she surmised, it was only a matter of time before he went back to the bottle. She was right.

Disheartened by his conversation with Mary, Frank went to the local bar that night, where he sat by himself and stewed in a bubbling sea of emotions. First he felt guilty, about what happened and that he was drinking again. Then he wallowed in self-pity. Then he started to convince himself that Mary's parents were the reason she was not coming home, filling her head with injurious thoughts about him. Then Frank started thinking about Eileen, wanting to find out where she was and put Victor's head through a wall. Then it was back to self-disdain.

On Monday, September 14th, Frank spent time at all of his three stores. When he arrived home around four o'clock, he saw Mary's car in the driveway and immediately lit up. She had come back! He was certainly glad that he had not had a drop to drink that day. With swagger in his step, he walked to the front door. "Mary, I'm home." It felt good just saying it.

Frank found Mary sitting at the kitchen table, crying, her head in her hands. He asked her what was wrong.

She lifted her head and for a second just looked at him, with long streaks of tears and mascara running down her ghostly white face. "I came home so we could talk and maybe—" She had to stop.

Now really alarmed, Frank knelt beside his wife and asked again what was wrong.

"I was here going through some of my things when there was a knock on the door. It was a messenger with a telegram."

"A telegram?"

Mary held up a piece of paper that she had been holding onto with her trembling hand. "It's Thomas. Oh Frank, our son is dead."

It was as if the world had stopped. At first, Frank stood there in shock for what seemed to him like minutes. Perhaps he was waiting to wake up from the nightmare he had just walked into. But this was reality, a cold, inexorable reality.

Mary leapt from her seat and threw her arms around him, collapsing in quivering tears. Frank felt like he couldn't breathe, as if the air was being sucked right out of him. His wife's tormented cries echoed in his head like the howls of hell.

Finally, Frank, too broke down in disconsolate tears. "It has to be a mistake," he wailed into Mary's shoulder. "God, this can't be happening!" But it was.

Mary broke free from Frank and ran to the bathroom where she threw up—for the second time. The two of them then sat around the kitchen table, completely helpless.

Eventually, Mary mustered up enough strength to break the news to her parents, and to Bob and Dorothy. But her first call was to Eileen. She had never before had to make such a difficult call. With trembling hands and a shaking voice, Mary told her daughter that her brother had been killed in action. Even Frank, who was standing over Mary, could hear Eileen screaming on the other end.

"No! No, it can't be! Not Tommy!"

Eileen came home late that night. After she cried into her mother's arms, Frank gave her a hug and told her how sorry he was for what he had done. Eileen was still angry with her father, but all that mattered now was Thomas. Everything else was a dialogue for another day.

For the next three days, while the Kellers made funeral arrangements and awaited the return of Thomas' body, the house was engrossed in a surreal, grievous cloud. Minutes seemed like hours, hours like days. Family and friends stopped by to pay their condolences and show their support. Every now and then the anguish of the moment would be broken by a forced smile or awkward mundane conversation. But mostly there were tears and pain. At night, there was little sleeping going on.

Frank loved his wife and daughter and part of him wanted to be strong for them and hold the family together. But another part of him just stopped caring about everything the moment he heard that his son had been killed. He would talk to friends and family who stopped by the house and held his wife when she cried, but inside Frank was a million miles away.

The night after learning about Thomas, Frank had what would become a recurring nightmare. He dreamt he was back in the Army, locked in an intense jungle battle. Bullets were whizzing by his head, flashes of gunfire and acrid smoke filled the air. Explosions and the frantic voices of men echoed through trees. It was sheer terror and pandemonium. Frank could not see the enemy so he just took cover behind a berm and fired his rifle in the same direction as his comrades were shooting. Then there was a massive blast, a bright flash followed by blackness. As muffled sound and blurred vision slowly returned, Frank looked around to see his fellow soldiers lying dead on the jungle floor, some torn apart. Some were still screaming for help as they bled-out. Then Frank turned his head and saw, lying on top of the berm right next to him, Thomas. His legs had been blown completely off and intestines spewed from his torso. Still alive, Thomas reached out for his father. "Please don't let me die here, Dad," he cried with the fear on his face only a dying man could know.

Frank leapt up in bed, covered in sweat and his heart beating out of control. It was enough to wake Mary up. She asked him what was wrong. With the vision of his son still crystal clear in his mind, Frank fought to catch his breath. "It's okay," he stuttered. "It was just a bad dream."

Mary asked what it was about. Frank did not answer; though she could only guess it had something to do with Thomas. It was the middle of the night, but Frank was not able to go back to sleep. In time, the nightmare would return again and again, causing many sleepless nights.

Having received his body back from the Army, Friday was the first night of Thomas' wake. Because of his wounds it was a closed-casket viewing. Appropriately, a large American flag was draped over the coffin. The funeral home was packed with family, friends, and neighbors. Of course, Alice was there with her parents. Need-less to say she was devastated about her boyfriend's death and cried the whole time, unable to be consoled. At different times all of Frank's employees showed up, including his ex-manager, Walter Rubenstein. Hubert Whittaker, who Frank had not seen in some time, came with his family. Frank and Mary were not without sup-port, and they appreciated it, but nothing was going to ease the immense grief and sorrow of knowing their son's forever-lifeless body laid inside that casket.

For Frank, Mary, and Eileen the night was an anguishing blur. But somehow they made it through it. However, they had another viewing in the morning, followed by the funeral.

Frank woke up Sunday morning after about three hours of total sleep. It was time for the funeral. Forgoing any breakfast, he put on his black suit and black tie. Then, in a dolorous state, he drove Mary and Eileen to the funeral home. On the short drive there, Mary talked to him about the day's arrangements, but her words went in one ear and out the other.

Exhausted, Frank stood in the foyer of the funeral home greeting many of the same faces he had the night before, exchanging the same routine words people say at a wake. After about a half hour, he had enough and went outside to get some fresh air. Frank, who did not normally smoke, bummed a cigarette off someone and lit it up. He then walked halfway down the block so that he did not have to talk to every single person that was going inside the funeral home. Puffing away on his smoke, Frank looked up at the sky. It was a beautiful, bright-clear late September morning. He then scanned the landscape. People were strolling down the block, enjoying maybe one of the last warm Saturdays of the year. Cars whizzed by, each on their way to some unknown destination. The world was turning, like it always did. Everyone but a select few were oblivious to Thomas' death. For them he was just another untold story, another name in a day's obituary. But Frank did not feel anger towards those people; rather he felt envious. Oh, how he wanted to be one of those millions of people just living another day of ordinary life.

As Frank pondered life and death, Hubert Whittaker came up to him. "I saw you down here having a cigarette. How you holding up my friend?"

Frank looked at Hubert, grateful that he had come. Frank not only liked Hubert, but respected him. "I'm okay," he lied. "Hey, how about going across the street to the bar? I could sure use a quick drink."

Hubert, who was unaware of Frank's drinking problem, agreed. He knew that if his son had just died he would need a drink, too. Plus, he only wanted to be there for his friend.

As soon as they sat down at the bar Frank ordered a Jack straight up and a gin and tonic for Hubert. Frank slammed his drink in one gulp and immediately ordered another. Hubert told Frank again how sorry he was about Thomas. The two then talked about Vietnam. As Frank downed his second, then third whiskey, he started to stew.

"It's not right, Hubert. These boys were just doing their duty, putting their lives on the line. Many of them volunteered. Then they come home to this—people calling them baby killers, spitting at them, comparing them to the Nazis."

Hubert sipped his gin and tonic. "Some people just don't have a clue."

"Like all those bigots when you came back from World War II. I mean, me and all the other white soldiers, they gave us a parade. But you fought just as hard. And what did you come home to? Jim Crow."

Frank put his hand on Hubert's shoulder and called for the bartender. "You see this man?" He yelled across the bar. "This man here is a war hero. Fought in the Ninety-Second during World War II. Was in battle after battle. Took a bullet in the leg for this country!"

Hubert looked embarrassed. The bartender, who seemed annoyed, just nodded.

Frank polished off his third Jack Daniels and went to order another one.

"Whoa, big fella, don't you think you've had enough?" Hubert told his friend. He then looked at his watch. "Anyway, don't you think you should be getting back? Mary's probably looking for you."

"You're right. Just one more."

The bartender did not seem thrilled to serve him another drink, but Frank assured him it would be the last.

By the time Frank stumbled back to the funeral home, with hardly any sleep the previous night, and four short glasses of whiskey in his empty stomach, he was completely drunk. Thoughts of Vietnam were running through his incoherent head, picking up steam like a freight train going down a slope without brakes.

A group of friends and family were already gathered out front of the funeral home and in the parking lot. Frank went inside and found Mary, who had Eileen by her side.

"I was looking for you. It's time to go to the cemetery. Where were..." Mary did not even have to finish her question. She could tell by his glassy eyes and smell of liquor on his breath that Frank was drunk. "How could you?" She lamented.

"Oh Dad, at Thomas' funeral," added Eileen. "Is getting drunk more important to you than..."

"How dare you talk to me about Thomas," he snapped at his daughter. "You're probably glad that he's dead."

Eileen looked as if her father had just hit her with a baseball bat. "How could you say that?"

"Now he can't slaughter anymore of your precious little Vietnamese. Help burn down their villages. You probably think he deserved to die!"

Eileen instantly broke down in tears, burrowing her head into her mother's shoulder.

Tears also swelled in Mary's eyes, but they were tears of rage. "You son-of-a-bitch! I never want to see you again! You take a different car to the cemetery—and don't you even stand by us. And then afterwards you go somewhere else. Go to your precious bar. Because I'm going home to pack up all my belongings."

With that, Mary walked off, with her still-crying daughter in tow. Frank tried to follow, but was stopped by Mary's father, who had overheard the whole thing. Words were exchanged and the two men, who used to be so close, nearly came to blows.

Frank found Bob and Dorothy in the parking lot and asked to ride with them to the cemetery. They could tell he was drunk and could only imagine what had happened. But in respect of Thomas' funeral, they did not ask any questions. Frank just squeezed into the car with Bob, Dorothy, Michael, and Diana, and was silent for the whole ride.

During the burial, Frank stood a few people down from his wife and daughter. At one point the priest asked if he wanted to say any last words. Frank just bowed his head and shook it no. As he stood there under the bright September sun, Frank had to fight from throwing up, not just from the whiskey mixed with an empty stomach and little sleep, but in angst over what he had just done. Finally the time came to lower Thomas' casket into the awaiting ground. As Frank watched, he feared that not only his son was being buried, but also his entire family.

After the ceremony Frank tried to get to Mary and Eileen, to drunkenly explain his actions and ask for forgiveness, but was stopped by Mr. Capelli and Bob. Not wanting to cause yet another scene, he watched helplessly as his wife and daughter scampered away into the awaiting limousine. By this time whispers of what happened at the funeral home were already making their rounds and Frank felt a hundred judging eyes upon him. Ashamed and broken, he found one of his employees to take him away.

Frank did not go home. Instead, he had his employee drop him off at a bar. He spent the rest of the day there, drowning himself in drink after drink until the bartender finally cut him off after Frank fell from the barstool. He then stumbled to another watering hole, stopping along the way to vomit in an alley.

Late the next morning, he woke up on his living room floor, having no recollection of getting home. Dehydrated, sick to his stomach, and with a knife-driving headache, he staggered around the house. There was no sign of Mary or Eileen. Moreover, most of Mary's clothes were gone. Frank sat on the empty bed and put his head in his hands. "What have I done?" He asked aloud.

# 30

# I USED TO BE
# A GOOD MAN

Giving Mary time to cool off, Frank waited a few days before he called her at her parents. But this time Mary would not even come to the phone. Mrs. Capelli pleaded with Frank to get help and not to call anymore. "Mary will call you when she is ready."

Mr. Capelli was not so polite.

One night, after getting wasted, Frank called the Capelli household at 2:00 a.m. and went into a drunken rant. That certainly did not help.

Either too drunk, too hungover, too distraught, or sometimes a combination of the three, Frank barely made it to work anymore. Some days he would just call his managers to see if everything was okay. Frank was no longer a functioning alcoholic.

One Saturday, Bob came over to check on his friend. He felt terrible about Frank's situation and wished to God there was something he could do for him.

Bob stopped by around noon and found both the house and Frank disheveled. The house, which had always been immaculately clean, was unkempt, with dirty dishes, glasses and empty beer bottles atop tables and counters. Worn clothes were draped over the living room couch. The kitchen was a disaster. The floors looked grimy. All the curtains and blinds were closed, windows shut, making the house look like a tomb, even though outside it was sunny. The stale stench of cigarette smoke hung in the air. Frank, who had always been clean-cut, was unshaven and wearing wrinkled, dirty pants and a tank top. His face looked pale and drawn, and dark, puffy half-circles drooped below his bloodshot eyes.

Like a zombie, Frank greeted his life-long best friend. He then went into the kitchen and offered him a glass of scotch. "Somehow I still have quarter of a bottle left," he said with a crooked smile and hoarse voice.

Bob could not believe what he was witnessing. Frank had always been a pillar of strength, confidence, and honor. He declined Frank's offer and suggested that he take a shower and wake himself up. Frank nodded, but poured himself a glass of scotch first.

"Frank, please, it's noon. And you look like you've tied one on pretty good last night. Why don't you skip the scotch and just take a shower? I'll wait for you."

"Noon, huh? At least it's not morning." Frank then slammed down the booze. "Relax, let me take a shower. I'll be out in a bit."

As Frank took a shower, Bob tried to clean up the kitchen. All the while, he wondered what he could do for his friend. Frank was in a hole and Bob was ready to do anything to pull him out, but feared that the hole was just too deep. And that killed Bob. It ate him up inside.

As Bob cleaned the kitchen, worried sick, Frank discovered an open, almost empty bottle of gin lying on the nightstand. Before going in the shower, he guzzled its last remaining drops.

After about a half hour Frank walked into the now clean kitchen. He was wearing clean shorts and a T-shirt. And his hair was washed and slicked back. Frank had also shaved, but had several, small wads of tissue on his and face where he had nicked himself. He thanked Bob for cleaning up and then asked if he wanted to hit the bar. Bob had heard and seen enough. He laid into his friend, giving him some tough love.

Frank was not expecting Bob's lecture, nor did he appreciate it. Listening to the tone instead of digesting the words and place they were coming from, Frank grabbed the bottle of scotch that was still on the kitchen table and slammed its remaining contents.

That infuriated Bob. "See, that's what I'm talking about! Look at you! You need some professional help!"

Already becoming more and more agitated with each word, Frank had also heard enough. "Don't you ever fuckin' think you can stand in my shoes and understand what I've been trough!" Once he started going, it was like a boulder rolling downhill. "You have no fucking idea what it's like to lose a son! Maybe Billy will die in that prison, then you'll understand!"

Bob knew it was the booze talking, but regardless, Frank had crossed the line. In a fit of rage he shoved his best friend to the floor. "I don't care what your excuse is! You ever talk about my son like that and I will kick your ass! No wonder why Mary left you!"

Fury shot through Frank's body. He picked himself off the kitchen floor and charged Bob. The two once inseparable friends wrestled each other to the ground, knocking over chairs and glasses. Grappling and choking, both men landed punches when the opportunity arose. Rolling on the floor, they made their way to the living room, smashing into an armoire, breaking some of its contents. Finally, after about ten minutes, Bob was able to free himself of Frank and get up.

"Don't you ever call me friend again!" With that Bob stormed out of the house.

One Sunday morning in mid-October, Frank's doorbell rang. Still half asleep and hungover, he put on pants and went to see who was there. It was a process server. Mary had filed for divorce. Though it certainly did not come as a surprise, it was nevertheless devastating. For nearly the whole day, Frank sat at the kitchen table, staring at the papers. So many thoughts ran through his tattered mind. He pictured him and Mary as teenagers, sitting at the soda shop, walking hand-in-hand down their old neighborhood, kissing under the school bleachers. He thought about them making love before he went off to war. He remembered clearly the joy on her beautiful face when he came back from Europe and surprised her at the factory. He thought about their wedding, moving into their very own house, the birth of Thomas and Eileen. He thought about the time they went to Hawaii and pictured the two of them having that candlelit dinner on the beach. Frank thought about all the promises they had made. Then Frank thought about how horrible he had treated her since Thomas had gone to Vietnam. He had abandoned her, lied to her, put her through a living hell at a time when she needed him most.

The truth was that Frank did love Mary, with every fiber of his being. And he wanted nothing more than for them to be together again and have things the way they once were. But that was not possible. Deep inside, Frank knew his actions were not worthy of his wife's—or daughter's—forgiveness. After staring at the divorce papers for hours while scouring through his mind, Frank signed them. With a simple swirl of the pen, he knew that it was the end.


There was not much to the divorce, nothing to fight over. Mary did not want the house. Eileen was eighteen and out of high school, so she did not ask for child support. She did not even ask for any of Frank's money or alimony. Mary didn't want anything from Frank, except her freedom. But Frank was not going to let Mary walk away with nothing. She deserved better than that. He called up Walter Rubenstein and asked if he was still interested in buying the hardware business.

Walter knew that he had his old boss over a barrel. He said he was still interested, but could only put together $130,000, less than half of what he had offered Frank a year earlier. Convinced Walter was trying to screw him, Frank said to forget it; he already had an offer nearly twice that. Walter knew his old mentor was bluffing. If Frank could have easily sold the business for double, he certainly would not have come to him. However, just because there was not another seller waiting in the wings, did not mean Frank could not go out and find one. Despite Frank's absence, all three stores were still doing extremely well. On the other hand, in Frank's current condition, the business could be run into the ground at any time and rendered useless. Any one of his managers could now easily embezzle from him. Also, though Walter was a shrewd business-man, and Frank had been an asshole recently, part of him felt sorry for his old mentor. Walter had always liked Thomas and for years, respected and admired his father.

Frank and Walter finally settled on the price of $185,000 for all three stores. Before the sale, Walter went through all the company books, to make sure that no one had been stealing money and that the business was still in good standing, which it was. After that, the deal went down fast. Within three weeks, Frank had relinquished all control and ownership to Harold & Son. It was a day that he had never imagined would come.

After paying some legal fees and the taxman, Frank was left with a little over $120,000. He also already had a substantial amount of money in several bank accounts, which he had saved up over the years. Fortunately, Frank's recent drinking and irresponsibility had not affected his financial status. Keep in mind that in 1970, $1,000 roughly had the same buying power as $5,700 in 2010 U.S. Dollars.


The Monday following Thanksgiving, Frank called Dorothy and asked if she could meet him that afternoon at a diner. At first Dorothy was surprised to even hear his voice. Frank would not tell her what it was about, but promised it was nothing bad. Frank sounded sober—which he was—so Dorothy agreed. Later that day, while Bob was still at work, Dorothy met Frank at the diner as planned. She asked how he was doing, but there was an awkward, strained feeling in the air. Both of them knew their close relationship—they had almost been like brother and sister—would never be the same.

Once they were in a booth, Frank wasted no time in reaching across the table and handing Dorothy a white envelope. Having no idea what could be inside, she unfolded the flap and pulled out its contents. She could not believe her eyes. "Frank, this is a check made out to Mary for a hundred and five thousand dollars."

"I knew I could trust you to get it to her. I know she didn't ask for anything in the divorce, but I want her to have this. It should be enough for her to live on for a while."

Her jaw still opened, Dorothy looked again at the check. "The hardware business must be good."

"Well it's been very well to me over the years. But not all of that is from savings. I also sold the business, all three stores."

Dorothy was completely taken aback. "But you built that business up from the ground. I don't understand, if you already had plenty of money why did you sell it?"

Frank let out a fleeting sigh. "Dorothy, I think you and I both know that I'm not in any shape to run a business anymore. At least I sold it while it was still profitable, before I ran it into the ground." Frank paused. "Besides, I need to get out of New York—just go somewhere and clear my head."

Frank then handed Dorothy a larger, manila envelope. "Here's the papers to the house. I paid it off and put it in Mary's name. She belongs there. I already moved everything I need into a storage container." Frank leaned over the table, closer to Dorothy. "Please, this is important, you have to convince her that she and Eileen belong in that house. She'll listen to you. It's not right that she's living with her parents. And Eileen shouldn't be living in some apartment with that guy." Frank pointed to the envelope. "This is their home. And tell Mary that I swear on my mother's and father's graves that I will never go there and bother them."

Dorothy looked at Frank. She knew how much it had to have pained him to let go of Harold & Son, move from his house, and admit to himself that there was no going back to the way things had been. "What about you Frank? What are you going to live on? What are you going to do?"

With his hands still clasped on the table, Frank leaned back. "I'll be okay. I still have money left over for myself. There wasn't that much money left on the house. As for what I'm going to do—I was thinking maybe heading out west. Maybe I can buy some cheap ranch out there. I've always loved horses."

Dorothy looked beyond the man Frank had become and remembered the devoted and loving husband and father, the hardworking entrepreneur he had been for so many years. To see him there now, broken, drove a stake through her heart. She put her hands atop his and leaned forward. "You're a good man Frank; you just need some help."

Frank gently pulled his hands away and looked down. "I'm not a good man, Dorothy. I used to be good man, but I'm not anymore."

Frank and Dorothy did not eat; they just each had a cup of coffee. Then, after walking outside together, Dorothy gave him a tight hug. "You take care of yourself, Frank Keller."

"You, too. And please tell Bob that I'm sorry for the way everything happened."

Dorothy let go of her embrace. "I will. You know he still loves you like a brother Frank and no matter what happens, he always will."

Frank nodded. "I know."

Dorothy held onto Frank's hands. "I'll pray for you Frank. And wherever you are, know that I'll be thinking about you. And I really do hope you find peace. I really do."

Frank smiled. "Bob's a lucky man. You're a great woman, Dorothy. And an amazing friend and mother. And I know Billy will come home safe to you. I know it in my heart."

Dorothy fought back tears. "Thank you." Then, after one last hug, they parted ways.

# 31

# TIMES SQUARE

nstead of heading out west like he had suggested to Dorothy, Frank made it as far as Manhattan. There, he rented a small apartment near Times Square on a month-to-month lease. He had no idea when he was going to pick up and head somewhere else. Even giving Mary over $100,000 and paying off the small amount left on the house, Frank had plenty of money. He was not broke, but he was most certainly broken.

Frank spent that Christmas, of 1970, at a local dive bar next to his apartment. There, he sat alone drinking the night away, his barstool his own little world. As he polished off beer after beer, Frank could not help but wonder what his wife and daughter were doing that Christmas night. He wanted so much to be with them, so much to turn back the clock to a time when they joyfully huddled together by the decorated Christmas tree and opened up presents. The image of it crushed his soul. Dwelling on it, Frank knew that if he was not in a public place he probably would have broken down in tears. But nevertheless, he was crying on the inside.

Nearly a week later, on New Year's Eve, Frank stayed in his

apartment with a bottle of whiskey, watching the ball drop in Times Square on a small, fuzzy, black and white TV. It had been a horrible, devastating year, but unfortunately, he knew that the turn of the calendar would bring even more misery and regret.


By 1971, the hippies, along with their mantra of peace and hope, were fading into cultural history. The Summer of Love somehow already seemed like a distant memory. There had been too much strife, too much civil unrest to even fathom some wished-for utopia. The last half of the Sixties had felt as though it lasted an entire generation. War, assassinations, and riots—now all anyone wanted was in some way or another to move on. As for Vietnam, there would soon begin a slow and gradual drawdown of U.S. troops. There was still much anger and dissent over the war. By now even the most adherent supporters just wanted it to be over.

Not only in America, but also across the whole western world, the times were changing once again. The Beatles had announced their break-up, to the disbelief and dismay of millions. Jimi Hendrix and Janis Joplin had died of drug overdoses. That year, Jim Morrison would follow their path into a young, drug-induced grave. Economies were stagnant. Cocaine and heroin were replacing marijuana and acid. Causes seemed more quixotic than ever. From New York to California, Kansas to London, Leeds to West Berlin, people were asking: "What's next?"

New York City in 1971 was…well, a shithole. It was certainly no place that you wanted to raise a family. Graffiti adorned nearly every train, was on walls and even billboards. Crime ran rampant. "Regular people" did not venture into Central Park at night. Certain places like Hells Kitchen and Alphabet City were ganglands. Time Square, far removed from a tourist attraction, was lined with prostitutes, peddlers, and peepshows. Unfortunately, Manhattan's darkest days were still ahead. It would be nearly two decades before the city's economy and streets would recover and it would once again become the tourism mecca it had once been.

One word has been used more than any other by commoners, writers, and scholars alike to sum up Times Square during the Seventies: Seedy. It had become a microcosm of the entire country at the time; directionless, careless, and vice-laden. Life was not measured by the possibility of tomorrow, but rather the reality of the hour. Times Square in the Seventies was a place where dreams came to die. It was a fitting place for Frank Keller. He was not as financially destitute as many of its inhabitants. Nevertheless, his despondency, anguish, and loneliness exuded the same forlorn air.

Frank was bitter at the world and bitter at himself. He not only kept drinking, but drowned further into the abyss. Now, the only days that he did not drink himself into self-loathing oblivion were the ones that he slept all day. He had come to realize that—sans Thomas' death—he was the lone culprit of his family's demise. But coming to grips with that did no help. In fact, it ate at him like a cancer of the soul. He missed Mary and Eileen so much. Of course, he missed Thomas as well, but his son's fate had been beyond his control. Mary's and Eileen's estrangement had been his own doing. So many days and nights he stared at the phone, aching to call Mary. But he never did. Frank had made a promise to never again burden his wife and daughter. He had caused them enough anguish.

Frank spent most of his time at a small, dank tavern named Jimmy's Corner, down the block from his apartment. A stone's throw away from his bedroom, it became his de facto home. He would sit on his favorite barstool and drink away the day and night. Although he had become a recluse, Frank inevitably made acquaintances with the bartenders and most of the regulars. They became his only friends, and the bar his only outlet for conversation and human companionship. But Frank had become beyond lonely. Sometimes, when he was at Jimmy's Corner, knocking down drinks, lost in small talk, the loneliness would subside for the moment. But alone in his diminutive, dark apartment, especially at night, that loneliness was crushing. He had never imagined that solitude could be so painful.

Like many of the pubs in New York during the early Seventies, Jimmy's Corner was mostly filled with men. However, there were a few women who were regulars, usually older, hard-drinking, weathered, take-me-home-tonight women. But near Times Square, younger, yet still weathered prostitutes were never too far away. The only time Frank really seemed content was when he was talking to a female. He was usually drunk, but the company of a woman took his mind off everything else, at least for a while. At first, he would just talk with them and then later go back to his apartment and masturbate.

But one night Jean, a thirty-something-year-old who looked years beyond her age, started getting particularly flirty. He had seen her at the bar a dozen times before, but usually she was hanging all over someone else. But that night was Frank's turn. He was drunk, she was drunk, and after hours of being touchy-feely, Jean bluntly asked if Frank was going to take her home. She quickly followed it up by whispering in his ear just what he could do to her. Frank, who had not had sex in some time and was naturally horny, paid his tab and away they went.

Frank was in his forties, but had been with only one woman his entire life. As unbelievable as that seems, it was not unheard of for his generation. But unlike when he was younger and the way he was brought up, this was not making love; it was sex. Frank slept with Jean that night, as well as several more times. But she was not a one-woman man—and Frank was not looking for a relationship anyway. However, his appetite had been wet. Frank was about to be introduced into the world of prostitution. And in New York City, in 1971, whores were as easy to come by as liquor.

Frank dabbled with several different prostitutes, usually taking them back to his apartment. These were streetwalkers, not any high-priced escorts. Frank never felt any attachment; it was merely an outlet for his pent-up sexual desire and took his mind off of everything else for a while. However, after trying-out several different women, Frank met a prostitute named Daisy, who became his regular.

Daisy seemed different than the other working girls. He met her at Jimmy's Corner, where she would come in every once in a while.

Tall, with big, poufy red hair and large breasts, she was in her mid-thirties. She always dressed a little tamer than most of the other prostitutes and looked less weathered. Frank would use her services a few times a week. But sometimes, when she was "off-duty," they would hang out at Jimmy's. Frank had no misconceptions about who Daisy was, but he enjoyed the companionship. Daisy, despite her situation, had a good sense of humor and actually made Frank laugh.

The first time Frank took Daisy to the apartment and undressed in front of her, she ran her fingers over the scar on his chest and asked what had happened.

"It was in a different life," he mumbled.

Daisy did not push the subject. In her world, keeping secrets was lifeblood. Everyone had a past from which they were trying to run. But in time, though still holding much back, Frank would open up to her more than he had anyone else since leaving Levittown. He would later tell her that he had been in World War II and had landed in Normandy, and that he had recently been divorced. He never did divulge all the details and again, Daisy never did pry.

Although Frank found spurts of contentment, he was still a bitter man, and most of his time was spent sulking, crying, or stewing. He was not always a happy drunk. One night, after he had been throwing down beers and shots at Jimmy's Corner for several hours, he accused the main bartender of shorting him. Frank swore that he had given the burly bartender a twenty, but the bartender insisted it was a five—which it was. It was not the first time Frank had gotten into it with the same bartender, but it would be the last. Half-past drunk, he went into a tirade of profanities and threatened to kick the bartender's ass. A younger regular tried to calm Frank down, but when he put his hands on his shoulder, Frank immediately swung around and punched him square in the jaw. The man staggered, but then punched Frank in the eye. A melee ensued, which ended with the bartender literally throwing a drunken, wounded Frank out the front door and warned him never to come back.

Jimmy's Corner had become Frank's watering hole, but the entire city was teeming with pubs and dive-bars. Usually a creature of habit, Frank started stopping at different places, sometimes hitting three or four bars in a day. He also started spending a lot of time just sauntering down the congested city sidewalks. Times Square was a spectacle at night. Under its famous, glowing neon lights the streets crawled with prostitutes, pimps, peddlers, dealers, junkies, conmen, and those just looking to indulge in its shady playground. There was always electricity pulsating through the air; not exactly a positive electricity, but electricity nonetheless.

Eventually, Frank met new characters at different bars, though none he would consider more than a casual acquaintance, a drinking buddy for the afternoon or night. Frank had not seen Daisy in over two weeks, and he was embarrassed by the black eye and swollen lip he had received at Jimmy's. But then he and Daisy started "seeing" each other again.

One weekday morning in late March, Daisy dropped by Frank's apartment unannounced. Still half-asleep, Frank was surprised to see her.

"Sorry, is this a bad time?"

"No, no." Frank waved her in. "Is something wrong?"

Dressed in blue jeans, sweater, leather jacket, and sneakers—not her usual working clothes—Daisy smiled as she entered the apartment. "No, nothing's wrong. I just figured we could do something off the clock for a change. I have the whole day. I never usually do this with my other clients, but well, let's just say you're different."

Frank smiled back. "Sure," he said in an upbeat voice, despite his hangover. "What do you want to do?"

Daisy stepped right up to Frank, who was shirtless. "Well, this might sound strange seeing as I have sex for a living, but I am feeling a little horny." She then put her hands around Frank's waist.

"Well, I think we can do something about that."

Frank and Daisy had sex. Then they had sex again. Then they actually fell asleep together for an hour. Frank enjoyed the sex, but it felt just as good to actually hold a woman in his arms again while he slept. When they awoke, most of the day was still left. After giving Frank a blowjob, Daisy asked what they should do.

"Come on, I'm taking you to lunch" he said with a smile, feeling the most content he had been in a long time. "Somewhere nice."

Frank took Daisy to an Italian restaurant in the Theater District that he had heard of. Before they even sat down Daisy was impressed. She had no idea that Frank had money. In fact, being unemployed, she wondered how he paid for her services and was always at the bar. But once again, in her world, people did not ask too many questions.

"Would you like a bottle of wine?" Frank hardly ever drank wine, but felt that being in an Italian restaurant it would be appropriate.

"Frank, you sure you have enough money?" Whispered Daisy. "This place is kind of expensive. And we don't need a bottle of wine. It's nice though, but…"

Frank smiled. "Don't you worry about it. Really, it's okay, I promise. And you order anything you want to on the menu."

Just then the waiter came over. Frank asked him for some recommendations from the wine list and ordered a bottle.

After the waiter returned with the bottle and poured them each a glass.

Frank held his up. "To a wonderful afternoon. Thank you for stopping by."

Daisy carefully met his glass with her own. "Thank you. I have to stop by more often," she said with a smile.

Over their drinks, Daisy told Frank a funny story about something that had just happened to one of her friends. In return, Frank told an amusing narrative about something that happened in the bar the other night. They then talked about the weather and how much Daisy was looking forward to the summer. Their conversation flowed, but it was never anything too personal or serious.

Someone sitting at another table looking over at Frank and Daisy, laughing, smiling, sharing a glass of wine, would never know it was a prostitute and a down-and-out alcoholic. But then again, what can you really tell about someone by gazing at them from across a restaurant?

"This food is excellent," Daisy said enthusiastically as she cut another piece of her veal parmigiana. Frank, who had ordered linguini and white clam sauce, agreed.

Daisy then put down her fork and knife. "Frank, I have to thank you again. This is really nice. I'm really having a good time."

Frank raised his glass and smiled. "I am too. It's been a while since I sat down and enjoyed a good meal in a nice restaurant with someone."

After they were done with lunch, Frank suggested they go have a couple of drinks.

Daisy looked at he watch. It was only 2:00 p.m. and she did not have to be at "work" until 9:00 p.m. "Okay, but I'm buying the drinks. You paid for enough already."

Frank realized that it was the first time in his life that a woman actually offered to pay for his drinks.

As they walked to the bar, it started to snow.

"I can't believe it's snowing," Daisy complained. "It'll be April in a few days. This has been the longest winter."

Frank agreed.

Daisy led Frank to a nearby cocktail lounge that she had never been to before, hoping that none of her clients would recognize and bother her. There, she and Frank ponied up by the bar and commenced their drinking. Frank tried to pay, but Daisy would not let him. Surprisingly, there was a good crowd for a Wednesday afternoon and the atmosphere was lively.

"Hey Frank," Daisy nudged closer, "did you hear what that couple that just left was talking about?"

Frank thought he knew the couple to which she was referring; a well dressed man and a woman who looked to be in their mid-forties and had been sitting at the bar next to them. But he had not picked up any of their conversation and shook his head.

"I overheard them talking about Las Vegas. They're planning a trip there." Daisy's face lit up. "Wouldn't that be amazing? Get out of this cold, drab city. I heard it's so exciting there. And it's probably so warm, even now, that you could go swimming outside."

"Sounds like you've thought about Vegas before."

Daisy smiled, as if she were envisioning herself there. "Oh yeah. I've always wanted to go to Las Vegas."

"So let's go."

"That would be great. Maybe someday."

"No, I mean right now, tonight."

Daisy looked at Frank for a few seconds then started laughing. "You're funny. I thought you were serious for a second."

Frank grabbed hold of Daisy's hand and stared straight into her eyes. "I am serious. Let's do it. Me and you by the pool, hitting the casinos, going out to dinner."

Daisy laughed again. "You're crazy. Or drunk. Or maybe both."

Frank said again that he was serious.

"I just can't get up and leave. Besides, I don't have the money for that."

"It's my treat. I have the money. You don't have to spend a dollar. Really, it's—"

Daisy cut him off. "I couldn't do that, Frank. Taking me out to lunch is one thing, but…that's very nice of you, but I can't."

"Listen to me, I have some money squirreled away. I want to do this. I want to go there with you."

Daisy shook her head, trying to not let herself get caught up in some fairytale. "Even if you pay, I can't just get up and leave for two or three days. I have work. You think I can just tell Jonny I'm not coming in tonight, because I'm going on vacation? It doesn't work that way."

Though Frank had never met Johnny, he knew from previous mentions that he was Daisy's pimp. "Fuck him. You're not his slave. He doesn't own you."

Daisy did not know if Frank was being naïve or benevolent. But again she told him that it did not work that way.

"Just tell him that you have a family emergency somewhere. It'll just be for a few days."

Frank motioned for the bartender, who came right over. "Here's five bucks. Can I borrow your phone and the yellow pages?"

The bartender thought about it for a second and told him just not to go crazy with any long distance calls.

"What are you doing?" Daisy asked.

"I'll make a deal with you: If I call and there's seats available on a flight out tonight and there's a hotel available, we go. If there isn't, I'll drop the subject for good."

As Daisy was pondering Frank's words, the bartender came back with the phone and the yellow pages. Daisy polished off her drink and ordered another round. "Okay."

Frank's face lit up and he immediately started thumbing through the phonebook, looking for airlines.

"It doesn't matter anyway. You'll never find a flight tonight." She looked at her watch. "It's already two-forty-five."

As Frank made some calls right there at the bar, Daisy started thinking about Las Vegas. It was such a crazy idea, but imagined herself lounging by the pool and sitting at the blackjack table, soaking up all the glitter and extravagance that Las Vegas had to offer. Daisy tapped Frank on the shoulder and said she was going to the ladies room. Once in the bathroom, she kicked herself for getting caught in some fantasy. Having some guy—a guy she really liked—spontaneously whisk her away to Las Vegas was something that only happened in the movies.

When she walked back to the bar, Frank was off the phone and waiting with a grin on his face. "TWA has two seats left on a seven o'clock flight tonight. It's a sign. I put them on hold. And I booked us a room at the Frontier, right on the strip."

Daisy wondered how long she had been in the restroom.

"A deal's a deal," Frank said.

Daisy stood there for what seemed like a minute. She then grabbed her drink and took a big gulp. "I'm gonna go outside and use the payphone. In the meantime, order me a shot of Jameson's."

After about ten minutes, Frank wondered if Daisy was coming back. Maybe he had spooked her and she just left. Or maybe Johnny was not going to let her leave. Suddenly, for the first time that day, he started feeling low. But after a few more minutes Daisy showed back up, though she had a poker face on, which Frank could not read. Before saying anything, she picked up her shot of Jameson's and slammed it down.

"Is this for real? Are we really going to Las Vegas?"

Frank jumped off his barstool and gave Daisy a bear hug, then a kiss on the lips. It was real. They were going to Vegas!

Frank and Daisy made plans to go to their respective apartments, pack, and then meet back up at Frank's and catch a cab to the airport. On the way to his apartment Frank stopped at the bank and withdrew enough money to cover the tickets, hotel, and one hell of a time. At 5:00 p.m. Daisy showed up at Frank's place, just as agreed.

"I can't believe we're really doing this," she said with a smile and two suitcases. For her, it was just like a movie.

# 32

# SIN CITY

Because there were only two tickets left on the plane, Frank and Daisy did not have adjoining seats. However, Frank worked his charm and the lady originally ticketed to sit next to Daisy was willing to move to her seat. After the plane reached cruising altitude, he and Daisy ordered a cocktail. It was hard to tell which one of them was more excited. But after a long day of drinking, they both soon fell asleep. As the plane gracefully glided along its turbulent-free route, Daisy rested her head on Frank's shoulder.

As the captain announced their initial descent, Frank and Daisy woke up from their slumber. It took Daisy a good thirty seconds before she realized where she was. Only eight hours ago she was planning to hit the streets, ready for another dreary night in Times Square. At the same time, Frank could never have imagined that by night's end he would be in Las Vegas. Nevertheless, there they were, twenty thousand feet in the air and descending on the legendary desert city.

Once Daisy shook off her drowsiness, she grabbed hold of Frank's arm. "Is this a dream? You have to pinch me."

Frank smiled and pinched her waist.

They both laughed.

Because of the time difference, it was only 9:45 p.m. when they landed. After getting their luggage, Frank and Daisy went outside to get a taxi to the hotel. It was still warm.

"It sure beats the snow, huh?" Frank joked.

By the time they checked into their room it was close to 11:00 p.m. But well rested, both Frank and Daisy were pumping with adrenaline. After freshening up they went to one of the hotel's restaurants and had dinner. Back in New York, on a Wednesday night, many places would have been closing up. But in Las Vegas, it was as if it was 8:00 p.m. on a Friday night. The casino was abuzz with people and the clanging sound of coins and ding-ding-ding of slot machines. Scantily clad cocktail waitresses sauntered down the aisles with trays of drinks. Assorted lights shone as bright as the afternoon sun.

Frank and Daisy found a home at a blackjack table. Frank tried giving her money to gamble, but she insisted on using her own. For a little while, Frank appeared to be on a hot streak and the chips started to pile up. Rounds of drinks were ordered. The table was full and electric. The one time Daisy had blackjack, she screamed with excitement as though she was a little kid on Christmas. After cards, they tried their luck at roulette. Daisy had lost her money at the blackjack table, but Frank insisted on her taking forty dollars. The roulette wheel was even livelier than the card table. Now Daisy went on a hot streak, in the end winning a $150. She tried to give it all back to Frank, but he talked her into keeping it to gamble with.

After roulette, Frank and Daisy stopped at one of the casino's bars and then hit the slot machines. The drinks flowed and the hours ticked away unnoticed. By the time they found their way back to the room it was 4:30 a.m. At that point drunk and finally exhausted, they passed out, foregoing any sex. In fact, Frank fell asleep still wearing his pants.

Daisy woke up dehydrated and in pain. She looked at the clock on the nightstand: 2:15 p.m. Hearing Daisy groan and move the blankets, Frank also woke-up. He felt just as shitty as his companion. Because of the long, thick curtains, the room was still dark. Frank asked what time it was and Daisy told him. Then she laughed. His head throbbing, Frank asked what was so funny.

"Are we really in Las Vegas? Or was all that a dream?"

Frank laughed as well. He suggested some food would make them feel better. But not in any shape to go anywhere just yet, he ordered room service. As they waited for it, Daisy gingerly opened the curtains. At first the light was blinding, but in an instant her languished demeanor changed. "Frank, did you know our room has a view of the pool? Come look, there's people down there in the water and just lounging around."

Frank slowly wandered over.

Daisy took hold of his arm. "Oh Frank, after we eat, do you think we can sit by the pool?" She asked with a wheedling smile.

"Of course."

After eating, which did make them both feel better, Daisy asked if Frank wanted to take a shower with her. It was an offer he was not going to turn down. In the shower Daisy gave him a blowjob, then they had sex.

It was 4:00 p.m. by the time Frank and Daisy made it to the pool. But the Nevada sun was still bright. Daisy immediately made Frank go in the water. Afterwards, they laid out on two lounge chairs and each ordered a Bloody Mary. By now, their hangovers were gone. Food, sex, sun, a pool, and a Bloody Mary will do that. Frank looked up at the clear, blue sky and then over at Daisy, who was blissfully soaking up the sun's rays. He then took a sip of his drink and thought for the first time in a long while that life was good.

That night Daisy insisted on taking Frank out to dinner. They then took a taxi to Desert Sands Resort and Casino to do some more gambling. It was another vibrant, fun-filled night. This time however, Daisy set the alarm clock in the room for 10:30 a.m. She wanted to spend the whole day at the pool. Frank joined her. It was Friday, their last day in Vegas. Frank surprised Daisy with tickets to see a show.

Inevitably, Saturday morning came; their flight was scheduled for 1:00 p.m. After waking up and having sex, Daisy laid in Frank's arms.

"I can never repay you for this," she said in a melancholic voice. "This has been like a dream come true. I wish we didn't have to back home."

Frank raised himself in bed. "What if we don't have to?"

Daisy gave him a crazy look. "What are you talking about?"

"To hell with New York. We can get a house here, you and me." Daisy asked him if he was still drunk.

"I'm serious. I have some money. Let's never go back."

Daisy climbed out of bed and started to put on a T-shirt. "Frank, I had such a good time here. And I love spending time with you, I really do. But I just can't get up and leave. I have a life in New York."

"Is that really a life you want to go back to? Working the streets?"

"It's not just that. I can't leave my little girl."

Frank was taken aback. "You have a daughter?"

Daisy sat back on the bed, next to Frank. "She's eight-years-old. I'm sorry, I guess I should have told you, but it just never came up. My mother, who lives in Brooklyn, raises her. But I see her all the time." Daisy looked at the floor. "I know I'm not the world's best mother. But I can't just leave her. And I can't take her away from my mother. Plus, I can't leave my mother either."

For the first time Frank realized how little he really knew Daisy. But then again, what did she really know about him? Of course, he also thought of his own daughter. Frank had estranged himself from her and it ate at him. He could not ask Daisy to do the same. "I understand," was all he said.

The flight back to New York was long and doleful. Though Frank and Daisy both had a great time in Vegas and would later look back fondly on the memories, for now they were just sad that it was over and were each thinking about the reality of the lives to which they were returning.

The plane landed after 10:00 p.m. at John F. Kennedy International Airport. After getting their bags it was close to 11:00 p.m. As

Frank and Daisy walked outside to catch a cab, they were hit by a blast of cold, windy air. They shared a taxi back to the city and then went their separate ways. Before doing so though, Daisy gave Frank a kiss and thanked him once more for the experience.

"It might have been just three days, but it's three days I'll never, ever forget," she added with a smile.

Frank may have been back in Manhattan, but his mind was still in Las Vegas. Though it was the beginning of April, New York was still brutal and, to Frank, never seemed more dirty, old, and drab. Besides the excitement of the casino, he thought about the desert warmth and how new and clean everything was. More than anything, he thought about how much more alive he felt in Las Vegas. After only a week of being back in New York, Frank had made up his mind: He was moving to Sin City.

Frank sold his car, which had been collecting dust in a Manhattan garage, and bought a 1969 Pontiac GTO. He boxed up all his possessions and fit them into the trunk and backseat. Frank was actually looking forward to driving cross-country. Of course, he had nowhere to live once he arrived in Las Vegas, but figured he would just stay at a hotel until he could find an apartment. As proven by his Manhattan dwelling, Frank did not need anything lavish.

The only person, besides his landlord, that Frank told about moving was Daisy. One Saturday morning she met him at a coffee shop in Times Square to say goodbye. She had mixed feelings about him leaving. Daisy truly did care about Frank and wished him luck and hoped he would find a new start in life. On the other hand, she secretly feared that he would quickly lose all his money in the casinos and be stranded. She was also going to miss him. As sad as it seemed, Frank had become the closest thing she had to a friend—or a lover. And although Daisy realized she knew only a fraction of Frank Keller, she was certain that inside he had a giant heart. After having some breakfast, it was time for the two to part ways.

Daisy gave him a kiss and then a tight hug. "You take care of yourself, Frank," she said, fighting back tears.

"You, too. And if you ever want to come out to Las Vegas, you just look me up you hear." Frank was sincere. But the two would never see each other again.


The drive across the country made Frank feel liberated; the open road seemed like a panacea. Of course, he had no timetable and could stop whenever and wherever he pleased and that's exactly what he did. Driving through the South, he would sometimes venture off the highway just for the hell of it and stop in some town that nobody but its residents even knew existed. Some of them seemed as if they thought the Confederacy had won the Civil War. In most towns Frank would just stay overnight, at some truck stop or roadside motel. But there was one place where he had always wanted to go and planned to stay a few days: New Orleans.

New Orleans was everything Frank had read and heard about. Getting a hotel not far from the French Quarter, he hit as many bars as he could, listening to live jazz music and soaking up the unique, electric atmosphere. He also fell in love with the food. At first, he only planned to stay for two nights, but wound up staying four. He hoped to make it back to New Orleans again, but it was time to get back on that open road.

After leaving New Orleans, Frank headed northwest, taking him through parts of Texas, New Mexico, and Arizona. Frank marveled at the expanse of the West and its majestic, mountainous backdrop. He could not help but think about how hard it must have been for pioneers trekking across the unforgiving land in horses and covered wagons. It must have been extremely arduous and, he knew, often deadly. But the landscape sure was beautiful.

One afternoon he stopped in Santa Fe. It was like a different world. Everything was so picturesque and open, such the opposite of New York. The air was crisp and clean. All the people seemed so friendly. After having lunch in a Mexican cantina, which he greatly enjoyed, Frank just walked around town for a while, taking in the sights. Of course, he had to stop into a local bar for a drink. It was like something out of a spaghetti western.

After more than two weeks on the road, Frank pulled into Las Vegas. Not knowing how long it would take him to find an apartment, he set up his temporary residence at a cheap motel in downtown that rented by the week. Then, after unloading the car, Frank cleaned up and hit the casinos.

Frank was able to find an apartment within a week. It was a humble, but clean and homey one bedroom in a new complex, about a mile from downtown. But if Frank had thought that he was going to relive the three-day lark that he and Daisy had spent in Las Vegas, he was mistaken. After about two weeks, Frank was as depressed as he had been living in New York City. All alone, a stranger in a strange land, Frank felt more removed from his family and previous life than ever before.

Frank spent much of his time hanging out at dive-bars and lower-end casinos in downtown Las Vegas, a place he soon realized was as shady as Times Square. There, he was just one of the other thousands of faces that blended into the background. When not out drinking or gambling, Frank was holed up in his apartment, mostly sleeping or watching mindless television, just wasting the hours away. Once again, he would sometimes look at the phone, part of him wanting to call Mary—or even Dorothy to see how she was—but he never did.

One night, after drinking nearly half a bottle of scotch, Frank broke out an old family album, which had been stowed away in a box. It was the first time he had looked at it since leaving Levittown. It was like looking into the window of a past life. There were photographs of him and Mary at their wedding, pictures of him holding Thomas as a baby, as well as Eileen. There were pictures of the kids at various ages. There were also photos of them all together as a family. The one thing all the pictures had in common were the always-present smile on all of their faces. As Frank slowly thumbed through the pages, tears poured freely down his face. After finishing, he put the album back in the box.

Eventually, Frank once again took comfort in the company of prostitutes. And in Las Vegas, they were even easier to come by than anywhere in New York. Sometimes the sex made him forget about his woes, but like everything else he did to dull the anguish, it was always fugacious. Bitterness, guilt, sorrow, grief, always churned within him. The only difference was that sometimes it simmered and other times it could not help but boil over.

By the beginning of July, Frank was getting restless. He had not worked in some time and felt as though he was wasting away. This was someone who had worked since the age of thirteen. Even when he had managers to run the day-to-day operation of his business, Frank went from store to store, helping customers, going over paperwork, and showing the younger guys how it was done. For a man who had spent most of his life always being busy and constructive, even the bars and casinos were becoming too monotonous. When in the apartment, Frank was starting to get cabin fever.

There was also the issue of income. Somehow, Frank had managed to keep his gambling in check and never lost an exuberant amount on any given night. He also lived modestly, really only splurging the time he and Daisy went to Vegas for a few days. The places he frequented had cheap booze and the hookers he slept with were not high-end. He had spent money, but still had a sizeable amount in the bank. Yet Frank realized that he could not live off that forever.

Frank ran into Jack Polinski, a single, thirty-six-year-old construction worker. A lanky, two-time loser who had a lengthy rap sheet and did a four-year stint for armed robbery, Jack happened to live two apartments down from Frank. The two had met at the bar several times. Although they certainly were not best buddies, while at the bar one evening, Frank told Jack about wanting to get a job. Jack had no idea about Frank's qualifications or anything about his past, but said that he could probably get him a job doing day labor with his construction company. Frank took him up on the offer and the next morning showed up at the job site. Having a laborer just quit on him two days earlier, the foreman didn't ask too many questions. Jack, who was no model citizen but a hard worker, had vouched for him. So just like that, Frank was hired.

It was a menial job and paid as such, but Frank did not mind. In fact, he felt good working with his hands again, putting in an honest day's work. It made Frank feel useful again, something he had not felt in a long time. Having to get up before daybreak, he also scaled down on his drinking for a while. But that's not to say he completely stopped. It was summer and because of the blistering Nevada sun, that meant the men were usually done by 11:30 a.m. Sometimes right after work he would go with Jack or some of the other guys to hit the bar. But now, instead of drinking to forget his name, it was drinking to socialize and unwind.

Frank was never late a minute for work and always busted his ass. He never complained and was liked by the other men. More importantly, Gus, the foreman of the site, appreciated his ilk. In fact, after the job was finished at the end of August, Gus hired Frank on his next project, a restaurant near downtown. But after only a week there were financial complications and the construction was put on hold. Gus and a few of the other men were able to move onto another project that the company was working on, which was already in progress. But there was no room for Frank or Jack. However, Gus promised both men that as soon as something came up he would give them a call.

Instead of looking for another job, Frank and Jack went on a bender. They hit the bars, casinos, and Jack introduced his new friend to the wondrous world of topless dancing. Although Frank had plenty of experience with prostitutes, and even went into several peepshows in Times Square, he had never gone into a full-blown strip club. With a plethora of topless, near-naked girls strutting and gyrating on stage, prancing around and ready to give anyone with a dollar their own vivacious lap dance, Frank instantly fell in love. Jack was going wild, spending all the money he had to his name. Frank was having just as much of a good time, but of course had money saved in the bank. And though he would sometimes pay for their rounds and even a few lap dances for Jack, he didn't reveal he had money.

On the second day of their binge, Jack asked Frank if he wanted to take some peyote. It had not been the first time someone had asked him to take drugs. Many times he had been offered marijuana. But no matter how drunk he was, Frank always equated any kind of drugs with the hippies and the hardcore anti-war movement, which he despised and thus always adamantly refused. Of course, he saw no similarities between smoking a joint or eating some mushrooms, and consuming enough liquor to forget who or where he was.

Over time Frank learned that no matter how much he had drank the previous day and no matter how bad he felt that morning or afternoon, there was no greater cure like the hair of the dog. In New York, he eventually could drink himself into oblivion every single day. So it was no problem keeping up with Jack. In fact, Jack was impressed with how much his neighbor could drink without falling down and passing out, especially without the help of amphetamines.

On the fourth straight day of their bender, Frank and Jack decided to drive down to a casino at the end of the Strip. Jack had an old, beat-up car, but had always wanted to drive Frank's GTO. Frank was already drunk enough to let him do it. Neither one really noticed that Jack was swerving all over the place, but a patrolman did. He pulled them over and gave Jack a field sobriety test. In 1971, it was still not uncommon for a policeman to let a drunk driver go with just a warning, but Jack was completely wasted, barely able to stand up straight. He was also being difficult. The two policemen arrested him on the spot and hauled him off to jail. Realizing that Frank was also drunk, they told him to park the car in the adjacent parking lot and walk home. Seeing what happened to Jack, he did so without argument.

The next morning Frank was woken by the ringing of the phone. It was a collect call from Jack. When taken into custody, they learned he had two outstanding warrants: One for possession of a controlled substance; and the other for burglary.

"I think I'm gonna be in here for a while buddy," was how Jack put it.

# 33

# A STRIPPER
# NAMED TRIXIE

I t was September 10, 1971, the one-year anniversary of Thomas' death. Frank visualized in vivid detail coming home to find Mary sitting at the kitchen table crying, with the telegram in her hand notifying them that their son had been killed in action. Although so many changes had happened in the previous twelve months, he could not believe that a year had already passed. He still could also not believe that Thomas was really gone—and was never coming back.

With the blinds drawn, Frank stayed inside his darkened apartment the whole day, nursing a bottle of scotch, dolorously reflecting on his son, wife, daughter, and a world he used to know. Tears flowed freely until he had no more left. The pain was so immense it was greater than any broken bone or physical cut.

Frank missed Mary and Eileen so much, but at least there was some solace in the fact that they could still live long and happy lives. However, Thomas never even saw his twenty-first birthday. He would never be able to marry, to have a family of his own, to find success. Thomas died before he even really had a chance to live. And for what? He died in some godforsaken jungle fighting someone else's war. Oh, how Frank had come to loathe that war. It had taken his son and destroyed his family—just as it had so many other families across the country.

Sitting there in that dank apartment, disconsolate and drunk, all alone in the world, Frank pulled out the family album. Flipping to a random page, he fixated on a picture of him and Thomas sitting in a rowboat together up in the Catskills, smiles beaming on both of their faces.

"Nooo," Frank cried aloud. "It's not fair! It's not fair!"

Unable to look anymore, he closed the album. Frank then happened to look towards the kitchen and saw an eight-inch carving knife lying on the counter. He looked down at his wrist. He thought about it. It would have been so easy. But for whatever reason, he decided to just crawl into a fetal position and continue crying instead.

For the next week and a half, Frank stayed in his apartment. If he was hungry he would order food and there were no trips to the liquor store. A combination of his over-drinking and the distress over the anniversary of Thomas' death hit him like a hammer. Physically and emotionally sick, he spent hours on end bedridden, either watching television, sleeping, or just thinking. In the dim apartment, each day seemed to last its own lifetime.

The first few days were the hardest, filled with crippling affliction. Frank spent most of the time reflecting on his past life. Both the good and regretful memories seemed just as painful. He mourned the loss of Thomas. He chastised himself for the way he treated Mary and Eileen. He loathed himself for ruining his own life. Frank looked at the future and saw nothing but a dark, lonely abyss. It felt as though nothing was left but to wait for the end.

Occasionally, Frank would doze off, but sleep would provide no relief. He would have nightmares about Thomas or even Mary and Eileen. Sometimes he would dream that they were all together as a family again, but when he woke up and realized the reality, it would cut like a jagged knife through his heart. Soon, Frank would fight to stay awake, but he was simply too exhausted.

After about four days the intense agony faded, leaving a tristful malaise. He was able to numb his mind at times by watching television and ordering in food, but was still too physically and emotionally drained to do anything else or go anywhere. Not even getting drunk sounded appealing. Frank wondered if this was it; if this was how he was going to live out the rest of his days.

Finally, after ten days, Frank could take no more. Either he was going to go out in the sunlight or he was going to kill himself. It was late September and the days were still long and hot in Las Vegas. When he walked out into the early afternoon, the heat and beaming sun made him sick to his stomach. But he knew it would feel even worse after spending any more time in his cave. Weak and still down, Frank decided to turn to his old friend, alcohol. At first, he stopped by the nearest bar. As he sat down on the barstool, he was still trying not to throw up. But after just three beers, Frank was beginning to feel better. In fact, after about an hour, he was feeling full of energy and decided to venture out and find another, livelier watering hole. Frank walked through downtown, hitting a few bars and casinos until he came to a seedy strip club that Jack had introduced him to called The Toy Box. It was there he spent the rest of the evening.


Now back to going out and drinking every day, The Toy Box quickly became Frank's new haunt. Becoming a regular, many of the girls recognized him and would often stop by to chat. It was not long before he took a fancy to one girl in particular. Trixie—at least that was her stage name—was a slender, alluring twenty-something-year-old with long, wavy black hair and green, hypnotic eyes. She had the look of the girl next door. Sometimes, in between dances, she would take a seat next to Frank and bullshit and flirt. Frank very much enjoyed her company but took the flirting as just a stripper doing her job. Then one night after her shift, Trixie asked if he wanted to get a drink. At first Frank thought it was a joke. When he realized it was not, he quickly accepted the offer. They went to a nearby lounge, had some drinks and laughed. Already after midnight when they arrived, they only stayed for about an hour. As they parted, Trixie gave Frank a quick, closed-lip kiss and said she would see him around. Frank had enjoyed himself, but figured it was a one-time deal.

A few days later Frank went back to The Toy Box. He was surprised to see Trixie working a rare afternoon shift. He was even more surprised when, after her shift, at 2:00 p.m., she asked him if he wanted to go out again. Like a little kid asked if he wanted an ice cream sundae, Frank eagerly accepted. Before leaving, they had a round of drinks at The Toy Box. While doing so, Trixie suggested that they go to Caesars Palace. Who was Frank to argue?

Frank and Trixie piled in his GTO and headed down the Strip. Caressing his leg, Trixie said how much she liked the car. Frank loved her hands massaging his thigh. They hit Caesars like a whirlwind, first going to one of the lounges for a few drinks and then playing some slots. Trixie mentioned how much she loved playing craps. Less than ten minutes later they found themselves at the craps table. It did not take long for Trixie to lose all her money, but Frank gave her thirty dollars to gamble.

That evening, all liquored up and still pumping with adrenaline, Trixie suggested that they go back to Frank's place "to fuck." As she said it, she grabbed his crotch. Frank could not get to the car fast enough. But Trixie decided not to wait until they got back to his apartment. While Frank drove, she unzipped his pants and gave him a blowjob. Once back at his place, Trixie quickly made him hard again and they had sex.

Trixie wound up spending the night at Frank's apartment. But early in the morning she woke him up and said she had to leave. Still half-drunk, Frank went over in his mind everything that happened the previous evening. As he did, he was left with one burning question: How much did all that cost him? Used to prostitutes, Frank could not believe that this young, hot stripper gave him a blowjob and sex because she was attracted to him. But then again, she did spend the night and Frank didn't remember her ever bringing up money. Plus they had gone out the other night and nothing happened. But then he went back to finding it difficult to believe that *she* would be interested in *him*. However, Frank did not want to insult her, by asking how much he owed, if she was not on the job.

After getting dressed, Trixie looked at him, still lying in bed. "Well, I had a good time," she said with a smile.

*Is this it? Is she waiting for money?* "I did, too."

"Well?" Trixie just stood there.

*Yes, this is it.* "Oh, I'm sorry," he said, grabbing for his pants.

Trixie saw Frank pull out his wallet. "What are you doing? You think last night was…you think I'm a whore?"

"No, no…I mean…" Frank didn't know what to say. "I…I'm sorry. I feel like such an ass," he said, climbing out of bed. "Fuck, I didn't mean…"

"I was just waiting for you to walk me out."

"Trixie, I'm so sorry. It's just, well…the truth is I just can't believe that a girl as hot as you would be interested in someone like me."

Trixie looked at Frank with a blank stare. "Did you ever think it was because I was just so shitfaced?"

Frank bowed his head. "Oh."

Trixie started laughing. "You should've seen your face. I'm just fuckin' with you. The truth is I had a really good time. And though I'm not looking for anything serious, I think you're handsome and a fun guy." She then walked up to Frank, who was wearing only boxers and grabbed his dick. "Besides, I like older men. They fuck better." She put her lips up to his ear. "And you fuck really good," she whispered in a seductive voice.

Feeling relieved and masculine, Frank walked Trixie to the door and suggested they go out again.

"Well you know where to find me. And you can call me by my real name, Tracy. But not at the club. We don't use real names at the club."

It was not long before Frank and Tracy were seeing each other all the time. But this was not Frank hanging out with some streetwalker at a dive bar or just taking a girl back to his apartment for a half hour. Frank put Tracy on a pedestal. She looked like a princess and he started treating her like one. They would go out for expensive dinners, see a show, rent a suite at Cesar's or the Flamingo for the night, and live the good life. At the casino, Frank would often give her money to gamble. Tracy never asked for Frank to shower her with opulence. She didn't have to. The truth was that he enjoyed his new life in the fast lane, with a beautiful, young lady always hanging over his shoulder. He enjoyed hitting the Strip at night and having wild, passionate sex whenever he wanted. Oh, how he loved the sex. Tracy was like a nymphomaniac and a pure tiger in the bedroom—or the car, or the elevator, or some back room.

Frank's new lifestyle with Tracy was exhilarating. Unfortunately it was also quickly draining his savings. However, he could not stop. Frank was getting addicted to the highlife, but more than that, he was addicted to Tracy and feared that if he could no longer provide her with the fancy dinners, hotel suites, and free gambling she would just find someone that could. Once someone has a taste of filet mignon it's hard to go back to McDonald's.

Although Frank rented the occasional hotel suite, he and Tracy usually spent nights at his apartment. Tracy expressed how much she hated her roommate and never wanted to spend much time at her place. One day in early December, Tracy really went off on a tirade, saying she could not stand to live with her "bitch roommate" any longer.

Seeing her in tears for the first time, Frank asked Tracy if she wanted to move in with him. She happily accepted. The next day he helped her move her belongings, which did not consist of much, mainly just a few suitcases. She also had her beat-up 1963 Plymouth Valiant. She spent many nights at Frank's anyway, so it was not that big of an adjustment. She also still worked at The Toy Box four to six days a week.

Although Tracy had slept over Frank's apartment many times before, it was not until moving in that she witnessed for the first time

Frank animatedly waking up in the middle of the night, out of breath and covered in a cold sweat. He had had the nightmare about Thomas dying in Vietnam, reaching out his hand and pleading for help. At first Tracy thought that Frank might be having a heart attack. But Frank told her it was just a bad dream and that he felt embarrassed.

"It's nothing to be embarrassed about," she consoled him. "Everyone has nightmares now and then. What was it about?"

"I don't know," Frank replied, still out of breath. "I don't even remember."

Tracy knew he was lying, but did not push the subject. She did think, however, that it might have something to do with his son. Frank had told Tracy that he had died in Vietnam, but she knew that he did not like talking about it. She knew he did not like talking much about his past at all.


Tracy had told Frank that her mother left when she was only twelve. Her father had died when she was seventeen and she was estranged from her only other sibling, an older sister. Like Frank, Tracy was without family. With only the two of them, Tracy suggested they go away over Christmas. She said it would not be a problem taking some time off work. They were both drunk when she suggested it, so Frank instantly agreed, saying it was a great idea. They immediately started brainstorming destinations. The winner was Acapulco. In the early Seventies, Acapulco was still one of the hottest beach destinations, with its expansive, luxurious resorts and miles of sandy coastline. It also sounded so exotic.

The next morning Frank woke up hungover and apprehensive about the vacation. He was very cognizant of his dwindling savings. However, he felt it too late to back out. So while Tracy was at work, he went to a travel agent and booked the trip.

The morning of Christmas Eve, they boarded a plane for Acapulco, where they would be spending four nights at a beachside resort. On the plane ride, Tracy finally asked the obvious question:

Without a job, how did Frank have all the money he was spending? Frank told her the truth, that he had sold a business he used to own and had money saved up. She asked him what kind of business and he told her. What Frank did not tell her was that the money was evaporating and that he would soon have to find steady income. It was a conversation that Frank knew he would have to have sooner rather than later, but figured on their way to Acapulco was not the right time.

When they arrived at their resort, it was even more lavish and beautiful than either of them had expected. Staff was there to wait on them hand and foot, and both the grounds of the resort and room exuded luxury. Then there was the beach, which looked right out of a postcard. Having never left the States, Tracy could not believe she was in such a place and kept on thanking Frank profusely.

Being in Acapulco with Tracy, there were moments when Frank could not help but think of the time he had taken Mary to Hawaii. But he pushed them aside and certainly never told Tracy.

Frank and Tracy had a blissful time in Acapulco, spending hours just laying on the beach, playing in the water, even renting jet skis. They hung out by the tiki bar and strolled down the beach, stopping at different resorts to check them out and get a drink. One day they rode around downtown, and Tracy excitedly browsed through all the shops and stalls. One night they went to a nightclub and Tracy even talked Frank into dancing. Another late night, when the beach was dark and empty, she even convinced him to go skinny-dipping. There, in the shallow water, under a serene, star-speckled sky, they made love.

On Christmas night, they celebrated by dressing up and going out to an elegant dinner. They also exchanged gifts. Frank had bought Tracy a gold bracelet. She gave him a watch.

Their time in Acapulco had been amazing, awash with luxury, pleasure, relaxation, and excitement. It was a paradise that neither of them wanted to leave. But their stay in paradise had been time stamped and the real world awaited their return.

Back in Las Vegas, Frank was faced with the reality that no matter how much fun he might have had spending most of it, his money was almost gone. He would have to get a job and certainly could not live the lifestyle that he had become accustomed to over the past three months. He wanted to tell Tracy. He needed to tell Tracy. But he decided to wait until after New Year's, which was only a few days away. On the whole plane ride home from Mexico, she kept talking about New Year's Eve. He figured they could live it up one more night.

On New Year's Eve, Frank booked a suite at Cesar's. That evening he and Tracy went out to dinner at an expensive steakhouse, gambled and joined a party in the hotel's convention center to countdown to midnight. As they ceremoniously kissed, 1971 turned to 1972.

On New Year's evening Frank finally told Tracy about his current financial situation.

She seemed surprised, yet supportive. In fact, she scolded Frank for not telling her earlier. "You should have said something. We didn't have to go to Acapulco. You didn't have to buy me that expensive bracelet. Frank, you should have told me you were running out of money. I'm not with you just because you can buy me things or take me nice places."

Frank was relieved by Tracy's response and told her he would start looking for a job.

The next night, Tracy said she had to return to work; she had been off for six days. But before going, she asked Frank if he could not go there anymore. "I've been meaning to tell you, but it's just that they don't really like the girls' boyfriends or husbands hanging out. One time, Destiny's husband came in and got into a fight with one of the customers, kicked his ass." Tracy paused. "Besides, well...to tell you the truth, now that we're getting more serious and have been together for a while, I feel kind of strange having to take my top off and dance for other guys with you in the club."

Frank nodded. "I understand. Believe me, it makes me feel weird too. That's why I haven't been coming in much. But it's alright, I won't come in at all anymore."

Tracy smiled and gave Frank a quick kiss on the lips. "Thank you."

"But you want me to drive you?"

"It's okay, I can take myself."

The next morning Frank bought a newspaper, sat down at the kitchen table and started looking through the classifieds. He made several phone calls, but a few of the listings of interest said apply in person. One in particular that caught his eye was a sales manager position at a department store. Though Frank had never worked at a department store, he certainly knew about sales, inventory, and managing. So without even a resume, he decided to give it a shot. The store was about a mile away, but it was a sunny, crisp, slightly cool January day in Las Vegas and he decided to walk. Before doing so, he took a long, hot shower and put on his only suit and tie.

Feeling positive, Frank walked to the store and talked to the thirty-something-year-old manager in charge. He explained how he used to own three hardware stores and was well experienced with sales and managing, as well as working with customers. The man listened and asked some questions. In the end, he took Frank's information down in the form of an application and said he should come back with a resume and references.

Frank left feeling dejected. He could easily put together a resume, but references? He could have put down Walter Rubenstein and even other managers he had employed. But Frank did not want anyone contacting them, especially Walter. He did not want anyone from his past life to know where he was or that he was trying to find some mid-level job. He had excommunicated himself from all those he used to know and wanted to keep it that way.

On the way back to his apartment, Frank stopped at a casino. There, he sat by the bar and ordered a screwdriver. One turned into two, then three and four. Before he knew it, it was 1:30 p.m. and he was already drunk. Frank had forty dollars left in his pocket and decided to do some gambling.

He usually played blackjack, craps, or roulette, but with drink in hand he decided to try his luck at the dollar slots. On his third pull, he won fifty dollars. Suddenly in much better spirits, he told himself he would stay at the machine until there was twenty dollars left. However, when that time came without winning anything else, Frank kept going. One pull, nothing. Another pull, nothing. Ecstatic just a few moments ago, he cursed himself for not cashing out earlier. But he figured what the hell, he might as well go for broke now. He was due at least a cherry. Discouraged, he played three coins and pulled the handle. One seven came up, then another, then a third one. As the fourth wheel did its final spin Frank thought, *Yeah right, what's the chances?* But then it happened—four gold sevens in a row! Frank thought he was seeing things, but instantly the light on the top of the machine started flashing and all kinds of bells and whistles were going off.

An elderly lady playing the machine next to him looked over. "You just won five thousand dollars!"

After signing some papers and collecting his winnings in hundred-dollar bills, Frank used the casino phone and called Tracy at the apartment. "I just hit the jackpot! I just won five thousand dollars!"

"What? What are you talking about? Where are you?"

Frank told her about applying for a job, winding up at the casino, and with his last few dollars, hitting the four sevens. He then told her to put something nice on and meet him at the casino—they were going to paint the town red!

Of course, the smart thing would have been for Frank to use all of the money to replenish some of his savings. And he told himself he would do that with whatever was left. But drunk, overflowing with adrenaline, and feeling lucky, it was first time to party! By the time Tracy met him it was close to 3:00 p.m. Tracy was hungry so they had a quick bite to eat then took a cab down the Strip to the Sahara and played some craps. Frank gave Tracy $200 to gamble. They wound up staying at the same table for about an hour and Frank walked away winning another $400. He was on a roll. He suggested that they rent a limo and take it down the Strip, stopping at different hotels. So that's what they did, drinking cocktails in the back, hitting the Riviera, Caesar's Palace, and the Frontier. They also managed to have a quick lovemaking session in the back of the limo.

Around 10:00 p.m., they stopped at an upscale Italian restaurant for dinner. Frank was still wearing his suit and Tracy was made up and had an evening dress on. By the time they say down to eat, having been drinking liquor all day, Frank was completely wasted, slurring his words and acting boisterous. Before even looking at the menu he ordered a bottle of Dom Perignon. He then ordered caviar and shrimp cocktails for appetizers.


The next day Frank woke up in his own bed, feeling like a train had rolled over him. The clock on his nightstand said it was 1:27 p.m. Frank had no recollection of getting home. The last thing he remembered was walking into some Italian restaurant.

Tracy was not in bed. Frank called out her name in a hoarse voice, but to no avail. Every part of his body aching, especially his head, he stumbled to the kitchen to get some water. Magnetically clipped to the refrigerator was a simple, cryptic note:

*I know you're going to be mad, but I really did enjoy our time together. Love, Tracy.*

Staring at the note, Frank sat down on a kitchen chair. *What the hell? Did Tracy just get up and leave in the middle of the night? Why would she do that? Everything seemed to be going well. She never even hinted that she was not happy.*

Frank sat there for a while, trying to figure out what was going on when suddenly it was as if he was hit by a bolt of lightning. Now wide-awake, he ran into the bedroom and checked his pants. His wallet was there, but no money. Even after the wild splurging the previous night, there should have been at least $4,000 left. Now in a panic, Frank tore his place apart, hoping that he had put the cash somewhere else in a drunken stupor. But it was gone. Tracy had stolen all his cash and ran off. But it would get even worse; Frank would soon realize that she had also taken his GTO.

Furious, Frank punched holes in his walls and threw things

around. After he was finished exploding, he was determined to track her down. But then it dawned on Frank that Tracy never as much as mentioned any of her friends. According to her, her father was dead and her mother ran off when Tracy was young. Her sister lived somewhere in Texas. She had never talked about any cousins or aunts and uncles.

Frank doubted Tracy would have been stupid enough to steal his money and car and then drive herself to work in it that night, but his options of tracking her down seemed limited. So early that evening he jumped in Tracy's beat up Valiant, which she had left behind, and went to The Toy Box to at least explain what happened and ask them to give him a call if she showed up. Before he even entered, he asked Jake, a big, burly bouncer who he was friendly with, if he had seen Tracy. He was shocked when Jake told him that she had quit nearly two weeks earlier. Freaking out even more, Frank told the bouncer what had happened. Feeling bad for Frank, Jake took him inside to talk to the manager.

Jimmy, a barrel-chested, thick-haired, slick Greek who managed The Toy Box knew Frank as being a regular and actually came to like him. He spent money there and never caused any problems. Plus, whenever the two men had talked in the past, Jimmy actually found Frank funny, often cracking sarcastic jokes.

But when Frank explained what happened, Jimmy knew it was no laughing matter. He confirmed what Jake had said, but with more details. "Yeah, she came in here three or four days before Christmas saying she needed some time off," he said in his thick, Greek accent. "We're open Christmas Eve and Christmas and usually the days off go to the dancers that have been here the longest. And Tracy's one of my newer girls. But she also brings in good money, so I told her she could have those two days off. Then she tells me she needs at least five days off. I told her I just can't do it. Then she starts arguing with me and finally she tells me to fuck off, that she doesn't need to strip anymore anyway."

Frank gave Jimmy his phone number. "Well listen, please just call me if she does happen to show up."

Jimmy looked down at the piece of paper. "With pleasure."

Frank left with his head spinning. He sat in Tracy's car in the parking lot, trying to figure out his next step. He realized it was time to call the police, but all of a sudden a light went off in his head. Why hadn't he thought about it earlier? Maybe Tracy was back at her old apartment. Wasting no time, Frank headed there.

A strange man answered the door.

Frank explained he was looking for a girl named Tracy.

The man said no one was there by that name. "What about Trixie?" He asked.

The answer was still no.

Ready to call the guy a liar, Donna, Tracy's old roommate, camè to the door. "Hey Frank, what are you doing?" She then looked at her guest. "It's okay, I know him."

The man shook his head and walked back inside.

"What's the matter, Frank? You look distressed."

"Donna, do you mind if I come in? Please."

Donna thought about it for a second and then led him inside.

"Have you seen Tracy?"

"No. Not since I kicked her out of here."

The onion kept unraveling. "You kicked her out? She moved out so she could come live with me. Because you guys didn't get along."

"Damn right we didn't get along. I had only known her for about three months and as soon as she moved in I just got this bad vibe from her. But when I caught her trying to steal some of my jewelry I told her she had to leave."

Frank told Donna what happened. She seemed disappointed for Frank, but not surprised. She put her hand on his shoulder. "I'm so sorry Frank. I would call the police right away if you haven't already. But I doubt you'll ever see that money, car, or Tracy again. She's nothing but a lowlife con artist. By the end of the week she'll probably already be setting up shop in some other town, setting her sights on some other guy to rip off." It was the truth, but Donna realized how harsh it sounded. "I should've told you about the jewelry when I found out she was moving in with you. I'm sorry, Frank. You seem like a really nice guy."

Frank went home and called the police. Late that night two patrolmen came to his apartment and took a report. But Donna had been right; he would never see the money, his car, or Tracy ever again.

# 34

# PEACE WITH HONOR

Frank had $780 to his name in the bank—and a beat-up, falling-apart car that he could not even drive, because it was not registered to him. Obviously, he was furious at Tracy, as well as himself for trusting her. In the end, their whole time together had been nothing but lies. But going back even before Tracy, Frank could not believe that he had frittered away all that money in just over a year. If he had been at all smart or responsible, it could have lasted him at least twice as long, probably longer. But for a while now Frank had been neither smart nor responsible.

Initially, Frank was so enraged and despondent about Tracy that it took him a few days before he could even go out and function again. But once he did, his first and only priority was to find a job. The first thing Frank did was buy a used typewriter and a book on resumes. After about seven drafts, he finally came up with one. The first place he took it to was the department store where he had applied for the sales manager. He was hoping they would not ask again about the references. However, it was a moot point; they had already filled the position.

Frank took his resume to a dozen other places, some of which resulted in an interview. Like the department store, most of the potential employers asked for several references, which was dead on arrival for Frank. A few said he was overqualified for the position for which he was applying. Others, in the end, felt for one reason or another that he was just not right for the job. Frank was dejected. How could no one want to hire someone with his experience? Frank thought back to a time when he hired employees and knew that if someone showed up with his resume and was able to present themself such as he was, it would be a no-brainer.

After two weeks of active searching, Frank finally found a job as a gas station attendant. The man who had built a business from the ground up and orchestrated its expansion and success for nearly two decades was relegated to pumping gas, making change, and washing windshields. It was minimum wage, but at least it was an honest, steady income.

Frank worked six days a week, and sometimes when needed, seven. Although he still went out for a few drinks sometimes after work, the full schedule kept him from flying off the handle and going on full-blown benders. His drinking continued, but to a much lesser extent. Frank was never late for work and never slacked off. The busy schedule also made time fly by. The weeks and months melted into each other and winter turned to spring, then summer.

Frank always worked efficiently, without complaints, and smiled for the customers. But inside he was in turmoil. There was regret. Frank thought about the money he had squandered, but more importantly, the family and life he had squandered. There was a sense of forlornness. What did the future hold but meaningless numbers on a calendar and the gradual descent towards the end? There was bitterness, not just towards Tracy, but also now towards all women (sans Mary and Eileen). There was also resentment. Frank would tend to seemingly happy couples rolling into the station with their expensive cars, new clothes, and stack of folded cash. Often they would look at Frank like a second-class citizen and treat him as such. To them he was a stereotypical cover on an inferior book. Of course, it was a book none of them had ever read.

Though Frank always managed to keep his cool at work, it was not easy. Never causing any problems and always working hard, his boss and peers always treated him with respect. But sometimes the customers, without reason, could be belittling and even downright belligerent.

A customer would say: "Come on guy, what's taking so long?"

"Watch this," a teenager said to his girlfriend. "Hey old man, you missed a spot on the windshield."

"See son, if you don't do good in school you'll wind up pumping gas like this guy."

"I know I gave you a ten dollar bill."

"Why you keep smiling at me? Is something funny about me?"

By September, Frank had enough of the gas station and Las Vegas. He was in dire need of a change of scenery. His rent at the apartment was not much. Also, since Tracy left, whenever Frank drank he either found a bar with drink specials or brought home the cheapest beer. Besides a small food budget, he didn't spend money on anything else. Somehow he had managed to stave off the heavy temptation of the casinos. So with the money he already had left in the bank and working sometimes seven days a week, Frank had managed to save up over $2,500.

After a week of searching around, Frank was able to buy a used 1967 Volkswagen Beetle for $420. He hated the car, because it reminded him of hippies. But though it's exterior and interior was in rough shape, it ran well, and Frank could see nothing wrong with the engine. Despite its look, it was the best he was going to get for that kind of money.

Frank had already decided his destination would be Dallas. He had read in the newspaper one day that a retail hardware chain named ACE was expanding its southwestern business and opening two stores in Dallas, as well as other locations. Frank called ACE's headquarters and eventually talked to a person who would be in charge of the hiring at the Dallas stores. Frank explained his background in the hardware business and mailed the man his resume. Unbeknownst to Frank, the company called one of his prior stores and actually talked to Walter Rubenstein. Though Frank would never find out, Walter actually praised his former boss and ACE was able to verify Frank's credentials. The man eventually told Frank that if he relocated to Dallas by September 25th, a week before the first store's scheduled opening, he could have a manager position. Frank happily accepted.

Frank arrived in Dallas on September 18, 1972. Fortunately, his Beetle did not break down once on the drive. With everything he owned packed into the car, he checked into a cheap motel and immediately went to work looking for a place to live. Frank's main concern was price. He was due to pull in a decent salary at ACE, but what if something happened and he was let go, or did not even given the job? Besides, he wanted to build up his nest egg.

After only a few days, Frank moved into an upstairs bedroom in a boarding house, which he rented on a month-to-month basis. A twenty-two-year-old construction worker named Carl rented one of the other upstairs bedrooms. A young couple that always seemed to be home lived downstairs. The actual owner of the house did not live there. Everyone had to take turns sharing the kitchen and Frank shared an upstairs bathroom with Carl.

On September 25th, just as scheduled, Frank went to the ACE Hardware store, which was still having finishing work done before opening to the public. He was much relieved when, as promised, he was officially given a daytime manager's position. A week and a half later, the store was open and Frank was again gainfully employed.

On October 10th, Frank was lying on his bed unwinding from work by watching the small black-and-white TV he had bought, when the evening news came on. The lead story was a report by the *Washington Post* that five men who had been arrested the previous June

breaking into, and trying to bug, the offices of the Democratic National Committee at the Watergate hotel had in fact been working for
President Nixon's re-election committee. The report went on to state
(which had already been rumored) that it was part of a massive plot,
directed by the White House, to eavesdrop on Democratic presidential candidates, with the hopes of being privy to their innermost strat-
egies, discrediting them, and ultimately sabotaging their campaigns.

Frank had loosely been following the Watergate story since
June and scoffed at it. "And this is supposed to surprise someone?"
He said aloud to himself.

Frank was still deeply patriotic, but had lost his trust in the government some time ago. There had been too many cover-ups, too
many changed stories, too many promises unfulfilled, too many
questions never answered.

Despite the *Washington Post's* story, one month later Nixon was
reelected in one of the largest landslides in presidential history. Of
course, Nixon continued to deny any involvement in the Watergate
scandal. However, the truth eventually caught up with him and on
August 8, 1974, Nixon became the first U.S. President to resign
from office.

Frank submerged himself in work. He did not quit drinking, but like
when he worked at the gas station, kept it manageable. Sometimes he would not drink for days at a time. He was back to being a
functional alcoholic. No one at ACE could tell of his problems. It felt
good for Frank to not only be employed again, but be in a signifi-
cant position. After Times Square, the debacle with Tracy, and being belittled at the gas station, he felt like a real man again.

At ACE, Frank was liked by both his employees and customers. If
there was a problem, he always seemed to work it out in a quick, ami-
cable way. To the customers he was congenial and to the other employees he was fair. No one really had an issue with Frank—except his
regional manager. Todd, a young college graduate who walked
around with a sense of entitlement, did not like Frank from the begin-

ning. But their relationship only went downhill. Frank would sometimes come up with good ideas and more efficient ways of doing certain things at the store. This did not go over well with Todd.

"I don't know how they used to do it in the Fifties," he would sarcastically say. He would always remind Frank "This isn't some mom-and-pop operation you're used to. ACE is a multimillion dollar company and I think they know how to run their business. Please don't make any changes to the store without my approval."

Though Frank wanted to smack the smirk right off of Todd's baby face, he always bit his tongue. He didn't want to cause any waves. Besides, at least Frank did not have to see Todd all the time. However, what Frank did not know was that behind his back, Todd often painted him in a negative light to the higher-ups.

When he was not at work, Frank kept to himself. At the house, he usually stayed in his room. He had no problem with any of the other tenants, but did not see any point with making friends with them. Frank just wasn't ready to get close to anyone again. If Frank did go to a bar, he sat inconspicuously in the corner. If he brought beer or liquor home, he would drink it in his room, on the bed, in front of the TV. Sometimes he would use the kitchen, but mostly ordered out food. However, after about three months the social isolation was too much and Frank would sometimes go out drinking with Carl. What he never did was go out for drinks with anyone at work. He kept his job strictly professional.

At the end of March 1973, the last remaining U.S. combat troops left Vietnam. Although some military advisors and Marines remained to protect U.S. instillations, it was the end of America's military involvement. In his address to the nation, President Nixon stated: "For the first time in twelve years, no American military forces are in Vietnam. All of our American POW's are on their way home. The seventeen million people of South Vietnam have the right to choose their own government...We have prevented the imposition of a communist government by force on South Vietnam."

Of course, history tells us that this was a lie. American prisoners of war were still being held in Vietnam and would be for some time. Some would never be returned home. As for the communists, they would soon control all of Vietnam.

America had been involved militarily in Vietnam for nearly a decade, but counting its "advisors" and sending of equipment to the South, even longer. In the end over 58,000 Americans lost their lives, countless others wounded, and families across the country torn apart. In his address, Nixon declared that the United States had "achieved our goal of obtaining an agreement which provides peace with honor in Vietnam."

For the hundreds of thousands of American men who had fought there, as well as the brave medics who worked tirelessly to save lives, they would never forget Vietnam. However, forgetting the entire war and putting it behind them was exactly what much of the country wanted to do. In fact, despite the heroism and sacrifices that so many young Americans endured during the campaign, countless people considered Vietnam an embarrassment, a black mark on the country.

As Frank watched the news that March 29th evening, he of course pondered the loss of his own son. He also thought about Billy, praying that he had made it home safely. But Frank's heart and thoughts ultimately went out to all those who had stepped foot in that place thousands of miles away, a land the majority of Americans had never even heard of before the war. Frank knew it was important for the collective conscience of the country never to forget what happened in Vietnam and chastised those who were so eager to turn the page—and their backs.

In late May the young couple who occupied the downstairs of the house where Frank was living moved and were replaced by another slightly older couple. The pair was also completely different than the previous tenants. The male, who went by the name Badger, belonged to a motorcycle club and they would often throw impromptu parties that lasted well into the night. At first, Frank found it a nuisance, though never complained. But after a while of Badger's and his wife's prodding, Frank actually began to join the festivities. In fact, a few of the regulars were veterans and Frank soon became a fan favorite.

As Frank spent more time partying with his new biker friends, he was back to drinking more and more. Inevitably, the late nights and severe hangovers started to affect him at work. Frank would come in pale and puffy-eyed, feeling like a pile of shit, not wanting to do anything but go back home to sleep. Not blind or stupid, his employees could figure out that he had been up partying hard the previous night. But they never said anything. More and more, they just stayed away from him. Sometimes Frank sat at his desk in a back room and actually fall asleep for a little while. Of course, he was the manager and still had to tend to various customer's complaints and issues. But he was becoming less and less effective.

One day, Todd came into the store and could tell that something was not right with Frank. Frank explained that he was sick, but Todd secretly started asking the store's employees about their boss. One of them, though saying he had no proof, said Frank was either a drunk or on drugs. Todd, who already had it in for Frank, started spending more time at the store. Afraid of losing his job, Frank did not stop partying, but tried harder to cope with his hangovers and put on a chipper demeanor. But one afternoon, Todd stopped by and caught him napping in the backroom. Todd told Frank he was writing him up and if Frank slipped up again he could lose his job. Instead of being concerned and shaping up, Frank was furious at his regional manager and took it out by going back to the house and getting shit-faced.

One Saturday in early August, Badger and his crew were having a big barbecue at the house. By 3:00 p.m. they had already gone through one keg, there had been two fights, and a wet T-shirt contest. Frank was having a great time. He even participated in a beer-slamming contest, with part of the crowd cheering him on: "Frank! Frank! Frank!" At one point a young, pretty blonde who he had seen at the house a few times asked if he could drive her to pick up her friend.

"I don't know if I should be driving. I've been drinking quite a bit," he said, trying not to sway.

The girl grabbed his crotch. "Come on, it's only about ten minutes away. I'll make it worth your while," she whispered in his ear.

Frank had not had any kind of sex since Tracy and he was not going to turn down the offer.

The one big purchase Frank had made since working at ACE was trading in his Volkswagen and buying a used Chevy Nova. He just could not drive around in a Beetle any longer. So he and the drunk girl piled in his car. Before he even turned the key in the ignition, she started to go down on him. *What a great day this is turning out to be*, Frank thought to himself.

After a few minutes, the act was done. The girl sat up in the seat and wiped her mouth with her hand. "Did you like that?"

"Oh yeah," Frank replied with a mile-long smile.

The girl started giving Frank directions and they drove off. As they gleefully headed to pick up her friend, the girl started asking Frank innocent questions about his background. Splitting his time between the road and the conversation, he told her about his job and living in Las Vegas. Frank was in the right lane, driving down a main road about to buzz past an intersection. Turning his head to answer a question, he caught the glimpse of a moving blur. Before Frank even had time to register what it was, there was an impact. The deafening sound of steel on steel screeched through the air as Frank felt like he had been hit in the side by a Mickey Mantle homerun swing. Not even realizing it, Frank had blown through a red light, right into the path of an oncoming car. The other vehicle slammed into Frank's car just behind the right rear wheel well, spinning it completely around.

Frank hit his head on the steering wheel and was thrust into the inside of the driver's door but never lost consciousness. His heart racing uncontrollably, he looked over at his passenger. She was moaning, and thick, red blood was gushing from her face.

"Oh my God, are you all right?" He asked in a panic. Upon closer inspection he realized she was bleeding from her nose and mouth, but there were no visible wounds to her head. Frank's mind then turned to the other vehicle. "Stay here, don't move. I'm gonna get help."

He then was able to force open the driver's side door and went to check on the other car. He was horrified to find a woman and a young girl in the front seat. They both appeared to be injured.

It seemed like the police were on the scene in a matter of minutes. Frank readily confessed to being the driver of the other vehicle. The smell of alcohol permeated from his breath and his eyes were completely bloodshot. After taking and failing a field sobriety test Frank was put under arrest for driving while intoxicated and taken into custody.

Frank's passenger had suffered a broken nose, and a dislocated right shoulder. The driver of the other car, a thirty-two-year-old mother of three, also suffered a concussion, and a broken leg. Her eight-year-old daughter, who luckily was wearing a seatbelt, came away with a four-inch-long laceration to her forehead that required stitches. The cause of the accident, Frank, suffered only a few superficial wounds to his face.

Two days after the accident, Badger and the other guys in the club posted Frank's bail. Frank was facing multiple charges, but his main concern was the wellbeing of the three victims, especially the little girl. He could not believe what he had done. What if he had killed that mother and daughter, he asked himself over and over again. Of course, he could not help but think about his own daughter. Locked in his upstairs room, Frank would lay on his bed and cry.

The accident made the local news and it did not take long for Frank's employer to get wind of the story. He was immediately fired. Seemingly on the right track, Frank had now fallen off a cliff. But if ruining his own life weighed on him, the gravity of almost ending three other people's lives was like a constant, crushing load.


While waiting for the court process, Frank moved out of the boardinghouse and into a cheap motel, rented by the week. He appreciated Badger's and the others support, but could no longer look anyone he knew in the face. He was too ashamed. Also, even staying in his room, he could not live in the party atmosphere anymore. Frank repaid Badger for the bail, using money he had saved up. Badger and his wife wished him the best.

As summer faded and autumn dragged on, Frank found odd jobs here and there, mostly as a laborer. One might think that the accident had made him go sober, but that was not the case. Frank would never drink and drive again, but the bottle seemed the only friend he had left. Now a complete recluse, Frank would buy the cheapest liquor he could find, often Mad Dog 20/20. He would just sit in his meager, rat-infested motel room and drink until he passed out. Once in a while he would stop in a bar for a few drinks. But be it the bar, the motel, or the jobs he worked on, Frank made an effort not to get friendly or close with anyone.

In the beginning of January, with his lawyer on hand, Frank accepted a plea agreement that sentenced him to six months in jail. Frank's main concern was his one box of most personal possessions, which contained his family album, wedding ring, the watch Mary had bought him, and other sentimental effects. He asked Badger if he would hold onto it for him while he was away. Badger told him not to worry about it.

A week later, Frank reported to the jail to start serving his time.

# 35

# THE STRANGER
# IN THE MIRROR

Frank had never before been behind bars, but he was not frightened. After all, he had lived through much more dangerous and precarious situations during the war. Though he was new to the world of incarceration, he knew to keep his senses always on high alert and stay out of trouble. However, that did not mean trouble never found him. During his third week, another inmate tried to push him around in the mess hall. The man was younger and bigger than Frank, about 6'3" with muscles and a rough face to go with his baldhead. Maybe just trying to test the newbie, the man walked over to the table where Frank was sitting and took his tray. He then called Frank out in front of the other inmates. Frank did not have to be a hardened con to know that if he did not do something, everyone was going to see him as a target. He stood up and without saying a word, punched the larger man right in the throat—something he had learned in the Army. The perpetrator immediately collapsed to the ground, gasping for breath. Frank then kicked the man in the face as hard as he could. By that time the guards came and broke it up. Frank was placed in isolation for a week, but the predator never picked on him again.

After that incident, Frank never really encountered any more trouble. He kept to himself, staying away from gangs, cliques, and deals. He never borrowed money or asked for any favors. Though inside he was distraught, outwardly he held his head up high and went about doing his time.

Though Frank purposely did not want to forge any relationships while behind bars, it was impossible not to converse with his cellmate. No stranger to the penal system, Josh Taveras, twenty-six, was doing a nine-month stint for drug possession. Josh was affable, but even in jail he had too much energy and was always trying to talk Frank's ear off, with his pleonasm and never-ending stories. At first it was agitating to Frank, but he soon realized that he could have had a lot worse for a cellmate.

Time moves slow when that's all there is. A month into his incarceration, Frank wondered about people doing ten, twenty years—even life. It must have been torturous, he thought. But in realty, no matter where you are or what you are doing, there are twenty-four hours in a day and seven days in a week, and time always forges on. Months fall and seasons change.

One morning, just as he always did, Frank woke up to the sounds of shouting guards and their clanking on the metal cell bars. Like an automaton, he climbed out of his bunk and readied himself for breakfast.

As he washed his face with the brownish sink water, Josh looked at the calendar that they had hanging up.

"Hey, it's April Seventeenth. It would have been my mother's birthday."

Suddenly, a bell went off in Frank's head. With his face still sopping wet, he stared into the small mirror above the sink. It was April 17, 1974—Frank's fiftieth birthday.

Looking back at his life Frank stood in front of the mirror and saw a stranger staring back. He had been a proud soldier, a volunteer, a loving husband and father, a successful entrepreneur, a leader in his community. Now there he was in a jail cell, homeless, without family or friends, nearly broke, and with no future. Frank thought of his father, who had played such a pivotal role in his up-bringing. How ashamed he would be, Frank thought. But right there, at that moment Frank had an epiphany. He could not get back his old life, but he could get back his self-respect and self-worth. Then and there, gazing into that mirror, Frank promised himself that no matter what it took, he was going to sober up and get his act together.

A week later, Josh was freed and Frank was given a new, quiet cellmate who kept to himself. Frank spent the rest of his time read-ing and thinking about what he was going to do once he was re-leased. He was convinced that a new start on life meant a new change of scenery. Josh had lived for a time in Phoenix, Arizona, and always went on about how beautiful it was there. "It's like the Old West there still," he could hear Josh say. "Dallas and other parts of Texas are nice, but you really want to go back in time and live the simple life, go to Arizona."

Frank's mind was made up.


Towards the end of May, because of overcrowding, Frank was re-leased several weeks early. He walked out of jail with no residence, no car, and $354 in the bank. He went to the old boardinghouse where, as promised, Badger had kept his belongings safe.

The next afternoon Frank boarded a Greyhound bus to Phoenix, on a one-way ticket. Once he arrived, he checked into a seedy mo-tel in downtown.

Early the next morning, Frank set out to find a job. It was not easy. In 1974, Phoenix was far from a booming economy. Much of the day-labor went to illegal immigrants who would congregate at certain corners and parking lots and work for less than minimum wage. Most employers were also not eager to hire someone with a criminal past. However, during that time, background checks were not routine.

While in jail, Frank's second cellmate had told him to never tell the truth about being locked up. "There's a chance they might do a check and find out you lied and, of course, they won't hire you. But if you tell them that you have a record no one is going to hire you. They'll show you the door right then and there."

With no car, Frank had to walk everywhere or take the minimalistic public transportation that existed in Phoenix at the time. It was approaching summer, and the Valley was already blistering with near triple-digit temperatures. But Frank was relentless in his pursuit of work. After a week and a half he landed a part-time job in a lumberyard, doing basically anything they asked him to do. A week later, he found a second, nighttime job as a waiter.

Frank was serious about staying sober. He knew that realistically he couldn't say: *Okay, I'll just have a few beers now and then.* He knew that if he was to clean up, he had to stop drinking altogether—and he was ready for that commitment. But he did not realize how difficult it would be. The urge was there every time he came home from a hard day at work, or walked passed a bar, or saw a beer commercial, or knew the other wait-staff at the restaurant were going to go out together after their shift.

In July, Frank started going to Alcoholics Anonymous, squeezing in meetings whenever he could. He had heard about AA when in jail and at first was skeptical. But then he figured, what did he have to lose? At the first meeting, Frank realized he had already conquered the first step, in admitting that he had a problem. But once a very religious person, he was still not ready to regain his faith, something that is a pillar of AA. Nevertheless, Frank found support in AA, knowing that he was not alone in his battle. In fact, the people at the meetings soon became the closest thing Frank had to friends or family.

Besides food, rent, and some clothes, the only thing Frank had spent money on was a used bicycle, to get him to and from work. Everything else went into savings. By the end of July, Frank was able to move out of the motel and into a one-bedroom apartment.

Frank had been keeping up with his AA meetings and winning

the war against alcoholism, but in mid-August he lost a battle and relapsed. Working in a restaurant made drinking and going out partying too tempting. The staff is usually close-knit and after a given shift at least several of them get together and let loose. When Frank started working there his coworkers would sometimes ask him if he wanted to join, but Frank always politely declined, usually saying that he had to wake up early for his other job. He never told anyone that he was battling alcoholism. After a while, they stopped inviting him. But on this particular night, another waiter asked again.

"We're goin' right down the block to Dugan's Bar. It'll be a good time. Jessie and Kyle are going, so is Yvonne."

Frank thought about the offer. He had a particular rough day, both at the lumberyard and at the restaurant. A large table he was waiting on was filled with assholes intent on breaking his balls just for the fun of it.

Yvonne, a voluptuous, young waitress walked over. "Come on, Frank. You never come out with us. It's two-for-ones at Dugan's to-night."

"Okay, sure, what the hell," Frank replied in a moment of weakness.

Not only did Frank go to the bar with them, but he thought he could still drink as much as when he was drinking every day. Besides beer after beer, the group kept feeding him rounds of Tequila shots. Frank was enjoying himself, but after closing time he threw up on the sidewalk in front of the bar. Barley able to stand, one of his fellow waiters gave him a ride home (praying that Frank would not throw up in the car).

The next morning, Frank woke in a world of pain on his bed, fully clothed, including shoes. On the carpet on the side of the bed was a pool of pungent vomit. He realized that he had left his front door wide open. His stomach churning, mouth feeling like it was full of cotton, and head pounding, Frank wondered what the hell he had done. Luckily, it was his one day completely off of work that week. He spent the entire afternoon and evening recovering and thinking about his actions.

At one point, Frank dozed off and had a dream about his father. The two of them were standing in an endless wheat field, the breeze peacefully blowing the amber waves of grain. "I'm disappointed in you, son. You made a promise to me—and more importantly yourself. But you can do it. This isn't the way I raised you. You're stronger than this." The scene vanished into white and Frank abruptly woke up, almost hearing his father's voice still echoing in the room. The dream had felt so real.

Early the following morning, Frank reported to work at the lumberyard. Though feeling better than the day before, he was still hungover and doing physical labor in the hot, August Arizona sun made him extremely queasy and dehydrated. Still, right after his shift and before going to the restaurant, Frank went to an AA meeting. Embarrassed, he told about his relapse. There was disappointment, only support. After all, there was probably not a single soul in the room who had not relapsed at least once, most numerous times.

After the meeting he was approached by a tall thirty-something-year-old named John, who he had talked with several times. John had been sober for over two years.

"I'd like to be your sponsor, Frank. I really think you need one. You know the drill; just call me if you feel you're going to break down and have a drink, or going through a particular rough patch."

Frank thanked John and took his number. However, he would never wind up calling him. He would never have the need. Frank's drinking days were over—for good.

When Frank went to work at the restaurant that evening his coworkers gave him a good-natured ribbing about the other night. Then they asked him if he wanted to go out again. Frank didn't mind waiting tables and liked most of the people with whom he worked. But he realized that the restaurant business was not a good environment for him. The busboys, waiters, cooks, and even dishwashers are either always talking about partying, or going out, or doing it. Frank knew he could not live in a bubble, but thought it best to remove himself from that setting.

Frank asked for and received some more hours at the lumberyard and quit his job at the restaurant. A few weeks later he started working the nightshift as a stocker at a grocery store. He still found time for his meetings.

One evening, in early October, Frank was at an AA meeting when a girl he had never seen before stood up and introduced herself.

"My name is Lynn Ross. I'm twenty-six-years-old and I have a six-year-old son. And I am an alcoholic." Thin, with flowing black hair and distant brown eyes, she spoke in a soft, ashamed voice. "I was married when I was nineteen to my high school sweetheart. We were in love, he had a good job working for his father, we moved into our own house, and I had just gotten pregnant. Everything was milk and honey. It was like I was living every girl's dream." Lynn paused and looked towards the floor. "Then in nineteen-sixty-nine, Gregg was drafted and wound up going to Vietnam." Tears started to streak down her pale face. "Six months later he was killed in an ambush. The moment I heard the news my entire life came crashing down. I started drinking shortly after that just to cope with being able to make it through the day…and I never stopped."

An older female stood up and handed Lynn a tissue. "It's okay, you've already made the first step."

Of course, Lynn's story struck a chord with Frank. It was as if he could feel the young woman's pain. After the meeting, he went up to her and introduced himself. "My son also died in Vietnam."

"I'm so sorry," she replied, fighting back more tears.

"I just want you to know that you can do this," Frank said, putting his hand on Lynn's shoulder. "It may not be easy, but Elaine was right, you've already made the first step."

Lynn smiled. "Thank you."

That night, as he worked at the grocery store stocking shelves in the backroom, Frank could not stop thinking about Lynn. He had seen so many different people stand up and tell their stories at the meetings, but none of them affected him like Lynn's. He wanted to know more about her. He needed to know more about her. But most of all, he wanted to make sure she received the help she needed.

Days went by, then weeks. Every meeting Frank would look for Lynn, but she was never there. Though he had only met her briefly that one time, Frank felt a sense of guilt for not getting to know her, trying to help her. Part of him wondered what he could have done differently. Still, he could not shake off the feeling. He just hoped that something terrible had not happened to Lynn and that she had not given up on herself.

Then, one evening in early December, as Frank was getting a cup of coffee and waiting for a meeting to commence, he spotted a sheepish-looking Lynn standing in the corner. He immediately went over to her. "Hi, you probably don't remember me. I met you one time at a meeting."

"Yes, of course I remember you," she quickly replied. "You lost your son in Vietnam."

Frank nodded. "Yes, that's right. I haven't seen you around."

"Well, I've been to a couple of meetings after that, but at a different location. But then I stopped going and…I don't know…My father-in-law pays for my apartment. I lost my job. He says if I don't go back for help and stop drinking he'll have me kicked out. He's said it before, but…" Lynn looked like she was ready to cry. "Besides, I want to quit for my son's sake. I need…I'm sorry, I don't know why I'm telling you all of this."

"No, no, that's okay. In fact, I've been thinking about you. Listen, I know I'm just some guy that you met once before in an AA meeting, but…well, I really want to help you. I don't know if you have a sponsor, if you even know what a sponsor is."

Lynn said she knew what it was, but did not have one.

"Well I would like to be your sponsor. I'm going to be perfectly honest with you; I'm kind of new at this, too. When my son went off to Vietnam I started drinking more and more. Then when he died, I just went off the deep end. That was in nineteen-seventy. I only stopped drinking about a year ago." He did not mention that five months of it was because he was in jail. "I had a relapse in August, but I've been clean ever since."

Just then the meeting started. Frank told Lynn that they would finish the conversation after it was over and she readily agreed.

After the meeting, Frank and Lynn stayed for a while and talked some more. Frank gave her his phone number and told her to call any time she needed help. Lynn took Frank at his word. She did not believe every story someone told her, but she believed Frank. In doing so, she felt a connection with him. Though they were decades apart, they both lost loved ones in Vietnam and in each of their lives it was the catalyst that drove them over the edge.

That night, while working at the grocery store, Frank's thoughts were once more consumed with this young woman he never even knew existed two months earlier. Frank was glad that he had run into her again and that she accepted his offer to be her sponsor. Part of him felt that he was not ready to be anyone's sponsor. After all, he was still trying to maintain his own life. But he could not escape the urge to try and help this girl. In fact, he wondered if it was fate that brought him and Lynn together. Frank was not sure anymore if there was a God, but if there was, maybe it was his plan for Frank to help Lynn. In the end, however, they would wind up helping each other.

The next afternoon, Frank was elated when he went to his meeting and Lynn was there. Over the next two weeks the two met at least every other day at a meeting and always talked before and after. Frank mostly did the listening. Lynn's father left when she was only six and there were only a few, vague memories left of him. Her mother was a drug addict and although she lived in Phoenix, Lynn saw very little of her over the past five years. But Lynn was not without family. She had aunts and uncles and cousins. However, it was her late husband's parents who provided the most support. Her father-in-law was a well-known civil defense lawyer who had worked on several high-profile cases over the years. In fact, when her husband Gregg's draft number came up, his father told him that he could pull some strings and get him out of it. Naturally, Lynn begged Gregg to accept his father's offer. But Gregg said it was his duty to serve and was adamant about not getting any preferential treatment.

When Lynn and Gregg were married, Gregg's father bought them a house in Scottsdale. After Gregg died, his father let Lynn stay there and paid the mortgage. But Lynn's drinking soon drove a wedge between her and her in-laws. Lynn started neglecting her son Kyle and was arrested several times, twice for disorderly conduct and once for driving while intoxicated. Finally realizing that she was in no shape to raise a child, she let Gregg's parents take custody of him. A year earlier, after repeated threats if she did not clean up her act, Lynn's father-in-law finally kicked her out of the house where she was living.

Over the past year, Lynn had lived in a studio apartment and worked various jobs, always doing something to get fired before long. Though Gregg's father had washed his hands of the daughter-in-law he once treated like his own child, his wife just could not let Lynn become homeless. So she talked her husband into paying Lynn's rent.

Frank felt terrible for Lynn, but knew there was no magical switch he could flip to make her stop drinking, get her life together, and mend her wounds. Healing is a process. But he wanted to be part of that process.

Five days went by without Frank running into Lynn at a meeting and he was starting to worry. He wanted to call her, but she had never given him her number and he felt awkward asking. It was a few days before Christmas and Frank knew that the holidays could be the hardest time of the year. It was for Frank, as he thought of a time past when he, Mary, Eileen, and Thomas went sledding or sat around the Christmas tree and opened presents.

It was Christmas Eve, and Frank had the day off from both his jobs. He would also have Christmas off. It was the first time in a long time that he would have consecutive days free. But the fact was that he would rather be working, to take his mind off the loneliness. He spent the day holed up in his apartment, reading a book and then watching TV. Then just after 4:00 p.m. the phone rang. It was Lynn and she was crying.

"I'm sorry to call you. I'm in this motel room down on Van Buren. I was with these two guys, but they left me here to go score some coke. I just don't want to be here anymore," she cried. "I just didn't know who else to call."

Frank got the name of the motel and room number and said he would come get her. He then called a cab. They said it would be ten minutes, but those ten minutes felt like an eternity. Thankfully, the taxi came on time and they drove the five or so miles to the motel. The whole time, Frank was a complete ball of nerves. *Was she still going to be at the room? Was she in danger? Should he have told her to call the police? What if something terrible happened to her?* Every block seemed like ten miles.

When they arrived at the seedy motel, Frank told the cab driver to wait for him and rushed to the room. His heart racing, he pounded on the door. To his relief, Lynn answered it. After looking through the peephole, she opened the door, still in tears. "I'm so sorry."

Frank took a peek at the small, dank room. There were empty beer bottles and an almost empty bottle of Jack Daniels on the nightstand. Cigarette butts littered every surface and a cloud of stale smoke hung in the air. On the dresser top was a small, smudged mirror with a glass straw. The bed had its covers torn off. Frank then looked closer at Lynn. She had no shoes on and her top was half buttoned. Tears and mascara ran in dark, muddy streaks from her red eyes. Her breath reeked of alcohol.

"Come on," he said, putting his arm around her shoulder. "Let's get you out of here."

Just then, two tall, lanky men showed up. They both had long hair, dirty clothes and looked strung out.

"Hey Lynn, what's going on?" One of them asked. He then turned his attention to Frank. "Hey old man, what are you doing? That's our bitch. What are you, her father or something?"

Frank snapped. He grabbed the twenty-something-year-old derelict and slammed him up against the concrete wall like a rag doll. "You listen here you punk, I've looked men straight in their eyes before and put a bullet right through their head. Now it's been a while, but I'd have no problem doing it again."

The young man looked at the rage in Frank's eyes and started shaking as his friend just stood there frozen. "Okay, okay. Lo...lo...look old man, just take her and go, all right? We don't want any trouble."

Frank kneed the guy in the balls, collapsing him to the ground. As he walked away with Lynn in his arm, he gave the other man a death glare.

Once in the cab, Frank told the driver to take them back to his apartment complex.

On the way there, Lynn cried into Frank's shoulder. "Thank you so much. I'm so sorry. I'm such a bad person."

Frank stroked her long hair. "Shhh, it's okay now. You're safe now."

Frank did not ask about what had happened in the motel room or about the two men. Part of him didn't want to know. Lynn did not volunteer what had gone on, but she did continue on an emotional, intoxicated rant. "I'm so worthless. It's Christmas Eve; I should be with my son. I'm such a horrible mother. I just can't take this anymore. I'm such a disgrace."

Frank tried his best to console her.

By the time they arrived at Frank's, Lynn was starting to lose steam. Frank laid her down in his bed and told her to try and sleep for a while. He then tucked her in like a child and turned off the lights. But as he was about to leave, Lynn grabbed hold of his arm. "Thank you so much. You're my guardian angel."

Frank smiled and told her to get some rest and that he would be right in the other room if she needed him.

Frank woke up on Christmas morning on his couch. He went to check up on Lynn; she was still sleeping. Frank went back in the other room and watched some television for another half hour. Then he went into the kitchen and started cooking eggs, bacon, and pancakes. Halfway through, an exhausted looking Lynn strolled out of the bedroom.

"Oh, good. I'm making some breakfast," Frank said with a smile, as he continued to cook. He turned to face Lynn. "By the way, Merry Christmas."

"Merry Christmas," she replied. The frenzy of emotions of the previous day now faded, Lynn was mostly embarrassed. She apologized to Frank and thanked him yet again for rescuing her.

He told her not to worry about it.

As they sat across from each other at the small table and ate breakfast, Frank said that he wanted to pay for a cab to take Lynn to see her son. "It is Christmas," he explained. He said he would also give her money for the cab ride back to her apartment.

"Thank you, Frank. That's very thoughtful, really. But I can't take your money. My in-laws live in Scottsdale. The ride would be at least fifteen dollars. Besides, you've already done enough for me. You really have."

But Frank would not take no for an answer. So after breakfast, Lynn called her in-laws and asked if she could stop by and see Kyle. It was Christmas and her mother-in-law could not refuse. Frank realized that Lynn could not show up wearing the same clothes that she had slept in and worn since yesterday. He called a cab, but first told Lynn that she had to go to her own apartment and get a fresh change of clothes (being Christmas, all the stores were closed).

Frank went in the cab with Lynn to her apartment and waited while she took a shower and put on appropriate clothes. He then put her in a taxi to her in-laws and walked back to his place, which was about three miles away. Lynn pleaded that at least have the cab take him back, but Frank insisted that he walk.

Lynn had given Frank her phone number and later that night he called to make sure she made it back all right. She had and thanked Frank profusely for seeing to it that she saw her son on Christmas. Lynn said it was the best Christmas present she could have ever received. Hearing her say that was the greatest Christmas present Frank had received since leaving Levittown.

Over the next few days, Frank checked in with Lynn at least once a day. He had also seen her twice at an AA meeting. Not only had Lynn given Frank her number, but he had given her the phone number at both the lumberyard and grocery store. In a time long before cellphones, Frank wanted to make sure that if there was an emergency, Lynn could always get a hold of him.

That New Year's Eve, Frank did not have to work at the grocery store and asked Lynn if she wanted to have dinner with him. He knew that New Year's Eve was one of the hardest nights to stay sober, when everyone was looking to go out and celebrate. Knowing that Frank was in the same boat, Lynn accepted. But they did not just stay at his apartment. Frank had made reservations and took Lynn out to a nice steakhouse. During dinner, they joked around and talked lightheartedly for a change. Lynn appreciated the gesture, but the truth was Frank enjoyed her company just as much.

After dinner, Frank had a cab take them back to Lynn's apartment. He did not want her to be alone when the clock struck midnight and a new year arrived. Of course, truth be told, he also did not want to be alone. Lynn made coffee and when the television announced midnight they gave each other a hug and wished each other a happy new year.

Then Lynn kissed Frank on the cheek. "I know I was kind of out of it Christmas Eve when you rescued me from that motel room, but I remember saying that you were my guardian angel," she said with a soft smile. "And I still mean it. I know this might sound crazy, but I think maybe God has sent you into my life. I know I still have a long road to go to recovery, but I don't know where I would be without you."

Frank fought back tears. He had not felt such a connection to anyone since leaving Mary and Eileen. It was not sexual, but pure love; like the love best friends have for each other, a brother has for a brother. Frank had just recently met Lynn, and for all he knew her stories were fabricated, but the heart feels what the heart feels. The soul feels what the soul feels.


Frank and Lynn talked to each other at least once a day. If they did not see each other in a meeting, they would talk on the phone. Whenever possible, Frank would ride his bike to Lynn's apartment and personally check up on her. Far from feeling it being intrusive, she appreciated the concern. Frank had become much more than her sponsor; he had become her savior. But it would not be a one-way street.

By May, Frank had stopped working at the lumberyard and was employed by the grocery store full-time. He had made his way from the overnight shift at the stockroom to cashier and then quickly to assistant manager. He was a hard worker and was well liked by peers, bosses, and customers alike. Other than his one-day relapse in August, Frank had been sober for well over a year. He was continuing to attend meetings and remained close with Lynn. But inside Frank, just below the surface, there was still this constant loneliness and guilt.


Lynn had started working at a shoe store and had been sober for five months, since Christmas Eve. She was seeing more of her son and even began repairing the relationship with her in-laws. She attended AA meetings several times a week and battled her inner demons daily. But Lynn felt that her renewed lease on life would have never been possible without the support of her so-called guardian angel, Frank.

On June 5th, Lynn invited Frank over to her apartment for dinner. Neither of them had to work that evening and she wanted to make him a home-cooked meal. Frank accepted.

Lynn was never much of a cook, but did her best, wanting once more to thank Frank for all his friendship and benevolence. She worked all day making homemade sauce, spaghetti and meatballs. It was actually quite good. During dinner, Lynn talked buoyantly about her job and son, but after a while noticed that Frank was not himself. She asked him if something was wrong. He said no, but she knew better.

"Are you sure, Frank?" Frank always insisted that Lynn call him by his first name. "I mean you've always been here for me. You can tell me anything. You know I won't judge you."

Frank looked down at the table and ran both hands through his still thick hair. "Today is Eileen's twenty-third birthday." Frank had told Lynn about Eileen and his past, but always in vague details. "I…I…I just…I'm sorry."

Lynn could see the pain on his face and hear the distress in his voice. She reached across the table and put her small hand on his forearm. "It's okay, Frank, don't be sorry. I've cried to you so many times. Please, let me be here for you. Please."

Frank started to fight back tears. "I told you that my daughter was opposed to the war in Vietnam. What I never told you was how much…how I held that against her. I was just…I mean Thomas was there fighting. Dammit, I was against the war, too." Frank paused and burrowed his head in his hand. "I know she loved her brother—she loved him as much as I did. It was just the times, the anti-war movement, the…I don't know." Frank wiped his eyes and stood up from the table. "I'm sorry, Lynn. The dinner was excellent. I should go."

Lynn also stood up and walked over to Frank and put her hand on his shoulder. "Frank, I'm here for you. I'm here for you like you've been here for me so many times. Let it out, it's okay."

Frank leaned on the kitchen counter and started to cry. "It's all my fault. Thomas was Mary's son too, and Eileen's brother. But I was so selfish that I thought my grief was so much greater than theirs. Even before he died, when he was just shipped off to Vietnam, I drowned myself in alcohol and pity. I abandoned my family. I abandoned my family when they needed me the most."

Lynn not only felt for Frank, but also could relate. Trying to be strong for the man that did so much for her, she fought back her own tears. "Don't blame yourself. You're a good person. It was just a difficult time."

"Lynn, you don't even know. I told my own daughter at her brother's funeral that she was probably glad he was dead." Now, the tears started running freely from Frank's eyes, like a faucet that no one could turn off. "You should've seen her face. And my wife's. We were laying Thomas to rest. They needed me more than ever—and I was drunk, thinking only of myself. How could I do that to them?" Frank collapsed into Lynn's awaiting arms.

"You have to forgive yourself. I know they've forgiven you."

"How could they ever forgive me?" Frank cried into Lynn's shoulder. "I'm so ashamed. Oh, Lynn, I miss them so much."

There was so much pain in Frank's soul, but it was finally being released. He had held it in for so long that as he cried, it was like a demon being exorcised from him. Just being there, allowing him to lift that weight, Lynn was as much of a guardian angel as Frank had ever been for her.

# 36

# YOU'RE NEVER TOO
# LOST TO BE FOUND

n 1975, though the United States' military involvement had already been over for two years, the nation watched news footage
of the last few Americans departing their embassy in Saigon via
helicopter, as thousands rushed the gates, also hoping to escape.
Newly appointed South Vietnamese President Minh had uncondi-
tionally surrendered to the North. As the last U.S. helicopter left the
embassy's rooftop, America was officially out of Vietnam and the
entire country had fallen to the communists.

By 1977, the upheaval of the Sixties and early Seventies that
nearly destroyed the country was finally over. One generation had
grown up witnessing a near nuclear war with the Soviets, the assassinations of a sitting president, a presidential hopeful, the most
iconic civil rights leader in history, riots, a long, bloody and divisive
war, and the only American president to ever resign from office.
People wanted to feel good again and just enjoy themselves. They
wanted music without any political messages, to gather for parties,
not protests or riots. They wanted to dance, not march. People
across America no longer saw themselves as part of some greater

cause. They just saw themselves as individuals searching for a good time. Enter the birth of the Disco Era—bad music, bad flashy clothes and jewelry, bad dancing, and a little, white helper called cocaine. Many of the same hippies who had congregated in fields all day to smoke pot and trip on LSD now had nine-to-five office jobs and unwound by going to posh clubs to listen to mindless, electronic music and snort lines in the bathroom.

Frank Keller was also moving on from the turmoil of the late Sixties and early Seventies. But his path ran counter to the disco culture. A world away from Studio 54—literally and figuratively— Frank was still living in Phoenix and still sober. Working his way up the ladder, he had become the head manager of the supermarket where he had started in the stockroom. Though not as often as previously, he also still attended AA meetings.

Frank remained close with Lynn, who had also been sober for some time. She had put her life together. She had mended her relationship with her late husband's parents and her father-in-law managed to get her a job as a travel agent, through someone he knew. But most importantly, her son Kyle, now nine, was back living with her.

Slowly, Lynn had made new friends and she purposely lost contact with her old cohorts. But Frank remained an important part of her life. He was also becoming somewhat of a father figure to Kyle. Sometimes the three of them would all go out together to see a movie, go to the waterpark, or Rawhide, a western-themed village, which Kyle loved. Other times they would go out to dinner. At a curious age, Kyle often asked "Uncle Frank" about World War II. He would answer some of Kyle's questions, though always leaving out any gory details.

Lynn's in-laws knew about Frank and were appreciative that he had played such a supportive role in helping her get clean. They even had him over for dinner once to thank him. Although nervous at first, Frank was glad he had met Lynn's in-laws. After all, they shared a common bond, having both lost their only son in Vietnam.

Mr. and Mrs. Ross told Frank how sorry they were about Thomas, and Frank said how sorry he was about their son. But that's all that was said about Vietnam during the visit. During dessert, Mr. Ross told Frank that if he ever needed anything to just let him know. Frank appreciated the gesture, but was not looking for any favors.

Lynn was happy that her in-laws had met Frank, a man she had told them so much about. But there was someone else she was even more excited for him to meet. Frank had told Lynn about his love of horses and about the American Horse ranch that he and Bob used to hang out by when they were kids. As it happened, Lynn had an Uncle Walter, on her mother's side of the family, who owned a small stable in nearby Apache Junction. One spring day in 1977, she finally took him there.

Lynn introduced Frank to her Uncle Walter.

"Lynn's told me a lot about you," he said in a friendly tone as they shook hands. "I want you to know that I really appreciate everything you've done for her. She said she couldn't have stayed sober without your support."

Frank looked at Lynn, who was wearing an embarrassed smile. "I don't know about that. She's a strong woman. I think she could do anything. Besides, she's helped me more than I think I've helped her."

Walter took off his cowboy hat. "Yes, Lynn told me about your son. I'm very sorry."

"Thank you."

Walter showed Frank around the stables. Lynn went inside and let the two men get better acquainted. As they slowly walked around the property, they talked about World War II, Vietnam, Lynn, and of course, eventually horses. At one point, they stopped in front of a beautiful, brown mare.

"Her name's Sunshine. She's the queen bee."

Frank was enthralled. "She's beautiful. Do you mind if I pet her?"

"Please, go right ahead, she'll love it."

Frank stroked the subdued Sunshine's neck and smiled as if he had just won a thousand dollars. "Back when I was a kid, before the war, there was this horse ranch called American Horse close to where my parents lived. My best friend Bob and I used to go there every chance we got. We would just hang out by the perimeter fence and watch the horses. We used to fantasize about one day buying the place. After a time we got to know the owner. After the war we both moved to Long Island, but one day we went back to visit him." Frank stopped stroking Sunshine. "He was very sick and was about to sell the ranch. I think there's apartment buildings there now."

Walter sighed and nodded. "Yeah, it seems the rancher is an endangered species. They need more and more land for houses, condos, and shopping malls. You'll see, it'll happen in Arizona too, soon enough. You already see signs that say *Save our desert* and *Save our land*. One day, this whole country will be some sprawling development." Walter paused. "It's the new American way."

The men walked around and talked some more. Before leaving, Walter told Frank that it was a pleasure meeting him and to stop by any time. Every once in a while Frank would take him up on that offer and over the next couple of years they would become friends.


Lynn appreciated her time with Frank. But she was a young, vibrant woman and also needed companionship of a different kind. First, losing her husband, then focusing all her effort on becoming sober, Lynn shied away from any serious romantic relationship. But after a long hiatus, she started going on dates again. The travel agency where Lynn now worked was predominantly women, but her co-workers and friends would set her up on various blind dates. It was not easy. In fact, early on she usually felt quite uncomfortable. The guy would usually want to take her out for drinks or ask if she wanted a bottle of wine with dinner. Lynn would simply reply that she didn't drink. But it was more than just the alcohol factor. Lynn had been out of the game for a while and felt awkward. However, after a while, she wound up going out with one guy for nearly three months, but dumped him after learning he was also seeing two other women.

Though they had been going out for less than three months, Lynn had started having serious feelings about him and the break-up left her down. She resisted finding solace in the bottle, but Lynn told her friends and Frank that she was through with men—forever. But after a few weeks, a co-worker wheedled her into going on a double date. Lynn had a good time and actually started seeing her date, a thirty-two-year-old car salesman named Ritchie. In fact, they soon became an item and by 1978, their relationship was turning serious.

Far from being jealous of each other, Frank and Ritchie actually hit it off. The truth was that if Frank had told Lynn that he received bad vibes from her new boyfriend, she would have cut him lose. Frank's opinion meant that much to her. But after hearing about him from Lynn, and meeting him a few times, Frank thought that Ritchie was a good guy, with his priorities straight. He was genuinely happy for Lynn.

Though Lynn and Ritchie were seeing more and more of each other, she still always made time for Frank; not because she felt obligated, but because he had become a pivotal part of her life. Sometimes Frank would babysit Kyle while Lynn and Ritchie went out.

Even before Ritchie, Lynn had been trying to convince Frank to date. "You're in your fifties, you're not dead yet," she would joke. "I'm not saying you have to get married. Just go out for dinner and see where it leads."

Frank had always politely brushed her off, but the fact was it had been too long since he had an intimate relationship—of any kind. So in April of 1978, he finally gave in and let Lynn set him up with a woman who worked at the travel agency, a forty-five-year-old divorcee named Brenda.

Frank took Brenda out for dinner and they seemed to hit it off. In fact, she went back to his place that night and they had sex. By the second date Brenda made it clear that fresh off a divorce she was not looking to get entwined in another serious relationship. She liked Frank and they could have fun together, but mostly he was merely a booty call. That was perfectly fine with Frank. After a few times, they skipped having dinner and went straight to the bedroom. Brenda had three children at home so she would always go to Frank's apartment, but would only spend the night on some of the weekends that her ex-husband had the kids. The two did also talk, but it was rarely a serious conversation. Sex with no strings attached usually doesn't last; feelings or other complications get involved. But Frank and Brenda seemed to have a good, easy thing going that fitted both their needs.

In early June of 1978, Frank saw an expose on *60 Minutes* about U.S. servicemen who were still missing in action and those still thought to be prisoners of war in Vietnam. Frank had heard the allegations before, but the *60 Minutes* piece really hit a chord with him. By the end of the show he was fuming. *How could the U.S. government leave so many of its own people behind?* Just the thought of it made him sick to his stomach. Of course, he could not help but think about Billy, wondering if he was one of those forgotten souls, still being held prisoner.

The next day Frank wrote a long, scathing letter to Senator Barry Goldwater stating that he was a veteran of World War II, that it was appalling for the government to leave these men behind, and demanded action. Before sending the letter he showed it to Lynn, just because both of them had lost loved ones in the war. Though she thought Goldwater would probably never even read the letter, she appreciated Frank's passion and felt much the same way about the Vietnam MIAs and POWs. She was also extremely impressed with the text of the four-page letter. It was critical, but eloquent. It was heartfelt and powerful, and at the same time, very articulate.

Lynn said how much she admired the letter. "You know, you should write a book," she added.

"A book? You mean about the government leaving our men behind?"

Lynn thought about it for a few seconds. "Perhaps. Or how about this? You should write a book about your life." Lynn had never really thought about it before, but instantly the idea made sense. "Yeah, you can write your autobiography, about everything that's happened."

Frank laughed off the suggestion. "Who would want to read my story?"

"Frank, you have a very interesting story. You can write about your experience in the war, about losing your son and how you lost everything, being in jail, then how you cleaned yourself up and turned your life around. Whether you realize it or not, it's an amazing story, Frank. It might not be easy writing about it, but in the end maybe it will bring you some closure."

"We'll see," he replied, just to appease Lynn.

"I'm serious Frank. It's an amazing story…and I can tell you're a gifted writer."

Frank sent his letter to Senator Goldwater. But Lynn's suggestion about writing an autobiography, which at first seemed ridiculous to him, would not leave his mind. Over the next week, Frank thought more and more about the idea until it transformed from a fatuous notion to a conceivable concept, and finally to an objective. He told Lynn that he was going to do it, and she was excited. That afternoon he bought a new typewriter and went to work.

Frank decided to start his story right before Pearl Harbor, with him and Bob hanging out at American Horse, discussing if America would become involved in the war in Europe. Sometimes at work he would remember details to put in the book, and when he came home, typed them down. The book began to occupy his every thought. He tried to talk about it with Brenda; she listened, but Frank started getting the idea that she was merely doing it to humor him, so he dropped it.

Early on, Frank realized that he was not just writing his own intimate autobiography, but also a biography of America. He wrote about his father struggling through the Great Depression, about Pearl Harbor, about Hitler, about the atomic bomb, and knew he would also be writing about the events of the Fifties, Sixties, and Seventies.

The more Frank wrote, the more excited he became about finishing the project. But that did not mean it was an easy task. Frank was ripping off the scabs of many almost-healed wounds and letting them bleed again. Writing about Mary made Frank smile, remembering the times they shared, but it also made him realize how much he still missed her. It made him once again curse himself for putting her through hell. He also understood that living through the most painful memories were yet to come. Still, Frank forged ahead.

In October of 1978, Lynn told Frank that Ritchie had proposed and she had accepted.

Frank was elated. "Congratulations," he said, giving her a tight hug. "I'm so happy for you. Ritchie is a real good guy."

"Thank you. That means a lot."

After what seemed like a minute, they slowly let go of each other. "There's one more thing."

"What is it?"

Lynn smiled. "I would be honored if you would walk me down the aisle and give me away."

Frank was taken aback. "The honor would be all mine," he replied, choking back tears.

This time, Lynn jumped into Frank's arms. "You've been like a father to me. If it wasn't for you, God knows where I'd be. I love you, Frank."

"I love you, too."

It was the first time Frank had said those words to anyone in a long, long time. But he meant them with every fiber of his being.

The wedding was that January. Lynn looked beautiful and as Frank walked her down the aisle he felt like a proud father. But most of all, he was proud of Lynn. She had come a long way from the depths of her despair. She had fought the demons of loss, alcohol, and self-pity, and won.

Understandably, Frank started seeing even less of Lynn, though they always stayed in touch. He missed spending more time with her, as well as Kyle, but he was content knowing they were happy. Plus, it was not like they *never* saw each other anymore. Sometimes Lynn and Ritchie would have Frank over for dinner. Now and then Frank would still babysit Kyle, so the newlyweds could go out.

In March of 1979, Brenda announced that she was going back to her ex-husband. Frank was not surprised, but was disappointed. It was not just the sex, but he enjoyed having a woman's company. When Lynn found out, she wanted to set Frank up with someone else. But Frank said he "needed a break for a while." Lynn persisted, explaining that it did not have to be anything serious, but he still politely turned her down.

By the summer of 1979, the United States was once again in dire straits. But this time it was not dissension that was crippling the country; it was staggering unemployment, skyrocketing inflation, and a shortage of oil. The oil crisis, due to Middle East turmoil, reached its pinnacle that summer when it became so bad that gasoline was rationed. Gas stations across the country were grid-locked with long lines of vehicles. In densely populated areas like New York, people could fill up only on certain days of the week, depending on the first letter or number of their license plate. There was no denying that President Carter's promise of "Change," on which he had run his campaign, had changed things for the worse.

Though Frank fortunately had a good job, like most Americans at the time, he was angry and concerned about his country. It was not just himself he was thinking of, but mostly of the younger generation. How were they going to be able to afford their own houses and get good-paying jobs, and pursue the American dream? Frank happened to be writing the part of his story where he and Mary had moved to Levittown and he had started Harold & Son. He had worked hard for his success, but the opportunity was there for the taking. Now, he looked around and wondered if that opportunity had become a forlorn dream.

The economy of the most powerful country in the world was in a shambles. But soon its citizens would have even more on their minds. On November 4, 1979, an armed mob of Iranian "students," followers of the Ayatollah Khomeini, stormed the U.S. embassy there and took 66 American hostages. News of the event instantly sent shockwaves across the entire United States. Unlike the divisiveness of the late Sixties and early Seventies, the country was united in its outrage and demanded the safe return of its fellow citizens. A few of the hostages managed to escape and several others were let go. But the remaining hostages would be held captive for 444 days.

People put up more American flags in front of their houses and businesses than had been seen since World War II. But even more than flags, it was a simple yellow ribbon that came to symbolize the hostage crisis and people's solidarity with their captive brethren. Almost every house across the nation had a yellow ribbon tied around a tree. Those without trees tied a ribbon around their mailbox post or fence. Living in an apartment, Frank kept his tied around the handle of his front door. Those millions of yellow ribbons did not come down until January 20, 1981, when on Ronald Regan's inauguration day, all the remaining hostages were officially released and flown out of Iran.


By the winter of 1980, Frank was in the middle of writing about Thomas going to Vietnam. This was starting the most painful part of the book. Frank felt more despondent than he had in quite some time. But by now, completing the story was something he felt he had to do. But it was difficult. Although he had not touched a drop of alcohol in years, Frank started going to extra AA meetings just in case. Lynn was also supportive. She periodically asked Frank how the book was going. When she found out that he had started writing about Thomas going to Vietnam, she called and saw him more often. It had been Lynn's idea for Frank to pen his autobiography. She now prayed that it would not pull him back to those dark days and unravel all the progress he had made.

With a sober mind, determination, his meetings, and Lynn's un-wavering support, Frank was able to make it through writing about his most desolate times. By May, he was on a chapter about meet-ing Lynn and almost finished. Frank figured he would end the story with Lynn's wedding.

One Sunday afternoon, off of work, Frank was sitting alone at a local café having a cup of coffee and reading the newspaper. His table was near the hostess station and at one point he heard a woman come in and ask the hostess for directions to the Sun Val-ley Apartments. That's where Frank lived, so he figured he would help. When he stood up and turned around, Frank's breath was taken away. The young woman looked just like an older version of Eileen. But…but it couldn't be.

The woman saw Frank and her jaw dropped. "Dad."

Before Frank could say anything, Eileen ran into his arms. In front of the hostess and curious eyes of patrons, the two held each other and both began to cry.

"Eileen, I'm so sorry for everything—the way I treated you and your mother."

"It's okay, Dad," Eileen cried into his shoulder. "I forgive you. That's why I came here to find you."

Frank let go of his daughter, his eyes red with tears. "What do you mean?"

"I hired a private investigator to track you down. I needed to see you again. I wanted to see if you were okay. I wanted to show you pictures of your grandchildren. I just hoped that after all these years you still wanted to see me."

Frank grabbed his daughter tight. "Oh, Eileen, of course I want-ed to see you. I love you so much. I've thought about you every single day. But after everything I did, I thought you would never want to see me again. I never wanted to cause you or your mother any more pain."

Eileen looked into her father's teary eyes. "All that's in the past. It was a long time ago…and I forgive you."

Frank and Eileen sat down at the table together. He asked how Mary was; Eileen said that she was fine. She had remarried, but had been divorced for several years. Though no longer in Levittown, she still lived on Long Island. She had known about Eileen's search for Frank—and actually approved of it. Before they went any further, Frank told Eileen that he had been completely sober for over five years.

"I'm so glad to hear that." Eileen put her hand on he father's arm. "Really, Dad, I'm proud of you. You look great."

"Me, look at you. My God, I still can't believe I'm sitting across the table from you. It's like a dream. You look so beautiful."

Eileen blushed. "So what else are you up to?" Eileen eagerly asked her father. "Are you married?"

Frank chuckled. "No, I stayed a solo act. But I'm doing okay. I have a nice apartment. I manage a supermarket. It's a good job." Frank quickly turned the subject back to Eileen. "So, you're married. You have kids. Do you have pictures of them?"

Eileen laughed. "Of course." She excitedly retrieved her wallet and opened it up. "This is a picture of me and my husband, Charles. He's a wonderful man. He's an accountant."

Frank pulled the billfold closer to get a better look. "You two look very happy together."

"We are." Eileen then flipped to the next photo. "This is your granddaughter, Kathy. She's six-years-old.

Frank was all smiles. "She's so beautiful. She has your eyes."

"Thank you." Eileen then flipped to the next picture, of a young boy. "This is your grandson, he's eight."

"Handsome young devil. I know he didn't get his good looks from me. What's his name?"

"Thomas."

Frank's eyes swelled with new tears. He took a deep breath. "Eileen, I know you loved your brother very much. The things I said, it was the alcohol talking. It's not an excuse, but…"

Eileen gave her father a soft smile. "I meant what I said before—all that is in the past. I know you weren't yourself." Eileen paused. "That's why I want to take you with me back to New York. I want you to meet Thomas and Kathy and Charles. And Dad...I know Mom would like to see you again, too. She's worried about you over the years."

Frank thought about it for all but a few seconds. "I would love to go back to New York with you." He could not believe what he was saying.

# 37

# REDEMPTION

The next morning Frank met with his boss, the regional manager of the grocery chain. Frank told him he needed to take a week off work. He told the truth about the reason. Frank actually had the vacation time coming to him but it was sudden and usually the company didn't like their managers taking more than a few days off at a time. However, after hearing the story, his boss could not haggle with him. Besides, Frank had been his best employee.

Later that morning, Frank and Eileen went to the travel agent together—this was still long before you could just go online and search for tickets—and Frank was able to get a seat on the same flight, leaving the following day.

Of course, Frank could not let his daughter leave town without meeting Lynn. He had called her and told of the news. Lynn was both floored and ecstatic. Ever since hearing Frank's story, she had hoped that he would some day reunite with Mary and Eileen and make amends. Frank had told his daughter briefly about Lynn the previous day at the café. They made plans to go out to dinner.

In front of the restaurant, Frank introduced Eileen to Lynn, and her husband Ritchie.

"I would like you to meet my daughter, Eileen." Just saying it filled him with pride and joy.

Lynn fought back tears. "It is such a pleasure to meet you. I've heard so much about you."

The four then went inside, sat down and became better acquainted. Though meeting her for the first time, Lynn felt she already knew Eileen. After some small talk, she got into the crux of her's and Frank's relationship. She told the story again about how he had rescued her and served as her guardian angel. Eileen was moved by the story. It had taken some time, but she truly had forgiven her father for the things he had said and done and for the lost years they were never able to spend together. Now, Eileen was happy just to see how far her father had come since the last time she had seen him.

Lynn also said how sorry she was for the loss of Eileen's brother. "I lost my ex-husband and father of my child in Vietnam," she explained.

"Yes, my father told me. I'm so sorry."

The two women, a mere few years apart, seemed to hit it off. Eileen realized how much Lynn cared for her father and also what a good influence she was on him. Lynn tried to stress how much Frank had thought and talked about Eileen over the years.

Ritchie tried to pay for the bill, but Frank would not let him. As they left the restaurant, Eileen and Ritchie chatted. Lynn saw her opportunity and pulled Frank aside. "I'm so happy for you. Eileen is such a wonderful person."

Frank smiled. "Thank you. I'm so glad that you were able to meet her. I still can't believe all of this. It's like a dream."

"Well sometimes dreams do come true."

As they parted ways, Frank told Lynn and Ritchie that he would be back in a week.

The next afternoon, Eileen dropped off her rental car at the airport and she and her father boarded a plane bound for New York. A gentleman was kind enough to switch seats with Eileen so the two of them could sit together. They used the time to catch up even more. There were certain things that Frank had already asked his daughter about. At the café, he had inquired about Bob, Dorothy—and most importantly—Billy. Eileen had explained that Billy had been released a few weeks before the war's end and returned home shortly thereafter. He was married and doing well. Bob was also doing well and still lived in Levittown. Unfortunately, after a long battle with lupus, Dorothy succumbed to the disease and passed away just a year earlier. Frank was heartbroken. Dorothy was a true altruist and Frank always adored her.

On the flight was the first time Frank told Eileen about writing his autobiography. She could not wait to read it. Eileen wanted to learn about all the things her father went through that he was probably not going to tell her. Naturally, she also wanted to read what he had put in the book about her.

Towards the end of the flight, Eileen fell asleep. As Frank sat there, for the first time, he started to get nervous about going back. How would Mary react to him? Would she even want to see him? What could he say to her after all these years?

"Ladies and gentlemen, we are about to start out initial descent into New York. We ask that you please return your seats to their upright position and make sure that your trays are up."

Groggily, Eileen lifted her head. Frank peered out the window and through a break in the clouds saw speckled lights below. This was it.

Eileen's husband, Charles, picked them up at the airport, minus the kids, who were with a babysitter. In 1980, you could still walk up to the gate to meet people and that's what he did.

All smiles, Charles greeted his wife with a big hug and peck on the lips as she walked off the plane. "I missed you."

"I missed you, too," replied Eileen. Then she turned to Frank. "Dad, this is my husband Charles."

"It's a pleasure to meet you, Charles," Frank said, extending his hand.

Charles firmly shook it. "It is a pleasure meeting you, Mr. Keller."

"Please, just call me Frank. Eileen speaks very highly of you."

"Well, I do my best. I have to tell you, your daughter is an amazing woman, and a great mother."

Eileen had wanted her father to stay at her house. Frank insisted on getting a hotel, not wanting to impose. But with the time difference, it was 9:30 p.m. by the time they retrieved their bags and left the airport.

Eileen and Charles lived in Massapequa Park, a few towns over from Levittown. As they pulled up to the house, Frank was impressed by its large exterior. As Frank and Charles grabbed the luggage, Eileen opened the front door. As she did, her two children ran to meet her. It had been the longest she had ever been away from them. It was a weeknight and they were usually asleep, but considering the circumstances, Charles told the babysitter that they could stay up.

"Mommy, is this Grandpa?" Kathy asked.

Eileen smiled. "Yes, this is your grandfather, my father. Dad, this is Kathy and Thomas."

Frank went down on one knee. He could not believe that he was actually face-to-face with his grandchildren. Two days earlier, he did not even know they existed.

"Mom says you live in Arizona," Thomas said in an innocent child's voice. "Is there real cowboys and Indians there?"

"Well, yes there are." Frank then went into his carry-on bag and pulled out two gifts he had bought them at the airport souvenir shop. "In fact, I brought this for you. It's a genuine cowboy hat."

Thomas held it and looked at it as if it were gold. "Wow!"

Eileen and Charles looked down and smiled.

"And this is for you," he said, handing Kathy a cowgirl doll.

Eileen and Charles let the kids stay up a little while longer before ushering them to bed. After doing so, Eileen suggested to her husband that they stay home from school the next day so they could spend it with their grandfather. Charles agreed. Eileen took her father on a tour of the house, which had four bedrooms and two baths.

"It's a beautiful house, Eileen. You and Charles really did well for yourselves."

"Thanks. He makes a good living."

The adults then sat around the kitchen table for a while and talked over a late-night snack. Frank told his son-in-law how impressed he was by the house. Charles told him a little about his job. Eileen was glad to see that the two of them were getting along. Finally, around midnight, it was time to go to bed.

Frank awoke late the next morning to the tantalizing smell of a home-cooked breakfast. He cleaned up and went into the kitchen, where Eileen was putting on the finishing touches. Charles had already gone to work. He greeted his daughter and then she yelled out to the kids to come sit down and eat.

After breakfast, Frank went out back with Kathy and Thomas and spent some time with them. Mostly they asked what it was like living in Arizona. Then, after a while, Thomas asked if Frank could play catch with him in the backyard. He might as well have asked him if he wanted to pick thousand dollar bills out of a bucket. As the two tossed the ball around, Eileen watched from the second-floor kitchen window with a permanent smile on her face.

Around 1:00 p.m. Eileen announced that they were going to Grandma's house. It was time for Frank to meet Mary. She also lived in Massapequa Park and though she lived alone, her house was as big as Eileen's.

As soon as Mary opened the door, Kathy and Thomas rushed to her. "Grandma!" They said in unison with their innocent, excited voices.

Mary greeted them and then stood face-to-face with the man whom she had thought she would spend her entire life. Though she and Frank had been closer than any two people could be for most of their years, awkward silence befell them. Then finally, Mary extended her hand like a long, lost friend. "Hello, Frank. It's good to see you."

Frank wanted so much to hug her, but refrained. "It's good to see you, too."

After a few more pleasantries, Eileen said she was taking the kids outside. Frank and Mary then sat down at the kitchen table.

"Before we go any further, I just want to tell you how sorry I am—for everything. What I did, how I acted, was abominable. And though I make no excuses, I want you to know that I've been sober now since nineteen-seventy-four. I haven't had as much as a drop."

Mary smiled. "Eileen told me. I'm very proud of you, Frank. Really, I am. And as far as what happened, well it's in the past. You had always been a good father—and a good husband. I know Thomas going to Vietnam put an incredible strain on you."

"But he was your son, too, Mary...and Eileen's brother. I abandoned the both of you when you needed me the most."

Mary sighed. "It was the alcohol, Frank. It had complete control of you. And I can't tell you how happy I am that you've sobered up and turned your life around. And I know that you're sorry about what happened. But I want you to know that I've forgiven you."

Frank hung his head. "So many times I wanted to call you and Eileen, but I was too ashamed. And I promised that I would never burden either of you again." He then lifted his head and fighting back tears, looked straight at Mary. "But I'm so glad she tracked me down. I'm so happy that she's happily married and has two wonderful children. And she tells me you're doing well too. You look great."

Mary blushed. "Thank you. You look very good too."

Frank and Mary spent the next hour and a half sitting around the kitchen table catching up.

Mary thanked him for giving her the money, saying it was not necessary. "I gave some to Eileen. I know you wanted me to move back into the house and I did for a while. But it just felt too strange." Mary explained that she sold the house and moved into an apartment in Bayside, near her parents.

Frank asked how her parents were doing. Sadly, Mary said that they both died in a car accident in 1974. "Oh Mary, I'm so sorry."

"Thank you. It was hard at first, but I've come to terms with it."

Mary then went on to talk about getting remarried. "He was a real estate developer. A friend introduced me to him. He was charming, handsome, and well off. Three months later we were married. But after only six months I found out he was cheating on me with his secretary. He swore it would never happen again and for whatever reason, I believed him. Then two years later I found out that he had been having several affairs all along. I filed for divorce."

"Well, I may have been a complete drunken asshole in the latter years, but I can honestly say, my hand to God, that in all our time together, I never as much as kissed another woman."

Mary just smiled in response. She then went onto explain that in the divorce she received half his wealth, which was substantial. "Plus I already had some of the money left in my saving that you had given me. So if you need—"

"Don't even say it. You know I could never take any money from you."

Mary then asked Frank about his life. Leaving out the parts about Times Square, Las Vegas, and being in jail, he started with getting sober. Frank told her all about Lynn. He explained that he never remarried nor was he in a relationship. He told her about his job and where he lived.

After a while, the kids finally came rushing into the house announcing that they were hungry. Frank suggested that he take them all out to lunch. Kathy and Thomas excitedly answered for Eileen and Mary.

After lunch, Frank said that he wanted to visit Thomas' grave the next morning. Mary and Eileen looked at each other and then agreed that the three of them should go together.


The next morning, as planned, Eileen, Mary, and Frank went to the cemetery. After parking the car in front of the appropriate lot, the three of them solemnly exited. Eileen and her mother both were carrying flowers. Frank had a small American flag that he wanted to place at his son's grave. It was a beautiful, warm late May morning in New York. The sky was blue, with just a few, swaths of thin clouds.

"It's over here," Mary said, leading the way, her voice fading into the otherwise silent cemetery air.

After passing a few more graves, there it was. For the first time since the funeral, Frank stood over his son's final resting place. As Mary and Eileen kneeled down and placed their flowers, Frank stared at the headstone, which read: *Thomas Michael Keller 1950 - 1970, 1st Calvary, Killed in Action in Vietnam, Loving Son and Brother.*

After they stood back up, they both looked at Frank. Mary took hold of her daughter's hand and without saying a word, she led her back a few steps.

Wiping away tears, Frank knelt down in front of the headstone and planted the flag into the hard, green ground. "I miss you so much, Tommy," he said softly aloud. "I'm so sorry that I haven't come to visit you before. I just couldn't bring myself to it. But I think about you every day son. Every day." Frank kissed his hand and then placed it on the gravestone. "I love you son."

Frank slowly stood up and turned around to face Mary and Eileen and started sobbing uncontrollably. "I'm so sorry."

They both went to him and put their arms around him.

"The way I acted at his funeral," he cried into Mary's shoulder. "I took away even being able to lay him to rest in peace."

Mary patted Frank's back. "I told you, I forgive you."

"That's all in the past now," Eileen added, choking on her own tears. "Thomas is resting in peace now."

They stood there for a few minutes, before letting go and wiping away their tears.

"Let's all hold hands and say a prayer together," Mary said. Then the three of them stood hand-in-hand over Thomas' grave and each silently said their own prayer.

After saying their peace, Frank was talking to Mary when he saw two figures walking towards them. It was Bob and Billy.

"I told them we would be here," Mary said. "They both wanted to see you very much. And they always come to pay their respects to Thomas."

At first speechless, Frank went to meet them halfway.

Bob smiled. "You're looking good. Older, but okay for your age."

Frank smiled back. "I'm only a few months older than you."

The two men, once inseparable, locked in an embrace.

"It's great to see you again, Frank."

"It's so good to see you again, too. Eileen told me what happened to Dorothy; I'm so sorry. She was a great woman."

"Thank you," Bob replied, stilling holding onto Frank. "She always thought about you. We all did."

Frank turned his attention to Billy. "Billy, I'm so glad you made it home all right," he said, fighting back more tears.

"Thank you, Uncle Frank. I'm so sorry about Tommy."

Frank wrapped his arms around Billy. "Don't you be sorry. It's not your fault. I just thank God that you made it home. I worried about you for so long. You know you were always like a son to me."

"I know Uncle Frank. And I always thought about you, too. It's so good to see you again."

After conversing some more, Frank, Bob, and Billy walked over to Thomas' grave together and shared a moment of silence.

Bob still lived in Levittown and after the cemetery, suggested that they all go back to his place. Frank could see Michael, who still lived with his father. Diana had married and moved to Florida. Frank was excited to see Michael again, but also couldn't wait to see the old neighborhood and how it had changed. On the way to Bob's, Frank, Mary, and Eileen passed their old house. Frank then asked to drive by his original hardware store.

"Are you sure you want to do that?" Mary asked.

"Yes, yes, it's okay. Really. I want to see if it's holding up."

Frank, however, was not satisfied just driving by the store, which was now called Better Hardware. He insisted on going in. The store seemed immaculate and had several customers in it. The young man behind the counter asked if he could help the wide-eyed strangers.

Frank explained how he used to own the store. The young man then said that he was Walter Rubenstein's nephew. Not only that, but Walter happened to actually be on his way to the store to pick up some papers. Frank waited for him.

About fifteen minutes later, Walter showed up and could not believe his old boss was there. As if the friction that had grown between them never existed, they talked for a while. Walter explained that he now had six stores across New York and the business was booming. Frank did not feel bitter. Having to sell Harold & Son was all Frank's own doing and he had put any hard feelings he may have harbored towards Walter behind him a long time ago. Frank congratulated Walter and wished him further luck.


That night, Frank had another dream of being in that dark, smoky jungle. However, this time, there were no sounds of gunfire, bombs, or men screaming out in pain. Back at that small, dirt hill, he looked over for Thomas but could not see him. Then he heard a calming voice sweep through the eerie silence. "I'm over here, Dad."

Frank looked up and the dense jungle had turned to an endless, sunlit, green field and right there in front of him stood Thomas. He was wearing his Army fatigues, but appeared unharmed. In fact, he was smiling. "It's okay, Dad. You can stop worrying about me. And you can finally forgive yourself. I'm in a better place now."

Frank went to reach out to him, but Thomas turned away and started walking out into the field. But after a few feet, another figure appeared out of thin air, holding Thomas' hand. They stopped and both turned to look at Frank. The other figure was Frank's father. Then, without either of them saying a word, they turned their heads back and continued to walk hand-in-hand further out into the green field. With each step they took, the backdrop became lighter and lighter, until it completely transformed into a soft white canvas.

The day before Frank was to fly back to Phoenix, he approached Eileen with an idea. After spending time with Eileen and Charles and his grandchildren, he could not just go back to Arizona and see them maybe once a year. He wanted them—he needed them—in his life. He wanted to be around to see Kathy and Thomas grow up. He asked his daughter what she would think about him moving back to Long Island. He said if she had any reservations about it, he would abide by her wishes. But Eileen savored the idea as much as her father.

Frank then called Mary, so as not to blindside her. He explained that he would not bother her, but felt the need to be a part of Kathy's and Thomas' lives now that he had met them. He also said that he could not walk away from Eileen a second time. Like her daughter, Mary approved of the idea.

Next, Frank did something he never thought in a million years he would do; he called Walter, told him he was moving back to Long island, and asked him for a job. Walter thought about it, but could not refuse the man who had mentored him and ultimately turned him into a millionaire.

Frank flew back to Phoenix the next day, and immediately started making arrangements to move to New York. Of course, he also had to tell Lynn. He took her out to dinner and told her the news. She was elated for him.

"I just feel bad about leaving you and Kyle," added Frank. "You've meant so much to me. You know how much I love you, Lynn."

A lone tear seeped from Lynn's eye. "I love you, too. And I'm going to miss you." She then gently placed her hand on Frank's forearm. "But it's time for you to go home now."

Frank spent as much time with Lynn and Kyle as he could before leaving. He promised that he would come back and visit—a promise he would keep.

That September, Frank returned to New York. He moved into an apartment in Seaford, not far from where Eileen lived. In a great ironic twist of fate, he began working for Walter at one of the hardware stores.

Frank now had a new ending for his autobiography and he had finished it by the time he moved back to Long Island. He titled it: *A Life With War…And Beyond.* After sending the manuscript to nearly every publisher and agent, it was finally picked up and published. Within three months of its release, it made *The New York Times* best-seller list. Before he knew it, Frank was doing the interview circuit and had become somewhat of a celebrity. *A Life With War…And Beyond* would ultimately sell over six million copies worldwide.

Frank used his newfound fame to join with Billy Davenport to promote awareness of those U.S. servicemen still left behind in Vietnam, and keep up pressure on the government to see to it that, whether alive or just the remains, every last soldier be returned home. Together, they made public appearances and went on talk shows. They met with congressmen and senators.

Eventually, Frank talked Billy into writing his own book, about his time in Vietnam and being a prisoner of war. It brought even more publicity and pressure to never forget those left behind on the battlefields of Southeast Asia.


Gradually, Frank and Mary started spending more and more time together. At first it started innocently, seeing each other when Eileen and the grandkids were around. Then, after a while they would go out to lunch and eventually even dinner. Perhaps inevitably, they once again became romantically involved. Then, one April evening in 1983, while taking Mary out to dinner, Frank knelt down on one knee, pulled out a ring and proposed. Mary accepted.

That August they re-married. Lynn, Kyle, and Ritchie flew out for the wedding. Bob was Frank's best man. For their honeymoon, Frank took Mary back to Hawaii.

Frank, Mary, and Eileen were once again a family.

www.ingramcontent.com/pod-product-compliance
Lightning Source LLC
Chambersburg PA
CBHW030030030726
47500CB00001B/29